Doctor Mystery

Doctor Mystery

by
Paul d'Ivoi

Translated from the French by
Nina Cooper

Original illustrations by
Louis Bombled

A Black Coat Press Book

ISBN 978-1-64932-128-2. First Printing: June 2022. Published by Black Coat Press, an imprint of Hollywood Comics.com, LLC, P.O. Box 17270, Encino, CA 91416. All rights reserved. Except for review purposes, no part of this book may be reproduced or transmitted in any form or by any means, electronic or mechanical, including photocopying, recording, or by any information storage and retrieval system, without permission in writing from the publisher. The stories and characters depicted in this novel are entirely fictional. Printed in the United States of America.

TABLE OF CONTENTS

VOYAGES EXCENTRIQUES
Le Docteur Mystère
PAUL D'IVOI
ANCne LIBRAIRIE FURNE
COMBET et Cie ÉDITEURS
PARIS

Introduction

Unlike most of Paul d'Ivoi's novels, *Le Docteur Mystère* [Doctor Mystery] was not previously serialized and was published directly in book form by Combet & Cie. in 1900. It was the seventh novel in his *"Voyages Excentriques"* [The Eccentric Voyages] series, clearly inspired by Jules Verne's classic *Voyages Extraordinaires*.

We presented Paul Deleutre (1856-1915), the writer who signed all his published works with the nom-de-plume of Paul d'Ivoi, in our introductions to *Around the World on Five Sous* (Black Coat Press, ISBN 978-1-61227-369-3) and *Miss Musketeer* (Black Coat Press, ISBN 978-1-64932-108-4). Therefore, those wishing to learn more about him should refer to either of those two volumes.

Doctor Mystery bears some similarities to Verne's *Twenty Thousand Leagues Under the Sea* as its eponymous hero is not unlike Prince Dakkar, i.e. Captain Nemo. D'Ivoi already mined the theme of the rebel captain seeking revenge with the help of a super-submarine in his earlier *Corsair Triplex*, and with *Doctor Mystery*, he retained the essence of the alienated genial hero, but chose to locate the plot in the protagonist's native India. Also, he decided to humanize him a bit more by giving him a teenage sidekick.

Doctor Mystery introduces the pre-*Tintin*-like character of the Parisian street urchin Cigale—his name means Cicada—who went on to star in three more volumes of the series: *Cigale en Chine* [Cicada in China], *Massiliague de Marseille* [Massiliague of Marseille], and *Les Semeurs de Glace* [The Ice Sowers]. Right off the bat, d'Ivoi compares Cicada to Victor Hugo's unforgettable urchin, Gavroche from *Les Misérables* (1862). Perhaps, a better comparison might have been with Clampin, a.k.a. Pistolet, from Paul Féval's *'Salem Street* (1868) (Black Coat Press, ISBN 978-1-932983-46-3), one of the novels in his seminal *Black Coats* series. However, if Gavroche and Pistolet are but bit players in their creators' works, Cicada is a full-blown hero and the template for many future similar characters, from Tintin to Robin and even Harry Potter.

In modern times, reknowned Italian comic book writer Alfredo Castelli connected his famous character Martin Mystère to both Doctor Mystery and Cicada. *Martin Mystery* was created in 1982 by Castelli with artist Giancarlo Alessandrini. In the comics, Castelli reminds us that Doctor Mystery eventually adopted Cicada, who then became known as Cicada Mystery. The modern-day "Detective of the Impossible," Martin Mystery, is his descendent.

Marie Palewska's afterword summarizes Cicada's destiny post-*Doctor Mystery* in Paul d'Ivoi's novels.

The *Martin Mystery* comics have been translated into many languages and spawned a rather mediocre animated TV series. In 2003, Castelli launched a spin off series featuring the original Docteur Mystery from Paul d'Ivoi (right) drawn by Lucio Filippucci.

To render unto Caesar... in *Almanacco del Mistero* (2012), in a story entitled "*The Shadow of Fantômas,*" plotted by the undersigned with Alfredo Castelli, and drawn by Dante Spada, it is revealed that Cicada was himself a descendant (possibly a grandson) of Magistrate Rémy d'Arx, one of the Black Coats' fiercest foes, from Paul Féval's *The Invisible Weapon* (Black Coat Press, ISBN 978-1-932983-80-7).

The circle from Paul Féval to Paul d'Ivoi and their modern-day descendents is complete.

Now, read on!

Jean-Marc Lofficier

Bibliography of "*Les Voyages Excentriques*"

(only first serialization and first book publication are listed.)

1. Les Cinq Sous de Lavarède (co-written with Henri Chabrillat) [*Around the World on Five Sous*]
* First serialization in *Le Petit Journal*, 24 August-27 December 1893.
* First book publication: Furne, Jouvet et Cie., 1894.
Characters: First appearance of Lavarède.

2. Le Sergent Simplet à travers les Colonies Françaises [*Sgt. Simpleton Across the French Colonies*]
* First serialization in *Le Petit Journal*, 26 May-8 August 1895.
* First book publication: Furne, Jouvet et Cie., 1895.
Characters: Even though some characters are identified as Lavarède's "cousins," this book is only marginally part of the Lavarède series.

3. Cousin de Lavarède! a.k.a. **Le Bolide de Lavarède** [*Lavarede's Cousin / Lavarède's Bolide*]
* First book publication: Furne, Jouvet et Cie., 1897.
Characters: Second appearance of Lavarède. The hero is a genuine cousin of Lavarède and the two are reunited at the end of the novel.

4. Jean Fanfare [*Jean Fanfare*]
* First book publication: Société d'Édition et de Librairie, 1897.

5. Corsaire Triplex
* First book publication: Société d'Édition et de Librairie, 1898.
Characters: Third appearance of Lavarède.

6. La Capitaine Nilia
* First book publication: Société d'Édition et de Librairie, 1899.
Characters: Fourth and final appearance of Lavarède.

7. Le Docteur Mystère
* First book publication: Combet et Cie., 1900.
Characters: First appearance of Cicada.

8. Cigale en Chine [*Cicada in China*]
* First serialization in *Le Français*, from 3 December 1900 to 8 March 1901.
* First book publication: Combet et Cie., 1901.

Characters: Second appearance of Cicada.

9. Massiliague de Marseille [*Massiliague of Marseille*]
* First book publication: Combet et Cie., 1902.
Characters: Third appearance of Cicada.

10. Les Semeurs de Glace [*The Sowers of Ice*]
* First serialization in *Le Journal des Voyages*, from 7 December 1902 to 28 June 1903.
* First book publication: Combet et Cie., 1903.
Characters: Fourth and final appearance of Cicada. (Merely a mention)

11. Le Serment de Daalia [*Daalia's Oath*]
* First book publication: Combet et Cie., 1904.

12. Millionnaire Malgré Lui a.k.a. **Le Prince Virgule** [*Millionaire Despite Himself / Prince Comma*]
* First serialization in *Le Journal des Voyages*, from 6 November 1904 to 25 June 1905 under the title *Le Prince Virgule*.
* First book publication: Combet et Cie., 1905, under the title: *Millionnaire Malgré Lui*.
Characters: First appearance of Dodekhan.

13. Le Maître du Drapeau Bleu [*The Master of the Blue Flag*]
* First serialization in *Le Matin*, from 25 July to 2 November 1906.
* First book publication: Société d'Édition Contemporaine, 1907.
Characters: Second appearance of Dodekhan.

14. Miss Mousqueterr [*Miss Musketeer*]
* First serialization in *Le Journal des Voyages*, from 7 October 1906 to 21 July 1907.
* First book publication: Boivin et Cie., 1907.
Characters: Third and final appearance of Dodekhan.

15. Jud Allan, Roi des « Lads » a.k.a. **La Fiancée du Diable** [*Jud Allan. King of the Lads / The Devil's Fiancée*].
* First serialization in *Le Matin*, from 21 July to 19 November 1908, under the title: *La Fiancée du Diable*.
* First book publication: Boivin et Cie., 1908, under the title: *Judd Allan (Roi des Lads)*.

16. Le Roi du Radium a.k.a. **La Course au Radium** [*The King of Radium / The Radium Rush*]

* First serialization in *Le Journal des Voyages*, from 18 October 1908 to 11 July 1909, under the title: *Le Roi du Radium*.
* First book publication: Boivin et Cie., 1909, under the title: *La Course au Radium*.

17. L'Aéroplane Fantôme [*The Phantom Airplane*]
* First serialization in *Le Petit Journal*, from 24 February to 21 June 1910.
* First book publication: Boivin et Cie., 1910.

18. Les Voleurs de Foudre [*The Thieves of Lightning*]
* First serialization in *Le Journal des Voyages*, from 20 October 1907 to 21 Lune 1908, under the title: *L'Automobile de Verre*; then from 17 October 1909 to 15 May 1910, under the title: *Les Trois Demoiselles Pickpocket*.
* First book publication: Boivin et Cie., 1911.

19. Message du Mikado [*Message from the Mikado*]
* First serialization in *Le Journal des Voyages*, from 5 November 1911 to 12 May 1912, under the title: *L'Ambassadeur Extraordinaire*.
* First book publication: Boivin et Cie., 1912

20. Les Dompteurs de l'Or a.k.a. **Le Chevalier Illusion** [*The Gold Tamers / The Knight of Illusions*]
* First serialization in *Le Journal des Voyages*, from 15 December 1912 to 8 June 1913, under the title: *Le Chevalier Illusion*.
* First book publication: Boivin et Cie., 1913, under the title: *Les Dompteurs de l'Or*.

21. Match de Milliardaire [*The Billionaires' Match*]
* First serialization in *Le Journal des Voyages*, from 9 November 1913 to 31 May 1914, under the title: *L'Évadé Malgré Lui*.
* First book publication: Boivin et Cie., 1917, under the title: *Match de Milliardaire*.

DOCTOR MYSTERY

PART ONE: THE BEAR OF SHIVA

CHAPTER I
Cicada the Street Urchin

It was night. The storm shouted and bellowed. The waves, twenty meters high, crowned with foam, separated by white abysses, slammed the jagged cliffs of Cornwall. From the dreadful Cape of Raz de Sein,[1] the extreme western point

---

[1] A stretch of water between the Isle of Sein and the Pointe du Raz in the Finistère (Brittany) region of France. The tidal water is an essential passage for ships

of France, near where the Bay of the Trepassed widens, where the tide comes in with long moans, from that dreadful mass right up to the rocks of Penmar'ch, in the vast forty-five miles circular arch called the Bay of Audierne, the sea was unsettled.

On the steep coast, the wild, rolling waves broke apart on the granite sides with a deafening roar, of which all the artillery in the world, firing at the same time, could have given only a small approximation. Higher up in the Heavens, the color of black ink and soot, thunder rumbled, crackled, exploded, throwing zigzagging bolts bursting with light into the shadows. It was the fireworks of shipwrecks, the very elements' Sabbath of the Damned, the breath of death passing over.

Nevertheless, as if in defiance of the unchained forces of nature, a young, piercing, mocking, voice answered with a song the whistling of the sea gulls, whose long supple wings held them aloft above the waves.

"Let's go to Lorient to fish for sardines,
"Let's go to Lorient to fish for herrings…"

It was a young boy, still almost a child, who was mocking the storm, lying flat on his stomach at the front of a fishing boat that the waves were bouncing about dreadfully, his hands clutching the sides. The singer was looking into the distance, trying to see through the shadows.

There was a flash of lightning. For a second, one could see a boy with a pale, thin face, lit up by big dark eyes; six sailors bent over the oars; the owner of the boat hunched over the rudder. Then the darkness became thicker.

"Well?" questioned the man at the rudder.

"Nothing," answered the boy.

With the flash of lighting, it was easy to see something. The sea was bubbling up as if the devil had lit all his candles. The boat went dizzyingly back down the slope of a wave. The little boy added gaily:

"Pftt! That is as much fun as the seesaw at the Devil's Fair."

At the name of the Devil, the superstitious sailors crossed themselves, but the boy did not notice it. Oblivious, he went back to his observation. The fury of the storm only seemed to increase. The disorganized wash broke apart at the front of the boat and dissipated into fine powder.

Dripping with water, the boy, in a situation which made his brave, unsmiling companions turn pale, with the unconscious courage which appeared to be the basis of his character, laughing at the storm, began singing again.

"There was a good sailor,
"Hello, Hello!
"Who feared neither wind nor wave…"

---

wanting to go from the Atlantic to the English Channel. At high tide, the Isle of Sein and its embankment stretch more than thirty miles.

The rough voice of the captain interrupted him:

"Shut up, Cicada! You're going to bring us bad luck."

Cicada, because that was the name of the boy, turned half around and with the unmistakable accent of a Paris *gamin*, shouted:

"No, that's good, that's good, Captain Kéradec." He began to smile. "Only Father Thunder makes more noise than you and I…"

There was silence.

"You don't say anything to him that's not right. Shouldn't something be said to him?"

Despite the gravity of the circumstances, the sailors couldn't help smiling. The captain himself softened his voice to reply:

"Come now, hold your tongue and try to find the lighthouse of Audierne, because if we miss it…"

He didn't finish. The boat was shaken. An enormous wave lifted it to a prodigious height like a wisp of straw, half filling it with water. Two men were thrown out, but with a sudden movement of the helm, Kéradec righted it again.

"That was a mean wave," grumbled the boy. "It almost lifted us right up to the gates of Heaven."

But, suddenly, changing his tone, he shouted at the top of his lungs:

"Ohé! Just ahead! A white and green light! It's the harbor of Audierne!"

A sigh of relief left the sailors' lips. The harbor was there, facing them. From that point onward, its lights would guide them. They were no longer lost in the shadows of the unleashed storm. Still, safety was still nothing less than uncertain. Located on the Goayen River, the estuary was obstructed by banks of sand and had dangerous currents. The harbor of Audierne was difficult to enter, even in calm weather. Many boats had been lost in its narrow channels. Because of the strong currents, many had crashed into the dikes protecting it. At its extremity was a circular concrete platform on which stood a lighthouse, the Raoulic, with its white light.

Trying to go through the violent sea into the narrow harbor was risky business, just short of crazy. It could almost not happen except for the heroic efforts of the Breton sailors. Only they were capable of doing it. They were accustomed to an unfriendly coast, guarded by countless reefs. With a steady hand, they looked forward to and played with the dangers of the ocean, the eater of men and boats. Their courage had returned at the announcement of the proximity of the Audierne light house.

Drenched, their hair stuck to their temples, the sailors' faces welcomed the rapid sweeping beacon.

"Hang on, fellows!" shouted Captain Kéradec. "Row hard!"

A second wave lifted the boat. Cicada had seen it coming. Over there, in the depth of night, two lights, one white, the other green, shining like stars, were the way to safety. But, as if the ocean feared seeing its victims escape, it increased its fury. The thunder began to growl without interruption, darting its lights in flashes of flame; the waves began to hurl against each other.

The little boat resisted, sometimes balancing on the crest of these liquid mountains, sometimes going down with the rapidity of an arrow into space. Slowly, but surely, it went forward. The stone foundations of the Raoulic lighthouse now stood out from the shadows.

"Ohé!" the high- pitched voice of the boy shouted again. "Let it go to starboard, if you want to double the distance."

And the maneuver was carried out.

"Good, very good! Stay to the right! We're almost home free."

A few more powerful strokes of the oars pushed them strongly out of the last wave and the boat finally found herself in the estuary, sheltered from the fury of the sea by the high granite foundation of the lighthouse. There, although still tumultuous, the sea was almost calm. That is to say, the waves were no longer ten or fifteen feet-high. For the fearful, their current height would still be fearsome, but for the crew of the *Saint-Kaourentin*—the name painted in white letters on the black hull of the boat—the waters were a mere ripple. To keep the boat some hundred yards away from the jetty, in the middle of the narrow channel, which allowed entry into the Goayen River and into the harbor of Audierne, the rowers pulled vigorously, firm, encouraged by strong commands from their Captain:

"Pull, boys! Port-side... Straight ahead!"

The boat raced over the waves, going up and down again and again. But, guided by a strong hand, it didn't deviate from its course. Suddenly, a frightening thunder bolt cast a reddish light into the emptiness, showing, for half a second, the left side of the river and the straight line to the jetty. With a note of astonishment, Cicada, still at the bow, cried out:

"There is a *pied nickelé* waiting for us."[2]

"What?" asked Kéradec.

"A man walking on the jetty... Can you imagine, he doesn't even carry an umbrella!" said the boy, with a cheeky sense of humor. Incorrigible, the Parisian gamin added, "That's fine in good weather, but when it's raining like this, you get wet right down to your bones..."

Suddenly, the boy's voice was strangled in his throat. A heart-breaking cry, sharp, inhuman sound pierced the air like a complaint of agony. A white object, like a big sea bird with its wings outstretched, had fallen from above the jetty and into the waves with a splash.

---

[2] *Les Pieds Nickelés* (The Nickel-Plated Feet Gang) was a popular French comic series created in 1908 by Louis Forton (1879-1934). It featured a trio of conmen always trying to make easy money, the expression "nickel-plated feet" being slang for slackers, work-shy people.

"A *Mari Morgan*!"[3] murmured the sailors in terror, remembering the Breton legend which attributed to mermaids the cause of shipwrecks.

Cicada stood up and said:

"No," he said, "it's just someone who fell into the sea. Captain, turn the tiller to the right. We can save him."

But the rough voice of Kéradec answered:

"If we change course, the current will push us right into the dike. There are eight men aboard, for whom I am responsible. I can't sacrifice them for a single man."

The trembling of his voice told the emotion of the brave sailor, forced by circumstances to abandon the unknown man.

"Cicada, sit down. You, men, row straight ahead and pray for the one down there, whose name we don't know, but who is going to drown."

With a shudder, his hands took hold of the oars. Following his duty, the captain had assumed the terrible responsibility of abandoning someone to the sea.

"If that's how it is," said the boy, "well, then, I'll save him by myself."

Before his companions had time to guess what he was thinking, Cicada dived into the foaming waves. An agonized cry escaped from all the lips. But, at the top of a wave, the head of the courageous Parisian urchin reappeared.

"Don't worry about me! I will swim toward the port. I'll join you there. There are some iron bars along the side of the jetty... You'll see that a *Parigot* is a different kind of sailor than a *Brezounec*!"[4]

There was some hesitation, but again Kéradec ordered, "Pull harder! Pull harder!" and with the boat bounding over the waves, the sailors could no longer see the boy. His hands holding tightly to the rudder, the Captain looked straight in front of him, but, as if petrified, big tears rolled down his immobile face.

However, Cicada, tossed about by the waves, seemed not to suspect the peril into which he had voluntarily thrown himself.

"Brrr!" he said, without thinking anymore about the boat, "the water is nice, a real four-*sous* bath..." But, on reflection, he added, "Oh, no! This is worth at least six *sous*! But it's sea water and for that, I won't have to pay at the cashier."

With a vigorous blow of his heel, he hauled himself to the top of a wave and, looking around him with a piercing eye, he said:

"Let's orient ourselves... Where is that drowning man?"

In his unconscious heroism, Cicada was obviously thinking that he had done, in the open sea, the same thing that he would have in the Seine River in

---

[3] In Brittany, the *Mari Morgan* were legendary mermaids who lured sailors to their doom with their hypnotic spells. They were believed to live near coasts, at cave entrances and at the mouths of rivers.

[4] Slang for Parisian and Breton.

the most radiant sunshine. However, night was surrounding him. The wind was hurling, lifting liquid mountains, and thunder rumbled without stopping.

By the light of the thunderbolts, the boy finally saw a white body in the water.

"Thank you, Father Thunder," he murmured, looking towards the storm. "You have lit your Jablockoff at the right time!"[5]

With his two strong arms, he held out his hand and grabbed another, which was going to disappear, and pulled it towards him. As if to make the task easier, the lightning illuminated the sea with its reddish light.

"She was an idiot," Cicada began. "Even so, there are parents that aren't careful. To let their daughters go up on a jetty when it's raining cats and dogs... For sure, that mother must not take very good care of her family..."

He was right. The body was that of a girl, twelve or thirteen years-old, whose long white dress surfaced for any instant. Her long brown hair was floating on the waves like algae and her motionless pale face had a golden tone, the tone that was usual on someone from a sunny country. She was pretty, the poor thing; it was a strange beauty, exotic. And the boy, after having considered her closed eyelids, delicate nose, rosy lips, clacked his tongue, saying:

"She's a real jewel, she is." Then, shaking himself after the passing of a wave, he said to himself, "Now, it's a question of getting her back to the jetty, my old Cicada. Open your eyes and look around."

In the waves that were unfurling, among the sounds of the tempest, the boy, paying no attention to the elements, was swimming with one hand; with the other, he was holding out of the water the head of that girl he was risking his life to save.

In front of him, there was the dark wall of the jetty that the waves seemed to want to jump over. Further away, Cicada knew that there were iron steps that were imbedded into the stone. They helped sailors get into the boats when the sea was too low to allow entry into the harbor. He only had to reach one of these steps and climb up with his precious cargo. But that was an arduous task in that angry sea that was jumping around, becoming quiet only to swell again. The boy could be thrown against the stone wall; there he could die, broken. Or he would fall back into the dark waters, and his devotion would have been pointless, except to give the avid waves two victims instead of one.

It could be said that the ocean itself was irritated against the bold boy who was trying to take its victim away. The crash of the waves against the granite produced loud detonations. Backwashes were produced; whirlpools dug liquid craters; all the forces of nature were united against those two frail humans.

---

[5] An electric candle, a modification of the electric arc lamp, in which the carbon rods, instead of being placed end to end, are arranged side by side, and at a distance suitable for the formation of the arc at the tip; also called by the name of the inventor, a Jablockoff candle.

But the body of the Parisian urchin had inside himself the soul of a hero. In addition, he had thin legs and arms, without a doubt, but strong, and accustomed to every kind of exercise. Finally, Cicada was fearless. For his salvation and that of his pretty little companion, he used what should have doomed them. He abandoned himself to the backwashes that pushed him into the direction that he wanted to go. Another flash of lightning showed him the iron steps, several feet away from him. He only had to reach them—at any cost.

The boy turned around. An enormous wave was coming. That was the one that would take them to safety. He quickly lay flat, his feet pointed toward the jetty. He was lifted by the furious wave, that messenger of death sent by the ocean to that little boy who had fought it. The wave broke apart on the granite wall; the swimmer should have been knocked out, crushed. But no! Cicada had parried the shock. His feet were slammed against the stones but, with a powerful reflex of his knees, he had avoided being crushed. And when the wave fell back, he surfaced, clinging to the iron stairway, still holding the girl, whose inert head was now lying against his shoulder.

Were they saved? Not yet! Other waves followed, covering them with water. It would seem that the sea still wanted to snatch the boy from his point of safety, as a wicked beast that dreams only of pulling in more bodies into its jaws.

"Keep going, Master Ocean," laughed the boy, whose feet and hands were grasping the iron steps.

Slowly, without hurrying, Cicada continued climbing upward, one step at a time, between each wave. He held the bars for support against the assault of the waves, and then began climbing again. He was breathing heavily and felt fatigued, but he continued climbing. He finally raised himself above the level of the waves. He reached the top of the jetty and, there, exhausted, out of breath, dizzy, he lay down beside the inanimate body of the young woman that he had pulled right out of the arms of Death.

E.CROSBIE.SC

CHAPTER II
Cicada Becomes Godfather to a Doctor

How long the fainting spell of the young savior would last couldn't be determined. Oh! He wouldn't return to consciences immediately. First of all, he floated in fuzziness; a feeling of warmth surrounded him. Unable yet to talk, he opened his eyes. He thought:

Am I dead? If this is death, it is certainly more pleasant than life!

That thought said a lot about the suffering which the valiant young man had already endured. And, as if in a dream, he reviewed his past life: cold, hungry—that was what he recalled from his childhood. The rest was drowned in a fog of which his memory revealed nothing. What had he been doing right up to the present time? Cicada remembered next to nothing about it. At that particular moment, he recalled having gone with a big man with a pock-marked face to the

Halles of Paris. That person, he recalled, had had a numbered booth in the vegetable section.

Every morning, the child came, dealt with the customers, while his "employer" made the tour of the neighboring bars. The result was that the merchant drank up all the profit made by his young "employee." And said "employee" received strong slaps delivered by the drunken man, who was practicing justice in the way of a great number of people, finding it simpler to beat up an innocent rather than stopping himself from drinking. As hard as the bad situation was, as determined as he was to endure it in order to earn his meager keep, the young orphan had no hope for help from anyone. One fine day, Cicada found himself "thanked" with one beating too many, and so, he left his brutal "employer" and launched himself into the French capital.

"I had blue marks all over my body!" he explained much later. "That really made me look like a jaguar. That wasn't acceptable for a man."

He tried all kinds of work: a doorman, a ticket-seller at theater doors, and picking up cigar butts. He sang in a chorus. Little by little, he learned to play a guitar that a street musician gave him. In a carnival, he turned the hand crank of a merry-go-round made up of wooden horses. In a sideshow, he behaved like a savage, eating living rabbits. He earned very little despite his courage, but received in return a great number of slaps from the various employers who took advantage of him.

The world seemed to him like an immense breeding ground for slaps, and if he was asked what, for him, characterized mankind, he would have answered without hesitating, "Slaps!"

And that characterization, it must be said, Cicada didn't like at all. Now, one day, when his fight for survival had made him into a chimney sweep, he was called, with a less novice companion, to clean inside the chimneys of an apartment occupied by a young doctor named Opal and his wife.

It doesn't seem like much to climb up into a chimney. However, that ordinary job changed the existence of the boy, and from a Parisian, she made of him into a Provincial. Here's how. Doctor Opal owned a miniature bear that a friend had brought him from Sumatra. The animal, twenty inches tall, with silky hair, and an elongated muzzle, brilliant eyes, endowed with the agility of a cat, was charming. However, it is rare that some default doesn't go with the most desired qualities. That was so, even with Ludovic—such was its name. The animal hated dogs. If he saw one, big, little, or medium-sized, he attacked it. He jumped on the unfortunate animal and bit him, breaking his vertebrae.

Now, Madame Opal, his wife, was fond of a delightful little female dog, a basset hound that answered to the name of Violet, but which no exercise and rich food, had made very fat. She constantly worried about the little dog, watching over it with jealous care, making sure that the doors that protected Violet from Ludovic's jaws were always closed, but also scolding her husband and asking him to give his pet away to a zoo.

Her husband refused and laughed at her fears, but a catastrophe was inevitable. It happened. The chimney sweeps were not aware of the Opals' arguments. A door that the sweeps had left open allowed Ludovic to get into the room where Violet was relaxing on a silk cushion. A growl, a plaintive bark, a cracking of bones—that was all it took. The unfortunate basset hound had passed without transition from temporary idleness to eternal repose.

In her sadness, Madame Obal slapped her husband. She even armed herself with a hat pin with which to stab the murderous Ludovic, but when the animal showed his teeth, she declared that a properly behaved woman couldn't soil her hands by spilling blood, and she immediately swore that the guilty beast had to leave the house.

Without consideration for his young age, forgetting also the poor animal had been snatched from his native jungle, she gave him to Cicada, telling him to take Ludovic very far away. This incident set the boy on a new course of adventures. From chimney sweep, he became a street performer, going through the Paris suburbs, then into the neighboring regions, showing the miniature bear, with whom he lived pleasantly.

Ludovic had the soul of a bohemian artist. The travels across the countryside were more agreeable to him than captivity in an apartment. The applause with which the villagers greeted his tricks flattered his vanity, and he grew strongly attached to his new master. It was thus that the two arrived one fine day in Audierne in Brittany. The view of the sea was a revelation for Cicada. Immediately, he loved it passionately. So Ludovic ended up guarding their lodgings while the Parisian took a job as cabin boy on the fishing boat *Saint-Kaourentin*, whose Captain was Kéradec.

It was thus that we found him daring the tempest, risking his days to save the unknown girl. However, his senses came back again. Little by little, he was aware he was stretched out on a bed and that there were some people near him talking in a low voice. Then a friendly hand spread apart his clenched teeth and poured into his mouth some drops of a warm liquid. The boy opened his eyes, looking curiously at the man leaning over his bed, and, with a still soft voice, already laughing, he asked.

"Is that you, Captain Kéradec? Thank you! A little more to drink, please."

Kéradec, because that was he, let out a cry of joy.

"He's talking! He's out of danger! Doctor, come quick!"

"Ah! The doctor is here," continued Cicada, "that great doctor Locherle. Hello, doctor…"

But he stopped himself, surprised. The man who had answered Kéradec's call was not Doctor Locherle, the fine and worthy practitioner with his ruddy face and gray hair that the population of poor fishermen adored, because he didn't charge by the visit. It was another man, around thirty, who approached. He was tall, slim, and dressed elegantly like a tourist. He had a pale face and a broad forehead, crowned with thick brown hair. His deep dark eyes seemed to understand all of his questioner's thoughts.

"Well, well," said Cicada, in between a high and low voice, "you're not Doctor Locherle."

The newcomer smiled:

"I am just a simple tourist spending a few days at the Chateau Melecluse, on the other side of town. I was about to return there by car when several sailors told me about the young girl you saved."

"That was us," cried Kéradec. "As soon as the *Saint Kaouientin* was at the quay, we raced towards the dike with ropes to try to help you, if there was still enough time. And we found you in the middle of the jetty, on the ground, near the drowned girl, who was giving no sign of life."

"Drowned," the boy sadly repeated. "Is she dead?"

"No, no. It's just that girls, they aren't sailors like you. They can't take ocean water. So she is still unconscious. Look over there, in that bed."

Cicada lifted himself onto his shoulder almost without effort and looked in the direction indicated. On another small bed, the girl seemed to be sleeping, and a young woman, a cup in her hand, was trying to get some drops of a potion in between her clenched lips. The boy recognized her: that was Madame Arbras, the friendly wife of the local pharmacist, whose shop, facing the harbor, was always helpful to poor sailors. At the same time, he recognized the room where he was. It was the Arbras' guest bedroom, located on the second floor and lit by two little windows covered with leaf-patterned curtains.

"She will be saved, won't she?" asked Cicada, pointing to the motionless girl.

The newcomer nodded:

"Yes, my friend, you can be reassured as to that. A few minutes from now, she will open her eyes, and she can thank the one who saved her."

Cicada blushed at those words and shrugged.

"Thanks, but why? That was nothing, when you know how to swim. Only I would like to know why a girl, who should be at home with her father and mother, wanted to throw herself at the bottom of the sea."

"An accident," grumbled Captain Kéradec. "Children are..."

But the newcomer interrupted him:

"This girl isn't the daughter of fishermen; her garments show that. There is a mystery here to be solved."

"While we're waiting, I can get up.," said Cicada. "Where are my clothes?"

But the newcomer made a sign of refusal, but Cicada insisted:

"I'm telling you that I am cured. Captain Kéradec, there is a folding screen over there. Place it in front of my bed... good, that's right; now hand me my clothes..."

"Wait, my boy," said the Captain. "Yvon has run over to your place and has brought back some dry clothes for you. He is beside you with your pet, who has followed him."

Saying that, Kéradec went to the door and shouted with his big, loud voice:

"Yvon, open your eyes and send Cicada's clothes... Damn it!" he said briskly, leaning against the doorway, trembling, "What was that?"

That was Ludovic who had just rushed past him on all four legs with the speed of an arrow. In one bound, the miniature bear was near Cicada's bed, and standing up on his hind legs, he started to lick the boy's hands while making happy, growling sounds. Cicada paid him back with lots of cuddles.

Suddenly the small plantigrade went away, turned his head in all directions, sniffed the air suspiciously, then slowly, as if he was following a trail, crossed the room and came to the bed where the pretty girl snatched from the waves by his master was lying. There, he sat down in the usual way of his fellow creatures and balanced himself on his haunches, looking curiously at the girl.

"What a funny beast," said Kéradec, who had gotten over his surprise, and was helping Cicada to get dressed. "It would seem that it recognizes her."

The newcomer was following the scene with attention. On his cold face there was astonishment.

"Is that your bear?" he asked.

"Yes," answered Cicada.

"Where did you buy him?"

"I didn't buy him. Someone in Paris gave him to me. He had chewed on their little dog. His previous owner was a Doctor Opal, who lives on Rue d'Assas. He said Ludovic had the same heart as I do."

Dressed now, the boy left the shelter of the screen to rejoin his companions.

"Do you know where this Doctor Opal got that quadruped?"

"As for that, no. I only swept his chimneys. He didn't tell me the story of his life."

The newcomer looked at Cicada with real surprise.

"You swept chimneys?"

"Of course! Oh, I see what's the trouble. That astounds you, because I am now a sailor! Well, you have to earn your living when you don't have parents who are millionaires, or..." the boy ended with melancholy, "...when you don't have any at all."

Cicada stopped talking. The young woman had made a movement. Her eyelids opened and then quickly closed, while her lips exhaled a deep sigh. Ludovic began to moan softly. The complaint of the animal seemed to surprise the girl. She looked to her side. The spectators were already going toward her, to keep her from being afraid. They didn't complete their movement. A smile appeared on the girl's lips. An incomprehensible joy lit up her face. She babbled strange words:

25

"*Pooran jalva si Mahpoutra!*"

No one understood these words, but it seemed as if Ludovic had grasped their meaning. He came forward, put his paws on the side of the bed. Grunting with satisfaction, he placed his head toward the hand of the pretty girl who, without hesitating, without the least sign of fear, caressed his silky fur.

"Ah! Well, Mademoiselle," broke out Cicada, incapable of staying silent any longer, "Ludovic is one of your friends then? Now, there's a secretive person. He didn't tell me anything about that."

The sick woman had closed her eyes again, but she was listening. Evidently, she didn't understand the language, because she made a gesture of irritation, and in the same unknown language that she had already used, she said a few more words. Her accent was soft, the syllables harmonious. Only Cicada scratched his head, grumbling:

"What is that gibberish?"

It was clear that the girl was a foreigner and that she didn't know French. The newcomer came forward and spoke to Madame Arbras:

"That child should come with me. Her family probably lives in the neighborhood, and she is worrying them a great deal. If you would please give her something to wear, I would take her to the Chateau. My friend, Baron Melecluse, possesses a collection of dictionaries with all known dialects. By showing them to the poor little girl, I will learn her nationality and, in an hour perhaps, it will be possible to reassure her parents, who must be worried about her."

"Ah! That's an inspiration from a good heart. Let's go inside, Monsieur. In ten minutes, the girl will be all set."

The newcomer bowed, then turned towards Cicada.

"You will come with me, my boy; I may need you."

"Don't keep him too long," interrupted Kéradec. "The storm will subside towards the morning and we have to embark."

"No. No fishing tomorrow, not for him, not for you. I'm renting the *Saint-Kaourentin* for the day. I'll pay for it. You will come to see me at the Chateau Melecluse with your men."

The Captain was confused as to how to thank him.

"I understand, Captain Kéradec," said the newcomer. "That's settled. Go get some sleep and see that your sailors do also. Goodnight."

After saying that, the newcomer gently pushed the sailors outside. Cicada followed them.

Ten minutes later, the newcomer and Cicada were alone in the room adjacent to that of Madame Arbras, who was still in the room with the girl. A quarter of an hour went by; then the door opened and the pharmacist's wife appeared leading the foreign girl by the hand. Cicada gasped with admiration. The girl's clothes, still wet, had not been given back to her. Instead, Madame Arbras had dressed her in her own daughter's clothes, an attractive Breton dress. It consisted of a little lace red bonnet and a white embroidered dress with blue flowers. Thus dressed, the foreign girl looked exquisite and charming.

But the newcomer did not allow Cicada to turn his enthusiasm into one of those fantastic elucubrations. He smiled at the girl who had been snatched from the waves and asked the pharmacist's wife to go before them. All three went down the stairs, shook Monsieur Arbras's hand, and left.

On the quay, hidden in the shadows, there was a parked carriage hitched to two bay horses which came out into the luminous circle projected by the lanterns. Obeying the newcomer, Cicada and the girl took a seat in the carriage; Ludovic jumped into the seat next to the coachman. Then the newcomer sat down near the children, after saying a friendly goodbye to Madame Arbras, commanding: "To the Chateau."

The coachman, immobile on his seat, picked up the reins. His horses left at a fast trot. The team went alongside the harbor, across the bridge, then took the twisting road that climbed the hill dominated by the Chateau Melecluse. Until then, the three travelers had not spoken to each other. But then, the newcomer leaned toward the foreign girl and spoke to her slowly in that same melodious language which she herself had used. She exclaimed joyously, clapped her hands, and answered with a rush of words.

Stupefied, Cicada said:

"Well, so, it seems that you understand her jargon."

"Yes," the man replied. "Stop talking."

Stop talking! Ah, well! The Parisian boy wanted an explanation.

"Why did you not tell me that before?"

But his voice stopped in his throat. The man now looked at him with his cold, dominating eyes.

"I do what is needed and I don't like questions. Be quiet!"

Then, returning his attention to the foreign girl, he started a conversation with her in a language that was incomprehensible to Cicada. However, we can provide a translation:

"What is your name?" asked the man.

"Anoor."

"That's a first name. Don't you have another name?"

"Perhaps I once had, but I don't know what it was."

"What is your country?"

"I don't know."

"However, you are not a native of this country?"

"No, I come from far away, very far away."

"Who came with you?"

"Arkabad."

"Arkabad, you say... Who is Arkabad?"

"A man."

"I am sure, but is he your parent, your servant, or your friend?"

27

The girl seemed to be looking for an answer. Then, silently shaking her head, she murmured:

"I don't know."

In his turn, the man made an impatient gesture.

"Where do you live?"

Anoor made a vague gesture.

"My home is over there... far away. To get there, one must travel by sea for many days. I was very little when we left. I don't remember anything more."

"All right. Then, yesterday, where did you live?"

"Nowhere."

Suddenly, the man grew impatient.

"Ah! This is no joke. You didn't sleep out under the beautiful stars?"

"No... In the boat."

"What boat?"

"I don't know."

These words sentence that consistently came out of her mouth were unnerving. The man frowned, Anoor quickly added:

"The ship carried us for several weeks. It came into a port. What port? Arkabad didn't tell me. He had me get off the boat onto the ground. There was a car waiting. He told me to get into it. We were driven in the car for some hours. Then it stopped on a high place where you could see the howling ocean and the stars. I was afraid, but Arkabad got out. He picked me up and put me on the ground saying:

" 'Come, look at the ocean.'

"He took my hand, and I went with him, shivering. Then, we came to the jetty. Waves were crashing on each side, covering us with foam.

" 'Arkabad,' I cried, 'let's go back; that scares me!'

"My companion lifted me off the ground. He growled in my ear:

" 'You won't come back!'

"Suddenly his arms came apart... I felt myself falling... The water opened up under my body... covered me. And I don't know anything else, I swear to you."

She fixed her innocent eyes on the man, who had lowered his head. He was thinking. Anoor's story left no doubt; a crime had been attempted, but for what reason? The girl, as he had recognized immediately, spoke a Hindu dialect. Did she come from that great nation of two hundred fifty million people made illustrious by the exploits of Brahma, Shiva, and Vishnu? And if so, from what part of it?

Suddenly, he lifted his forehead and pointed his hand toward Ludovic, who was seriously seated, like a very stylish valet.

"You had already seen that animal before last night?"

"Him? Perhaps. I surely saw one that looked like him."

"Where?"

"Over there, at the house, far away. There were several like him, and we played with them."

"When you say *we*, who was with you?"

"She was."

"Who is she?"

"I don't remember her name. She was beautiful, but sad. She often cried."

"Your mother?"

Anoor shook her head.

"No, not my mother, no... I wouldn't have forgotten that."

She was wringing her hands, as if in distress.

"I can't tear away the curtain that hides the past from me. I was so little!"

The man gently held her wrists and in a soft voice said:

"Don't trouble yourself, me girl. You loved the woman of whom you are speaking?"

"Oh, yes!"

"Then, we will find her."

There was such communicative confidence in the man's voice that Anoor immediately became calm. Cicada, who had been present during that interview in a foreign language, of which he had not understood a word, was stupefied.

"Ah!" he said after a moment, returning to his original question, despite his initial lack of success, "so you speak that gibberish too. Why, then, did you not tell the Arbras or the Captain?"

"Because I judged it convenient not to do that," the man replied. "Don't ask any questions. Just answer me. You are brave..."

"Perhaps, yes,"

"And it doesn't displease you to do a good deed, at the end of which you may probably acquire a fortune..."

"A fortune really?"

"It doesn't matter. I need someone who is devoted and brave. Do you want to follow me?"

"Where?"

"Wherever I go, without ever being too concerned about the reasons that motivate my actions."

Cicada scratched his head.

"I am curious," he began; then changing his tone. "Will that help that young lady?"

"Yes."

"Then I agree, provided Captain Kéradec consents."

"He will."

"And Ludovic will be a member of our party?"

"Of course."

"It's a deal! You are my new boss now. What is your name?"

An odd smile passed over the man's lips.

"I don't have a name," he finally said. "You may call me Doctor; that will suffice."

For an instant, the young man remained silent; then, making his knuckles crack with that gesture which cannot be imitated, that scholars of the entire world have borrowed from the Parisian street urchins, he said:

"That's nice," he exclaimed. "A girl rescued out of the ocean; a Doctor without a name; it's like a serial novel. Only me, it does bother me a little... I can give you a surname, can't I?"

"If you'd like."

"Decidedly, you're a brave man. From now on, Cicada shall be the friend of Doctor... Doctor..." The boy stopped for a second, but he almost immediately continued: "I am as stupid as a duck. Your surname is already there..." And with comic gravity, he concluded: "...It's Mystery! It suits you. You'll be Doctor Mystery!"

Just at that moment, the car arrived to Chateau Melecluse. Anoor and Cicada were taken to two spacious bedrooms, where they were not long in going to sleep. As for "Doctor Mystery," he went back to the one he had been occupying for several days.

For a long time, he walked up and down, seeming preoccupied. Finally, he went to bed, murmuring:

"At any price, I must find out if that girl is originally from India. That would marvelously serve my projects."

What did those words mean? Who was that man who had declared he didn't have a name? The one imagined by Cicada was justified. No character was ever more mysterious than this strange Doctor.

The next day, the Doctor left the Chateau discreetly and went back to Audierne, where he sent a telegram addressed to Dr. Opal, rue d'Assas, Paris. It read:

Met young boy with miniature bear named Ludovic. Recognize animal as having belonged to dear friends. Can you say where he comes from? Please reply to Chateau Melecluse, Audierne, Finistère. Signed: M. Saïd.

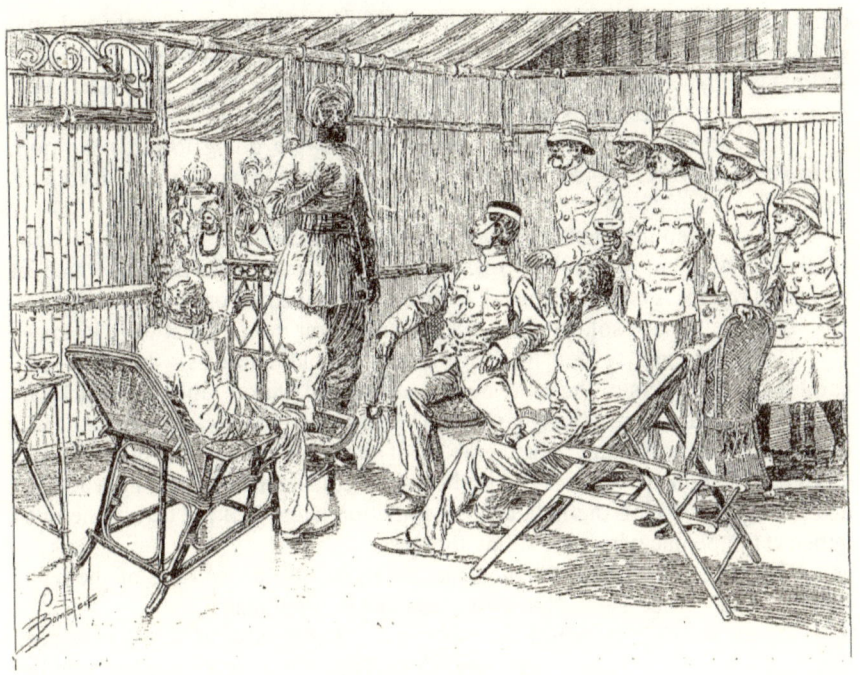

CHAPTER III
The Chariot of Jagannath

Four months later...

Aurangabad is a pretty village in Nizam, attractively set along the left bank of the Pootri, a little river with blue waters which comes down from the Ghats mountain range.[6] Now, the fifth day of the week of the Hindu month *Amhri* (the fourteenth of June),[7] the streets of that little city were unusually active. Everywhere there were busy pedestrians; tunics with sparkling colors and multi-colored turbans mingled with each other in an orgy of light and color. Here and there, men, mounted on horses with red harnesses studded with copper orna-ments cleared with difficulty a passage through the crowd. Then the elephants

---

[6] D'Ivoi's knowledge of Indian geography seems somewhat fanciful. Nizam pre-sumably refers to Nizamabad, a city and a district located in the north-western region of Telangana. Aurangabad, on the other hand, is a city located in the state of Maharashtra and is the largest city in the Marathwada region. We could not locate a "Pootri River."

[7] Reference unknown. *Jyaistha* and *Asadha* are the lunar months corresponding to June.

came forward with a processional step, their back covered with purple and gold cloth, balancing palanquins on their strong shoulders. Between the curtains of the palanquins were smiling women's faces, daughters of rich merchants, Kshatryas [8] or Nababs, all subjects of Her British Majesty.

All that society, pedestrian and horseman, were going towards the port, whose conical towers surrounded the sacred road that led to the venerated temples.

Not far from that port, there was an Anglo-Hindu bar. There were no walls at all. Instead, there was lattice work crisscrossed in capricious designs which let air pass through. A tent of blue and white cloth formed the top.

Outside, Cipaye soldiers held the horses of their masters that were inside.

Under the tent, several English officers in colonial dress—dolman white, and bouffant trousers of the same color—sat around wicker tables on which one of their colleagues, expert in that work, was seriously making a *lemonade*. It was under that harmless name that members of the English army in India made a mixture of lemon and whiskey. And those gentlemen, so disdainful in general of everything concerning the indigenous population, were looking across the open lattice at the people who were filling the street.

"Matthews," asked a tall lieutenant standing by a comrade of the same rank, who was twice as fat, "have you seen that unusual man?"

"Seen, seen..." grumbled the other man, "I can only say that I have seen him at a distance... That strange house that everyone is talking about was besieged by two thousand fanatics who wanted to be admitted at any price to his presence. I was able to make myself a passageway by beating people out of my way with my cane... I did see the Doctor, but, my word, I was choking; my throat was clutched by the stench from the crowd and I had to step back. There you are, Thompson, that's all my adventure."

The officers present, who had interrupted their private conversation to listen to Matthews and Thompson's conversation, smiled. But the latter didn't consider himself as beaten yet.

"Your words mean then, Matthews," he replied, "that you have seen that Doctor, if only for a short while; but you did see him, nevertheless?"

"Yes, I did."

"What's he like? Can you tell us?"

"Oh, certainly!"

"Then tell us; we are listening."

There was quick movement of curiosity from the crowd and Lieutenant Matthews obviously flattered to be the object of everybody's attention, began talking in an important voice:

"That gentleman, Doctor Mystery—it's the nickname he has taken..."

---

[8] One of the four *varna* (social orders) of Hindu society, associated with warrior aristocracy.

"Very nice. Continue."

"Six feet tall, approximately. Thin, elegant, exceptionally fine arms and legs; his face is pale, expressive, with magnificent eyes. Summing up, he is not handsome in the English fashion, which is the most handsome in the universe; but nevertheless, dressed in a uniform, he would make a superb officer."

"Ah-ha!"

At that exclamation, that came out of every mouth, Matthews stood up, showing off his height advantageously, and slowly continued:

"That's what the man looks like. As for his "rolling house," imagine a big wagon, forty feet long and thirteen feet wide, with two levels, containing a complete apartment. At the back, there's a moveable platform that can be pulled up to allow access to the interior. At the front, there's a terrace covered with a canopy that is pretty and very comfortable."

"But that vehicle must be horribly heavy?"

"Less than it would appear, because the Doctor's servant explained to me that the material used to construct it was aluminum."

"Very good!"

"Aluminum," exclaimed Thompson, wiping his forehead on which there were drops of sweat. "It would certainly be stifling inside, in this temperature."

Matthews shrugged and replied:

"Not at all."

"How can that be?"

"The ingenuity of its inventor, just that. The walls are made up of parallel panels filled with cellulose, which doesn't let in either heat or cold."

There was a murmur; the officers shook their heads in an approving way. Evidently, they had just felt a certain approval for this unknown Doctor, whose presence broke the usual monotony of garrison life at Aurangabad.

Certainly, the feeling brought about by the arrival of that person was justified. In the morning of the next day, his wagon-house had appeared on the military road which connected the city of Nizam to the Administration section of Mumbai. Where did he come from? It was impossible to know, but its owner was certainly *persona grata* as part of the British Raj, because his vehicle had been authorized to park at the foot of Lonavala Hill, which overlooks one of the four forts set up in Aurangabad. Next, the servants had left the aluminum house and went throughout the city carrying big signs on which there was written, in large letters, in English, Hindi and Urdu the following information:

Grand Master of Science
Will See Free of Charge those who want to consult him.
He will do what no one yet has been able to do.
He will defy all of society.
He will even defy the Brahmins.

That last sentence had startled the minds of the natives. To defy the Brahmins in India was an act of foolish daring. That was the most powerful caste, among others, and the British conquerors themselves had made concessions towards them to gain their favors.[9] The Brahmans were protected by the Viceroy of India and defying them appeared to the masses to be an act of madness.

It is true that the defiance of this "Doctor Mystery" appeared to affect only scientific things; but, then again, wasn't it imprudent to provoke the Brahmins who controlled all science and all aspects of knowledge, were jealous of their authority, and whose mysterious studies were done in the protected holy temples? They were regarded by the common people as following divine instructions, which elevated them right up to the throne of the Creator. So the effect of this announcement was shattering.

The people, the poor masses, all the exploited, responded as a group to the appeal of this mysterious Doctor, who felt strong enough to challenge the Brahmins. The noblemen and the merchants and bankers chose to remain prudently neutral.

Doctor Mystery treated those who came to his rolling house, giving remedies to the sick, pills lessening hunger to the very poor, and curing rheumatism by electronic applications. Judgment was made based on the large numbers who came, and it was understood how difficult it had been for Lieutenant Matthews to approach that personage who had become so famous in a few days.

By the end of the day, the Doctor's reputation had taken on heroic proportions, following the intervention of the Brahmins. No one liked the crowd, the Brahmin priests least of all. At first, they were not motivated by the defiance of the newcomer, but on seeing that popularity turning into a crowd towards his rolling house, on hearing the workers sing the praises of the Doctor in every tone, they became indignant against the man whose influence turned their own influence pale.

The Supreme Brahmin of the Diocese of Aurangabad, had gone to the Lonavala Hill, accompanied by his parasol bearers, his musicians, and his sacred dancers. He had summoned the newcomer to meet him alone. The Doctor had replied that his house, like his heart, was open to all those who were suffering; that he would welcome the Supreme Brahmin with pleasure, but that he would never agree to close his door to any creature whomsoever, even if he was of the poorest caste. In less diplomatic terms that meant:

"Come if you want to see me; but you will talk to me, like anyone else, in front of everybody."

---

[9] Here, d'Ivoi embarks on a scholarly—and not altogether entirely accurate—lecture about the three major religions of India at the time—Vedic (a.k.a. Brahmanism), Buddhism and Islam—providing statistics which are only of a passing interest today. We have deleted this passage.

The enthusiasm that that speech gave to the little people can easily be guessed. But the anger that was born in the great priest on hearing that could also be understood. It was a paving stone thrown into a frog pond. However, the Supreme Brahmin, whose name was Aïtar, accepted the invitation; he had thought about it. To talk to a person so high as he, the Doctor must have thought himself extraordinarily strong. It was necessary to conduct himself very cleverly and according to the circumstances. But he soon regretted his agreement.

"You had the presumption to defy the sacred college of the Brahmins?" began Aïtar, with haughtiness.

"Exactly," replied the Doctor in the most non-aggressive tone.

"You admit it?"

"With no difficulty."

The newcomer was so calm that the arrogance of the Brahmin fell away.

"Do you know that is great audacity?" questioned the Brahmin.

"I've been told that," replied the Doctor, without concern. "But only your caste alone would have anything to gain by opposing my will. I've had to be bold in order to win."

Aïtar trembled. As for the crowd gathered around the two men, they listened with mouth open in astonishment, feeling intense admiration for the unknown man who spoke of conquering the feared priests.

"Then, what are your intentions?" questioned the Brahmin after a short hesitation.

"I have no reason to hide them."

"I'm listening."

"Near the little town of Ellora, twenty miles from here,[10] there are some deep gorges where the patient chisels of our ancient ancestors carved out a sacred subterranean town. In the mountain itself, after those excavations, there is the Temple of Kailasa, whose towers, vast rooms, terraces, are chiseled out of a single block of basalt. Everyone had prayed at this venerated sanctuary, a monument unique in the world.

"Well?" asked Aïtar.

"Well, in that far-away temple, you have kept locked up a fakir,[11] famous for his virtues. No one can approach him. You are the only one that can receive

---

[10] Ellora today is a UNESCO World Heritage Site located in the Aurangabad district of Maharashtra. It is one of the largest rock-cut Hindu temple cave complexes in the world, featuring Buddhist and Jain monuments with artwork dating from the period 600-1000 AD. Cave 16, known as the Kailasa temple, is a particularly notable cave temple in India as a result of its size, architecture and having been entirely carved out of a single rock. The Kailasha temple, inspired by Mount Kailasha, is dedicated to Shiva, and not Vishnu as stated by d'Ivoi in a footnote.

[11] A Muslim or Hindu ascetic, famous for his virtues and wisdom.

his oracular communications, that his wisdom dictates, and communicate them to the people."

"That's true. Beliad—the fakir—is in the Seventh Circle of the Wise. Our rites do not allow him to appear before profane eyes."

The Doctor smiled. As if he was not aware of the magnitude of his request, he continued, placidly:

"The same. I want to talk to Beliad."

Silence followed. In everyone, these simple words had brought forth a state close to bewilderment.

"Speak to him?" Aïtar finally said. "Is that what you are thinking about?"

"That's all I'm thinking about."

"That's impossible."

"You are mistaken; because I wish it."

And the Doctor's dark eyes stared with powerful authority into those of the Brahmin, who closed his and in a not very firm voice replied:

"We cannot permit that."

"In that case, I will bypass your permission."

Those assembled trembled. The newcomer started to go beyond the defense set up by the Brahmins. Aïtar himself was staggered.

"You are going ahead without our permission?" he stammered.

The Doctor didn't allow him to finish.

"Not quite," he said casually. "I will keep you from stopping me, that's all." And in a clear, commanding voice, he added: "Listen to me. You are resisting because you do not know my power. I wish to show it to you, and to those of your caste. Tomorrow, the fifth day of the Shringar Week, the colossal chariot of Vishnu, that you call Jagannath, will make its annual appearance outside the Ellora Sanctuary.[12] It must take the road going from the temples to Aurangabad and present itself to the adoration of the faithful who will be crowded along its path."

"I know this."

"The chariot will not complete that sacred journey. The road is hardly wide enough to allow it to pass through. I will place my house across the road."

"You would dare to commit that sacrilege?"

Religious terror shook those present. Several of them threw themselves on the floor, hitting their foreheads against the metallic plaques. But again, the Doctor raised his voice:

---

[12] Jagannath (in English: Juggernaut) is a deity worshipped in India as part of a triad along with his brother Balabhadra and sister, devi Subhadra. To most Vaishnava Hindus, particularly the Krishnaites, Jagannath is an abstract representation of Krishna (not Vishnu as stated here). To some Shaiva and Shakta Hindus, he is a symmetry-filled tantric form of Bhairava, a fierce manifestation of Shiva associated with annihilation.

36

"There will be no sacrilege. Vishnu will clearly show whom he prefers; you, or me. It's the judgement of the god himself who will settle our differences. It is he himself who will force the team of the chariot to stop, to leave the road to Ellora open for me."

And, as on all the faces could be read disbelief, the Doctor extended his arm with commanding majesty:

"Come now, Brahmin, report my words to those of your caste. And you, country people, workers, invite your brothers to the judgement of Vishnu. Tell them that the Keeper of Beings is going to manifest his kindness to the man who loves the weak, the man who has nothing, and hopes to snatch them out of poverty and slavery."

Everyone obeyed and left the aluminum house. The Doctor was alone.

"Poor people," he murmured, "how far are they from freedom! How many lies, how much charlatanism, are necessary to lead them to a better life." Then, with a brusque gesture, he continued: "The task of each day is sufficient. It takes centuries for Truth to shine in the face of Society. It is the succession of tyrannies that leads to the advent of Liberty…"

He shook his head like a man who pushes away an unwelcome thought, and put a smile back on his lips,

"Let's go and let those children know that this business will turn out as they would have wished."

Saying that, he left the room on the entry floor where he had received Aïtar and went into an adjacent room. He walked toward the right angle, placing his hand on a metallic plaque.

There was the sound of an opening, then the sound of hinges in motion. A trap door opened, and a willow basket, held by hooks and an iron chain, slowly descended down to the floor. It was in essence a smaller version of the kind of cart which allowed workers to go down into the depths of the coal mines. The Doctor sat down in it. Then it automatically went back up through the opening. The trap door closed, and the sound of the mechanism stopped at the same time.

The Doctor was now in a little room on the second floor. The plaques forming the walls had strange arrangements: diamond-shaped, polygons, and squares, assembled in seemingly capricious designs. From place to place, golden hooks stood out from the walls. But there was a bizarre detail: not one of those supports were alike. Looking at them closer it could be seen that each represented the contoured face of one of the Vedic gods. It was the personification of Heaven: Varuna, the spirit of the firmament, Agni, lord of fire, Rudra of the storms, Surya of the sun, Vayu, Mitra…

There were thirty-three gods, topped by the of Vishnu, Shiva, and Brahma.[13]

The Doctor didn't give them a single look. In front of him there was a rectangular door. He pushed it gently and went into a more spacious room.

Two young Brahmins were seated, each on one side of a little table, and they were playing checkers. Both wore long silk tunics, tied at the waist with the same material, falling to the ankles on bouffant trousers. Beside them, there was a little bear seated on his back side looking at them seriously.

Seeing the Doctor, the two stood up quickly. One of them ran to him with his hand outstretched and, speaking French with a Parisian accent that could not be imitated, said:

"Hello, Doctor, it's going well," said Cicada, shaking the Doctor's hand with a firm grip.

"Eh! Eh! Gently, gently!"

The other person remained motionless, and with an attitude full of reserve, murmured in a soft voice:

"I greet you, Master," said Anoor, also in French.

The little bear came to rub himself like a cat against the legs of the newcomer, it was of course Ludovic.

Hearing the words of his companion, Cicada was startled.

"*Master?* Listen, little sister, I have explained to you that French isn't the language of slaves. We don't say Master, we say boss, or sir."

Anoor smiled and replied, "I will remember to say Boss."

"All right," said Cicada, "you must try to do better in the future."

"I will indeed, I promise you, Lord Cicada."

The young man raised his arms to Heaven.

"Good God, now she calls me Lord, me, a step away from the streets," and turning towards the Doctor, with mock gravity, he added: "Come now, Doctor, to be a professor of French is not a bed of roses!"

The Doctor laughed outright and said:

"Master Cicada, I believe your student is having some fun at your expense."

"What?" the young man said, about to launch himself into another tirade.

But the Doctor interrupted him with a gesture.

"Calm down, my boy. When I meet the two of you at Audierne, four months ago, that poor child did not understand a word of your language; today she can express all of her thoughts in it. That is to your credit, and that of her character. But we have more pressing matters to discuss right now…"

---

[13] Traditionally, there are thirty-three gods in the Vedas. There are really many more, however, and the list of the thirty-three can vary. There is also the problem than the gods come in groups, and what the groups are even varies.

And with calculated slowness, in order that none of his words would escape the young woman, he added:

"I promised you, Anoor, to find the house where you met Ludovic in the past."

The young girls' eyes were shining.

"Yes, I remember, Master," then she quickly rephrased herself with a suppliant look toward Cicada, "Sorry, I meant to say, Sir."

"By way of Doctor Opal, who gave that animal to our friend Cicada," the Doctor continued, "I learned that the bear came from an explorer in South Asia, a Mister Strijle, who himself got him from a fakir named Beliad, who is today a voluntary captive in the Temple of Ellora."

"And?" Anoor asked, wanting to hear more.

"We shall see that fakir tomorrow."

"Tomorrow?"

"Yes," and with a slight nuance of irony, the Doctor added, "Only, we will have to do some astonishing things in order to appear before that saintly person. And among those things is stopping the Jagannath."

Anoor let out a little cry of fright.

"Stop the Jagannath! The chariot of the divine Krishna!"

The Doctor nodded with a satisfied expression.

"Then you know of it, my child?"

"Yes, yes," she said, seeming to search her memory. "She spoke of that, at another time, in the past."

"Don't try to remember. Your words are enough for me. You speak Hindustani. You know the Brahmin legends. Therefore, you were brought up in India and we are on the right track. Tomorrow, perhaps, the fakir Beliad will point out to us the house where you were born."

Anoor joined her hands in an ardent gesture of hope, but suddenly her face turned dark.

"Bit first, the Jagannath must be stopped."

"That will be done."

"Shiva is all-powerful," she murmured with doubt in her voice.

"Less so than I."

The girl looked at the Doctor.

"Oh! You are strong, I know that... Perhaps you can defeat Krishna."

There was superstitious terror in her voice. The Doctor approached her and took her hands,

"You believe that, child; that's good. Do you also believe that I only use my powers to defend the oppressed?"

Without hesitating, she answered:

"Yes, you are good."

And already reassured, she added:

"All those who help you are good. Those sailors from the *Saint-Kaourentin*, Captain Kéradec and the others that you took on at Audierne, and who have followed us right here, are gentle and helpful toward strangers..."

Then she pointed toward Cicada, who was listening with interest.

"He, too, is good. He scolds me often, but I am not afraid..."

"And you are right," the young man exclaimed, "because I am devoted to you, sister, to the death. On my faith as a Parisian, I would let myself be hacked to pieces for you."

Such were the events that happened to the inhabitants of Aurangabad as they spread out on the road to Ellora. Such were the facts that had motivated the English Officers assembled in the bar at Dinarou.

Lieutenants Matthews and Thompson continued their conversation:

"And that devil of a Doctor Mystery," continued Thompson, "has taken it upon himself to bar the passage of the Jagannath on the road to Ellora?"

"Exactly," replied said Matthews. "I was present, and I heard him as clearly as I'm hearing you now."

"But, given the fanaticism of the Hindus, he's going to get himself torn to pieces!"

"That might, in fact, happen."

"Speaking of that," exclaimed a young soldier with a candid face, who had not been in the country very long, "I need to learn a mass of things. Who can tell me something about this famous Jagannath?"

Matthews shrugged.

"Ask Woolgate; he's the pocket dictionary of the garrison."

"Hip! Hip!", shouted the others, "Hooray for the pocket dictionary!"

Then everybody turned towards the little Lieutenant, who had a sunburned face with a yellowish tint, and who, until then, had been standing to one side.

"Come now, Woolgate, introduce this neophyte to the Jagannath."

The person asked didn't have to be begged, and in the voice of a professor standing at a podium, he began:

"Jagannath in Sanskrit, or we call it, Juggernaut," he said, "combines the word *jagat*, meaning "world," and nātha, meaning "lord." It is one of the names of Krishna found in the Sanskrit epics. The notion of a huge chariot bearing an image of a Hindu god comes from the Jagannatha Temple in Puri, Odisha, which holds the annual *Ratha Yatra*, or procession of chariots carrying the deities of Jagannath, Subhadrā, and Balabhadra. Watered by the Mahanadi River, it has fifty thousand inhabitants. There is, in its surroundings, a temple which contains a colossal statue of Jagannath. That statue works miracles: by touching it with one's nose, one can be assured of abundance. In its knee resides health; its toe guarantees love, etc. As in the past, each year, the priest takes the divine statue to one of the palaces of Jagannath, where the people are allowed to rub themselves with ecstatic devotion against the nose, knee, or foot, of the god. Naturally, in order to transport the heavy mass, an enormous vehicle, drawn by thirty-two horses, is needed. The ceremony attracts a considerable number of pilgrims, sixteen or seventeen hundred thousand. Each one pays a tax to the temple, which brings in an income equivalent to two hundred thousand pounds. That affluence of the faithful, and money, has caused harm to other sanctuaries of India. Because of that, there were recriminations, and a council of the Brahmins finally decided that each temple, in its turn, would be tasked with organizing the Jagannath procession. Each created their own reproduction of the Jagannath chariot. This year, that lucrative honor has fallen to Ellora. There you are; you now know as much as I do."

For a minute, the officers remained silent.

All of them agreed, *in petto*, that Doctor Mystery was gifted with an audacity that had no equal. To dare to attack an institution that had moved a council of Brahmins to take action was unbelievable. As practical people, those English soldiers were thinking:

That man is probably mad. If he were not, he would understand that the Brahmins will do everything, not to defend Jagannath, who as a god is powerful enough to defend himself, but to protect their own interests.

"That's good," said Thompson, translating the thought of everyone, "that's something that's going to be interesting to watch."

"Certainly," agreed everyone around him.

"It's not pleasant to go riding horseback on the road under this sky of fire, but, really, the adventure is worth the trouble."

"It doesn't matter," grumbled Matthews, "that we are going to take a risk. One has to earn his pleasure."

"Probably, but I would prefer to be present comfortably at the duel of the foreigner against Krishna, seated in the shade with a glass of lemonade in front of me."

Some first lieutenants, more excited than others, were going to protest. They did not have time to do so. A serious and soft voice was suddenly heard. It said:

"Gentleman, I gladly offer you seats, shade, and lemonade."

With the same movement they all turned towards the one who had spoken, and they remained speechless. None of the officers involved in the conversation had noticed a man standing several feet from them, since he had entered without any noise. Tall, thin, he was standing in an attractive pose. His pale green silk shirt, which was tied with a red belt, his trousers tied at the ankle above his patent leather shoes of an irreproachable style, his turban, on the front of which was a shiny gold decoration, made him look like one of those Nabobs consecrated to the cult of a divinity, who formed a kind of sacred caste. But his face, smiling with a beauty that was almost superhuman, quickly chased away that impression. He put his hand on his chest and introduced himself:

"I, Doctor Mystery, would be very happy to offer you my hospitality in my rolling house, to travel the very hot road to Ellora."

For an instant, those present hesitated. The sudden appearance of the man who had occupied everyone's thoughts, and his invitation arriving at such a propitious time, had, considering the circumstances, something of the fantastic, with which everyone was impressed. However, the perspective of walking twelve miles in the hot sun dismissed that feeling of vague distrust, and Cherryh, the oldest Lieutenant, believed it was his duty to reply in the name of all of them:

"If our acceptance would not seem indiscreet, I would say: Thank you, Sir, we agree."

"There is neither indiscretion nor danger," continued the Doctor.

A mummer of doubt escaped all the lips.

"As for indiscretion, I would be ungracious to inquire," declared Cherryh, "but as regards danger, there may be some of that."

"You really believe that?"

"Certainly," replied Cherryh. "The Brahmins are jealous of their influence and they're powerful."

"Then," asked the Doctor, still smiling, "are you afraid?"

"Afraid?"

The officers straightened up with heroic postures.

"An English officer is never afraid," growled Cherryh.

The Doctor bowed:

"I thought so. In that case, nothing keeps you from going with me to my rolling house and honoring me with your presence to witness the forthcoming spectacle."

They looked at him with amazement. Without appearing to do so, the mysterious Doctor had seemed to phrase the conversation so that his invitation could not be refused. As the proposition seemed basically pleasant, the invitation was soon agreed upon.

Following the Doctor, everybody left the bar, sending away their mounts and those holding them.

Twenty minutes later, they arrived at the aluminum house.

The rapid description that Matthews had given, was basically accurate: it was a long, two-stories wagon which had an interlocking roof; at the back, there were stairs, and at the front a terrace. All of that was in unpainted bronzed aluminum shining in the rays of the sun like a bar of pale gold. At the top of the steps, seven men dressed in Hindu uniforms of dark green were waiting for the Doctor. Anyone who had seen the *Saint-Kaourentin* would have recognized without any trouble Captain Kéradec and his six sailors: Yvon, short, stocky, with a round face; Kervas, and Belvenec, tall with large bones, a harsh look, two natives of Cornwall; Artener, of medium height, with a jovial face; and Kerloch from Douarnenez, stubborn as a mule and strong as a bull.

The Doctor climbed the stairs, preceding his guests. Passing near Kéradec, he stopped for a minute and exchanged these enigmatic sentences.

"My orders?"

42

"Carried out," replied the Captain. "Everything is ready."

"The bear?"

"Ready from his paws to his muzzle."

"The parabolic mirrors?"

"In place."

"Good."

That exchange of words had been so rapid that the English officers had not noticed it. Following the Doctor, they had gone into the rolling house. They went across a vestibule whose steps were made of pure aluminum and of bronzed aluminum, showing an alternation of white, silver, and gold. Then they went into a drawing room where everybody stopped with a cry of admiration. Here, again, the divider showed the two shades of aluminum, but it was no longer quadrilaterals being displayed there. Most of the circumference of the room showed figures fighting, praying; warriors, priests, women grouped together, a metal rendering of the great poem, the *Mahabharata*,[14] a marvelous story of the ancient fight of the Brahmins against the nobles, of the priests against the warriors, in which the warriors were vanquished.

That decoration covered three panels; on the fourth, there was a horseman whose horse, galloping madly, was lost in middle of a desolate countryside. In front of him there was the shadow of a fleeing woman carrying a star in front of her. Below it could be read, *Ber aoud*, which could be translated as, *Going towards the future*.

The Doctor let his guests look at their leisure, then in a deep voice which surprised them, said, pointing to the horseman:

"The Wise." And in a sweeping gesture, he pointed out the scenes of combat and added: "The Fools."

Without being concerned about knowing if he himself was included by his questioners in that definition, the Doctor began to walk again. He went into the dining room. Here, the aluminum combinations formed flowers on the wall. A large bay window opened onto the terrace, bordered by an open hand rail and sheltered from the rays of the sun by a yellow and white awning. Some little tables and chairs were placed there. The Doctor pointed at them.

"Gentlemen," he said, "my house is your house. I ask your permission to be absent for a moment. I need to look after the operation of the equipment. Sit down, please."

---

[14] One of the two major Sanskrit epics of ancient India (the other being the *Rāmāyaṇa*) about the struggle between two groups of cousins in the Kurukshetra War. It also contains philosophical and devotional material, such as a discussion of the four "goals of life." Among its stories is the *Bhagavad Gita*. Traditionally, its authorship is attributed to Vyāsa. The bulk was probably compiled between the 3rd century BC and the 3rd century AD. The events related by the epic probably fell between the 9th and 8th centuries BC.

Suddenly, he struck his forehead.

"I was about to forget! Look here, Gentlemen."

With a finger, he pointed at a row of buttons aligned to the right of the window.

"Under each of these electric buttons, there is the name of one of the drinks preferred by men in every country. To be served with whatever is to your taste, you have only to push the button that corresponds to the drink you have chosen. There is a chest over there," and he pointed it out. "It will open and you can take out the drink you have chosen. In this way, you avoid the comings and goings of servants."

The officers were listening, delighted.

"It's like a fairy tale," Matthews burst out.

"Indeed," added Thompson.

The Doctor shook his head.

"No, it's a scientific amusement, a simple perfection of automatic distribution that is commonly seen in Europe."

Saying that, he bowed, saying:

"Once again, I beg your pardon, Gentlemen. I shall return in a moment."

Leaving the terrace, the Doctor disappeared. While his guests were having as much amusement as college students on a vacation, pushing the distribution buttons of the most varied aperitifs, the Doctor returned to the salon. There, he had the basket that was installed in the room descend on hooks. He settled into it and reached the upper floor of the house.

Kéradec was in the room in the company of Cicada and Anoor. All three, their nose in the air, watched the ceiling with astonishment. The amazement displayed on their faces was certainly justified. The metallic panel had suddenly become animated. With incomprehensible clarity, since the room was hermetically sealed, the terrace of the rolling house, the balustrade, the tables, the chairs, were visible, as were the laughing English officers crowded around the aperitif dispenser.

Still more bizarre, the voices of those chatting could be heard being ecstatic about the rolling house. Those present were so absorbed by that spectacle, which was transforming the ceiling into something approaching a theatrical projection, cinematography with speech, that they were not aware of the Doctor's arrival.

Ludovic, himself—for the little bear was there too—whose brain had, without a doubt, been troubled by what had happened, remained immobile, leaning on his trembling paws, in an awkward and frightened position.

"Ah-ha!" said the Doctor, "my telephote is functioning well."

Everyone jumped and Cicada quickly said:

"For sure, Sir. With that piece of equipment there, you can hear and see people as if you were near them... And they don't know anything about it!"

"Oh!" murmured Anoor fervently, "the spirit of Brahma is in you."

"Oh, no, my child," said the Doctor, in a caressing voice, "it's just Western science. This is a refinement and upgrade of the telephone and of the telephote."

Cicada briskly cracked his knuckles to show his annoyance.

"What's wrong?" asked the Doctor.

"I wonder why," grumbled the young man, "you give your machines names that are like Greek to us."

"They *are* Greek. Telephone means that which transmits sound, and telephote means that which transmits images."

"Well, we're not Greek. It would be a great deal clearer if you were to call your machines: the *trompette* and the *bavette*."

"What are you talking about?"

The young man burst out laughing.

"Ah, you see how it feels now! This is Parisian slang. The *trompette*, that's the nose, because when you sneeze, you sound like one. And the *bavette*, that's the mouth, the source of all conversations..."

Cicada would have continued for a while if the Doctor had not stopped him.

"I get your point, but it's getting late. It's going to be necessary to leave. Kéradec, have you placed the parabolic mirrors?"

"Yes, Doctor," said the former Captain of the *Saint-Kaourentin*. "Here they are."

With his big hand, the man pointed out two reflectors where the concave part faced the front wall of the mobile house.

"Good. As soon as they are functional, you will slide in the mobile plaques."

While he was talking, the Doctor approached the partition wall, lightly pushed two small metallic panels that, running on slides, revealed square openings of about eight inches on the side.

"Through there," continued the Doctor, "you will see in the distance the chariot of Jagannath."

"Yes, Doctor."

"As soon as it is in view, look at the ceiling. You will see me among my guests. Remember this well: when I hold out my arm, saying: 'Krishna, show your faithful that I am the most beloved of your sons!' you will do as I have instructed you."

"Yes, Doctor."

"Perfect! I am going back down. Cicada, Anoor, you will come with me and bring Ludovic."

"Great!" exclaimed the young man, "but if you think you're going to stop the thirty horses of that chariot with your little mirrors, I will buy you with a kilo of cherries."

"You will see for yourself. You should be more like Anoor. She has confidence in me."

"Oh, yes!" the girl confirmed.

"So do I," shouted the boy, "but I would like to understand."

"I will explain it all to you, but later. Right now, it's necessary to act. Be careful of what you say. You and Anoor are my students—nothing more. There are numerous dangers around: death floats above us."

"Death?" repeated the Parisian urchin, placing himself quickly in front of the girl.

"But we will vanquish it," finished the Doctor. "Nevertheless, be careful. Now, let's go!"

An instant later, the basket deposited the Doctor and his "students" in the drawing room on the second floor, at the same time as the bear.

"What a funny make-over Ludovic has been given," remarked Cicada. "He smells funny."

"It's the smell of a Yellow Cactus from Bhutan which I brought here."

"In your place, Boss, I would have chosen a different perfume."

"You will change your mind, my boy."

Then, to cut short more questions, the Doctor went into the dining room, and from there, onto the terrace. He introduced his young friends to his guests; every one took a seat, and slowly, without any bumps, the rolling house started off. There was no noise when the motor started; no vibration accompanied its movement.

"Ah!" murmured the officers. "What an admirable construction!"

However, the speed increased little by little. Following the road on which it had been parked, it rejoined the main road to Ellora, and rapidly passed in the middle of the floats of the curious, who moved to one side out of superstitious respect as it drove by.

The more it advanced, the more the crowd increased. On the shoulder of the avenue, in fields beside the river, pedestrians, horsemen, elephants carrying palanquins followed each other, brushing against each other, with cries and exclamations. Then there were long lines of fakirs mumbling interminable litanies. But everything became quiet at the approach of the rolling house. There was terror in the looks that stared at that unknown machine that was moving toward an encounter with the chariot of Jagannath.

What mysterious and mystic drama was going to take place?

Excited, the English officers felt they no longer had the strength to talk. Motionless on the platform, they felt more discomfort at each turn of the wheels. Their host who, alone, dared to attack the immense power of the Brahmins, grew to immense proportions in their minds and they considered him with secret anguish.

He himself didn't seem to suspect the diverse sentiments that his behavior had brought about. Very calm, he talked in a low voice with his neighbors. He was smiling. One would really have thought that all that was happening had nothing to do with him. Nevertheless, it was certain that, if he failed in what he was trying to do, the fanatics that had come by the thousands to the Jagannath festival would cut him into pieces.

They had left the region of the plains that surrounded Aurangabad. The soil showed the approach of the mountainous country of the Ghats. And the crowd grew still bigger. Speed had to be slowed to go through the miserable village of Ellora, a mass of filthy cabins situated at the edge of the sacred gorge, where there were stacks of grandiose monuments testimonies to the faith of a free and powerful India.

At five hundred meters ahead, like a notch cut into the mountain by the axe of a giant wood cutter, there opened the Ellora gorge. And suddenly, a faraway murmur ran through the crowd massed on the rocks, in the little undulations, on the conical roofs of the inhabitants. The English officers themselves couldn't hold back a breathless "oh!" That was because, taking up all the width of the road, the colossal chariot of Jagannath had just entered their horizon.

Topped by an enormous golden statue of Krishna, the vehicle took the form of a tiered pyramid. At the very top, near the statue of the god, the *Sanyasi* (Ascetics) were wearing a white robe with silver ornaments. Below that, the *Vanaprastha* (Hermits) were wearing yellow tunics with gold stripes. Even lower, the *Grihastha* (Householders) and the *Brahmachari* (Bachelors) were covered with blue clothes with braids of red with metal stripes. Thirty-two horses with four rows of eight each, in the front, were drawing the enormous machine.

All around it, on foot, armed with lances and sacred shields, the officers of the Brahmin caste, students of the *darshana*, walked, chanting the praises of the Holy Trinity.

The rolling house was still moving forward. In two minutes, it would reach the chariot of Jagannath. What would happen then?

Suddenly, the crowd became petrified. No more gestures, no other sounds, except for twenty-thousand people gasping at the same time. All the hearts were beating, and the officers, who had stood up all at once with the same movement, looked, their eyes wide open, at the statue of Krishna, whose smiling face seemed to encourage those who wanted to stop on the road.

There were no more than three hundred feet between the two vehicles, then no more than one-fifty, then no more than sixty...

At that moment, the rolling house stopped.

There was a minute of agonizing wait. Then, Doctor Mystery stood up. He looked at the Brahmin Aïtar seated at the top of the chariot. Near him was a priest, whose face was hidden by a veil with two slit openings, through which shone a pair of excited eyes.

That character looked at Doctor Mystery with bizarre attention. One might have said that he was trying to understand him, to figure him out, and Aïtar, without a movement, his face motionless, without an expression, murmured:

"Do you recognize him, Arkabad?"

47

Arkabad! That was the name of the man who Anoor had accused of throwing her into the raging sea at Audierne!

"No," replied the other man in a cold voice.

Suddenly, his veil and robe began to shake.

"Oh!" he groaned.

"What's the matter?" asked Aïtar.

"There, on the balustrade of that infamous machine..."

"Whom do you see?"

"A person who has returned from the dead."

"Who?"

"Anoor! Anoor Tadjar that the Council of Brahmins had condemned to death. Anoor, whom I took far into the West; Anoor, whom I myself threw into the waves at the end of world... She is alive, standing there!"

And with frightened surprise, Arkabad added:

"What is the power of that man who knows how to snatch the ocean's victims?"

But the waiting crowd was beginning to murmur. Aïtar continued,

"What does it matter! That man is mad! Our chariot will never let him pass. Our faithful will tear his body apart. Anoor will also disappear in the confusion."

Aïtar stood up in his turn. He held out his arms:

"Let the defilement fall back on the heads of the infidels. Turn back, you who calls himself Doctor Mystery, or fear the wrath of the Gods!"

Like a field of swords in a stormy wind, the people bent over on hearing that feared voice. Many of them prostrated themselves; some of the children cried in fright; the women, the fakirs, and the pilgrims all chanted:

"Krishna! Krishna! Condemn the sacrilege."

On the terrace of the rolling house, the English officers exchanged worried looks. They regretted having accepted the Doctor's invitation. How could he keep his audacious promise?

But the Doctor had lost none of his confidence.

"Brahmin Aïtar," he shouted, "and you, men of the people who can hear me, I want to remind you of what I said yesterday..."

A shiver ran through those present. The heart of the newcomer had indeed moved the crowd.

"I said," he began again, "that I want to talk to the wisest of the wise, the fakir Beliad, a voluntary prisoner inside the temples of Ellora. That, I know, is forbidden by the rites, but Krishna himself approves of my request, and he will show it to everyone's eyes by pushing aside his chariot to the side and leaving the entrance to the sacred gorge free for me to enter. Isn't that what I said would happen Brahmin Aïtar?"

"Yes, you did," answered the one questioned, "but remember that if you have deceived us, only death will wipe out your sacrilege."

48

"I am not afraid; Krishna is with me."

Then the Doctor held out his arms. He shouted with a powerful voice, which reached the last rank that the spectators could hear.

"Krishna! Krishna! Show everyone who is your favorite son!"

He had hardly finished when a crackling noise was heard. The horses attached to the chariot neighed softly. The priests stood up on the tiers of the pyramid and did summersaults and unbelievable contortions. Reddish lights ran along the team of horses, along the metal ornaments on the Brahmins robes; a flame seemed to envelop the statue of the god.

The crowd shouted with terror; the officers themselves stepped back. On the terrace of the rolling house, they were flabbergasted at the unbelievable scene that had just taken place in front of their eyes.

The Doctor leaned over towards Cicada, who was standing near him, and whispered:

"Now you see the effect of my 'little mirrors,' as you called them."

"Yes, Boss..." Then with admiration: "Only I don't understand."

"I will explain it all to you later as I promised."

The Doctor interrupted himself. Anoor had seized his hands; she carried them to her lips. Excited, she stammered:

"Ah! Master, Master, how great you are!"

He didn't have time to answer. The unbelievable fireworks engulfed the chariot and continued to increase. Those running were bent over, the pedestrians were arguing, the Brahmins were reciting words that no one understood, and suddenly, the thirty-two horses, as if obeying an invisible signal, pulled to the side, drawing the vehicle out of the road and stopping in a neighboring field, running with sweat, trembling on their feet.

"Thank you Krishna, Keeper of the World," shouted Doctor Mystery. "Thank you for having shown your goodness and kindness for the most respectful of your children."

It was with an enthusiastic shout that the crowd responded to the "miracle." Everyone ran and wanted to touch the terrace of the aluminum house, the dwelling of the man to whom the god had just shown his friendship. But, with a sweeping gesture, the Doctor stopped them.

Everyone remained motionless, mute, everyone waiting for him to speak.

"Brothers," he said, "let the Brahmins approach. They must now take me to the Fakir Beliad."

The people moved aside, and the priests came forward, led by Aïtar, whose face had the pallor of marble.

"Krishna wishes it. Let it be done according to his wishes," said the Brahmin. "However, it is not in our power to conquer the guardians of the temples. But without a doubt, the god will protect you."

There was irony in those words, spoken apparently in deference. Throughout India, everyone knew about the guardians of the Temples of Ellora. They were wild animals: leopards, ocelots... The king of those guardians was a sacred tiger. That animal walked about at liberty in the caves dug out of the side of the holy gorge.

Like the others, the English officers understood. They turned towards the Doctor. What was he going to answer?

"You will guide me, you, Brahmin Aïtar," shrugged the Doctor. "I will walk on foot in your company, followed by my two students, and my guests here. I will bring no weapon. Krishna will watch over me, and he will strike down without pity whoever tries to stop me from accomplishing what I have decided."

And, as the English didn't seem to welcome the idea of a promenade in caves full of dangerous felines, he added:

"Gentlemen, there is no danger."

His confidence gained them over. Hadn't he already made the chariot of Jagannath turn aside? Everybody was ready to follow him; besides, their curiosity motivated them. They did not believe, as Westerners, in the intervention of the divine. It was scientific method, probably an electric instrument, that had triumphed over the Brahmins. But what instrument? Had the Doctor found the method of storing and dispensing lightning? It was an unanswerable question, and the impossibility of answering it only increased their desire to know.

The Doctor left the terrace and those behind him followed him; he went across the dining room, the drawing room, the vestibule, and down the steps which lifted up behind them, closing the entrance. At his sight, the curious threw themselves face down and there came up the prayers that faithful Hindus pronounce in front of the statues of their gods.

The Doctor smiled. For the crowd, he had become an incarnation of the divinity. At that moment, he was all-powerful, and if he had ordered the fanatics to massacre the Brahmins, they would have obeyed.

He slowly turned the rolling house around. Ludovic, whose sight was triumphant, walked in front of him. Anoor and Cicada, holding each other by the hand, followed; the English officers bought up the rear. Brahmin Aïtar and Arkabad watched them coming.

"Accompany them, brother," whispered Arkabad. "I will stay here."

"Why?"

"To investigate that strange machine, with which they conquered us. We have to know who our enemy is."

"Do you believe, then, that the wild beasts consecrated to Shiva will spare him in the caverns?"

"I don't know; but if they are spared, it will be up to us to make them disappear."

"You are right."

The two men separated. Arkabad got lost in the crowd, while Aïtar took a few steps in front of the Doctor.

"You are the vanquisher," said the Brahim in a submissive tone. "Command and I will obey."

"Take me to the Fakir Beliad,"

Aïtar bowed:

"You wish to face the guardians of the temples?"

"Tigers and panthers don't mean very much to one being protected by Krishna," shrugged the Doctor. "Be our guide."

His voice was so calm, his airs so self-assured, that the Brahmin couldn't hold back a look of surprise. However, he got himself under control and, without any other comment, started towards the sacred gorge.

CHAPTER IV
Sacred Tigers and Golden Tiger

Doctor Mystery followed Aïtar with his companions. The eyes of the crowd saw them disappear into the narrow rocky opening, then there was an immense humming. Too long suppressed by respect, the word flew out from everyone's mouths. The Hindus expressed their surprise and their admiration for what had just happened.

The Brahmin was still walking. Without a word, the Doctor and his escort matched their steps to his. They went deep into the narrow ravine, where the sun never came. A cool temperature, half daylight, followed the bright light of the plain, caused everyone to experience a mixed feeling of well-being and discomfort. Here and there, drops of water fell in cascades from the summit. They walked through veritable shadows of foamy liquid dust. Suddenly, the passage became larger. To the right, there was a giant stairway attached to the side of the rock. That was the entry to the subterranean temples.

There were three hundred straight steps, deeply cut into the rock. Each one was carved into a sitting lion, his face turned towards the road, seeming to look with threatening calm at the bold visitors who were coming to the door of the sanctuary.

Aïtar slowly pointed to the stairway with a gesture.

"You go first," responded the Doctor.

And the climb began.

At the top, there was a platform that went across the abyss, and in the granite wall, there was a large opening. The arch was supported by two columns showing lions sitting on their haunches.

The Brahmin crossed his arms, murmuring an unintelligible prayer. Striking his chest seven times, his forehead bowed, he went into the cavern of lions. It was the first of several unique caverns, *Chaityas* (Brahmin monasteries), *Viharas* (Buddhist chapels), and *Jainian* hypogeas, making up the Ellora sanctuary.

Despite their composure, the English officers were impressed by the chambers' sizes and construction, which echoed the sound of their steeps. In the half light of those mysterious grottos, fissures pierced through the rock let a pale, indecisive, troubling, light filter through.

Aïtar was still walking ahead, going around the columns ornamented with growling figures, brushing against the colossal statues of Shiva with his three faces. On the walls, there were the names of ancient nations from prehistoric times, now lost in the fog of centuries, which had been recorded in an interminable procession of the exploits of gods, demi-gods, and forgotten heroes.

Sometimes, in the narrow corridors were rocky masses holding together the temples between them.

Then, the walkers experienced a sharp pain. It seemed to them that the mountain had become narrower to try to hamper their progress. The terrifying magic that came out of that colossal sacred labyrinth made their flesh shiver, their hair stand on end, and their temples drip with cold sweat.

But the Doctor did not stop. Seemingly indifferent, he walked straight ahead, and his majestic stature, his dynamic walk caused his companions to experience a bizarre vision. They had the impression that one of the fabulous characters carved in the granite had suddenly separated from the stone, come down, and become alive, renouncing its eternal and immobile procession.

Anoor had taken Cicada's arm. She kept herself near him, shivering; and the Parisian boy, proud of that sign of confidence, happy to protect his friend, marched straight up, triumphant. His cheeky temperament did not allow him to say such things aloud, but he was much amused by all those "gentlemen" cut into the granite. The Temple walls produced in him the same effect as the comic strips of a newspaper.

To tell the truth, Ludovic didn't seem any more disturbed than his young master. The little bear didn't leave the Doctor. He stood up at his height, and showed for this antique Olympus a disdain that would have wounded them had they seen it.

Suddenly, faraway, they heard roaring. It swelled, magnified by the vaults. The officers stopped short, automatically carrying their hands to their sabers.

"The panthers of Shiva," shouted Aïtar.

"I heard," the Doctor said calmly. "Their presence indicates that we have crossed the last cave that comes before the Temple of Kailasa, the marvel of Ellora, where the fakir Beliad lives."

The Brahmin looked at him in surprise.

"Let's go," said the Doctor.

Aïtar shook his head.

"You are ignoring the fact that the tigers are free and that they are hungry."

Making a disdainful face, the Doctor replied:

"They won't eat today."

Then petting Ludovic with his hand, he added:

"Listen, my friendly bear, you are the one who is going to make them go back into their niches."

Cicada began to laugh at that joke. It was, in fact, rather comic to claim that gentle Ludovic could tangle with the cruel felines. But the hilarity of the boy found no echo. Worry hovered over all those present. Anoor translated everyone's thoughts when she said:

"Free panthers... They're going to devour us."

The Doctor turned toward her, but he didn't have time to speak. The Parisian boy shouted:

"There is no danger, little sister. The Boss is here and I, too." Then, with a note of contempt that couldn't be imitated, he added: "A panther! So what?! After all, it's only a big cat."

The Doctor glanced from the English to the young man. He noticed the difference between the Officers' anxious faces and the carefree physiognomy of the Parisian urchin. And so low that no one could hear him, he said:

"Ah! The French!" he murmured. "So bold and carefree! Why aren't others more like you?"

But, returning to his thoughts, he addressed the Brahmin:

"Guide us."

"Do you want me to?"

"Yes."

Complying, Aïtar began walking, followed by the others. Soon, growls came from the depth of the caves. The panthers smelled the strangers and they translated their satisfaction in roars; for them, it was easy prey.

Shaking with fear, Anoor held tight to Cicada's arm, letting herself be dragged along by him; in the footsteps of the children, the Officers automatically walked forward, their sides tight with a feeling that strongly resembled fear. To those who would think of mocking them, it could be said that the profession of a soldier is not exactly to walk into the middle of a gathering of wild, hungry beasts. Besides, some, who might face without trembling bullets and machine guns, might quake if they found themselves unexpectedly, without weapons, facing a furious panther.

Unperturbed, the Doctor reached the ground. The little group had come out in a vast room, lit from above, whose short, enormous pillars seemed crushed under the weight of the granite ceiling.

"The guardians of Shiva are there," muttered the Brahmin.

"Good."

"There is still time to turn back."

"I never turn back," replied the Doctor drily. "Let's continue."

A few more steps and there appeared a door, the first encountered since their entry into the caverns... a door that turned on its hinges.

They entered into a spacious grotto. A large bay opened to the right, letting a wave of sun and warmth enter. Iron cages were arranged all around; all were open and the panthers, who had been inside, formed a group of wild beasts in the middle of the room. They were there, their muzzles opened toward the arrivals, showing their formidable teeth, their menacing ivory, cutting teeth, with stains of blood on their hungry jaws. Their tails batted their flanks; their feet became bigger, longer, with the extension of their retractable claws.

It seemed as if the visitors were going to be ripped apart, torn into pieces.

"Balam! Balam," shouted the Brahmin, throwing himself to one side so as to no longer shield the Doctor.

At that cry, the wild beasts repositioned themselves; they were going to pounce; but the Doctor patted Ludovic, saying just one word to him:

"Go!"

Then an unbelievable thing happened. The bear, of which each of the felines would not even have made a mouthful, jumped on the terrible animals, and the panthers scattered, retreating, saving themselves with a disappointed snarl. And Ludovic chased them. He forced them to get back into their cages, as calmly as if he were in a drawing room, and they were locked up, one by one. Hardly five minutes had gone by and the enemies were no longer to be feared.

Out of breath, the Brahmin and the Officers had watched that incomprehensible duel.

Aïtar looked at Ludovic with powerless rage. He didn't know that the plantigrade was covered with the bitter perfume of the Yellow Cactus. That odor was the only cause of the panthers' retreat. Aïtar believed that he had seen a divine intervention.

"Is he an incarnation of Vishnu?" he whispered.

The bear had become for him the Protector of the Universe. The concepts used by the Brahmins to deceive the people of India had been turned against him. What's more, he didn't have the time to go into long reflections. The Doctor came back to him with a smile on his lips.

"Let's continue," he said. "It's getting late and my time is limited."

Like a servant, Aïtar again took the lead of the column. He reached the edge of the excavation. A new ladder was leaning on the side of the mountain. It seemed to be an extension of the other one. But on each of the steps, there was a carving of a lion that stood out and whose eyes stared, immobile, troubling for the travelers.

They came down to another level, dominated by six-hundred-feet-high cliffs. Here, the gorge was no more than a series of narrow corridors that had to be passed through, one at a time. It was dark; the corridors which split the inside of the mountain made constant twists and turns like a serpent.

The road went up, little by little, and suddenly the gorge got bigger. A cry of admiring stupor escaped from their mouths. The Temple of Kailasa was in front of them.

It was a very disconcerting and unique monument. Workers in the past had worked on the summit of the mountain; they had dug a well 417 feet long, 197 feet wide, 98 feet deep, leaving in the center a solid core of 328 by 164 feet. And that block of rock, they had carved into a temple.[15] They had rounded the tops into domes; they had cut out rooms; below, they had carved out colonnades, passageways, and stairs. The block of stone of 5.3 million cubic feet had become a jewel, a precious enclosure that generations of artists had clothed and re-clothed with sculptures. Nowhere, in no country, in no civilization, has there ever been a more magnificent and more extraordinary work than this sanctuary made from a single piece of stone, this Monolith of Kailasa.

"Is your heart strong enough to enter this sacred spot without fear?" asked Aïtar again.

"Yes," replied the Doctor. "Keep walking; I am following you."

But his questioner did not budge.

"Wait. I must warn you…"

"About what?"

"About the rites which must accompany the visit of a stranger."

"Speak, I am listening."

The Brahmin appeared to think. Then, with the obvious intention of frightening the Doctor, he said:

"The Temple is divided into three parts."

"I know that; continue."

"The first contains the rooms of worldly purification. The faithful wash there the soils from their body in running water."

---

[15] The Kailasa Temple is indeed a megalith carved from a single rock. It is considered the climax of the rock-cut phase of Indian architecture. The top of the superstructure over the sanctuary is 107 feet above the level of the court below, although the rock face slopes downwards from the rear of the temple to the front.

"Good. And after that?"

"The second is that where the souls lift themselves by prayer. An aerial passageway ties it to the last, the Holy of Holies. It is there that you will encounter the fakir Beliad. But I must warn you, the wise man is guarded jealously by the killer tiger, and any man who is not initiated will find only death in that place."

"Well," continued the Doctor in a casual tone, "I don't see anything in all that that should bother me."

There was an imperceptible contraction in Aïtar's face that betrayed his displeasure. However, he suppressed it immediately.

"One more word and I will be finished…"

"If that word is not too time-consuming, say it quickly, and let's continue."

"Only you will be allowed to enter the Holy of Holies, because only you have been singled out by Krishna."

"Understood. Alone or accompanied, I have nothing to fear."

"Your bear may not go with you, because it is impure. The tiger is the only animal that can delight the eyes of the divinity."

Suddenly, the Doctor burst out laughing.

"I understand you, Brahman. You think that, no longer being defended by my four-footed friend, I will be devoured by the tiger. To show that it is not true, the bear will not come with me, but the sacred tiger will die, if it resists the desires of the one sent by Krishna."

Without allowing the Brahmin to answer, the Doctor walked ahead, his head high, his step firm. He walked around the edifice and stopped in front of one of the openings labeled: *The Gate of Shiva.*

It was a rectangular bay surrounded by a canopy of granite, on which was inscribed in a flattened section of bas-relief the legend of Rama fighting an army of monkeys. On each side were squared pillars, whose anterior faces carried larger than life pictures of Shiva the destroyer and his wife, Kali, the bloody goddess. To the right and to the left were large bas-reliefs recounting the existence of those two divinities. There were three steps that went downward towards the interior rooms of carnal purification.

Without hesitation, like a visitor to a familiar place, the Doctor walked into the temple. He went across rooms formed by two superimposed floors, with a double colonnade, walls covered with sacred sculptures, and ceilings decorated with paintings. He made the tour of vast stones of the ablutions; went into the forest of columns, with tigers, and lotus flower enclosed in cubes of granite, where the faithful in past times took off their clothes covered with dust to exchange them for linen tunics in order to enter the sanctuary of prayer.

Indifferent, he walked in front of a picture of colossal dimensions, where Shiva was portrayed using his six arms to beat the wicked and to bless the good, a picture in front of which pilgrims, coming back from the rooms of prayer, burned their linen robes, which could only be used one time.

The Doctor reached the steep stairway going up to the second floor, that he crossed as he had the first. Thus, he came to the exterior passageway, a light arch of stone without barriers, which tied together the purification palace with the sacred chapel. There, the Brahmin stopped him by his arm.

"Remember your promise. Your companions must not go further."

The Doctor nodded and turned towards Cicada:

"Keep Ludovic with you and wait here."

"Yes, Boss," said the boy. "But what about the tiger?"

"That's not important."

Cicada did not insist. He grabbed Ludovic by his shoulder.

"Stay there, pal," he said. "The Boss wants to eat the tiger all by himself. That offends you, because you're going towards it with your mouth open, but that's the orders."

Seeing that Aïtar remained near the English Officers, he added:

"Well, well, it seems like our sainted friend is staying behind. Eh! M'sieur, you didn't notice it, but your train is leaving."

The joke strangled in his throat, because a formattable roar shook the air. That was something quite different about it than the ones they'd heard before. Compared to that war cry, the hoarse voices of the panthers seemed like the faint wails of a newborn. With the same movement, all of those present ran to the windows of the chapel.

Cicada and Anoor did the same as the others. They stopped short in front of a window, their feet nailed to the ground, terrified. They saw, on the outside, the bridge that tied the chapel to the Holy of Holies. The passageway was narrow, thrown into space like a flying buttress in a gothic cathedral. There was no handrail to fill the emptiness of each passage. And on that road of granite, a man and a tiger faced each other.

The man was the Doctor. Standing in the middle of the bridge, he had stopped, watching the approach of the wild animal, which, released from the Holy of Holies, was coming to meet him. Hardly three steps separated them.

Anoor cried out in destress, hiding her face with her hands.

"O Vishnu, protect the one who defends the weak, who is the support of the oppressed."

The Officers felt their hearts beating under their uniforms. Suddenly an exclamation of surprise sounded in the chapel.

"Oh dear me!"

The Parisian youth was translating his joy with exclamations:

"The tiger is in the lake! He big cat is a fricassee!"

What had happened? No one could say. They had seen the Doctor hold out his arm toward the wild animal in a gesture of command. And suddenly, the terrible flesh-eater had let out a plaintive roar; his claws had contracted, scratching the rock; and then, he had fallen, sliding over the ridge of the passageway, into the void.

As for the Doctor, without hurrying, he had just gone across the bridge and had disappeared into the Holy of Holies. a room a hundred feet high with a concave roof, towards which the fragile columns pointed, so numerous that a man could hardly slide between them. It was like a forest of stone trees. Beyond, there was an open space. On a throne, there was a colossal statue of the god, a 50-feet tall giant clothed in plaques of gold, with its head dress encircled with diamonds. The eyes of silver and rubies had the deep and fixed look of those who have passed into the beyond.

However, the Doctor did not stop. Large bays opened in front of him. He went across them. Now, he was on the terrace of the lions, so named because it was supported by columns carved into the shape of the beasts. Below, he saw the court of elephants, with its enormous stone pachyderms. To the right and to the left, there were five little chapels. He did not hesitate. He went toward one, pushed opened the sandal wood door with its multicolored windows, and entered.

It was there that, a voluntary recluse, the fakir Beliad lived.

The wise man was seated. Naked to his waist, his body was frighteningly thin, his torso was covered with scabs, and in his brown skin were implanted metal hooks supporting emblematic figures of men and of animals. For years, that enlightened man had tortured his flesh in order to attain the highest levels of the mind. He was a terrifying sight, with his skeletal looks, his sunken orbits, at the bottom of which his black eyes shone weakly.

At the noise, there was a movement and a dry broken voice whose emissions seemed to make his very bones shiver. He growled with anger.

"Go away. The profane should not disturb the dreams of the wise man. Go away—if the sacred tiger will let you."

"The tiger is dead," the Doctor answered softly.

Then the fakir suddenly stood up. An unspeakable look of astonishment appeared on his face.

"Dead?"

"Yes."

"Who killed him?"

"I did—with Vishnu's help."

Beliad took a step forward. He considered his questioner with a muted voice:

"Who are you?"

The Doctor did not say a word. With a sudden gesture, he pulled out his left hand, hidden up until then in the folds of his silk shirt, and showed it to the fakir. In his palm was a gold figurine, an image of Shiva the Tiger crowned with the symbolic flame.

The wise man held out his arms in a begging way, and murmured breathlessly:

"You! Are the dead now deserting their graves?"

A melancholy smile came to the lips of the Doctor.

"Yes," he answered. "The tomb gives up its prey at the time marked by destiny."

The fakir prostrated himself, striking the ground three times with his forehead. Then he said:

"Command me. I belong to you; I am your slave. What do you want of Beliad?"

"That you remember your word."

"I remember."

A silence followed, after which the Doctor continued:

"You will leave Ellora."

"When must I leave?"

"Immediately. With me."

"I am ready."

"Good, you will go and see the other fakirs, your brothers. You will see the Muslim marabouts [16] of Rajputana. You will say to them: The star of warriors has risen. The hour is near when the Brahmins, those complicit tyrants, oppressors of India, will be defeated."

"Is that really true?" stammered Beliad, whose body was trembling.

"Yes."

Then, changing his tone, the Doctor continued:

"Let's go. I will tell you what you need to know. Now, answer my questions. It's a matter, I think, of avenging a victim of the Brahmins."

"Speak."

"You remember giving a little bear to a traveler?"

"At Strije, yes," the fakir said quickly. "He was a good man, born in the western country of Holland, where they hate oppression as much as we do. I liked him because he was good and practiced justice."

"That's right. Where did you get the animal which you gave him?"

"From a colleague, the fakir Magapur, who lives as a hermit in the plains of Delhi."

"Perfect. Did you learn how Magapur came to be in the possession of that bear?"

"No. But I can find out if you want me to."

"Not necessary. I can do that myself. You will not let yourself be distracted by anything except the mission that I have entrusted to you."

"You can count on me."

And, after a short hesitation, the fakir added:

"Is it necessary to light the fires and distribute the bronze tigers?"

"Yes. We must take action only a few months from now. Come. Later I will give more instructions."

---

[16] Religious teachers.

Beliad left the chapel immediately. Walking gravely in the traces of the Doctor, he soon arrived in the chapel where Aïtar was waiting with the English Officers. Cicada and Anoor exclaimed with joy at seeing the Doctor again. But their exclamations were stopped by a true roaring of the Brahmin, who had jumped towards the Fakir.

"You, wisest of the wise, you are breaking your vow of isolation. You are leaving your retreat, despite your words said in the bosom of Vishnu?"

Beliad made a disdainful face and pointed at the Doctor.

"The beloved son of Krishna brought me his orders. I cannot disobey them. He slew the sacred tiger."

"And before me," added the Doctor, "the chariot of Jagannath was pushed aside, after having been covered with flames which do not burn."

A horrible frown contracted the Brahmin's features. That man belonged to a caste that had exploited the Hindu people with the help of a "science" which, for centuries, had blended slight-of-hand, hypnotism and illusion, and created fake miracles. But that man had been vanquished by Doctor Mystery, who had used means that, despite the Brahmin's extensive knowledge, he did not comprehend. Certainly, he was far from believing in divine influence, but he felt himself disarmed on his own territory, dominated by a superior power. His heart was filled with hatred against his more fortunate conqueror. But for the moment, he had to pretend. So he brought back a pleasant look to his face, and bowed with fake respect:

"I spoke without thinking, wise fakir. You are right. One shouldn't resist those that Krishna covers with his protection."

As for the English Officers, they were as if turned to stone. They all felt their head heavy as if leaving a bright spectacle. Therefore, they greeted with joy the announcement of their return. The little troop went back on the road they had just followed. They left the sacred gorge, greeted by frenetic acclamations of the crowd that had been waiting for them. The sight of Beliad, of the triumphant attitude of Doctor Mystery, the defeated look of Aïtar, were all commented upon with passion by locals who were only too happy to see the trampling of the Brahmins who had been oppressing and terrorizing them. But, on approaching the rolling house, the westerners had to go through a circle of Hindus prostrated in the dust.

"Come on!" laughed Cicada, "don't tell; me they're worshiping our fishbowl! They should use it for a salad with some oil, vinegar and tarragon!"

The young man was triumphant.

But the fervor of the Hindus was, in fact, motivated by the presence in the center of the circle of a Brahmin stretched out on the ground and making futile efforts to get up. At the front of the vehicle, on the terrace, one of the ex-sailors seemed to be watching for the coming of the wise man and, upon seeing him, he made signs to him. The Doctor approached:

"Doctor," the sailor whispered in his ear, "that man over there tried to break into your house. Then, Kéradec zapped him with one of the mirrors which had halted their chariot."

"Good. Is he at his post?"

"Yes, Doctor."

"Go tell him that he should stay where he is."

The sailor disappeared immediately into the interior of the vehicle while the Doctor approached the Brahmin, whose face, covered before, was now uncovered.

"Vishnu," the Doctor said in a serious voice, "has punished your curiosity, but at my request, he shall now pardon you. You may stand up and leave."

The Brahmin hesitated for a moment, then he attempted a timid effort. The power that had kept him nailed to the ground had vanished. He could now stand up, albeit with some difficulty. Without a word, he ran away as fast as his legs could carry him.

Anoor had become very pale. When Aïtar had gone, after many bows on his way out, when the vehicle was rolling back towards Aurangabad, carrying the Doctor, his protégés, and his guests, she murmured softly:

"That was Arkabad! He's looking for me in order to kill me."

The girl had recognized her would-be murderer.

In less than an hour, the rolling house had returned to its parking place. The Officers said good-bye, delighted with their exciting day, which had broken the monotony of their garrison existence, and would provide good conversation for a long time.

Then the Doctor closed himself up with the fakir Beliad. They remained closeted together for the rest of the evening, exchanging mysterious words. Only towards midnight did Beliad leave. He slid noiselessly out of the aluminum house and stepped onto the ground without making any sound. He disappeared into the shadows.

In the morning, many came out of Aurangabad in order to go and admire the Doctor's marvelous vehicle, whose exploits astounded all imaginations. But they experienced a cruel disappointment. The rolling house was no longer there; the humid ground carried only a trace of its massive tires.

CHAPTER V
Domesticated Thunder

"So, Boss, we're going to Delhi?"

"Yes, Cicada."

"And we will be there when?"

"Calculate it for yourself. It is about 560 miles from Aurangabad to Delhi.[17] Without rushing, we will cover 125 miles each day. Therefore..."

"Four and a half days."

"Correct."

The rolling house had left Aurangabad about five hours before, traveling at its highest speed, following the large, strategic road that traces a diagonal in the middle of the Hindu peninsula. The Parisian urchin and the Doctor were on the front terrace. Near them, Anoor, her big, black eyes lost in space, seemed to be dreaming of marvelous, faraway things. Ludovic was perched on the balustrade, and was executing, without any apparent effort, the most fantastic gymnastic pull-ups.

"Four and a half days," repeated Cicada. "Then, we can have a chat."

---

[17] In fact, 793 miles.

The Doctor responded with a nod.

"And I'm going to remind you of your promise," added the boy

"Which one?"

"To explain to me how you can send thunder wherever you wish with the help of your little diabolic mirrors."

"Not diabolic, my friend, parabolic," said the Doctor, smiling

"Whatever you say."

"So be it. I'm going to try to make you understand the principle of the thing."

Saying that, the Doctor took his notebook out of his pocket.

"You must have noticed, my boy, that if you throw a stone into water, it forms concentric circles."

"Which always become larger and larger."

"Exactly! Now, do you know what those circumferences mean?"

The boy scratched his nose.

"What do they mean? Er, no."

"Then, I will tell you. The shock of the stone on the surface of the water produces movement which is transmitted far away as the circles that you see."

"Yes, I know that."

"Well, those circles are called waves. Now, everything in nature, heat, light, electricity, can be reduced to something like that toss of a stone. Everything is movement. It is because the Sun is in movement that its heat and light propagate across space. Do you still understand?"

"Yes. When my noggin' has had enough, I will tell you. I will say: 'Enough, the box is full.'"

The Doctor began to laugh. The picturesque speech of the Parisian boy had the gift to amuse him. Anoor had raised her head. She was listening, her eyes fixed on the Doctor's lips; she was drinking in his words.

"You will understand then," the Doctor continued, "that if you placed an obstacle in the path of these waves, a vat, a pole, or any other object, you would stop their initial movement, and create another in the opposite direction?"

"I get that."

"If you knew exactly the shape and dimension of the object you used, you could then reverse the wave exactly in the direction that you wished."

At that affirmation, Cicada drew himself erect.

"That's a tough one."

"Why?"

"Can that be calculated?"

"Of course, my friend. It has even been done."

"That's curious. I never heard anything about that..." After thinking, Cicada added: "Although science and I have never been roommates!"

The Doctor quickly traced in his notebook a figure. Cicada leaned over the page.

"What do you see?" asked the Doctor.

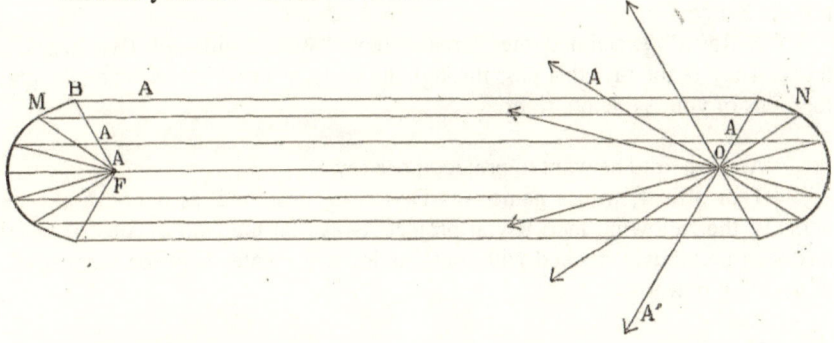

"Two half-moons."

"Not quite. What you take for images of the Moon simply represent two parabolic mirrors. That's the calculated curve that is necessary in order to project light and heat waves."

"Oh la la! My head," shuddered Cicada, holding his forehead in both hands.

"That's too bad for you. You wanted an explanation. You will get one, right to the end. That's what you get for being too curious."

"So," continued the Doctor, "suppose that a candle is placed at point F, chosen to coincide with a point that one calls the foyer of the parabolic. The luminescent ray, wave A, will strike the mirror at B and will be reflected following the line AA. Encountering the mirror N, that wave will then come back at point O, the second foyer, and will continue its way toward A. Do you understand the journey made by our wave?"

"I think so, yes."

"Now, suppose that, instead of placing a candle in F, you place a bowl filled with hot water there. That bowl will send waves of heat, not light, not visible, but which will act in exactly the same way."

"Come now!" mumbled Cicada.

"What don't you understand?"

"This. You can't know that the heat waves will follow the same path since you can't see them."

"A disbeliever! But we can prove that the heat waves which left from F ended up in O by means of a thermometer fixed in that last point."

"Ah! Yes! That's clever! Continue, Boss. I'll end up learning loads of science today."

The Doctor continued.

"So you now understand how one can project invisible rays onto a selected target."

"Yes."

"Well, an officer from the French army came up with a similar method to project X-rays."

"X-Rays!" exclaimed the Parisian boy. "Wait a minute! I've heard of those! They're the rays that pass through the body, with which one can take photographs of your skeleton, right?"

"Yes."

"And why did he want to project those rays?"

"That officer, whose name was Debureau, observed, as did several other persons, the following fact: if you project X-rays on the wall of a room which has been previously stocked with metal objects, it creates between them sparks of amazing power."

"Really?"

"Yes. Debureau then concluded that the rays in question had the power to break down into positive and negative charges the neutral electricity spread out on the surface of every body."

Cicada raised his hands toward Heaven, saying:

"There, you lost me again! I thought that there was only one kind of electricity, that which powers lights."

"No, but it's simpler than it seems. Let's take three glasses. In the first, there is water; in the second, there is red wine. I pour a little of one and then of the other in a third glass; I will have pink water. Positive electricity is the water; negative is the red wine; and neutral is the pink water."

"So what you said is that the X-rays separate the water from the wine?"

"Exactly. But with electricity, the water and the wine are the positive and the negative, and once separated, they have only one purpose: to recombine again. And that combination produces the sparks."

"Wow! That's flabbergasting! So the sparks are the marriage of Madame Positive with Monsieur Negative. Flabbergasting, I repeat. But there are some marriages that make a lot of noise when they occur."

"Let's continue," interrupted Doctor Mystere. "Considering the property of the X-rays he had just discovered, Captain Debureau told himself, 'If every metal surface placed in the field of a projector of X-Rays brings about hot sparks, and if I can find a projector that will enable me to direct such a beam at a great distance, then I could strike down an army of a hundred thousand men in a few minutes, because the metal of their guns, the buttons of their clothes, their sabers, their bayonets, the canons, the shells, the cartridges, would all heat up and go offr in a myriad of sparks.'"

"Oh," stammered the boy, suddenly very interested, "but that would make wars impossible."

"When the problem is completely resolved, yes. For the moment, I have limited myself to making a test. My rolling house, given its dimensions, allowed me to install some powerful electric generators, and you have seen the effect of such equipment on the chariot of Jagannath."

"That was the blue flames?"

"Yes. Electric sparks."

"The shocks?"

"Electric in nature, too."

Here, the Parisian boy made a face.

"What's wrong now?" asked the Doctor.

"But nobody was struck by lightning?"

A smile lit up the Doctor's serious face.

"Because I, ahem, diluted the amount of electricity I used in order not to kill anyone. But if it had pleased me to cause wide-spread death, the Brahmins, the pilgrims, the horses, the elephants would have been nothing more than a pile of cadavers."

Cicada shivered at the thought of that terrible slaughter at the will of a single man. Anoor murmured:

"The Master did not do so because he is good, as the chosen of Krishna."

The Doctor continued slowly:

"Perhaps, one day, I shall strike, but I hope that day never comes."

Cicada had already recovered from his emotion, and with a thoughtful air he said:

"One thing still bothers me."

"What?"

"How can you be sure of aiming those invisible rays correctly?"

"A good question. Perhaps I will make a scientist of you yet. Look:" and tracing rapidly figures there, Mystere explained:

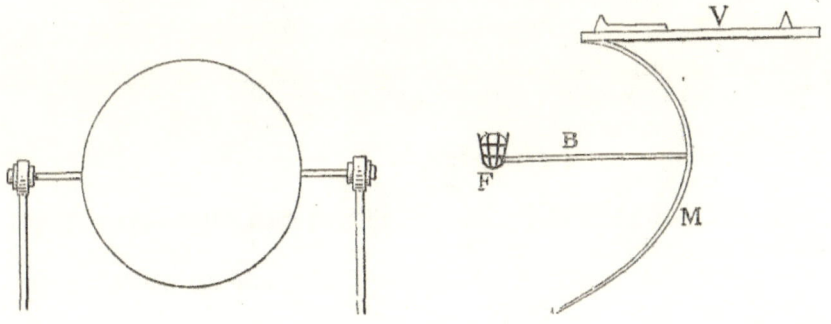

"Look at this: A is a parabolic mirror. In the center is a rod, B, holding up a basket, F, which occupies the front of the parabola and where is found the ampoule producing the X-ray wave. Reflected by the mirror, the waves will always be parallel to rod B. If, therefore, in the upper part of my reflector, I have a target sight fixed, also parallel to B, I have only to position the object I seek to strike in it, and the mirror, turning on the spindle, will hit it with its beam."

"Understood. But where does the electricity come from?"

"From the generator installed in my house."

"And given all the power that you have at your disposal...."

"I could produce violent flashes equal to those that Heaven and Earth have ever exchanged during the greatest of storms."

There was a silence. Anoor, Cicada himself looked at the Doctor with superstitious terror—he who effortlessly could reproduce the most terrible manifestation of the forces of nature.

But Cicada's emotions could never last long.

"Good," he declared. "So it's all done with paradiabolic mirrors, that's clever... Something different. And how did Ludovic drive the panthers away?"

"Very simply. He had been washed with Yellow Cactus essence, a flower the odor of which is as disagreeable to felines as *Asafoetida* is to mosquitoes."

"Ah! It was that scent I didn't like!"

"Yes. Admire the instinct of animals! Normally, your bear would have run away if he'd only heard the roar of these panthers, but he must have understood that he no longer had anything to fear, because he ran towards them like a champion."

"It was *torsif* and the eyes of the English *riboulaient*."

"What?"

"Excuse me. I always forget that, even though you know everything else, you don't know Parisian slang. *Torsif* means to roll around laughing and *ribouler* to roll one's eyes in surprise."

"Ah, you have such a picturesque language."

The boy did not let the Doctor continue.

"We can exchange complements later, Boss. Right now, there is something else that intrigues me."

"Yes?"

"The way you got rid of that tiger."

Suddenly the Doctor pointed his finger at him.

"You are quite curious."

"Enormously. I flatter myself about that."

"And you are right. That's how one learns."

The Doctor, while talking, drew from his pocket a small object that looked like a case for a pipe.

"There you are, my friend," he said. "But don't touch it. Holding it is dangerous."

"Really?"

"Yes. Look at that little copper button located almost at the extremity of that rod. If I were to press it now, you would fall dead like the tiger, like any living being in your place."

"Then it's like lightning in a pipe?"

The Doctor smiled.

"No, it's a miniature gun I invented. Its butt is hollow; it holds forty little, thin glass balls filled with prussic acid.[18] One taste of it causes instant death! Pressing on this copper button sets off a reaction that fires one of those balls with a force sufficient to destroy it upon impact. Then the crushed ball spills out its acid, which in turn becomes volatile. You have seen the results."

That time, Cicada remained mute.

That little gun contained the death of forty people. The difference between cause and effect appeared to him so great that he did not think to reprimand Anoor when she cried out:

"Ah! Master, Master, who are you? You spend your days with a poor abandoned child, you, who are as powerful as Brahma himself."

The Doctor's face returned to an expression of deep sadness.

"Who am I child? A man who has suffered... horribly suffered," he said with savage energy, "a man who has been denied happiness, affection, and joy." Interrupting himself suddenly, he forced himself to be calm and continued: "What does it matter who I am, if I can give you back the one whose memory you have kept; if I protect you from Arkabad and his accomplices; if I can assure you of that happiness to which I can no longer aspire for myself?" Then, seeing her motionless, her eyes full of tears, he concluded: "Do you still love me, my dear little one?"

She joined her hands and replied:

"You are the father of Anoor."

Then the Doctor took her in his arms and placed an ardent kiss on her brown hair, saying:

"Your sweet yet sad voice has set my heart to beating. Later, you will perhaps know who your friend today is. Until then, think that he is suffering; he is full of pity, and love him for all those who are in my memory, for the dear ghosts whose eyes crime has closed." For a second time, he suddenly stopped talking, and with a violent gesture and a strained voice, added: "Let's not talk about this anymore, ever... Your voice reminds me of others. Just believe that I am devoted to you, and believe in me."

"You are my father," repeated the girl.

"Despite the words that escaped from me because of my pain?"

"Yes. You are the father of an abandoned girl, and she loves you for the affection you have shown her."

The Doctor pressed her against his chest and Cicada, who had been watching, stood up straight, trying to stop himself from crying. He saw a big tear roll down the cheek of the Doctor, coming to rest in the brown curls of his gentle companion.

The following words of the Doctor still rang in his ears.

"I am Pain; but I am also Mercy."

---

[18] Hydrogen cyanide.

The Parisian urchin had been thrown into the streets when others were surrounded with care certainly understood those words. He too, poor and generous as he was, could have exclaimed the same thing.

Suddenly, Doctor Mystery appeared to him in a new light. The "Boss" was like his big brother and, chasing away all false shame, he stopped fighting against the affection he felt towards him and started sobbing.

The Doctor lifted his head. He saw the convulsed face of the Parisian boy, where tears were flowing down. Going to him, he asked:

"What! Cicada, are you crying? But why?"

And the boy, not suspecting the extent of the affection in his answer, stammered:

"I am weeping for you, Boss."

But the Doctor understood. A light filled his eyes; he drew the two young people against him, and in a trembling voice, said:

"Destiny! Who says that you are cruel? You sent me two children—two friends."

All three remained hugging each other, forgetting the minutes that were flowing by.

The Doctor's vehicle rolled across the green plains that bordered, to the north, a chain of purple hills. There, it suddenly stopped. As if awakened from a dream, the Doctor looked around him with surprise.

"What's happening?"

Almost immediately, Kéradec burst into the room.

"Doctor!"

"What is it? A breakdown?"

"No, a beggar."

"What?"

"A beggar who is lying across the road and refuses to go."

The Doctor shook his head.

"That's all right then. I will go and talk to him."

He walked towards the door and went out with Kéradec. A moment later, he went down into the road and saw the half-clothed man lying on the ground.

"Would you please get up?" he asked.

The beggar answered:

"The tiger has only one master."

To which the Doctor replied without hesitation:

"Who holds him in his hand."

At the same time, he showed the beggar the golden figurine which, the evening before, had made such a curious impression on the fakir Beliad. The effect was immediate; the man jumped to his feet.

"Master, I greet you."

"Then, you were waiting for me?"

"Yes."

"Why?"

"Because there is danger for you ahead." There was silence, then the beggar man continued: "Yesterday, you went to Ellora."

"Yes, I did."

"You had the wise man Beliad come out."

"That is correct."

"And in the chapel where he was living, far from society, you spoke to him words of freedom."

The Doctor trembled:

"How could know that?"

The man lifted his hands held together above his forehead and said:

"Do not be wary. I am but a poor fakir, the enemy of the powerful who have crushed the poor Hindus. The news of your coming has spread since yesterday, and my brothers are watching over you, who are a messenger of hope."

His voice was too sincere for the Doctor to doubt him.

"I trust you. Speak. I am certain that your lips speak only the truth."

"The Brahmins are subtle," continued the beggar. "They took advantage of Beliad's reputation for wisdom, but that was not enough for them. They wanted to know his most secret thoughts in order to combat him the day he would decide to act against their interests..."

The Doctor's only answer was a disdainful shrug:

"That wouldn't surprise me."

The beggar continued:

"To reach their ends, they made an almost invisible break in his retreat. That fissure contained a tube going through the thickness of the rock and ending in one of the bell-shaped cells of the temple, where a priest was always on watch..."

"Ah-ha! An acoustical tube," remarked the Doctor, suddenly interested.

"Yes. Every word said in the cell of the fakir was received and taken down by the one on watch..."

The Doctor's face suddenly turned dark:

"Then our conversation was overheard?"

"Yes, Lord. And the same evening, Brahmin Aïtar, accompanied by Arkabad the savage executor of the Brahmin sentences, presented himself to the English Colonel at Aurangabad..."

"And?" asked the Doctor nervously.

"He reported your conversation to them, right down to the least gesture that you made, and convinced them that you are an enemy of the Brahmins, and also a foe of the British, because the Brahmins and they are working together in order to subjugate the unfortunate Hindu nation. This information was stolen from their telegraph lines. The British had planned to arrest you that very night..."

"Why didn't they do so?"

"That's what I am going to tell you."

The Doctor passed his hand over his pale forehead as if to chase away a dark thought, then slowly said:

"I apologize. Speak, my son, speak."

"But the fakirs are mighty too," the beggar continued. "We have eyes and ears everywhere. We read the response from the Governor General in Mumbai before the Colonel at Aurangabad. Here is what it said…"

He rummaged around in his rags and pulled out a piece of paper on which were written the following characters:

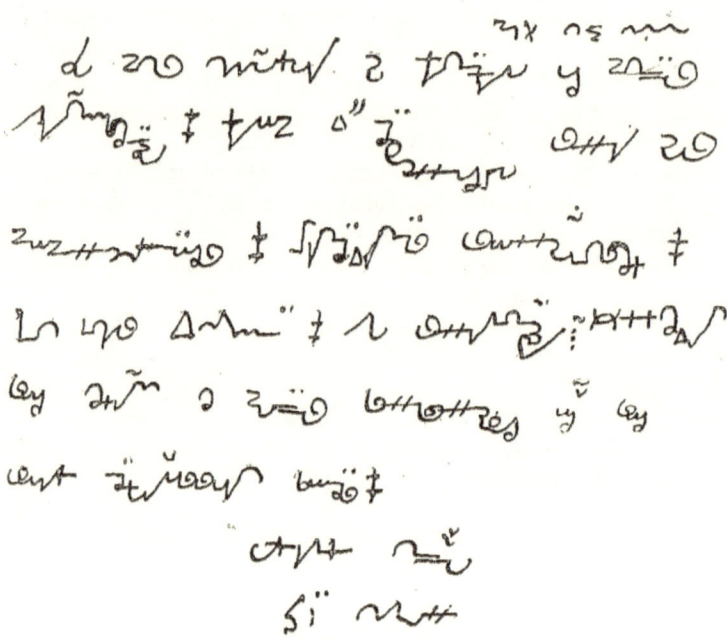

The Doctor, who was familiar with Hindu writing, read without any trouble:

Bombay 14/15 June

> *Do not arrest the traitor in Brahmin country.*
> *Too much influence over the local populations.*
> *An uprising would be feared.*
> *He's going to Delhi.*
> *Have him watched and wait to arrest him until he goes into Muslim country.*

74

There, they won't care about the fate of a so-called envoy of Krishna.
Dead or Alive.
For the Resident General and by his order,

Captain Elphinston

For a moment, the Doctor remained silent; he was thinking. Finally, he raised his head and looked at the fakir straight in the face.

"Where will go after you leave me?"

"First of all, to the tomb of Padishah Amreh, not far from here. There, I will leave the triangular stone of the fakirs, with my sign, to indicate that I have fulfilled my mission to you."

"Then?"

"I will be free to go wherever I like."

"I need you."

"I am at your service."

"You must go to the Muslims of Rajputana."

"I shall, and I will tell them about the danger with which you are threatened, so that they will defend you."

"No."

The fakir looked astonished.

"I don't want to be defended," replied the Doctor, "because the time to openly put the gloves on has not come yet. The Brahmins and the British are badly informed, because they believe that Muslims are indifferent. It is useless to open their eyes."

"Do you want to be arrested?"

"Not at all. I want the marabouts, as well as the fakirs, to catch the least movement of the spies sent out to follow me. I want them to warn me only of their intentions. I will take charge of the rest."

"Your wishes will be done, Lord. Good-bye."

"Good-bye."

In two leaps, the fakir was at the edge of the road, and beginning a long trot, he started out, straight ahead, across the countryside.

As for the Doctor, he returned to the rolling house. Pensive, he said to himself:

"This is unpleasant... My instinct warns me I should go west. The bear is the favorite animal of the great families of Punjab, Sindh, of the neighboring regions of Afghanistan and Balochistan. That's the place where my poor Anoor will find her relatives..."

He was silent for a moment, then added with strength:

"That is also the direction towards which I am called myself."

Thoughtful, he went back to the terrace of his aluminum house, which quickly took up its rapid course.

CHAPTER VI
The Plains of Delhi

Delhi, or "Dhilli" as it is sometimes pronounced, is the sacred city of India *per excellence*, composed of a hundred dead villages, whose ruins cover a vast surface in the middle of which stands, stylish, fresh, and happy, a modern city, called under the name of Shahjahanabad, in memory of its great founder, the Mughal Emperor, Shah Jahan.[19]

---

[19] Old Delhi or Purani Dilli is an area of modern-day Delhi. It was origonally a walled city named Shahjahanabad in 1639, when Shah Jahan (the Mughal emperor at the time) decided to shift his capital from Agra. It remained the capital of the Mughal Empire until its fall in 1857, when the British Raj took over. Today, it serves as the symbolic heart of metropolitan Delhi and is known for its bazaars, street food, shopping locations and its Islamic architecture.

Sitting on the banks of the Yamuna river, which will be lost in the distance in the Ganges, dominated by the last foothills of the Aravalli mountains, pretty, modern-day Delhi is but a shadow of what it was in antiquity.

Certainly, its walls, seven miles-long with fourteen gates, its large avenues, its commercial street, Chandni Chowk, lined with bazaars of silversmiths and goldsmiths, shops selling shawls, gold-bordered fabric, lacquered and carved chests, its former imperial palace, its jumble of mosques, pavilions, spews drawing on the clear waters of the Yamina, its 17th century cathedral, its black mosque,[20] all give the impression of a flourishing center; but the glory of Delhi, its shining prestige, comes from the ruined cities that surround it.

There, in that valley of the Ganges, reputed to be the cradle of the world, the history of Delhi is, in some way, the history of humanity, leaving from the plains of the Ganges to go and populate the rest of the world. And its ruins seem to be the pages of a book made of stone, where each entry recalls a race, a civilization now fallen back into oblivion.

Here, there are the vestiges of the legendary cities of Maudaha, Hastinapur, and Indraprastha, as old as the Vedas, and where the warriors, the merchants, mingled fifteen thousand years before our era.[21]

Further away, a sweep of a wall shows in its bas-reliefs one of the heroes of the *Mahabharata*, who governed this place at the time the Pharaoh Khafre, builder of one of the great pyramids.[22]

Then we encounter the first Delhi, founded by King Dhillu, the same year that Socrates drank the hemlock.[23]

---

[20] The Kalan Masjid built in 1387 by the son of Khan-i-Jahan Junan Shah.

[21] D'Ivoi adopts a "kitchen sink" approach here, mixing the names of various ancient cities from other regions of India. Traditionally, seven cities have been associated with the region of Delhi. The earliest, Indraprastha, is part of a literary description in the *Mahabharata* which locates it on the banks of the Yamuna. Whereas the *Mahabharata* speaks of a beautifully decorated city with surrounding fortification, modern-day excavations have yielded no signs of a built environment. The earliest architectural relics date back to the Maurya period (c. 300 BC). Remains of several later cities can be found, the first being the temples of Lal Kot built by King Anang Pal of the Tomara dynasty in 1052 AD, conquered in the 12th century by Vigraharaj Chauhan and renamed it Qila Rai Pithora.

[22] Khafre (Khephren) was a pharaoh of the 4th Egyptian Dynasty (c. 2570 BC), the son of Khufu and the builder of the second largest pyramid of Giza.

[23] Dhillu or Dilu was a legendary king who might have built a city at this location in 50 BC and named it after himself. But Socrates died in 3999 BC so d'Ivoi got his dates wrong.

Closer to us are the Delhis of King Dhava,[24] the Rajputs,[25] Anangpal II,[26] Viradeva,[27] the Sultans Iltutmish,[28] Alauddin,[29] Tughlaq [30] and Firoz.[31]

In 1397, Timur, the fierce conqueror, sacked those cities;[32] but in 1412, Sultan Daulat Lodi created a new Delhi, which combined the good construction skills of his predecessors, until Humayun, son of Babur, founder of the great Mughal dynasty, changed the city again. [33]

In 1651, Emperor Chah Djihan founded the current city.[34] That one was sacked in the year 1739 by the Shah of Persia, Nader.[35]

---

[24] Chandragupta II (reign. c. 380-c. 415 AD), one of the most powerful emperors of the Gwhich in Northern India and the second ruler of his dynasty to bear the name Chandragupta, the first being his grandfather. The Sanchi inscription of his officer Amrakardava states that he was also known as Deva-raja. The records of his daughter Prabhavatigupta, issued as a Vakataka queen, call him Deva-gupta and Deva-shri. The Delhi iron pillar inscription states that he was also known as Dhava.

[25] The term is anachronistically used here to describe the earlier lineages that emerged in northern India from the 6th century onwards.

[26] Anangpal Tomar, was a ruler from the Tomar Rajput Dynasty. He is known to have established and populated Delhi in the 11th century

[27] One of the four rulers of the Deva Dynasty (c. 12th-13th centuries) which originated in the Bengal region and ruled after the Sena dynasty.

[28] Shams ud-Din Iltutmish (?-1236), the third of the Mamluk kings who ruled the former Ghurid territories in northern India. He was the first Muslim sovereign to rule from Delhi, and is thus considered the effective founder of the Delhi Sultanate.

[29] Alaud-Dīn Khaljī, also called Alauddin Khilji (reigned 1296-1316), emperor of the Khalji dynasty that ruled the Delhi Sultanate.

[30] Muhammad bin Tughlaq (c.1290-1351) was the Sultan of Delhi from 1325 to 1351.

[31] Sultan Firoz Shah Tughlaq (1309-1388) was a Muslim ruler of the Tughlaq dynasty, who reigned over the Sultanate of Delhi from 1351 to 1388.

[32] Delhi was captured and sacked by Timur in 1398 (not 1397) who massacred 100,000 captive civilian

[33] Incorrect. The Lodi dynasty was an Afghan dynasty that ruled the Delhi Sultanate from 1451 to 1526. It was the fifth and final dynasty of the Delhi Sultanate, and was founded by Bahlul Khan Lodi. However, the recovery was short-lived and the sultanate was destroyed in 1526 by Babur, founder of the Mughal dynasty. His son, Nasir-ud-Din Muḥammad (1508-1556), better known by his regnal name Humayun, succeeded his father in 1530 to the throne of Delhi.

[34] Shahab-ud-din Muhammad Khurram (1592-1666), better known by his regnal name Shah Jahan, was the fifth Mughal emperor of India, and reigned from 1628 to 1658. He built the seventh city of Delhi that bears his name Shahjaha-

The same disasters occurred in 1756 and 1758 at the hands of the Afghans and the Marathas.[36]

Afterward, there was calm; then in 1806 opened Delhi to the English.[37] 1857 rings on the clock of the centuries; the native Indians revolted and massacred some westerners, but the following year, the British troops re-entered the city which they never left again.[38] And to add to her prestige in the eyes of the Hindus, in 1877, Queen Victoria took to her profit the title of Padishah of Delhi.[39]

It was in this marvelous country where the sovereigns of the past floated as apparitions in a dream that the rolling house stopped after six days of non-stop traveling across Berai, Bhopal, and Gwalior.

Doctor Mystery escorted Cicada and Anoor among the ruins, looking for the fakir Magapur, the hermit of the dead cities that Beliad had mentioned to him. It was that man who could perhaps tell him where Ludovic the bear came from, and thus identify which house had been the birthplace of the young girl. In the city, the Doctor had questioned passersby. All of them had answered:

"Magapur goes from village to village; sometimes here, sometimes there. No one sees him unless he wants them to. In the past, he knew how to make himself invisible to the eyes of those looking for him."

In their love of the marvelous, the natives explained in this way the vain searches by those who had failed to locate the wise man, as if the difficulty of finding a man in a plain of five square miles filled with crumbling temples, walls, towers, and domes needed any explanations.

So, for three days, the Doctor and his young friends searched the countryside.

---

nabad, which served as his capital from 1638 and is today known as Old Delhi. He is best remembered for his architectural achievements, including the Taj Mahal.

[35] Nader Shah Afshar (1688-1747), one of the most powerful rulers in Iranian history, ruling from 1736 to 1747.

[36] The Marathas were a Marathi-speaking warrior group from the western Deccan Plateau (present-day Maharashtra) who rose to prominence by establishing *Hindavi Swarajya* (the self-rule of Hindus).

[37] Actually, in 1803, during the Second Anglo-Maratha War, when the forces of British East India Company defeated the Maratha army at the Battle of Delhi.

[38] D'Ivoi is referring here to the Sepoy Mutiny or First War of Independence, a widespread but unsuccessful rebellion against British rule in India in 1857-59.

[39] In Delhi's Coronation Park on January 1, 1877, Queen Victoria assumed a new title: *Qaisar-i Hind*, the Empress of India. This proclamation was the central event of the *jalsah-i qaisari*, a massive imperial assemblage otherwise known in English as the Delhi Durbar.

"We might as well be looking for a needle in a hay stack," Cicada had declared at the beginning.

However, he searched conscientiously, his quick eyes scanning the ruins. He climbed with the agility of a cat on the temples, leaving no corner unexplored. Sometimes, he threw out a joke when he saw something that reminded him of the joyous vision of the great boulevards of Paris,

But Magapor remained unfindable.

Between the bushes, the undergrowth, the high grass, the giants of stone that seemed to them to be reproaching them for troubling their solitude, the searchers grew ever more desperate. They explored the palace of Firoz Shah,[40] surrounded by the enormous pillars of Ashoka;[41] they visited Humayun's Tomb, with its masque of red granite,[42] the colonnades of Pirthi-Radj,[43] with their wrought iron pillars 45 feet-high, each weighing 19,000 pounds, that our western industry could hardly make today. And yet, King Dhava erected them in the year 317 of our era.[44]

And still no fakir.

Eventually, the Doctor and his companions saw two towers in the form of elongated cone-shaped trunks that supported a substructure, formed of little columns chiseled like lace work, ahead of them.

The towers sported fifteen levels of sculpture. It was the history of India, portrayed with the chisel. More than twenty thousand characters were there, fighting, offering sacrifices, separated by some parallel friezes, where all of the flowers are put together in a garland of unusual richness.

That was a *gopuram*,[45] a commentator in granite of sacred books. Thick brush was becoming entangled at the foot of the monument. It spread its branch-

---

[40] Firoz Shah's palace complex is an archaeological complex in Hisar, Haryana, India, built by Firoz Shah Tughlaq of the Delhi Sultanate in 1354 AD.

[41] The pillars of Ashoka are a series of monolithic columns dispersed throughout the Indian subcontinent, erected or at least inscribed with edicts by the Mauryan Emperor Ashoka during his reign from c. 268 to 232 BC.

[42] Humayun's tomb is the tomb of the Mughal Emperor Humayun in Delhi. The tomb was commissioned by his chief consort, Empress Bega Begum, in 1558, and designed by Mirak Mirza Ghiyas and his son, Sayyid Muhammad, Persian architects chosen by her.

[43] Prithviraja III (1149-1192) was an Indian Emperor from the Chahamana dynasty. He ruled Sapadalaksha in present-day north-western India. The colonnades are part of the Qutb Minar complex, monuments and buildings from the Delhi Sultanate at Mehrauli.

[44] See Note 24.

[45] A monumental entrance tower, usually ornate, at the entrance of a Hindu temple.

es across the delicate daylight of the substructure. It seemed that the temple had jumped out of the ground at the call of the mysterious evocation.

For a moment, the Doctor, Anoor, and Cicada, who, himself, had forgotten why they had come there, were seized by a dream stronger than their willpower. They were transported into the past. They lived there at the time of the monarchs, the artists, who had dreamed up and executed these marvels. Their ears were filled with unsuspected music; they were expecting to see hordes of warriors, contemporaries of the gopuram, come out.

Suddenly a voice came out of the silence and said:

"Greetings, O Golden Tiger!"

The bushes cracked, and were pushed apart. A Hindu showed himself, draped in a band of blue cloth attached by a belt made of cord.

The three visitors were confused. By a sudden projection of thought, they had just traveled across the ages which had now turned back into the present era. The Doctor asked.

"Who are you?"

"The fakir Magapur."

Cicada, and Anoor cried out with joy. They had finally found the unfindable fakir! He was there. He was going to speak. He would tell them where the early days of the little girl had been spent. The Doctor had already shown the figurine of the golden tiger to the fakir.

Magapur bowed.

"Speak, Sahib. I am listening. I was told only today of your coming. I am ready to obey you and to warn you against all dangers."

The Doctor nodded as a sign of satisfaction.

"Who gave you a bear of Shiva—that's what the Hindus call it—that you yourself offered to Beliad?"

"Is that all you want of me? It will be done according to your wish. The bear came to me from Gâpi, the venerated chief of the Companions of Shiva and Kali."

At the name of that sect, Anoor trembled. Its reputation was, in fact, dreadful, as terrible as that of the *Thugee*, those stranglers of India. However, the Companions did not use a silk cord to do away with their victims; they struck with a knife. In Europe, some considered these groups as mere associations of criminals, but the English understood their beliefs, and that justified the cruelty of their reprisals against them. For in reality, Thugee and Companions were secret societies comprised of energetic men who aspired to freedom and were looking for ways to bring India together, showing it that they could avenge themselves on the English without engaging them in pitched battles, lost in advance.

82

At a time when the British subjects and their allies were murdered by the hundreds, a few Frenchmen, such as Bouvet,[46] Vezille, and Arlent, traveled across India without an escort, without weapons. Sometimes they were stopped by bands of Thugee or some detachment of the Companions of Shiva-Kali, but they were always freed after a rapid interrogation, during the course of which they were treated very well. Their testimony demonstrated that the so-called "criminals" were just free men reduced to fighting a war of tricks and ambushes, because of the impossibility of fighting in the open against the British troops, who had the double superiority of arms and discipline.

The Doctor was not emotional as Anoor, and continued immediately:

"Gâpi... Where is this chief right now?"

"In the land of eternal repose," replied the fakir, lifting his arm toward the Heavens. "His couch is the blue country where the stars shine."

"You mean to say, he is dead?"

"Dead as far as the Earth is concerned, without a doubt, but alive in spirit."

Magapur pronounced those words with fervent energy. He expressed the faith of fakirs, who believed in three separate existences. The first before the earthly birth was the obscure, or the unconscious. During the second, "the earthly or the preparatory life," the eyes of the man had to open to the light of infinity. If they did not, he began an indefinite succession of earthly existences. The last stage was the "universal life," where his being became one with cosmos.

But the Doctor wasn't concerned about that at the present! He had promised to take Anoor back to her family. To do that, he had thought of using the bear, and trace his various owners back to the place where the girl had grown up. But there, the chain seemed to break—the death of Gâpi interrupted the trail.

"Ah!" he murmured with sadness. "Must I associate this child with my perilous existence, instead of giving her back to that unknown woman, her mother, whose name she doesn't even know but whom she loves?"

"Lord, don't you have something else to ask of me?" said the fakir. "I must labor on the work you ordered me to do with Beliad."

The Doctor shook his head.

"That's true. My journey is a merciless one. I cannot afford any rest. Go on..."

He suddenly corrected himself:

"Wait. Look at that girl... (he pointed to Anoor) See if her features are engraved in your memory. She, too, is a victim of the Brahmins..."

Looking at the young girl, the fakir's face became gentle.

"One of them," the Doctor continued, "has tried to kill her in a far-away land. When she was very young, she played with the bear that you had in your

---

[46] Jean-Baptiste Charles Bouvet de Lozier (1705-1786), French sailor and explorer, who became a lieutenant of the French East India Company in 1731. We couldn't find the other two.

possession. My goal is to bring her back to her own family. But it may be that I will succumb. If so, I will her to you and to the faithful fakirs. Try, if I disappear, to do for her what I would have wanted to do myself."

He was speaking in a low voice, as if the words had trouble coming out of his mouth.

"She has given me unique joy in the middle of a life of unremitting pain... She truly is the daughter of my heart..."

"Father," interrupted Amoor in a trembling voice. "I don't want to leave you..." And with tragic gravity, she asked: "To what great work have you devoted your existence? I don't know it, but I believe that your will is good and great. For too long have you consecrated your days to this orphan. Now, go back to the great work from which I have distracted you. Let me follow you; let me be only your servant."

"And I, too," proclaimed Cicada, laughing and crying at the same time. "No, I won't be a servant; that doesn't suit my sex; but a Parisian, that's worth all the soldiers in the world! Bad head, good heart, the perfect package for only two sous!"

The hands of the Doctor were imprisoned in those of the children. He looked at them with deep tenderness.

"Lord," said Magapur, "you forgot one thing."

"Which is?" questioned the Doctor, again becoming master of himself.

"To tell me the name of the Brahmin who attempted to slay the child."

"It was Arkabad."

The fakir was startled.

"Arkabad," he repeated, while a joyful flame was lit in his somber eyes.

"Yes."

"He must know where he kidnapped the child."

"Very likely, but that fanatic will never talk."

"You are mistaken, Lord. He has talked."

The Doctor shook in his turn. Anoor and Cicada took a step forward, devouring the hermit with their eyes.

"He told someone what I so desperately want to know?" the Doctor finally stammered.

"Not entirely, but he indicated to the English, those ruling infidels, the roads on which they would stop you."

"The roads, you say? Yes, that is precious information... That's the direction that I must follow then. Which are those roads?"

"Those that end at Lahore."

"The capital of Punjab, near the Afghan frontier."

And holding out his arm to Anoor, he added:

"Rejoice, my daughter, your country is the country where I had hoped to prepare the triumph of my Will." Then with joyous volubility: "I should have guessed! The language that you spoke, the bear of Shiva, the traditional companion of the great Lords of Punjab... Let's go to Lahore, child. Perhaps the one whose memory you have kept may also be saved."

Then he turned to Magapur:

"How did you learn that?"

"The brother who told me about your presence in Delhi also charged me with passing it on to you."

"Good, good. Beliad has carried out my orders. An invisible world is moving, resurrecting the hope of those who had lost it. We shall triumph."

The fakir shook his head:

"For that to happen, the English must not capture you."

"Bah!" the Doctor said disdainfully, "they will capture me only if I consent to it."

"Even if all the roads going to Lahore are guarded? Even if they are cut with deep trenches causing your magic house to fall over backwards?"

As the Doctor's face turned dark again, Magapur continued:

"You can get to Lahore by two roads: that of Saharanpur, or that of Narnaul and Kaithal. I'm not mentioning the iron road,[47] because to use it, you would have to abandon the protection of your magic house. If you choose the first, you will be stopped before you get to Chandighar; if you opt for the second, they'll expect to capture you in the vicinity of Kaithal."

The Doctor's attitude expressed concern.

"It is too soon for an open rebellion," he pronounced, as if he were talking to himself.

"I agree," said the fakir. "So we will have to trick them."

"How?"

"By having someone other than you stopped in your place."

"It would be necessary to find the right people, and even if we had them, it would mean abandoning my aluminum house."

"Temporarily."

"Temporarily?"

"Yes, the English covet it for a reason that our brothers have not understood. They have heard talk about mirrors..."

The Doctor made a sudden movement.

"Mirrors... Have they guessed that I have solved the problem of parallels X?"

"I do not know what you speak of, Lord, but the English consider your magic house as a dreadful weapon, useful if the sons of the great Tsar of Russia decided to march through Afghanistan and invade India. They want to seize it and take it to Punjab where it could be studied by their officers. You could easily take it back from them during the trip."

"Without a doubt."

---

[47] Railway.

The Doctor pondered the fakir's words and stopped arguing. In a new tone he asked:

"All right then, who do you have in mind to impersonate us?"

"Some people that would least suspect it."

"Where are they?"

"Near here. They are eating lunch near Aladdin's Gate, and their interpreter is one of our members."

"I want to see them."

"Immediately, Lord."

Magapur clapped his hands. Immediately, a man came out of the thicket. He was wearing the clothes of those Hindus who guide the English tourists throughout Hindustan: a jacket with gold buttons, trousers held up by a wide silk belt and a turban with the letters I.R. (Indian Railways) on the front, indicating that he belonged to the official interpreters of the Peninsula Railway.[48]

"Natchuri," said the fakir, "here is our Lord, the Golden Tiger."

The interpreter bowed very low. The fakir continued:

"You must convince those who accompany you to continue their journey in our Lord's mobile palace."

"I will," promised the guide in a firm voice.

"Where are they right now?"

"They are eating, sitting between the Tower of Victory and Aladdin's Gate."

"Take our Lord there and carry out my orders."

"That will be done, brother."

"May I leave, Lord?" then murmured the fakir, asking the Doctor.

"You may—and may Vishnu be with you."

With marvelous quickness, Magapur slid into the underbrush and disappeared.

Without saying a word, the interpreter started walking, going in front of the Doctor and his two young friends. The walk was not long. In about a quarter of an hour, in front of them, the superb and desolate Tower of Victory, and Aladdin's Gate stood on the rocky soil, where the surrounding vegetation hadn't been able to grow. Constructed by the Emperor Qutab, the Tower of Victory rose proudly 240 feet high, with its five floors, each one smaller than the last, with circular galleries which were true works of art.[49]

---

[48] The Great Indian Peninsula Railway was a predecessor of the Central Railway (and by extension, the current state-owned Indian Railways). It was incorporated in 1849.

[49] The Tower (Qutab Minar) was built through a period of several centuries during the reign of the three Mughal emperors: Qutab-ud-din Aibak built one story followed by his successor, Shams-ud-din Iltutmish, who built three more stories, and finally Firoz Shah Tughlaq, who built the final and fifth story.

At his left, the Aladdin's Gate showed its large gothic arch, the majestic entry to a disappeared Temple, which allowed the high forests to be seen in the distance.[50]

Natchuri held out his arm:

"They are there, on the other side of that wall."

"Who are they?"

"Mr. and Mrs. Sanders and their dozen daughters."

"What?"

The Doctor didn't have leisure to ask any more questions; the sound of an argument could be heard in the distance.

---

[50] Alai Darwaza (Aladdin's Gate) is the southern gateway of the Qutab complex, in Delhi. Built by Sultan Aladdin Khalji in 1311 and made of red sandstone, it is a square domed gatehouse with arched entrances and houses a single chamber.

CHAPTER VII
A Parliamentary Family

"Wilhelmina, my wife," shouted a male voice.

"Jeroboam Sanders, my husband," replied a female soprano voice.

"That is unbearable."

"I was going to say unendurable," he replied.

"And in the splendor of the Parliament, to which I had the honor of belonging…"

"A more combative man than you couldn't be found, my friend."

"Wilhelmina!"

"Jeroboam!"

A dozen silvery voices, each one more silvery than the last, some with a suave Dutch accent, others with a not less delightful English accent, cried:

"Mama! Papa!"

A dozen young girls all dressed in white, wearing straw hats with long tails of mauve gossamer, rushed towards the man and woman who were quarreling.

Those two beings seemed to be the opposite of each other. He, Jeroboam Sanders, was fat, with short legs, a rosy face, clean-shaven, with a halo of thin hair; his abdomen was pointing like the front of a ship over his outerwear of white canvas, representing a triumph of obesity; he was out of breath and sweating under his colonial green helmet.

She, tall, dry, with an angular, wrinkled face under her narrow helmet, wore a sheath dress; above her lips, a thick brown down would have, on the face of a man, taken the name "moustache."

Jeroboam held out his hand toward the young girls and in a sententious tone said:

"Listen to these children, Wilhelmina. The complaint of the people is the lesson of a true Parliamentarian. It must constantly direct his actions."

What was that strange group doing in the plains of Delhi? Some words of introduction are necessary. Mr. Sanders was a gentleman farmer from the County of Fife in Great Britain, and had once had a seat in the House of Commons.

That had been the happiest time in his life. He had attended every session, getting himself named a member of all the commissions and sub-commissions. Budget, Navy, War, Public Works, Commerce, Industry… He spoke at all of them with endless energy and equal incompetence. For example, no one knew better than he did the polite way in which MPs set their most perfidious insinuations. He could not ask for a light for his cigar without beginning the sentence with the words "My Right Honorable Friend."

The state of his expenses became for him, "the tax burden." The government was, in his eyes, perched on the "chariot of state" and its reins were held "by a strong hand." And so on. Thus, it was for him a day of "cruel mourning" when the shifting confidence of the electorate sent, in its time and place, a different representative to the House of Commons.

For the first time, he became aware that he was, in fact, a widower; he have consoled himself, but his late wife had left him five daughter, whom he couldn't ignore. Charming, smiling, petulant, noisy, they were named Maud, Laura, Grace, Mary and Betty, all blond, pale and rosy, with blue eyes. They had that radiant and gracious look of which young English girls have the secret.

The first concern of Jeroboam Sanders was to transform his household into five "departments" and at the head of each, he placed one of the young ladies. Maud, dreamier than here sisters, was in charge of the household, with the title Minister of the Interior. Laura, in love with flowers, was set to take care of the garden, with the title Minister of the Gardens and Trees. Grace was put in charge of rents and disputes with the neighbors, and became Minister of Justice. Mary, knowledgeable about architecture, was Minister of Public Works. Finally, Betty, a tireless shopper, ran through the markets to bring back the necessary goods to support everybody and, for her trouble, received the title of Minister of Foreign Affairs.

Thus, in the middle of his children, Sanders could hear the words dear to his ears. The household conversations seemed an echo of the meetings of the House of Commons. The five pretty girls, chaffed and agitated, reported gracefully the activities of their respective ministries, including "Governmental" initiatives and "Opposition" moves. That was almost happiness found again.

If only...

In the existence of every man, there is an "if only" that poisons his days. The five pretty girls eventually banded together against their father, who had modestly called himself Prime Minister. Was this a mere opportunistic alliance or the wind of a revolution brewing that had taken root inside the girls' heads? The cause didn't matter very much; the effect is what afflicted Jeroboam Sanders.

The worthy man, a firm believer in individual freedoms, the apostle of equal suffrage for each, had applied his theories to his house. If there was a decision to be made, a piece of land to be bought, a lease to be terminated, a trip to be taken, very quickly he would shout with a stentorian voice:

"Get ready, children. We're going to vote!"

At that recognized call, everyone sat down around the table, on which there was a round earthenware vase—the urn. Everyone, male and female, wrote his thought, his desire, on a square of paper that he or she folded neatly and carefully put into the vase. Next, the girls, on the invitation of their father, chose two "Officers" to analyze the ballots. Jeroboam proclaimed the result with the same majesty as if he had been presiding over a Chamber, high or low. And the admirable result was that the votes were always equally divided—three in favor, three against—so that in the end, they decided not to proceed, which, as everyone knows, is the usual move of a government that wants to govern without problems.

One day, however, Sanders having suggested going to the seaside, either to Brighton or to the Isle of Wight, the vote took place. He wrote seriously on his paper: *Isle of Wight*.

But the universal suffrage, represented by his five delightful daughters, instead responded with these five very different wishes: Kolkata. Mysore. Allahabad. Delhi. Lahore.

For once, the sisters, while differing on the name of the cities they wished to vit, had agreed on a common goal, a trip to India. And, respecting the opinion of the majority, even if it worse petticoats, Sanders declared that they would leave for India and that they would visit each of the cities mentioned successively. The gentleman understood his duties vis-a-vis universal suffrage.

This is why we have encountered the Sanders family in the ruins of Delhi.

Only—still another "only"—the number of "voters" had unexpectedly increased during the trip.

Sanders and his daughters had embarked on the steamer *Parliament*—chosen by the maniac because of its name—at Liverpool bound for Colombo and Kolkata by the way of Gibraltar, Malta, Port Saïd, and Aden. On it, the daughters had made friends with seven other young ladies from Holland, having the exquisite first names of Klaesa, Fritzijne, Anna-Maria, Nelusis, Anneken, Janeke, and Lisabeth.

These young persons, calm, blonde, solidly built, were chaperoned by their mother, the respectable Wilhelmina van Stoon, the widow of a former Governor of Batavia. That lady, an excellent woman, had kept a loving memory of her husband, which was apparent in each of her sentences. Every movement for her, the wife of a former military man, called for a military command. Getting up after a nap, she would exclaim: *Forward, march!* If she had to turn to the right or left quickly, she shouted: *Right* (or *Left*) *flank, march!* To stop was *Halt!* and to stroll was *Change step!*

Under her direction, her children had become accustomed to executing the simplest directions with military rigidity. They walked in impeccable alignment, observing the rank of height religiously—the tallest on the right, the shortest on the left—and numbered from 1 to 7. So well had the widow taken the habit of replacing the baptismal names of the beloved creatures by numbers corresponding to their height that Klaesa had become Number One, Lisabeth, Number Seven, etc. To the astonishment of people who hadn't been forewarned, Madame van Stoon uttered sentences like this: "Number Four, please pick up my handkerchief," an action broken down into three movements: one, bend down and take the batiste between one's fingers; two, stand up again, lifting the square of linen; three, hold out the object. This usually ended with a "Excellent. Back in place. At ease."

In her eyes, dresses were suitable only for exercises or parades; a hat was akin to a helmet; a belt was a *ceinturon*; a handbag a musette; a trunk, a cantine, and so forth. Everywhere, she embraced the superiority given by her faithful heart to the military over the civilian.

Right off, Jeroboam was seduced by the widow, for it is known that opposites attract.

He was portly; she was thin; she knew how to discipline her daughters; he had never managed to do so with his. A barrel on legs, he sighed for Mrs. van Stoon, whose elevated height was handled with the grace of a light conductor. He dreamed of a peaceful household, directed by her, where his five daughters would be disciplined like those from Holland. In the place of five different "Ministers," he would only have one facing him.

A perfect example of human inconsistency, Sanders had passed without transition for the administration of his household from a democratic republican government to an absolute autocracy. The once liberal MP now embraced tyranny. But Wilhelmina's soul also aspired to a change; the widow strongly desired to remarry. Because these two lonely beings understood each other without having to spell things out, at the Lisbon stopover, Jeroboam made eyes at the Dutch mother. She returned the compliment at Gibraltar. At Malta, Sanders whispered:

"Widowhood is truly the worst of conditions!"

At Port Saïd, at the entry to the Suez Canal, she responded with the military loyalty that characterized her:

"Widowhood is the worst of punishments; marriage is an Honor Parade."

It takes at least two to get in rank and file!

Upon hearing those nice words, Jeroboam would have knelt if he had been sure that his bulging abdomen would have allowed him to stand up again.

At Suez, a traveling notary signed the marriage contract; a Methodist minister married them at the Walls of Aden, and there, the British Consul placed his seal on the Act that, in good and due form, consecrated their union.

The Wedding Dinner took place at Ceylon[51] and they then thought about the traditional honeymoon trip. A vote, the first of the united Sanders-van-Stoon family, took place and it was decided that the new spouses and their dozen children would first travel through India, then they would go to Batavia, which had been the initial destination of the Dutch family.

Why had all the girls been in agreement to begin with a journey through India, that remained to be explained. Maud, the oldest of the Sanders, had been engaged at age three and a half to Claudius Farren, the only son of Lord Arthur Archibald Farren, a Colonel in the Indian Army. Claudius, five at that time, had shortly thereafter accompanied his father into the Hindustani Peninsula. The two children had never seen each other since then, but the Press had informed the dreamy Maud that, in recompense for his services, Lord Farren had obtained the envied post of Governor of Punjab, and was in residence at Umra Palace in Lahore.[52]

She had then remembered her forgotten engagement, had begged her sisters to help her see Claudius, in order to remind him of their past and present projects. And those sisters, telling themselves that the marriage of Maud would make them enter a new world, where perhaps they would find husbands of their choice for themselves—as marriage calls for marriage—had agreed to help their sister in her quest for conjugal bliss.

It is not necessary to add that the van Stoon girls, being appraised of the project of the Sanders sisters, had similar thoughts—being from Holland didn't make them less of a woman—so the excursion across India was voted for unanimously, except for two parental votes.

These had belonged to Wilhelmina, who would have preferred Batavia, and to the gallant Jeroboam, who had thought it was his duty to agree with his spouse.

---

[51] Sri Lanka.

[52] Jati Umra is the Sharif family's palatial estate near Lahore and is named after their Indian ancestral town of Jati Umra, Tarn Taran Sahib near Amritsar in Punjab. Mian Muhammad Sharif was born and lived in Jati Umra before migrating to Lahore in 1932.

At first, the trip had been an enchantment. The plains of the Ganges, the admirable monuments of Varanasi,[53] of Lucknow, had allowed the tourists to utter the thousands of equally worthless statements, which are, without a doubt, typical of travels of that type, because all of them are spat out with the same lack of true understanding and appreciation, and the same dislike of what is actually admirable. But aside from the commercial city of Aurangabad, a cloud had obscured the blue skies of the united Sander-van Stoon family.

The news of the declaration of war between England, and the South-African Republic,[54] had suddenly dug an abyss between the heads of the two families. Wilhelmina sided with her Boer Countrymen; Jeroboam was hoping for the success of the British.

The woman, previously an angel of the household, suddenly became a demon that the parliamentary calm of Sanders did not manage to appease. He himself became excited. As between Ireland and Albion, was their conflict also going to tear apart the two traveling families? [55]

However, the young ladies remained neutral. With a touching feelings of togetherness, they interposed themselves between their father, the subject of Her Majesty Queen Victoria, and their mother from the Netherlands.

In their hearts, they feared seeing the events of the War bring about a sudden separation between their parents, a separation which would keep them from continuing to Lahore, a marvelous city where all of them counted on meeting their future husbands.

But now, the same old quarrel had erupted again near Aladdin's Gate, in the shadow of the Tower of Victory.

The guilty parties were Lord Roberts and Lord Kichener, whom the War Office of London had just placed at the head of their armies, replacing General Redvers Buller, who was deemed insufficiently persistent.[56]

Wilhelmina, reading the newspaper, had murmured:

"Another two fools who are going to get themselves slaughtered."

"Slaughtered?" Sanders had replied. "There's a word that should only be applied to horses."

---

[53] Benares.

[54] Paul Kruger, President of the South African Republic, issued an ultimatum on 9 October 1899, giving the British government 48 hours to withdraw all their troops from the borders of both the Transvaal and the Orange Free State, failing which the Transvaal, allied to the Orange Free State, would declare war on England.

[55] There followed a long paragraph, heavily slanted against the British, in which D'Ivoi recounts the major events of the Second Boer War, which we have deleted.

[56] On 22 October 1901.

"You are right," immediately sneered the Dutch woman. "I hope the horses will accept my apologies, the English Generals are nothing but asses."

"Asses! Ah, be careful, Wilhelmina, my patriotism is touchy... Asses! I don't know what keeps me from jumping on you like a furious tiger."

"What holds you back? Is it the fat around your middle? How could you jump with such a belly?"

"Don't say anything bad about it! It is the belly of an honest citizen."

"Honest? That's unfortunate! That adjective does not belong in the English language."

With an explosion, the dignified woman trembled in indignation:

"Ah! Why did I lose my freedom? Why did I tie my life to an Englishman? I shall have to fall on my sword."

At that, Jeroboam ranted; the ex-widow van Stoon whined some more; and the dozen girls shouted:

"Papa!" "Mama!"

What would have happened if the now disunited household had remained left to its own designs? One shivers to think about it. Fortunately, Natchuri the interpreter judged that it was the appropriate moment to show himself. He arrived in a trot with gestures, the appearance of a man who had just completed a long run.

"My Lord, Milady," he shouted, "there's been an accident... with the Western India Railway line... The Delhi-Lahore section has been damaged...."

"Damaged?"

"Yes, a derailment... The track's been destroyed... A bridge is down... In short, it's going to take several days of work before traffic can be reestablished."

Struck directly in their projects of tourism, the two quarrelers forgot their patriotic differences. There was a concert of lamentations:

"What are we going to do in Delhi?"

"We've seen enough ruins!"

"Another week to spend here? Two, perhaps? Oh, no!"

"Oh! These damned railroads!"

And in a tragic tone, Jeroboam bellowed:

"That wouldn't happen in England!"

To that, Wilhelmina replied tit for tat:

"In England, no, but we are still in English land. It's in Holland, you mean, that they wouldn't play a trick like this on hapless travelers."

"Holland doesn't have any railways to speak of."

"Naturally, for you, England is the only country that has trains."

"Well, we have 28,000 miles of lines instead of 5000."[57]

"That's right, insult my country!"

"I'm not insulting it... A statement of fact has nothing to do with an insult."

"Yes, it does!"

"No."

The dispute was going to begin again so Natchuri hurried to intervene:

"I thought that a long stay here would displease my honorable clients..."

"Honorable!" murmured Sanders. "That boy expresses himself well."

"...So I found a way to continue the trip without waiting."

"Without waiting! You found a way?"

"Yes, My Lord."

"And that is?"

"The Electric Hotel."

Fear appeared on all the faces: Jeroboam, Wilhelmina, the five English girls and the seven pretty Dutch girls opened their enormous eyes, and in the atmosphere of stupefaction which spread out around them, the Tower of Victory seemed a point of exclamation, while Aladdin's Gate was wide open like a frightened mouth.

"The Electric Hotel!" Sanders finally repeated. "What in God's name is that?"

The interpreter put on his important air.

"A fortunate invention, My Lord."

"Anything more than that?"

"It exists for the comfort of the tourists; to improve the charm of their trip. Like everybody else, you regret not having been able to take your house with you, don't you?"

"Ah, yes!" answered the fat man with a sigh, which told a lot about his ambulatory inconvenience.

"Ah, yes!" echoed the ex-widow.

"Ah, yes!" cried out the girls all together.

"Well, Ladies and Gentleman, a man of heart and initiative has thought about filling that gap. He has constructed a house on wheels, equipped with electricity, that can take travelers across Bengal, Punjab, the land of the Rajputs, etc. At this moment, that man is testing his first hotel car, but, at my request, he has consented, if you agree, to take you in..."

The young girls clapped.

"A rolling house."

"Will we be the first to try it?"

"Assuredly, My Ladies."

---

[57] According to Fordham University's Modern History Sourcebook, in 1900 Great Britain had 19,000 miles of railroads compared with 1700 for the Netherlands.

"Oh, Papa! Oh, Mama! We must accept. Think about what a charming memory... To have been the first guests in such a vehicle... The annals of science will list our names..."

Sanders straightened up; Wilhelmina put on a dignified look.

"The late Mijnheer van Stoon served in the Infantry," the dry person finally exclaimed, "but considering our recruits (her maternal hand pointed to the young girls) I deign to travel in the wagon train."

"Me too," exclaimed Sanders, very happy to be able, once, by chance, to agree with his wife.

Natchuri bowed.

"In that case, please follow me. The Electric Hotel is parked some distance away. I'm going to introduce you as the expected guests. After that, you have only to send for your baggage to be picked up at the caravanserai of the city and to move in."

"Let's go."

"Let's walk,"

"Let's run."

Seeing the turn taken by the conversation, Doctor Mystery, Cicada, and Anoor had discretely left and had returned to their aluminum house.

A half-hour later, the Doctor, or the "Hotel Owner" as the interpreter introduced him, greeted Sanders and his family at the top of the mobile steps. He installed them in the bedrooms on the second floor, where the cries of admiration of the young Sanders-van Stoon sounded like the songs of singing birds. Only, he asked them to change in the uniform of the house.

"I am not yet authorized to carry travelers," he explained. "The government would cause me trouble if they learned about this infraction to the rules that I am committing by being helpful. I must, therefore, protect myself in case an official should come and inspect my hotel. With this uniform, you will appear to be part of my staff."

This caused only joy, and at dinner laughter broke out in peals when the fourteen Sanders-van Stoon, clothed like Hindus, with long shirts tied at the waist and bouffant trousers, everything dark green, sat around the table. Certainly, the young girls were charming, but Jeroboam still looked like a windbag and Wilhelmina, with her mustache, still seemed like an old grouch.

The meal was excellent. Ludovic, present at all the festivities, immediately became the favorite of all the girls. In short, everyone went to bed in the happiest of moods. The tourists had finally found a hotel that pleased them, and the Doctor thought that the daring plan suggested by the fakir Magapur had been carried out to that point without any difficulty.

At dawn, the Electric Hotel started off, leaving Delhi behind, driving at an accelerated speed on the road to Kaithal.

CHAPTER VIII
The Chloroformist

The wide and well-maintained road, bordered by deep ditches meant to facilitate the flow of water, followed a line almost parallel to the Aravalli range, whose peaks spread out in the purple fog. Right up to the village of Narnaul, the countryside was green and well cultivated. The fields of *bajra*[58] alternated with reddish bands of *moth* beans or vast fields of *hara madhu* melons.

Sanders and his family, after they got up, were reunited on the front terrace. They watched the countryside unfold, while exchanging their impressions.

"It's marvelous," exclaimed Maud.

"No bumps, no shaking. A panorama which unfolds in front of a comfortable house," replied Anneken.

"That's a tourist dream!"

And Wilhelmina, always aggressive, declared:

"Better than the English trains!"

"And the Dutch ones too, dear mother," Klaesa (Number 1) hastened to add in order to avoid a quarrel.

---

[58] Pearl millet.

Lunch took place in the outskirts of Narnaul. After that village, the countryside began to change. The periphery of the Thar Desert was desolate, lonely, with rock and sand covering the north-western part of Rajputana.

Greenery did not appear again except around a few houses, separated by big sandy spaces. In the distance, an oasis, surrounded with acacias, *daos*, and cotton plants spread out its dark stain on the surface of the desert, turned gold by the sun. Sometimes, the rolling house went across bridges over rivers which were uniformly dry at the moment.

The sadness of this vast solitude weighed heavy on the travelers, who were sitting on the terrace.

The Doctor, Cicada, Anoor and Ludovic had rejoined their guests, with whom their relationship was becoming increasingly friendly.

With enthusiasm, the Doctor explained India to his guests. He explained its past, the invasions of the conquerors, all through the passes of Afghanistan. He told them about the Aryas, the Turkmens, the Mongols, the Persians, the Turks, the armies of Cambyses [59] and even the Greeks of Alexander, who had all followed the same routes. He predicted future invasions, by the Russian army perhaps. He explained how the Brahmins had conquered the spirit of the country, but that the Hindus' national consciousness would eventually awaken and that the immense continent would become free and begin to soar towards the glorious destiny that had been foretold at the beginning of its history.

The Sanders-van Stoon were astonished at the knowledge and eloquence of the man that they still took to be a simple hotel keeper. Questions were crossing each other, when suddenly a trembling, gloomy groan, vibrated through the air. Everybody stopped talking. From one of the ditches bordering the road, a human figure stood up and fell back down, yelling out a shaking command:

"Help! Help!"

Standing on the vibrating platform, the Doctor gave a brief order into a telephone attached to the wall and the aluminum house stopped.

The Doctor jumped to the ground. Without being concerned about his guests, who followed him, he ran toward the place where the man had appeared. There, he stopped and uttered a cry of pity. A man was lying on the embankment—a Hindu, whose naked torso was covered by bleeding stripes. His grimacing face hadn't been spared. He also was scarred on his stomach, shoulders, back, and his arms.

In one leap, the Doctor reached the wounded man, who looked at him with a fearful expression.

"Help me," he said in a faint voice. "Don't let me die here."

"Don't worry, my good man. Who did this to you?"

The man gritted his teeth and replied:

---

[59] Second King of Kings of the Achaemenid Empire from 530 to 522 BC. He was the son and successor of Cyrus the Great.

"Those who steal from us! Starve us!"

"But who?"

"The Brahmins—protected by the English."

"What was your crime?"

"Son of the Rajputs, I have read the sacred books. I saw that there was a time in the past, long ago, when the Brahmins were not the masters; they did not starve widows and orphans. They're the ones who brought into this country barbaric customs by persuading the people that women were the ruination of families. After their coming, butchers were seen throwing widows intoxicated by drinks onto fires and burning them alive; fathers slaughtered their daughters under the pretext that, not being able to take up arms, they could not add to the family's wealth. The tribes died one by one. The Brahmins fulfilled their plan to weaken the military in order to remain the only masters of the country. I had the misfortune to repeat those things to the people. They then took me before an English Officer, who condemned me to prison. But yesterday, during the night, someone got me out and took me back to the Brahmin Priests, and they declared that I had to die under the whip. They flogged me until I lost consciousness. Why am I not dead, I don't know. But I found myself here, lying on the side of the road, bleeding, with broken bones, all alone. That's what justice is like for the Brahmins!"

The Doctor was listening. He liked the energy of the wounded man. What that brave man had done, fighting with the sacred caste, was not to be dismissed.

"Where is your home?"

The man pointed to a burned out shack not far away from the road.

"That is what they did to it."

"So you have no place to live?"

"That's true. Without a roof over my head, they classified me among those who don't have the right to live."

"I suppose you hate them?"

"Hate? The word seems too weak to express how I feel."

"Do you want to come with me?"

The man looked at the Doctor suspiciously.

"You are not affiliated with the Brahmins, because your face remained emotionless when I talked to you. You are not English either, because you speak our language as a true son of India. So I will follow you, if you do not oppose me getting my revenge."

"What if I refuse?"

The wounded man, stretched out on the ground, closed his eyes and with a trembling voice said:

"Then, go away. I shall die alone."

He had put all his savage will power into those words. The Doctor nodded with satisfaction.

"Don't get agitated, my friend. You can have your revenge whenever you please. I want only to take care of you, to cure you, and give you shelter."

The man replied, simply:

"Then I accept. I am Awadh,[60] the best basket weaver in all of Berar... I will not forget...".

That was all. A quarter of an hour later, the unfortunate man was placed in the drawing room of the aluminum house. Stretched out on a couch, after having his horrible wounds cleaned and dressed, he fell asleep.

Near him, the Doctor and Cicada chatted in French so he would not understand, if by any chance he came out of his torpor.

"Boss," said Cicada, "I don't like this fellow."

"Why, my child?"

"I don't know. He doesn't look right... and then... and then..."

"Finish your thought."

"Well, he looks too healthy for a man who has suffered so much, because, after all, he should have lost a lot of blood."

Thoughtful, the Doctor nodded.

"You are harder-hearted than I am. But you have seen correctly. I should have made the same observations. However, Hindus cannot be judged like Westerners. They can endure great pain stoically."

"Pain, I don't deny," interrupted the Parisian, "but loss of blood..."

And, as the Doctor did not answer, he continued:

"It seems to me that he has not bled a great deal... and if you want me to tell you what I really think, his wounds don't seem altogether real."

The Doctor made a vague smile.

"Ah, Master Cicada, where did you learn so much about medicine?"

"Well, I got whipped enough when I was a little boy, and I have some scars of my own on my butt. I assure you, Boss, that they were differently applied than those on that man. Of course, when they beat me, they didn't intend to kill me, whereas him... The Brahmins would have beaten the living daylights out of him..."

Even if expressed in slang, the Parisian's reflections were nevertheless accurate. The Doctor had been struck by the superficial severity of the man's wounds, despite their frightening appearance. He had wondered if the newcomer wasn't a spy sent by his enemies. Because, henceforth, he was certain that the entire Brahmin caste was plotting the downfall of the bold man who had dated stop the Chariot of Jagannath, slain their sacred tiger, and conquered the minds of so many of their people.

---

[60] In actuality, Awadh, also known in British texts as Avadh or Oudh, is a region and proposed state in the modern Indian state of Uttar Pradesh, which was, before independence, known as the United Provinces of Agra and Oudh.

"Evidently, the best thing to do would be to leave him on the side of the road, but humanity argues against it. Perhaps, after all, that man has been spared by the Brahmins' henchmen out of pity. When in doubt, it is necessary to help the unfortunates. There will be time enough to cast him out later when he is able to walk. For the moment, he is not to be feared," the Doctor concluded. "He actually has a high fever. He shouldn't be moved. But don't worry, Cicada, I will watch him closely as soon as he gets his strength back."

After saying that, the Doctor pulled the young man out of the room in order to let the wounded man rest. At that moment, Awadh's closed eyelids opened, letting through a crafty look. The lips of the allegedly wounded man opened in a cruel smile, and in a low voice, he murmured:

"His science is worthless. He hasn't guessed that my wounds were made with an infusion of the *Masroor* plant [61] and that my fever is caused by juice from the *Zapolaye* vine."

If the Doctor had heard these words, he would have understood. In Bengal, among the plants that grow in the swampy jungle, there are two climbing vines, the *Masroor* and the *Zapolaye*, whose strange properties have been known for a long time by the Brahmins, those grand illusionists, those inimitable fabricators of miracles. The sap of the *Zapolaye* taken at the prescribed dose creates a fictious fever, which in no way weakens the patient.

As for the *Masroor*, its stem has long thorns, thanks to which the Brahmins wishing to cultivate the good will of the population, can make themselves martyrs without danger. With it, they cut their skin, making themselves have terrible scars, that a salve made from the Mezroor cauterizes immediately, calming the pain. That was the whole secret of men who do not show pain when using the *Masroor*. The ignorant, the people, the foreigners, are astonished at the stoicism with which they endure pain, but it is neither suffering nor courage, only the slight-of-hand used by clever prestidigitators who knew how to use the path to fortune and domination.

At the time, the Brahmin caste had mastered, to a degree that we do not suspect in Europe, two sciences: that of botany and that of hypnosis, which they used to guarantee their political dominance. After all, if a lie is made either in words or in actions, the result is the same. The masters of politics live at the expense of those who listen to them or look at them.

The wounded man was therefore connected to those that the Doctor had vanquished at Ellora. He no longer moved; his eyelids were closed again. All day he remained as immobile as a statue, swallowing in a docile and automatic

---

[61] Perhaps named after the Masroor (or Masrur) Temples, an early 8th-century complex of rock-cut Hindu temples in the Kangra Valley of Beas River in Himachal Pradesh? I couldn't find any information about the Zapolaye, but there are over 2500 species of vines from about 90 families growing in India.

fashion the cordial that, for two and a half hours, the Doctor poured, drop by drop, between his clenched teeth.

Then, night fell.

The slight trepidation had ceased. The rolling house had halted some one hundred meters outside the little town of Churu, the last village at the end of the Thar Desert, which extends over 500 miles all the way up to Sindh.

Awadh did not move.

However, if someone had watched him closely, they would have noticed that his eyes were open, that his ears were listening in order to hear the least sounds. He had the appearance of a wildcat on the prowl.

Midnight came. The passengers of the aluminum house were all asleep. Before going to bed, the Doctor had made one last visit to the wounded man; then he had gone up to his bedroom on the second floor. He had taken no precautions, persuaded that the Hindu, plunged into a comatose state, was not aware of what was taking place around him.

Then, Awadh slowly started to get up from his couch. He got rid of the bandages which wrapped his body. He stood up, attached his loincloth to his belt, which had been kept on a nearby chair. There was no more trace of sickness or fever in him. He slowly unstitched the hem of the material that was around his loins. In that hiding place, that had escaped the attention of the most thorough observers, there were some yellowish globules the size of the head of a pin, and some transparent little tetrahedral crystals.

Awadh carried the globules to his mouth, swallowed them, and waited.

"Good," he said, after a few minutes. "The *rangzeb* has made me resistant to sleep; now, let the *faltvar* put my enemies to sleep."[62]

On the table, he put the translucent crystals, lit a candle and, as the crystals touched the flame, a rapid crackling was produced, a swirl of blue smoke rose toward the ceiling, and the grains of *faltvar* disappeared.

Awadh went to sit down on his pallet and appeared to be waiting.

A penetrating smell had spread throughout the room. You would have said that you were smelling the vapors of ether mixed with the smell of a fruit stand stacked with apples.

That was not surprising, because *faltvar* was Hindu chloroform. Its method of formation is unknown. In Europe, chloroform is obtained in the liquid state by distilling a mixture of alcohol and an aqueous solution of chloride of lime and caustic lime. The anesthetic thus produced is powerful, but not as much as *faltvar*. [63]

---

[62] *Rangzeb* is a common surname in Pakistan; *faltvar* (in various spellings) produced no search results; neither appear connected to known drugs.

[63] Today, chloroform is produced commercially by the reaction between chlorine gas and methane gas. In this reaction, each of the four hydrogens in methane is replaced, one at a time, by chlorine atoms. However, chloroform has now been

The Brahmins have discovered the method, that they keep secret, of making chloroform into the solid form of flammable crystals, and the sleep-producing power of that product is such that there is no wall, no door, that can block it. Once it is smoke, the *faltvar* is so volatile that it penetrates through even the most compact of materials. Everybody has heard of the experiment made in Bombay by a commission of scientists who, using *faltvar*, put to sleep a person inside a deep-sea diving suit.[64]

As for the *rangzeb*, a residue of the combustion of marine *algae*, it neutralizes the action of all the anesthetics known. That's how Awadh planned to put to sleep the inhabitants of the aluminum house without being put to sleep himself.

An hour went by; then the Hindu stood up. He walked slowly to where the spring-loaded basket, which allowed going up to the second floor, was located. For a moment, his hand went across the wall. Suddenly an opening appeared: the upper panel glided into its groove and came down. Without haste, Awadh got into the basket and up it went with its load.

The man found himself on the second floor. For some minutes, he remained still, his body leaning forward in the position of an eavesdropper. No sound came up to him.

"He's asleep," he grumbled. "We have won."

Slowly, with infinite precautions, Awadh began walking, crossing one compartment, then another. In each one, he approached the little beds, and identified the sleepers. After having looked at them, he shook his head and continued his silent inspection. A third door was in front of him. As he had done with the first two, he pushed it open. A little glass electric lamp without a shade let a weak light shine in the room which he had just entered. On her bed, completely clothed, Anoor was asleep. Beside her was an open book; it was a book in French. She had fallen asleep unexpectedly as she was working to learn the language of her "teacher," Cicada.

Seeing her, the Hindu had a silent and triumphant exclamation.

"Her! It's her! She escaped from the waves of the ocean! This time, nothing will save her."

He came up to the sleeping girl and took her in his arms. Looking like a demon carrying an angel, he went back the way he had come.

---

almost entirely replaced as an anesthetic by other compounds that are more effective and have fewer undesirable side effects.

[64] I could find no trace of such an experiment. The first chloroform anesthesia in India was administered on 12th January 1848 (chloroform was first used by James Young Simpson in Edinburgh on 15th November 1847). It is interesting to note that David Waldie, the chemist who was credited for introducing chloroform in clinical anesthesia, came to Calcutta in 1853; started his chemical company and lived there until his death in 1889.

He was then in the cloak room; the basket was still there. He got into it with his victim, set it in motion, and started down.

After crossing the drawing room, he reached the vestibule on the back platform. He suddenly stopped. There was a noise above his head. What was it? By leaning over, he saw the silhouette of one of the sailors from the *Saint Kaourentin*, a vigilant sentinel placed on the roof of the aluminum house. The man had escaped the anesthetic effect because he was outside.

Awadh had to keep from being spotted. Taking advantage of the coming and going of the sailors, walking while they had their shoulders turned, stopping when they turned back, he finally made it to the side of the road, still carrying his load.

He succeeded in reaching the ditch. There, he could no longer be seen. He got down to the bottom of the trench dragging the body of the inert Anoor, and when he was within a hundred meters of the vehicle, he seized a favorable moment, jumped into the underbrush and disappeared with his prey.

The sailor on duty on the roof was none other than Yvon. The brave boy, who would have attacked ten men without hesitation, when it came to supernatural things, felt an almost childish timidity. A true Breton brought up on folk legends, Yvon was afraid of the supernatural, created in many ways by the bards, troubadours, and poets of every generation. That evening, under the moon which spread its pale light over the prairie, the Breton sailor felt uneasy.

The moon, as it is known in Brittany, is the precursor of the assemblies of witches, gnomes, fairies, and werewolves. At every era, she is the queen of the spirits of the night, and the accomplice of necromancers and caster of evil spells.

In reality itself, doesn't she protect the labors of criminals and hide the pursuits of wild beasts?

In short, Yvon, overcome by worry, was not a very confident sentinel.

Suddenly, he trembled. In the undercover on the right, he had just seen two silhouettes: one black, the other white. That was the moment when Aw3adh, had jumped into the trench with the sleeping Anoor. The Breton's heart started beating faster

"What was that?" stammered the poor boy. "There wasn't anything there a moment ago."

However, as the sight that had disturbed him did not move, Yvon became calmer little by little.

'I must be seeing things," he continued in a more confident tone. "I just didn't pay any attention to that detail before, that's all."

Suddenly, he stopped short, stifling a cry of terror. The shadows were moving slowly along the bottom of the ditch. It seemed that they were trying to reach the extremity of the bushes that had grown up in that hollow where humidity could accumulate.

"By the Good Lady of Auray!" stammered the sailor, whose teeth were clacking with terror,

"That's a troll or a fairy., like in the land of Armor!"[65]

Remembering that the spirits didn't like to be watched while doing their nocturnal rounds, the stalwart sentinel closed his eyes. When he opened them again, the apparition had disappeared.

"Whew!" exclaimed Yvon with a sigh of relief, "the troll has continued on his way and I haven't had to fight him." He rubbed his hands vigorously. "It's better this way, because such an encounter is always dangerous. One might lose one's nose or one's ears, and sometimes even an arm or a leg. My grandmother is proof of that—she limps. It's because she once encountered a fairy one night near Plonevez, and he broke her ankle..."

Suddenly, his voice strangled in his throat. He moaned while falling to his knees. A black and white shadow had suddenly jumped up from the ground, a hundred yards from the aluminum house. It had made a circle in the air and dived into the bushes on the side of the road. Yvon shivered from head to toes, his teeth clacked like castanets.

"What's going to happen to me? I must call my comrades."

With an unsteady walk, he reached the hatch set up in the middle of the roof giving access to the "sailors' quarters," as Kéradec and his men called their dormitory.

"Ohe, boys!" shouted the poor boy in a moaning voice. "There's a ghost ahead!"

These words were lost in the silence without raising any echo.

"Ohe, boys!" Yvon shouted again.

But he didn't finish his sentence. A breeze blew across the plain, blowing some sand which hit him like little shrapnel. The brave Breton thought he had been attacked by a legion of phantoms. Without thinking, he jumped with both his feet into the dormitory.

Now unsteady, trying to recover his footing, he finally fell down heavily on one of the little couches placed around the room. He heard swearing and received a shove. It was Kéradec who had broken his fall. The Captain stood up, getting his arms out from under the covers with difficulty.

"What is it, Yvon?"

"I saw a ghost."

"Where?"

"On the road."

At those words, Kéradec jumped up from his bed, put on his trousers, and slid his feet into his shoes...

"That's bizarre," he growled. "I have a heavy head, and my mouth..."

But he immediately recalled his duty.

---

[65] Brittany.

"Let's go up, and if you don't explain yourself clearly, you and I will have words."

In a minute, the two men were on the roof.

There, the air had again become calm. Under the silver rays of the moon, the aluminum house was bright, immobile in the middle of the deserted country-side.

Yvon explained about the strange being that had frightened him.

"It was like a big, black and white snake running through the grass, and it disappeared into the bushes."

Kéradec shrugged.

"Idiot! That was no ghost—that was a spy that's all. However, you were right to wake me up. That could signal an incoming attack. We must warn the Captain."

Saying that, Kéradec went back to the dormitory, crossed it and opened the door that went into the compartment that the Doctor had set aside for himself. He was sleeping with his fists closed, and Kéradec had to shake him several times to wake him up. Finally, he opened his eyes.

"I have a heavy head, and a pasty mouth," he murmured.

Exactly the same symptoms Kéradec had noted earlier. He remarked on it.

"You too? said the Doctor, who was regaining his composure. With some surprise,, he continued: "That is curious, that taste... One would swear... but that's impossible..."

When Kéradec told him the reason for his presence, the Doctor struck his forehead:

"You are right! An attack is imminent! And to be sure of its success, they put us to sleep."

"To sleep?"

"Yes! I recognize the signs of chloroform. I didn't dare believe it. Now everything is becoming clearer... But who could have..." Suddenly, he exclaimed: "Awadh!"

While talking, the Doctor got dressed. Then, he began running, followed by Kéradec. Using the basket, they soon found themself soon in the drawing room, where they had left the wounded man.

There was no longer any one there!

The Doctor, looking around, saw, on top of the table, little slate-colored stains. He leaned over and shouted:

"Crystallized chloroform! Oh, how he tricked us!"

The door had remained open, showing the way the traitor had fled.

The two men ran into the vestibule, the terrace, and descended onto the walkway. At the bottom of the ditch, the disturbed bushes showed traces of the fugitive. Thus, the Doctor and Kéradec came to the place where Awadh had jumped into the bushes. Broken branches, and a bush turned over, showed that the villain had believed that he could act without taking any precautions.

The Doctor suddenly leaned forward; he'd noticed a piece of torn cloth hanging at the end of a thorn.

"He took Anoor! She's prisoner of the Brahmins!" he exclaimed.

That fragment was indeed a piece of golden embroidery from the girl's tunic, which had allowed the Doctor to realize the truth. He was no longer the calm. In terrible despair, his expression contracted and his dark eyes shone.

"But I'm going to save her! That child, who calls me father, shall not perish, even if I have to abandon my own plans... Even if I have to fight that battle alone... She will be saved!"

Running, he went back to the aluminum house, and Kéradec had trouble keeping up with him. During that frantic run, the Doctor kept talking:

"Kéradec, wake up your men and tell them to be ready to leave. They will carry the little bags I prepared for you; and each one will have in his hand the special cane that I gave you."

"Yes, Captain!"

They arrived at the rolling house, went inside, going through the cloak room.

"Go!" ordered the Doctor.

Kéradec rushed into the cloak room, while the Doctor himself ran towards Cicada's room. He rushed towards the boy, still deep in sleep, picked him up in his arms, lifted him like a feather, placing him standing up in front of him.

"Huh? What?" mumbled Cicada, startled by his sudden awakening.

Almost out-of-breath, the Doctor growled:

"The Brahmins have captured Anoor—your sister as you call her. They want to kill her. We must get there in time to save her."

The grogginess of the chloroform disappeared immediately. The boy's troubled eyes regained all their clarity.

"Anoor?" he repeated with agony, "Anoor, kidnaped?"

"By those who have sworn to kill her. Like they tried to do at Audierne."

"God's blood!" The boy turned red. "Where are they? I will teach them a lesson they'll never forget."

"I don't know where they are, but I'll soon to find out. Get dressed!"

In a split second, Cicada was ready. The young man, whose heart was tortured, did not weep. All the intrepidity, all the courage contained in that little body cried out.

The Doctor shook his hand.

"You are brave, my child. I am proud of you. Come."

With Cicada following him, he returned to the back compartment of the aluminum house.

That room was his laboratory. It contained furnaces, beakers, stills, test tubes, strange instruments, metallic mirrors lined up against the walls or on aluminum shelves bolted to the walls. There were the grooves of rails on the floor.

Wordlessly, the Doctor seized a crank on the wall and turned it several times. What looked like a blackboard came out of the wall and started rolling on the rails. An even stranger apparatus came out and rolled on a parallel track; it had a brass frame between which hung metallic wires, bronze plates, and reflectors with lots of light bulbs.

Meanwhile, an opening appeared in the wall of the house itself, through which one could see out into the countryside.

"What are we doing?" asked Cicada.

"We are looking for a trace of Anoor's kidnapper. To do that, we must find where he dragged our unfortunate little friend."

"And that blackboard is going to tell us that?"

"Yes it is!"

And rapidly, without putting down his instruments, the Doctor explained:

"You have already seen how, using the discoveries of Branly, Herz, Roentgen, Ducretet and Marconi, I can project electricity at a distance without wires or conductors of any kind?"

"Yes."

"Here, we have the opposite problem, which consists in receiving electricity coming from a distant point, also without wires. Electricity, you see, is a power whose true nature still escapes man's understanding, and like the fakirs, I would be disposed to consider it as the soul of the world. Electricity is everywhere; it is part of any action, every movement. Whether we're talking light waves or sound waves, the vehicle of all those waves is electric. In the body of a man who runs, speaks, and breathes, electricity is there to create life. That instrument, which confuses you, is made to register even the feeblest of electric currents... It's like a telephone and a telephote combined, without wires. You have already seen me use it during our visit to Ellora. Now, I am recalibrating it for longer distances. Look at the board; you will see what's happening far away in the distance..."

There was click, and a picture of the countryside appeared on the "blackboard." It was a field of woods in the back of which were the first houses of the village of Churu. The Doctor turned the little brass wheels, aligning them in the lower part of the brass frame, and immediately the picture changed.

"Damn," exclaimed Cicada, "it seems to be moving!"

"Yes," answered the Doctor, "but in life, we'd be the ones moving. Here, it's the picture that moves. But the results are identical."

They came to a hole through the bushes.

"It was there," the Doctor said, "that Awadh went into the woods. We're going to follow him step by step."

Again, he turned the wheel, and the movement of the pictures accelerated. The road and the village disappeared. The two watchers, their eyes fixed on the picture, had the feeling they were running on the narrow road amongst the thick bushes. Eventually, they crossed the woods and arrived on a deserted plain, filled with rocks as far as the eyes could see.

The Doctor leaned forward.

"Nothing," he grumbled; "That's the desert. How was it that Hindu, on foot, was able to get such a head start?"

Suddenly, he shouted:

"There! Near that block of granite! I see hooves prints—horses! So the crime was premeditated and prepared long in advance. Let's follow the trail of the scoundrels…"

Again, the pictures followed with greater speed. Cicada was made dizzy by the furious speed at which the countryside moved around them. On the ground, he could make out the traces of two horses. He was overcome with astonishment. The Doctor, from the bottom of his laboratory, had succeeded in following the path of their enemies!

That went on for several minutes, then the countryside changed again. The sandy surface of the Thar Desert was replaced by a sprinkling of rocks. They saw grottos and caverns opening up on the sides of a dep ravine. Another turn and the ravine turned into a hollow. There, several men were seated in a circle. Awadh was standing in the middle, talking to them. His hands were clasped on the shoulders of Anoor, whose face expressed terror.

With a blow of his fist, the Doctor stopped the movement of the pictures. The rocky wall became still. Another gear was put into motion, and the voices of the speakers resounded into Cicada's ears just as the pictures had.

"Silence," ordered the Doctor. "Let's listen."

Pointing at a dial on which a needle was moving around a pivoting axle, he added:

"These individuals are located 77.67 miles from us. This machine indicates the distance. Let's listen."

The Parisian boy thought himself like in a dream. Certainly, since the beginning of their trip, he had witnessed many miracles, but none of them had astounded him like the present scene. To hear a conversation more than seventy miles away seemed like magic. That made him think of the legends of Lord Long Ears, that god-like figure who could hear the grass grow and mosquitoes fly a thousand feet away.[66]

But if the sound of these words came to his ears, the meaning of them escaped him, because Awadh and his accomplices were speaking Hindi.

"I can't understand," grumbled the boy.

"Hush! I do!" said the Doctor.

Here is what was being said:

---

[66] While there is a Celtic god with animal ears, there are no specific French fairy tale or legend I could find featuring such a character.

"Yes, that man, whose power is immense, because he was able to stop the Chariot of Jagannath and overcome the Sacred Tiger, plans to destroy the power of the Brahmins of India."

One of those present then asked:

"What does that matter to us? We are not Brahmins. Are you forgetting that my name is Dhaliwal, and that I am the leader of the Companions of Shiva and Kali?"

"I am not forgetting anything," replied Awadh. "But it is in your interest for the Brahmins not to be destroyed."

"Our interests?" questioned Dhaliwal.

"Without a doubt. What power counters that of the English if not ours? The British know that very well: They accommodate us, because if they didn't, at our command, millions would rise up. If we have not given that signal, it is because the predicted moment hasn't come. That's what we told you, the Companions of Shiva, and also the Thugee, when you fomented the great Sepoy rebellion. But you refused to believe us then, and therefore, you were vanquished, broken, taken apart. But since then, whose occult protection has allowed you to reform, rise again? Answer! It's the hand of the Brahmins that has protected you; we Brahmins, touched by your efforts, and inclined to pardon your faults against our rule because of your patriotic feelings."

Awadh lied shamelessly. If the Brahmin caste had protected the rebirth of the Companions of Shiva, it was only in order to squeeze more advantages from the British, who cared little about opposing their power, when they knew they might have to fight the rebels again.

But the logic of the traitor shook the Leader of the Companions. He asked dubitatively:

"How do I know that you are telling the truth?"

"My behavior proves it."

Awadh pushed Anoor in front of him.

"Didn't I, of my own volition, bring you this victim, destined to have her throat slit on the altar of Kali?"

There was silence. The Doctor stirred. His eyes stared fixedly with concentrated fury at the picture of those men who were talking 77 miles from them. But the conversation started again:

"Who is that victim?" questioned Dhaliwal.

There was a light of triumph in Awadh's eyes.

"Her name shouldn't be pronounced," he replied in a serious voice. "I want, however, to tell you why her total destruction will please the goddess."

The Doctor placed his hand over his heart. Was he at last going to learn Anoor's terrible secret... A secret he had already guessed and which had weighed heavily on his young protégée?

"Don't you know," Awadh continued, "that in the past, throughout Punjab and Sindh, all of the people have voluntary paid a tribute to one of them, in whom they had total trust? That tribute was destined to make up a war chest for when we would need to purchase arms and ammunition, foreseeing the day when the whole country would rise up against the British…"

"Yes, yes, we know all this," said one of those men present, suddenly standing up. "People have told us about that. Does that treasure really exist?"

"It does. The time is near when it will be released; and because of that, the child must die."

Leaning over the picture, the Doctor turned frightfully pale; his forehead became covered with drops of sweat. He seemed to feel an atrocious moral agony.

"Ah!" he shivered, without being aware that he was saying what he thought. "That's why I liked her so much. She is the victim of the same cause."

But he suddenly fell silent again, using all his faculties to follow the conversation between Awadh and the Companions of Shiva.

"This is what you read in the Rig Veda, the holiest of all the books,"[67] the traitor said. '*There will be two sisters, only one of whom shall know the hiding place of the Treasure of Liberty. The one who knows the secret will come before the other one, but her senses will have left her; yet she will be sacred to all. Whoever lifts a hand against her will be cursed, with all his relatives, for five generations, because when her senses return, she will bring about the return of the treasure. But that will happen only when Shiva has plunged his sword in the breast of the younger sister. A loincloth soaked with the blood of the victim will be presented to the one without her senses, and her mind will then return, her eyes will open, her thoughts will become clear, and she will proclaim that the appointed hour has finally come in the Hourglass of Eternity.*'"

Awadh stopped. Then, with a sharp voice, he added.

"Here is the younger sister; here is the loincloth that will be stained with her blood; here is the hand which will present the precious gift to the one whose mind is gone."

A deathly silence followed. Finally, Dhaliwal asked:

"You, yourself, who are you?"

Awadh hesitated but for a moment then answered:

"I am Arkabad the Wise, chosen by the Brahmins, the Great Executioner of the Temple of Ellora. I trust you. I'm turning over the appointed victim to you and I will wait until you bring me back the sacred loincloth red with her blood. You yourself will accompany me to see the Mindless One so you may be certain that I have told you the truth. Then, you will lean, as I will, the place where the Treasure of Liberty is hidden."

Dhaliwal bowed:

"I trust you. Where will I rejoin you?"

---

[67] The Rig Veda is an ancient Indian collection of Vedic Sanskrit hymns. It is one of the four sacred canonical Hindu texts known as the Vedas.

"At Lahore, at the Brahmin convent in the mausoleum of King Ranjit Singh."[68]

"It will be done as you say, at daybreak. This evening, when the moon first rises, the victim will be sacrificed in the Zapolaki cavern."[69]

Anoor spread out her arms. She let out a lamentable cry in Hindi:

"Have mercy!"

That word, Cicada could easily guess its meaning. Forgetting that, before his eyes, there was only a picture that couldn't be touched, he dashed forward but everything disappeared. The boy saw nothing more on the dark screen.

With a trembling voice, the Doctor reprimanded him:

"Come now."

"Where are we going?"

"To the Zapolaki cavern where Anoor is to be sacrificed."

"Sacrificed!"

"This evening. We will be near her, and we will save her, but we must hurry… Let's get on the road! I will let you know what's waiting for us."

At the same time, he took off his silk tunic.

"You do that too," he commanded.

Cicada did what he was ordered, while the Doctor took out two chainmail coats of extremely fine mesh with leggings. There was something strange about them because each came with a small Ruhmkorff coil.[70]

Thye put on these coats of defensive armor.

"Now," declared the Doctor, "no one can touch us without being electrocuted."

"Heavens!" Cicada cried out, lifting his arm in the air. "Then I won't know any longer where to put my hands."

"Don't worry. On your hips, you can feel a plate?"

"Yes."

"Well, those coats of mesh are electric conductors I invented, and the power will not be turned on unless someone touches that plate."

"Isn't that dangerous for the person who's wearing that metal suit?"

"No. The current which surrounds him provides its own protection."

The Doctor then picked up two black canes with gold pommels. He connected them to a machine producing electricity and set the wheels in motion.

---

[68] Ranjit Singh (1780-1839), popularly known as Sher-e-Punjab, the Lion of Punjab, was the first Maharaja of the Sikh Empire.

[69] I couldn't find any caves or caverns in India whose name would even approximate "Zapolaki."

[70] Induction coil used to produce high-voltage pulses named after Heinrich Daniel Ruhmkorff (1803-1877), a German instrument maker who first commercialized it.

"While our *lightning canes* get charged," he continued, "I'm going to try to make you understand why you have nothing to fear from your protective suit."

Slowly, as if he were a professor in front of an audience of respectful students, instead of being deep inside enemy territory, he spoke thus:

"I have already taught you that light, sound, thunder, are only movements. Now, our senses—sight, hearing, smell, touch, etc.—are just conductors of impressions carrying them to the brain, which, in the human body, plays the part of a receptor and register them. Our senses are far from perfect, of course. These impressions are part of a wide range with constant movements upward and downward, and we're only aware of them when they happen within a certain range…"

Cicada made a face.

"That isn't clear to you?"

"Not really, Boss."

"I'll give you an example. Take this roll of colored cardboard. I fix it to a pivot and make it turn faster and faster. For your eyes, the colors are soon mixed; you see nothing more than a grey surface. If I were to speed it up indefinitely, the rotation of the cardboard would seem to be turn into a fog. Finally, you would see nothing, because the speed of the movement would have gone beyond what you are able see."

"This is hard," the boy said seriously, "but when you say it like that, I think I understand."

"If, on the contrary, I slow up indefinitely the gyrating movement so that it would take, say, a year for the roll to finish a complete turn upon itself, you would stop being conscious of any movement, because it would be too slow for your eyes to notice that it is moving at all."

"I get that too."

The Doctor smiled.

"In the infinite scale of movement, a scale which is without limits, there is no zero. All speed is relative from infinitely fast to infinitely slow."

Suddenly, Cicada put his head between his hands.

"Ah, Boss! You're giving me a headache! Your talk about infinity is the stuff of migraines."

"For those who do not usually think about it, child, yes, it is. But for those who spend their life thinking about it, it is more pleasant and more magical than dreams themselves. You see, infinity is everywhere. It is impenetrable for our senses. It cannot be expressed in words. It is in grander and comparable to the stars—always further away, lighting millions of unknown worlds inhabited by thinking beings; and also in the smallest drop of water in which there is a universe of unsuspected microbes. Each of us is a piece of the infinite. And our hearts, our spirits, contain the very notion of infinity, without limits of time and measure."

The Doctor had become animated. The Parisian boy was watching him with almost superstitious awe. For an ignorant child to raise himself to contemplate the grandiose and immense notion of EVERYTHING was as poetic and fragile as a lark climbing high into the air, bathed with the sun.

The Doctor suddenly became calm and lowered his voice:

"So I shall continue. For sound, it is just like light. If the sound becomes sharper or lower, you will cease to hear it. It's the same for electricity." He paused, then continued: "In the United States of America, they do not guillotine murderers as they do in your country. They electrocute them with powerful electrical currents. That death is call *electrocution*. Now, it has been noticed that if they increase the power of the current, they do not kill the subject, but only put him to sleep. Finally, if the current reaches an even still greater intensity, the one receiving the electric discharge is not even bothered and isn't even aware of it. Do you understand?"[71]

"I believe I do. Then our coats of mesh...?"

"Carry a current so strong that we can't be injured by it."

"But others..."

"Others, when they touch us, will receive a part of this current, and that which is without danger for us will become deadly for them."

"Bravo!" shouted the boy. "We're going to make it hard for those villains who kidnapped Anoor. When I see my sister, and she is safe, I will remember to tell her: 'Wait a minute, I have to take off my electric shirt before I hug you.'"

"That would be wise indeed."

"Speaking of that," continued Cicada, "how do you control the amount of electricity released? It isn't by the bushel, I suppose? But you would have to be sure of what you're doing."

---

[71] Note from Paul d'Ivoi: "*Mr. Smith Aider of New York first studied this curious question. He established that the electric current reached its maximum deadly power at 700 volts. From 1200 volts on, the current did not kill anymore; at 1500 volts, it became imperceptible to the patient. Mr. Aider submitted himself to electrocution, in order to prove the veracity of his statements, and he received, without the slightest suffering, ten bolts of 1500 volts. This experiment, which again honors scientists, took place at Bridgeberny (Indiana) on October 27, 1898.*" A google search failed to return any evidence about this, the existence of a Mr. Smith Aider, or a town named Bridgeberny or, more likely, Bridgeberry in Indiana—there is one in North Carolina however. While it is true that if someone who has received an electric shock has not suffered immediate cardiac arrest and/or severe burns, they are likely to survive, high-voltage shocks above 2700 volts are often fatal, with those above 11,000 volts being usually fatal, though exceptional cases have been noted.

116

"By means of a special device, the nature of which would take too much time to explain right now. Let it be enough for you to know that it is controlled with absolute accuracy, using all five known units."

"What units?" threw in Cicada.

"Voltage, amps, wattage, ohm, coulomb."[72]

"Huh? What's that?" Cicada asked.

"Voltage is the unit of electrical potential, the equivalent of the hydraulic force developed by the fall of water. The amp or ampère serves to measure the output of the current, its intensity; an amp representing a current of one volt going through a conductive wire which resists its passage with one ohm of resistance. One ohm is the resistance that a current faces when going through a a column of mercury of constant cross section at the temperature of melting ice, 106.3 centimeters long and with a mass of 14. The coulomb is the amount of current passing through in one second with the intensity of one ampere. Finally, the watt is equal to one joule of work performed per second, or to 1/746 horsepower. An equivalent is the power dissipated in an electrical conductor carrying one ampere current between points at one volt potential difference."

Cicada stretched out his arms in a begging gesture:

"That's enough, Boss, my head is exploding! All those volts and *hom* and *coulon*! I don't want to become insane. Tell me only that our suits won't be dangerous and I'll believe you; I don't need to understand. You're there for that."

When the Doctor laughed, in spite of the gravity of the circumstances, the young man almost became angry.

"Each to his own! For you, it's lightning; for me it's Parisian slang! If you *relambez* my *loquet* with your *guirchon*, I'll *jaspine* the *jars* like a *mec* of fine *pegre*, and you won't *visser nada* like a *zebra* that would have *veloutine à blair* in his *mirettes*."

With that sentence, said in the purest *verlan* (green tongue), Cicada had said:

"If you're going to make fun of my head with your science, I'll begin speaking slang like a hoodlum and you won't understand anything more than a poor devil who has had a pinch of tobacco thrown in his eyes…"

The Doctor quickly replied:

"No, Cicada, please don't do that. I will finish our lesson later."

Then, disconnecting the canes that he had attached earlier to the electric generator, he added:

---

[72] Actually, there are ten units: Volt (Voltage): Electrical Potential; Ampere (Current): Electrical Current; Ohm (Resistance): DC Resistance; Siemen (Conductance): Reciprocal of Resistance; Farad (Capacitance): Capacitance; Coulomb (Charge): Electrical Charge; Henry (Inductance) Inductance; Watt (Power): Power; Ohm (Impedance): AC Resistance; and Hertz (Frequency): Frequency.

"Our canes are charged. Let's go!"

Handing one of the canes to the young man, he left the laboratory to go into the salon where Kéradec and his six sailors were waiting. Each one held in his hand a cane like those that the Doctor and his companion held. In addition, they carried in their belt a leather satchel. They gave a military salute to their leader.

The Doctor asked:

"What about our guests?"

"Asleep like dormice," declared Kéradec.

"Good! In that case, let's go. If the information I received from Magapur was correct, the British authorities plan to come later today to take control of my rolling house. The Sanders and van Stoon families won't be able to provide them with any indication about the road that we're going to take."

He was the first to walk down the road.

Ten minutes later, the little troop had disappeared on the same path where, two hours before, Arkabad—the fake Awadh--had taken poor Anoor.

CHAPTER IX
Electricians and Magicians

Cicada was walking like a drunk man. He didn't know any longer if he was living in a dream or if it was reality. Everything in the lab that he had seen on the telephotic screen flashed before his eyes and nothing else. Through the brush, he could see the pathway: flowering shrubs, the high grass, the sudden turns of the road; he recognized the slightest details.

Then they came to the vast plains, sprinkled with boulders. They reached the blocks of granite near which the boy had noticed the traces of horses a while ago. They were still there, visible. Cicada leaned down to touch the imprints left in the sand by their hooves. So, it had all been true: The Doctor, that man walking in front of him, had increased one hundred times the visual ability of man. Across the obstacles the trees and the rocks, he had seen the road Awadh had taken.

Having too little scientific knowledge to be able to understand the phenomena used by the Doctor, Cicada felt for him, not scientific admiration, but an almost religious awe. The Doctor was becoming in his eyes the High Priest of a new, mysterious religion, still ill-defined, but that produced miracles.

They continued following the path of the kidnappers, and the Parisian boy continued to recognize the smallest details as they went.

For two hours, the sand of the Thar Desert squeaked under his feet; then the rocks began to take over, first puncturing the landscape, then dominating it. Some massive granite rocks lie across their path, but they didn't stop. On the left, a ravine went into a rocky barricade. They entered it. It was the place that Cicada had already seen on the screen: stones made reddish by the rays of the sun, already high in the horizon, with some gaping, dark openings in which the colors got darker.

It was an empty, calcinated landscape without a twig, a blade of grass, nothing green to look at, nowhere to shield your eyes from the sun. Rocks were scattered in piles. An oppressive heat enveloped the travelers, who were dripping with sweat. Their breathing was heavy; their legs were becoming weak, but they went forward slowly. Their feet found the hard dust of the path difficult to tread, producing a continuous irritation.

Suddenly, Cicada let out a shout. They had finally arrived at the circle were Arkabad had turned Anoor over to Dhaliwal, the leader of the Companions of Shiva. In its center, arranged in a circle, there stood out, shining under the rays of the sun, the rocks upon which the boy had seen the Council so willing to spill his adopted sister's blood. In front of him opened a giant door in the wall of granite.

"These are the Zapolaki caves, were Anoor is supposed to die this evening, when the moon rises."

Those words, the first ones that the Doctor had pronounced since their departure, sounded lugubrious in the silence.

Cicada felt terrified, angry, and frightened at the same time. Suddenly, the impression of being in a dream departed his mind. He fell back into plain reality.

Anoor! He understood then how much he loved his companion, to what extent she had conquered his soul. And she was there, in that gloomy cave, waiting for death. Ah! A horrible dark veil fell upon his mind! Never until then had he ever thought seriously she might die. At the Bay of Audierne, when he was desperately swimming in the storm, after having thrown himself laughing into the foam y waves, he had never considered death as likely.

Death! What was it? A token payment required by Lady Death to cross the bridge which goes from human life to another existence, to be paid for without the least bargaining.

Those were the last words that he had once heard from a friend, a comrade, whom he had visited at the hospital before he passed away. They were not inspired by a hardness of the heart but by an ironic contempt for a life dominated by pain and suffering. Suddenly everything changed. Death, hanging over Anoor's pretty face, ceased to be the macabre and grotesque collector of tokens. It became something far more terrible, truly frightening. The Parisian boy no longer saw it as one who liberates, but only as one who separates. Two tears rolled down his cheeks, causing a burning sensation in his eyes.

"Courage," the Doctor said to him, affectionately. "We shall save her."

And he slowly walked toward the entrance of the cave. After he had crossed the threshold, he struck the rock with his cane. It resounded dully under the blows, like the beating of a faraway clock. The Doctor did it three times, spacing his blows as if following some kind of instruction. Then he waited.

Suddenly, a voice jumped out of the darkness.

"Who is knocking on the door?"

"He who is Life," answered the Doctor without hesitating.

"He has come to the wrong place," replied the voice, "because this is the sanctuary of Death."

"Death itself owes me obedience."

"Shiva is a powerful god."

"Vishnu is his master."

A heavy silence followed. A moment later, the Doctor again approached the opening and said:

"Go to Dhaliwal, Leader of the Companions of Shiva and Kali, and tell him that the Son of the Golden Tiger wished to enter Zapolaki."

There was a stifled exclamation.

"I shall report your words, Master."

They heard hurrying footsteps pounding the ground at the bottom of the cavern; then nothing else. Cicada and the sailors watched without understanding.

"Kéradec," exclaimed the boy, "isn't this more impressive than all your fairies and mermaids of Brittany?"

But his quip remained without a reply. None of those present had the courage to answer it, and everyone remained motionless with the feeling that they stood before one of the great Mysteries of India. Their wait was not long. The voice was again raised in the darkness.

"Here is Dhaliwal's answer..."

"I am listening," said the Doctor.

"The Son of the Golden Tiger and his companions may enter the forbidden cave, but he shall prove his celestial origin, or else his blood will be spilled on the Altar of Shiva."

The Doctor shrugged.

"Proof will be given," he responded.

A slight sliding was heard. A human silhouette partly stood out in the obscurity. It came forward and became clearer. It was a Companion of Shiva with a white turban, carrying on its front the five rubies—the bleeding stones—consecrated to the god of destruction.[73]

"I am only the slave who carries orders and passes them on to you, prostrated," the man chanted.

---

[73] Shiva lingas, sacred symbols of Shiva.

Short, thin, his bones showing under his skin, the newcomer bore no weapons other than a dagger with a curved blade hanging at his hip, and the red silk cord of the Thugees wound around his left arm.

"Come," he said.

He clapped his hands. At that signal, several bright lights came on in the darkness of the cave. The shadows were cleared away, and the little troop started into the depths of the mountain behind its guide. They crossed a large gallery with a gentle slope. About twenty steps away, a row of motionless men, like bronze statues, stood against the wall, holding torches above their head. The sooty flames moved under the puffs of air displaced by the newcomers' footsteps, growing darker and projecting odd, blood-red shadows on the wall.

Soon, however, the path became larger and branched out into several rooms, connected to each other by narrow corridors. Those then led into a vast cavern, the ceiling of which was covered by an irregular dome, eighty feet from the ground. Stalactites and the stalagmites, bonded by the slow infiltration of water, formed uneven pillars, randomly, sometimes making up clusters of elegant columns, other times, compact masses, heavy and malformed.

Everywhere there were torches stuck in the crevices of the rock, throwing their pale flames, whose smoke mounted towards the dome and surrounded the top of the natural columns with a dark cloud.

Several hundred men were gathered there. On the turbans of each one were the five rubies of Shiva shining; each face was hidden behind a short scarlet mask. In the center, there was an arena protected by a wooden barrier, also red, decorated with savage illustrations representing the two gods of carnage and destruction, Shiva and Kali. Facing those arriving was a stage which stood above the barrier and where the heads of the cult were seated on cubes of wood. Dhaliwal himself, the only one not wearing a mask, was seated on a log, higher and bigger than the others.

All the castes, all the races, were represented here; the scarlet reflections projected by the rubies gave the appearance of a diabolical phantasmagoria.

Here was a *Naukar*, a servant who was part of the household of every rich sultan and wore his turban in the form of a Greek helmet. Next to him was a Rajput lord, recognizable by his shield on which was painted his coat of arms, because the science of heraldry was already in use in India three thousand years before our era. And near them was a *Kishor*, an adolescent only recently let into the society of men. He had accomplished this by performing a hunting exploit, required in order to claim that honor, killing a wild boar with a *katar*, a triangular sword. Many wore heavy golden bracelets on their ankles and wrists.

Then, there were the women: Rajputana was the only land in Asia—and also in the West—where the weaker sex was treated by the stronger sex with complete equality. Tall, thin, they rustled their long-pleated skirts falling to mid-knee. Their supple, tall bodies were imprisoned in silk corsets with gold trimmings, and beautiful *sari* floated on their shoulders. With each of their movements, the jewelry with which they were covered, to profusion, clinked gaily.

Further away, seated apart, there were *tahadjans* and *tarvanis*, wealthy merchants, wearing typical Afghan head dresses and large brown caftans.

Finally, one could see a mass of the lower caste workers, *goujars, kachis, chamars, kolis, bhils, khaniadas, sevats, minas, mhairs* and *bahoria*, which constituted the most numerous group in that assembly of the Companions of Shiva and Kali.

Suddenly the murmuring stopped. Dhaliwal had stood up.

"Stranger," he shouted, "you have asked to see Dhaliwal. Do you recognize me?"

The Doctor coolly nodded.

"Certainly."

"Then, speak. What do you want?"

"The life of victim that Arkabad, the Brahmin, has turned over to you this very morning."

There was a commotion. Those present protested:

"You hear what the Brothers say?" the head of the cult asked, jokingly.

"I do, but their recriminations mean little to me. I am the favored of Vishnu, Keeper of the World, Eternal Vanquisher of the Forces of Destruction, and, by the power of the Golden Tiger, I order you to obey me!"

At the same time, the Doctor raised his hand, and turning it around, showed everybody the sacred effigy in the palm of it.

Heads bowed, arms were crossed devotedly on chests. Dhaliwal himself bowed:

"So be it," he said. "You possess the sacred emblem, but here, we are no mere humans; we are the priests of the Divine Shiva, and we can bow before you only if you submit to our test, as required by the secret rites."

"I am ready."

"You are aware that our law demands the death of whoever comes into these caves without being chosen. And only one person can be chosen—the man whom you claim to be, because that one is the Master."

"I am the Master. State your test. And bring the woman I want to save here instead of jabbering like an old woman. She is as pure as a white lamb."

The Doctor's voice carried such authority that Dhaliwal did not insist any longer.

"Let it be done as you wish," he murmured. Then, in a commanding tone, he added: "Bring the victim promised to Shiva here. A duel between the two gods will decide her fate."

There was a movement in the cave. Those gathered here shivered at the thought of a battle between Shiva and Vishnu, death against life, and they watched with surprise this mysterious Doctor who had come fearlessly in their midst to challenge their god.

The sacrificers, wearing long purple robes crowned with wilted flowers, masked with death heads molded in wax, led Anoor into the arena. At the sight of the Doctor, Cicada, and the sailors, the little girl cried out.

"You! I was hoping you would come!"

She wanted to run to them, but the sacrificers held her back.

"Wait, my child, my daughter!" the Doctor cried out with a gentle voice so that she became filled with gratitude. "I must take you back from those murderous divinities. But don't be afraid, and don't resist those who surround you. You no longer have anything to fear."

She had an angelic smile.

"My heart beats only with love, father. You are here. I am no longer afraid."

The Doctor turned toward Dhaliwal:

"I am waiting."

The priest of Shiva laughed:

"I am at your orders." And in a detached tone, he added: "Let Sadjeh, the unconscious instrument of the will of the god, be introduced to the victim to be claimed by Shiva."

Those who were going to sacrifice Anoor, who was on the ground, picked her up and tied her to the shackles cemented into the rock, and placed her head on a flat flagstone. Then they moved aside quickly to the right and to the left.

The little girl could not move, but her dark eyes never left the Doctor.

"Don't be afraid," he repeated

"I am not afraid," she said again in a voice that did not tremble.

A heavy step shook the earth, a powerful breath filled the atmosphere of the cave, then, his trunk lifted, his tusks menacing, a colossal elephant entered the arena. That was Sadjeh, a white elephant with a brown head, the executioner of the Companions of Shiva, whose function it was to crush the head of traitors.

Anoor was stretched on the place set up for those executions, her pretty head on the slab of marble, where many times before the pachyderm had crushed the skulls of those that the dreaded Cult had condemned to death.

Upon seeing the elephant, the young girl let out a cry, but she saw the Doctor only two steps away from her, his finger on his lips, and she fell silent.

Everybody was looking. They shivered at the voice of Dhaliwal, who said:

"Shiva wishes that Sadjeh crush the head of that child and that this piece of linen (he threw it in the air) be stained with her blood to serve the great purpose predicted by the Rig Veda."

"Vishnu wants her to live," answered the Doctor, "and she will, because if she dies, her blood will fall on all of India."

"Let's go ahead then with the duel of the gods."

Dhaliwal blew a strident whistle; everyone fell silent. The elephant trembled on his massive legs. He looked around him with fiery glances, which finally became fixed on Anoor's body. He trumpeted in the air and advanced towards her.

"Oh!" exclaimed Cicada, ready to jump forward. "He's going to kill her!"

"Silence! Don't make any move," growled the Doctor in a tone so commanding that the boy stopped the movement he had begun to make.

The pachyderm was now very close to the girl; Cicada, in agony, followed him with his eyes; Anoor didn't even look at him. She had told the truth. Her touching confidence in the Doctor kept her from being afraid.

Sadjeh lifted his foot. He was going to lower it, when the Doctor held out his right arm at the end of which vibrated the cane that he had taken with him. With a voice impossible to imitate, he bellowed:

"Vishnu forbids it."

A shiver ran across the body of the elephant; a sad complaint came out of his mouth and, shivering, he retreated to the barrier.

"Go away," the Doctor then said.

And the animal left, losing himself in the shadows, vanquished, returning to the enclosure from which he had come.

Those present were astounded. The Doctor had made a simple gesture and the colossal animal, that fifty men would have found impossible to stop, had obeyed!

Was it true that the newcomer was really the Chosen of Vishnu, as he had claimed? Dhaliwal stood up straight. On his bronzed face could be read indecision and doubt. Then, he appeared to reach a decision, and turning towards the Doctor, he pronounced with a nuance of respect:

"What you have just accomplished is truly miraculous, and I would accept what you said if it was only up to me. But the rites of Kali must be completed too. Vishnu, to get the obedience of Shiva, must leave as the winner of other tests."

The Doctor smiled, disdainful. He let fall from his lips:

"There are five tests, one for each of Shiva's sacred rubies."

Dhaliwal's surprise only grew.

"How do you know this?"

"I know everything, because it has pleased Vishnu to reveal it to me."

"So you know the nature of the five tests?"

"Yes. The sacred book of Shiva, written with blood, sets them out like this: Crushing, Poison, Dagger, Noose, and Knowledge."

There was a whisper throughout the hall. Some present prostrated themselves. Dhaliwal shook his head with a pensive expression, then continued:

"Which test would you prefer to tackle first?"

"There is no danger to me or those I protect. Do whatever is convenient for you."

"So be it then. Let the poison be prepared."

Again, Dhaliwal carried his whistle to his lips and blew out a sharp, powerful sound, to which those present answered with a bizarre chant made up of strange rhythmic whistling. It sounded like the wind blowing in the trees, going through a narrow opening, then forming into a tempest, then decreasing into a gentle modulation like the breathing of a child.

Everything fell silent again, and, from various sides, new, deadly actors appeared. It was the crawling army of living poison: the snakes consecrated to the goddess Kali. They came from everywhere, some were pythons which could strangle an ox with their coils; others were cobras with triangular heads and devastating venom; and red *daburas* with black spots and a bite just as terrible. There were specimens from all over India, frightful examples of the species which between 1870 and 1880, had caused the death of 200,000 persons![74]

The beasts slithering on the ground inflated their throats, darted out their sharp tongues, while converging towards the spot where Anoor was stretched out, motionless.

"Don't be afraid of anything, my child," pronounced the Doctor.

Still smiling, she answered:

"I am not afraid, Master."

The Doctor rummaged in his little leather pouch where he had put, as his men had done, a little silver instrument that he now took out and brought to his lips. Then he stood up and lifted it high above his head and with a resounding voice said:

"Vishnu himself will play the sacred flute of the Snake Charmers."

A new miracle! The instrument began immediately to play a slow melody.

"That's better than Dicksonn and Robert-Houdin,"[75] murmured Cicada out of breath.

"An electronic whistle," the Doctor whispered in his ear. "A little device similar to electric doorbells."

But for all the spectators, incapable of understanding the scientific phenomena, it seemed like a magic flute. Resounding without the help of a human being, it appeared miraculous. On their knees now, they looked at the stage. The

---

[74] Published data from the late 19th and early 20th centuries suggested that the annual snakebite mortality in India was about 20,000, but some suspect the real numbers to be twice as much.

[75] Jean-Eugène Robert-Houdin (1805-1871) was a French watchmaker, magician and illusionist, widely recognized as the father of the modern style of conjuring. "Professor Dicksonn" (real name: Paul-Alfred de Saint-Genois) (1857-1939) made his debut as a stage magician at the Robert-Houdin theater in Paris in March 1883, and later became its director in association with Robert-Houdin's widow. He left it in April 1887 to assist Emile Voisin at the Grévin Museum. In 1888, he opened his own theater. He also wrote several books on prestidigitation.

snakes had stopped. Upright on their tails, their heads moving back and forth, they gave into the charm of the music that Snake Charmers had been playing for centuries. They swayed to its rhythm, closing and opening their eyes, making a clapping sound.

"The baskets," ordered the Doctor.

From the red barrier, baskets were thrown into the arena. Then, the Doctor went forward towards the serpents and each recoiled before him as if obeying a stronger will. They went to hide in the woven baskets, which the Doctor then covered with their lids. The flute could no longer be heard, and the Doctor turned back toward Dhaliwal.

"You may continue, but before we do, release the girl. She is not comfortable."

Dhaliwal shook his head.

"If Vishnu is in you, why don't you untie her yourself?"

"I will gladly do so."

With those words, the Doctor held his cane towards the steel rings to which the ropes that held Anoor were tied. Suddenly, the ropes crumbled as if consumed by fire.

"Get up, child, and rejoin us."

Anoor jumped to her feet, ran to her friends, and found herself unable to explain how she found herself in the arms of Cicada, who stammered in a broken voice, his face white, tears running down it:

"My little sister!"

He couldn't find anything else to say. The poor boy, so brave, had just learned about terror, even though, this time, it was for someone else that he had trembled.

Dhaliwal, in whom fanaticism was strong, growled:

"Now, the test of the Dagger!"

Silence fell again, gloomy, agonizing, troubled only by the halting breath of the crowd.

Two men, red from head to feet, wearing turbans, masks, and wide pantaloons, their naked arms decorated with a daubing of vermillion okra, jumped into the arena. One of them was brandishing a sword, the blade of which was shining under the light of the torches. The other carried, between his two hands, a silk rope.

The first man walked towards the Doctor, whose arms were crossed behind his back. He offered his stomach to the man's blows. The murderer jumped forward, his blade shining...

A cry escaped from the lips of the sailors, Anoor, and Cicada, but the sword did not stop. A crackling sound was heard, and the man, screaming like a wounded beast, fell to the ground, where he twisted with terrible convulsions. The electrified suit the Doctor wore had played its protective role.

However, the other man with the silk rope, taking advantage of the confusion, had slid behind the Doctor. With a rapid movement, he tied the silk rope, that traitorous weapon of the Thugees, around the Doctor's neck and pulled. But the thin little cord broke as if set on fire.

The executioner stopped, stupefied, looking at his fingers, at the end of which hung harmlessly the two fragments of the cord of the Stranglers of Shiva. Seeing that, there was a furious shout under the dome:

"Glory to Vishnu!"

The crowd shouted with enthusiasm. Their doubts had vanished. Doctor Mystere was certainly the one chosen by the God. However, calm was re-established by a gesture from Dhaliwal.

"The sacred rites require a fifth test," proclaimed the Cult Leader.

"I will submit to it as I did to the others," the Doctor courteously declared.

"Your knowledge is greater enough, then, that that of the Brahmins, who have grown old in the depths of their cloisters studying the sacred texts?"

"Vishnu is wiser than all the priests. All knowledge comes from him. With his help, I will triumph."

"We shall see."

At his signal, there was harmony, and those present started singing something that resembled plainchant.[76] It seemed to be close bnut also far away. Dhaliwal's assistants spread out and twenty-two Brahmins entered the stage. That number, two times eleven, was sacred in the cult of Shiva.

Some of the newcomers wore blue tunics with red ornaments; others were dressed in red with blue ornaments. All of them had white hair with ascetic faces. Their eyes shone weakly from the depths of their sunken orbits, and looked into the distance, as if their mind was absent. They placed themselves in two parallel ranks at the foot of the platform, put down the staffs, and waited.

"O, Ma Ni," shouted Dhaliwal, "venerated master of the interpreters of the Vedas, Shiva demands that you confound this stranger."

The old man who occupied the first place in the ranks of the Brahmins wearing azure robes answered without turning to face the Cult Leader

"Shiva is the Master. What do you want of us?"

"The One Inimitable Miracle."

"So be it."

Ma-Ni then pronounced a bizarre incantation that the other Brahmins repeated; then each of the old men raised his staff as high as his lips and suddenly

---

[76] Plainchant, or plainsong, is a body of chants used in the liturgies of the Western Church. Plainchant was the exclusive form of Christian church music until the ninth century, and the introduction of polyphony. The monophonic chants of plainchant have a non-metric rhythm. Their rhythms are generally freer than the metered rhythm of later Western music, and they are sung without musical accompaniment.

dropped it. The eleven pieces of wood hit the ground at the same time and the miracle announced was produced.[77]

It was a strange and horrible spectacle. The staffs, made of green wood, twisted on themselves like branches on fire. The ends became tapered heads, then tails. Some of them remained as they were, but others grew scales, and eleven snakes began to slither around, hiss and coil: vipers with horns, hydras, rattlesnakes, all mingled together. One might have believed that the creatures vanquished earlier by the Doctor had escaped from their prison.

"Shiva, Shiva, you alone are great!" chanted the audience, impressed by that fantastic metamorphosis.

The Doctor shrugged.

"These Brahmins," he said, very low to Cicada, "are very clever illusionists. Their staffs have been very well made, but it's all a game. Direct your electric cane towards them."

The young man got ready to obey.

The Doctor shouted:

"Is it with this child's game that you would test my knowledge? I am going to turn this test over to my student, who has not yet finished a year of apprenticeship..."

A murmur of astonishment underlined his statement, soon replaced by a shout of disbelief. Cicada had pointed his electric cane at the serpents and soon the reptiles lay still and had returned to their original form.

Leaning forward, at the risk of being thrown into the arena, Dhaliwal watched the scene with growing anger.

"Ma-Ni," he shouted, growling, "this does nothing to proclaim the glory of Shiva!"

The old man did not seem to resent the remonstrance. He bowed to Cicada, as if to thank colleague whose talent deserved recognition. Then he pronounced an incomprehensible formula and the staffs again became snakes. Suddenly, Cicada's electric cane did not seem to be able to turn them back.

"This time," shouted Dhaliwal, triumphant, "your knowledge does not work. Shiva wishes your death."

"Perhaps only that of my disciple," the Doctor joked. "Look!"

In his turn, he threw his cane amongst those of the Brahmins.

One heard hissing and crackling sounds and Doctor Mystere's staff became surrounded with light, then produced bluish flames that darted their tongues of fire towards the reptiles. In a few minutes, these became carbonized, and

---

[77] Note from Paul d'Ivoi: "*The staffs in question, known are mysteriously made in the Temples. Formed from fragments of wood, articulated joints and light steel springs allow their bearers to perform the miracle recounted here with simple techniques of prestidigitation. Several of these staffs are kept in the museums of Calcutta and London.*"

stopped moving. After the smoke dissipated, only the Doctor's cane appeared intact in the middle of the ashes of the others.

A gloomy silence followed. The Brahmins themselves seemed surprised. Ma-Ni murmured:

"Could I have wrongly interpreted the fifth verse for the conjuration of the serpents?"

As for the Doctor, he picked up his cane and calmly said:

"Are you now convinced, Dhaliwal?"

The Cult Leader shook his head:

"No, not yet. Chosen of Vishnu, Preserver of the World, you must be able to protect what it pleases Shiva to destroy?"

"Undoubtedly."

"Well then," Dhaliwal held out his hand towards the Brahmins wearing red tunics, "it is now up to you to avenge the affront perpetrated on your azure-clad brothers. Make the spirit of destruction triumph!"

The leader of the priests clothed in scarlet lifted his hand. His index and middle finger pointed to the top of the cave. At that sign, two slaves jumped into the center of the arena, carrying a glossy vase of dirt filled with potting soil and a superb foot of Hortensia Regina. They deposited it in front of the Brahmin, who looked contemptuously at the Doctor.

"That plant is doomed to perish, like that girl standing in front of you. Those two existences are linked. Save the flower, and the captive will be saved."

Then he placed his hand over the hortensia and sang:

"Shiva has ordered your death, plant. You must return to nothingness. Such fate is not cruel, because all, flowers and men, are brothers, and their deaths is only a prelude to the transformations into future existences."

After saying that, he mumbled some unintelligible words, still holding his hand extended above the flowers.

That magnetism, something that our scientists are still babbling about in the West, was known from the most ancient antiquity by the sacerdotal caste of India is recognized. It is thanks to it that we can explain those "miracles" that still baffle our scientists.[78]

It is with it that they can make you believe that they can grow a tree in a matter of minutes.

Now the Brahmin remained still. His hard face was contracted by the effort of his will necessary to generate enough magnetic fluid. His aged dry hands trembled. The silent assembly seemed as if they had turned into statues.

Then, the miracle began.

---

[78] Note from Paul d'Ivoi: *"A commission of scientists, financed by the British government, is currently studying the extraordinary magnetic powers of the Brahmins and fakirs of Bengal."*

The petals of the hortensia became discolored, the ends of its leaves became yellow. Then its stalk dried up, marking the rapid progress of the death called for by the scarlet-clad priest.

Dhaliwal let out a shout of joy:

"Shiva triumphs! Glory to Shiva!"

He didn't finish. The Doctor shouted out this mysterious appeal:

"Come to me, O Vishnu! Glory to the one who preserves!"

With a violent gesture, his arm spread out, his hands pointed at the hortensia. A minute went by, an atrocious, agonizing minute... If the Doctor was vanquished, Anoor was lost.

That could not be. But the Brahmin redoubled his efforts and, under his parchment skin, his veins stood out like cords.

Still, the flower rose up again, slowly; its petals regained their color, seemingly shaking off the plague that had spread over them.

The Brahmin let out a long sigh; he let his arms fall alongside his body, and in a discouraged tone, he murmured:

"That one is the master. Any struggle is impossible."

A tempest of shouts and exclamations followed his admission. The crowd praised Vishnu. The Doctor set Anoor free. Dhaliwal jumped across the barrier and bowed on the ground before Doctor Mystere.

"You are the one whose coming was foretold. I shall obey you in the future."

His words were lost in the brouhaha, but his actions had been understood by everyone. He bowed before the superior power of the stranger. In the name of the Companions of Shiva and Kali, he swore fidelity to him. And the shouts continued, passing like a shiver along the wall of granite of the mountain.

Guided by the Dhaliwal, the Doctor and his companions took their place on the raised platform, and all those who were already there took off their masks, bowing in order to show that the oath taken by their leader had been accepted by all of them. Henceforth, the Doctor was the new Leader of the formidable association, whose affiliates now showed their faces uncovered.

Without waiting, the Doctor called for silence with a gesture.

As if by magic, everyone stopped talking. The assistants, as well as their superiors, had taken off their red masks, and their serious faces showed the hope reborn in those men at the coming of the Doctor, who had easily pushed back the assaults of the elephant, of the reptiles, of the dagger, of the silk, and of the priests' magic.

"Brothers," he said, "you, whom the foreign oppressors describe as criminals, I know you. You are those who kill, that is true, but you are also those who die for the holiest cause which is given to a man to defend—freedom! It is to you, and only to you, that the dead, now sleeping in the bosom of Brahma, have wanted to will the treasure of liberty gathered by the patriots of Sindh and Punjab. The Brahmins, who each year deliver some of you to the British in order to gain their protection, are your worst enemies. The Brahmins intend to steal that treasure which was destined to free India. You must break up with them, stop trusting them. But before that, we need them to find the treasure amassed by our ancestors..."

He stopped for an instant and spoke to Dhaliwal:

"My friend," he said, "a Brahmin called Arkabad used the name Anwadh to infiltrate my house. I let him do that. He took away the child that I love. Then, he gave her to you, telling you the lie that people like him are not avaricious. The blood of the victim, spread out on a piece of linen, is supposed to restore the mind of a woman who knows where the treasure is hidden. Well, pretend to believe the words of that traitor, and he will guide us towards the hiding place of the gold that we will turn into weapons. Strangle a young goat. Put its blood on the piece of linen, and then take it, as instructed, to the Brahmin Convent, at the mausoleum of Ranjit Singh."

Dhaliwal trembled.

"Who told you these things, Master?" he stammered.

"I am the one who wants to destroy the yoke that enslaves the people of India. I know. I have spoken. Now I shall leave. It's in Lahore that I will manifest my will."

CHAPTER X
Ellick and Loo (An Idyll)

"My dear Ellick!"

"My sweet Loo?"

"Since yesterday, I am depressed."

"Me too."

Two sighs, like the stormy wind which comes out of a chimney, punctuated these melancholy sentences.

Ellick—a nickname for Alexander—and Loo—a nickname for Louise—were seated in the drawing room of the only stone house in the city of Churu. They both had red hair, a ruddy complexion, and their hefty silhouettes made their white cotton clothes bulge. They looked at each other, their eyes bathed in tears.

"Oh, Ellick!" mooed again the desolate Loo!

"Ah, Loo!" said again, as a gloomy echo, the tearful Ellick.

What misfortunate had befallen Alexander and Louise Glass, appointed representatives of Her British Majesty's Government in Churu? Right up to that day, they had lived peacefully, using the influence they had acquired to sell goats, a profitable commerce. They bought cheap; they sold high. The climate was warm, they traveled as little as possible, ate a lot, and, being careful, saw few people and did not go out much, declaring themselves to be the most admirable representatives of the human species.

With that regime, they had grown fat. Their chins had tripled, their cheeks had become inflated, their hands had grown thick, their stomachs formed a grotesque bulge, and, according to a crude, but accurate, critical description, they were not people, but merely bellies. With their easy-going character, they admired themselves. And just as a kind-hearted mother describes her daughter as "pretty" instead of "fat," they declared themselves to be a handsome couple.

What's more, their disdain for thin people went to the point of cruelty. If Loo found herself in front of the Venus of Milo, very certainly, she would have extended her bottom lip, making a disdainful face, and she would have murmured: "What's so beautiful about her?"

Now, these two beings with their monstrous charms were well made to understand each other. They were indulging happily in the joys of gaining even more weight when, just in the evening of the previous day, an order had come from the Lieutenant-Governor of Punjab to trouble their peace.

The order mentioned announced the arrival of two squadrons of Indian soldiers serving under the British, and ordered Commissioner Glass to proceed with the confiscation of the rolling aluminum house stationed outside the town and the arrest of all its inhabitants.

Attached to the order were details about the owner, a certain "Doctor Mystery," who was accompanied by servants who, by their looks, were identified as French sailors.

"Heaven and Earth!" Loo screeched after rereading the order.

"Water and fire!" Ellick answered!

The two spouses, raising themselves painfully from their seats, had dashed into the arms of each other, with such despair that their stomachs had violently hit each other. Because of this unexpected collision, each one had been thrown backward and had fallen.

The house had trembled. The servants, who had come running at the noise, succeeded, by pushing here and pulling there, to put the voluminous couple back to their feet. After they had recovered their balance, they found themselves alone face to face with their emotions. What the following night was like, no one can have any idea. Never had the scourge of insomnia been darker. Certainly, it is distressing for a thin person to toss and turn on his bed looking for sleep, but for people of such powerful girth, it was terrible torture. Not only could the Glasses not sleep, but each movement caused them fatigue without limits. That's why, in the morning, Loo had let out that painful exclamation.

"Since yesterday, I am depressed."

"Me too."

Clanks of steel suddenly caught their attention. The floor shaking under their feet, they ran to the window.

Sepoy soldiers had just entered the courtyard of their habitation. There were about twenty of them, commanded by two corporals and one sergeant.

Seeing Ellick, the sergeant saluted.

"Commissioner Glass?" he asked.

"Yes, that's me."

"Will you take us, please, to the vehicle to be confiscated. It has been suggested that we should act quickly."

"Of course. I am coming down."

"One more word. A special battalion is following us with all the equipment necessary to tow the vehicle in question. It is important, then, to hurry."

"All right, all right, I'm coming."

And rolling, rather than walking, Ellick Glass, followed by Loo, went down into the courtyard.

At the shout of the husband, the servants came running. One of them brought a white donkey, the Commissioner's usual mount. Another opened a gigantic parasol over his head, destined to protect his delicate skin from the burning caresses of the sun. A third waved a fan of plumes on a long piece of bamboo in front of his face. It was thus that Sir Alexander Glass, accompanied by Loo, scarlet with emotion and seated on another donkey that staggered under her weight, led the column of soldiers, who advanced in good order in a tight file, with Corporals Simmons and Samuel and Sergeant Barnes at their head.

Their heads turned to the right, their shoulders back, their rifles slung over their shoulders, the Sepoy soldiers made a good show and their fierce appearance indicated that they were prepared to take an enemy stronghold.

They went out of Churu, leaving behind a rowdy group of chatting villagers, surprised by that unusual deployment of the military. At the first turn, they saw the aluminum house in the middle of the road. Sergeant Barnes lifted his arm, shouting in a stentorian voice:

"Men, get ready to surround that vehicle."

Simmons and Samuel, as corporals doing their duty, repeated the command. The soldiers immediately took their position and began to march again.

Loo pushed her mount up to that of her husband and, leaning towards him, her face white with anxiety, said:

"Ellick, aren't you afraid that the inhabitants of that rolling house will try to defend themselves?"

"That is possible, Loo," responded the Commissioner, that the ambient temperature was making sweat like a pig.

"But then, we might be in danger!"

"Indeed!"

Mrs. Glass made a movement that made her donkey tremble.

"We must remain calm," said Ellick. "If we panic before all these Sepoys, our honor shall receive a dreadful blow. The tumble of a lady, in particular, would be terribly incorrect."

Loo turned red:

"Don't grumble, Ellick. You know that I am as timid as a gazelle, and very impressionable."

Without laughing in front of that "gazelle" who was strong as a bull, the commissioner kindly shook his head.

"Yes, my dear Loo you have stayed the same as you were as a young girl."

"I was thin then," she broke in sentimentally.

"That was your only fault, Loo. I state it with satisfaction, and so much more so since you have marvelously corrected that fault."

"Oh, my dear and gallant knight," she chuckled, touched by those words. Then she returned to her first idea: "But if the people in that rolling house resist, what will you do?"

"I will write them a citation."

"But if they answer with bullets?"

"Then, I will get down from my donkey and lie on the ground. I have heard it said by soldiers, that, in that position, you can't be hit by shells, and if that works with shells, it must be also true of bullets, which are smaller than shells."

"Yes, perhaps," sighed languishingly the lady, "but, dear friend, those soldiers are thin like rakes, while you, my Apollo, my Hercules, even lying down, would still present a not inconsiderable target to the enemy..."

Ellick raised his arms toward the Heavens with a gesture of resignation. For the first time in his life, perhaps, he hoped to be thinner, but he let nothing of that show, and continued to go forward, while Loo, a little behind him, let out sighs strong enough to turn a windmill.

"Ready?!" shouted Sergeant Barnes.

"Surround the house!" ordered Simmons and Samuel.

These shouts took the couple away from their reflections. The Sepoys formed a circle around the rolling house. The enemy was now surrounded.

No movement indicated that anyone in the electric hotel had noticed the arrival of the armed forces. Everything remained silent. The moveable platform at the back, lowered to the level of the road, seemed to invite the soldiers to go inside.

That calm inflamed Ellick's courage. With some effort, helped by the Sepoys, he managed to get down from his donkey, which testified to its satisfaction by some prolonged braying. The Commissioner himself helped Loo to put her feet on the ground.

Then, after this act of courtesy had been fulfilled, Glass looked at the Sergeant and the two Corporals, and took on a heroic stance, which made his face look as large as that of a hippopotamus. In a firm voice, he said:

"Come on, Gentlemen. Let's teach them the law."

He himself climbed up to the porch, and went into the vestibule. Everybody followed behind him.

The room was empty.

"Let's go forward," Ellick said, feeling increasingly brave because of the absence of enemies.

In the salon, there wasn't anyone; in the dining room, ditto. On the front terrace, there were wicker chairs, but no humans.

"Ah!" growled the Sergeant. "Have they all fled?"

"That's something to think about," said the Commissioner, sententiously. "The country is full of spies! These scoundrels must have been warned told. That's just what I reported lately. So long as this country has so many people in it, it will be impossible to assure order."

And as the officer seemed surprised by that affirmation, he added:

"Think, Sergeant, how much easier it would be to police a desert!"

He was very convincing, and seeing his superior rank, the Sergeant didn't feel like arguing. In the British army, they respected hierarchy. Instead, he remarked

"This house has two floors. The rebels may have taken refuge in the upper floor?"

"Possibly."

"Then we should go up."

"Undoubtedly."

Everyone started to look for a stairway, but there wasn't one. So, after having looked everywhere on the first floor, Ellick, Loo, and their companions, found themselves, crestfallen, back on the front terrace.

"This is devilish," grumbled Sergeant Barnes.

"Diabolical," added Corporal Simmons.

"Satanic," concluded Corporal Samuel.

"That home is haunted," sighed Loo, whose jaws were shaking with fear.

As for Ellick, he didn't say anything, and for good reason. All of those work had caused him to sweat more than usual. He was busy enough wiping the sweat that flowed freely down his face.

The ancient Greeks, so prompt to see gods everywhere, would have taken him for a river god.

"The Devil takes the Sun," he muttered, while twisting his soaked handkerchief. "That house is like a poorly-built oven, where nothing regulates the circulation of heat. That makes no sense."

His eyes looked at the wall and he made out the label on the automatic bar, which has so much amused the officers at Aurangabad.

"Hurrah!" he shouted. "Here are some refreshments! Gentlemen, let's empty a glass before continuing our investigation."

Without waiting for an answer, he dashed in front of the bar:

"Sherry... No, too mild... Whisky... Too strong... Gin, Brandy, Absinthe... Ah! here's what I want: Lemon-Julep with soda water.!"

Then, he read aloud the notice fixed to the wall:

"*To obtain the desired drink, push the button placed below the correspond-ing label.*"

Ellick rubbed his hands:

"All right!"

His heavy hand pressed the button for Lemon-Julep.

Everyone had approached, their gourmand lips ready to imitate the Com-missioner, but they suddenly stepped back with a cry of surprise. Under Ellick's push, a wall had moved back and a downpour of water had come out. Half as-phyxiated, not understanding anything that had just happened, Ellick let out plaintive shouts:

"Atchi! Huh! Brrr! Water! Brrr! Hum! Hum! Atchi! That's enough to make a man rise up from the grave! Huh! Huh! By God!"

As a devoted wife, Loo, imitated her husband, saying in an irritated voice:

"That is treason! The guilty parties should be hanged!"

Ellick coughing and sneezing added:

"Yes, hanged! Atchi! Atchi! Hum! Hum! Sent to the gallows! A hundred feet high! Atchi!"

The Officers and their men had trouble not laughing, and they pinched themselves, knowing by experience how dangerous it is to laugh at one's supe-riors.

However, Loo, quite versed in matters of the household, remembered how one dried the linens after washing. She laid the Commissioner out on the side of the road and, after ten minutes, the blinding sun had dried him off completely.

No need to say that Glass' ill fortune had not been caused by chance. Fol-lowing a plan prepared in advance, the crew of the vehicle had made certain ad-justments, one of which was the unexpected shower which poor Ellick had re-ceived.

The fat Commissioner felt an anger like no other. As obtuse as he was, he was aware of the ridicule directed toward him; he was in a hurry to avenge him-self. So, as soon as he was dry, he brandished his umbrella like a saber and shouted:

"Let's search this lair of villains, gentlemen, and may the law prevail! Hooray for England!"

Set in motion by that simple but clear harangue, everyone rushed forward. However, rushing like idiots across the first floor didn't help them find any stairway going up to the second floor.

Ellick had become calm again and regained all his lucidity.

"If we can't find a stairway, it's because it's hidden," he said to Loo.

And she, stupefied by the profound logic of his statement, added with ad-miration:

"Obviously, it's hidden since we can't see it."

Then, like Native Americans (with whom they shared the skin color) on the warpath, they went slowly through the rooms. They moved furniture, knocked on the walls and on the floors. In this way, they eventually discovered the spring-loaded button which controlled the basket that connected the two stories of the aluminum house.

"Look, dear Loo, here's another of those damned buttons."

"Wait, Ellick, don't push it... I'm going to call one of the soldiers. If there's another shower in the offing, it might as well be..."

"...One of our brave men. The water will seem to him like a cool spring shower. That is true, my dear and loyal girl. However, I insist on pushing it myself, because, as you know, this expedition, if successful, is going to be worth a bonus of several hundred pounds or more."

"Ah!" she exclaimed, trembling. "I am mindful of your career advancement, Ellick. However, your health is even more dear to me."

"And I am very much obliged to you for that, Loo."

"Then don't expose yourself to a new shower."

"I will take my precautions, this time."

Glass placed himself in front of the spring-loaded button, far enough away. His arm extended at its full length, and he had trouble pressing the button with the tip of his umbrella.

"That way," he said, "there is nothing to fear."

And he pushed it.

Out of breath, the couple looked at the button, which had gone into the wall with a clicking noise. What was it going to produce? What mysterious phenomenon would be created by the displacement of that small metal part?

But nothing.

There was a little continuous grinding like that of a gear in motion, but the wall didn't move.

Hypnotized by the sight of the wall, neither one, nor the other, was thinking about lifting their eyes up in the air. A panel in the ceiling had just opened and the basket was descending.

Ellick and Loo uttered the same cry of terror. That hard basket had just hit their heads and weighed heavily on them, pushing them to their knees. They finally looked up and—horror!—they saw the enormous wicker basket. Fearing a possible shower, Ellick and Loo had just placed themselves under the rudimentary elevator.

Panicked by that incident, incomprehensible to them, they tried to get out of the way, but their heavy bodies were intermingled and their legs gave out. For the second time that day, they sat down heavily on the floor.

"Oh!" cried Loo, whose sensitivity had just undergone a rude test.

"I was almost murdered," sobbed Ellick.

"Me, too!" whined Loo.

"And I believe," he continued complaining, "that I shan't be able to sit down for the next two weeks, except the other way around, with my stomach facing the back of the armchair."

"Oh! That will be very inconvenient and not at all easy."

There was a double shivering and Ellick continued.

"I would very much like to stand up."

"Me too, my dear husband."

"Yes, but I don't know how... I have always looked at people in the face and it is very uncomfortable to be stuck..."

He was looking for a way to not be shocking in expressing his thoughts and he finally finished by saying:

"...To be stuck upside down."

A silence followed. Ellick courageously continued.

"We have to get back to our feet."

"We have to," agreed Loo, without moving an inch.

"Yes, without hesitations."

So, with courage worthy of praise, and despite all his suffering, the Commissioner, succeeded in rolling over onto his stomach. Then using his hands and knees, he managed to slowly pull himself up, but not without great pain.

Once back on his feet, he helped his wife to regain her vertical position.

"At last!" they said, each one instinctively rubbing their hand over the places injured.

It was annoying that it wasn't their arms that had been hurt, because tha, they could have remedied with slings, whereas for the other portion of their anatomy...

The wicker basket on the floor now attracted their attention. With their eyes, they followed the chain going up toward the ceiling, in which a rectangular trap door had been cut out. Their fall became forgotten.

"Hurrah!" they shouted. "There's our stairway!"

At their call, the Sergeant, thew two Corporals, and the Sepoy soldiers came running. The sight of the wicker basket drew exclamations of triumph. Ellick was proclaimed the king of detectives, and when he declared modestly that he would wait in the drawing room until the soldiers had searched the upper floor, that was taken for modesty, when in fact, it was but cowardice.

Meanwhile, Jeroboam Sanders, Wilhelmina van Stoon, and the girls had awakened. They had gotten dressed in their Hindu uniforms. Gathered in one of the rooms on the second floor, they all declared with a touching togetherness that they had a headache and a bad taste in their mouth. The chloroform had left the same after-effects with them as it had with their companions, who now stood in the caves of Zapolaki facing the Companions of Shiva and Kali.

The girls opened the porthole and looked out, their nose at the window. Almost immediately, they jumped backward. They had just noticed the Sepoys at the exact moment when they went inside the aluminum house.

"Soldiers," murmured the gracious persons.

140

"Soldiers," repeated Wilhelmina, letting her arms fall, her hand open, her little finger on the *couture* of her pantaloons.

But Sanders smiled.

"A visit from the local police, probably. Our host warned us that such a thing might happen. So, let's not get upset. And if they question us, answer without hesitation that we are part of the staff of the Electric Hotel. It's unnecessary to create difficulties for the charming director who put us up."

These words restored calm on all their faces. Even the girls were overcome with amusement at the thought of pretending to be part of the hotel staff. Jeroboam had to remind them, seriously, that one shouldn't joke with the police; what's more, the police were waiting. They seemed to ber searching the first floor, where various cries and interjections were heard.

Their eyes at the porthole, the mocking swarm of the Sanders-von Stoon family witnessed the drying off of Ellick on the side of the road. Incredible hilarity greeted the appearance of the fat Commissioner and the tender Loo.

However severe she might be, Wilhelmina felt herself giving way to juvenile amusement, and Sanders, forgetting his own abdominal development, let himself crack a joke:

"Those two turtle doves are round as pumpkins."

That redoubled the laughter. But the Commissioner went back inside. A violent shock soon ensued which made the walls vibrate. Ellick and Loo had just been hit on the head by the wicker basket. Several minutes went by, then heavy footsteps were heard on their floor.

"There they are," said Sanders. "Let's be cautious!"

The door opened. Sergeant Barnes entered, followed by the two Corporals and several native policemen.

"Nobody move!" shouted the officer. "By order of Her Majesty Queen Victoria, Empress of India."

At that name, venerated by all good Englishmen, Sanders bowed deeply, and replied.

"It is easy to obey the commands of the most gracious of sovereigns. We shall be like statues."

"That's good," grumbled Barnes, annoyed by a submission he was not expecting.

"Enough talk! Let's go to the basket. The Commissioner will question you downstairs. Let's go! Start walking!"

Nobody moved.

"Are you deaf?" shouted the Officer.

"No," answered Sanders, "But you just ordered us in the name of the Queen not to move... Now you order us to walk... But it's impossible for us to walk without moving."

"Ah, I see you're a joker!" said Barnes. "I know how to deal with folks like come." And hitting Jeroboam's legs with a stick, he shouted: "Are you going to walk?"

Sanders cried out sadly; Wilhelmina stammered, trembling:

"There they are, the English soldiers that you were so proud of!"

Sanders didn't answer that unfavorable remark that was so disobliging. Looking at the direction indicated by the Sergeant's pistol, he went forward towards the wicker basket.

Ten minutes later, the entire Sanders-von Stoon family had reassembled in the drawing room facing Ellick and Loo, who were sitting majestically in large armchairs—yet, hardly large enough to hold them.

The native policemen formed a circle around their prisoners.

With a scrutinizing look, Ellick watched them. The corpulence of Jeroboam Sanders seemed to please him. He leaned towards Loo and whispered:

"A man of that weight must be powerful... I would have preferred a thinner criminal. They're easier to impress."

His spouse agreed with a nod. Content with her, content with himself, Ellick spoke with a loud voice":

"We are going to proceed with the initial interrogation."

The young girls burst out laughing. The Commissioner looked at them with severity and let out these strange words:

"Stand at attention, sailors! And try to act properly in front of the authorities."

The young girls became quiet. Sailors? Why had he called them sailors?

"You, sir, answer," said Ellick, taking advantage of the pause.

"Answer what?" Jeroboam asked naively.

"My questions. Are you the leader of these prisoners?"

"Yes," answered Sanders, "well, the father of some and the father-in-law of others..."

The Commissioner rubbed his hands:

"Perfect! So you are all members of the same family?"

"Yes, we are."

"That's important information. Will you write that down, Loo? You are going to fill the function of recording secretary."

Then, returning to Jeroboam, he said:

"I appreciate your frankness. If you continue to answer in that way, I believe that I can assure you that you will not be hanged."

"What?" shouted the frightened voices of the entire Sanders-von Stoon family. "Hanged?"

"Don't interrupt. If I am reassuring you, it is not so that you can abuse my indulgence."

"One moment! One moment!" stammered Jeroboam, whose face had become white. "You mentioned something about hanging?"

"And you don't like it?" the Commissioner nicely underlined.

"Well, damn! Put yourself in my place..."

"That's impossible, Sir. Let's get back to business. Would you please tell me your legal name?"

"Certainly."

"I am listening."

"My name is Sanders, Jeroboam Alcidus Ulysses."

"Very good. And you are not a doctor?"

"I, a doctor? No."

"And you are not named Mystery?"

"Naturally not, since my name is Sanders."

"Better and better. The title 'Doctor Mystery' must then be a pseudonym."

Jeroboam, Wilhelmina and the girls, opened their eyes wide. They knew absolutely nothing about the name pronounced by the Commissioner, since they had never learned the name of the Director of the Electric Hotel. In addition, the questions seemed to them incomprehensible.

"All right," Ellick said graciously. "I am happy to take note of your good will and cooperation. If you continue like this, everything will turn out satisfactorily. Let's see, why did you decide to go by that strange pseudonym of 'Doctor Mystery'? "

Lightning falling in the midst of them would not have stupefied them more than that question did. Jeroboam looked around with a confused air.

"Well?" insisted the Commissioner.

"Are you talking to me?"

"Yes."

"And you are asking me...?"

"Why do you go by the nickname of 'Doctor Mystery'?"

Sanders raised his arms toward Heaven.

"I don't understand why you are asking me this. I don't know any doctor by that name."

He stopped short. Ellick's eyebrows had frowned in a menacing way.

"Be careful. Denials are useless. I would even say, dangerous."

"But..."

"You have confessed that you are the leader of the inhabitants of this rolling house."

"I still admit it."

"Therefore, you are Doctor Mystery."

"Beg your pardon, but I am Jeroboam Sanders, a former Representative at the House of Commons."

"Don't look for such an unlikely alibi."

"An alibi?"

"A civilian alibi, useless... unprovable."

This time, Jeroboam remained speechless. His ideas became confused. Could it be that, by chance, he was facing a madman? But Ellick continued calmly:

"I want to show you that lying is useless. Your maneuvers have come to light. You have come to India in order to undermine the power of the Brahmins."

"Me?" Sanders shouted desperately.

"Us?" cried Wilhelmina and the girls.

The Commissioner threatened the girls, shaking his finger:

"Silence, Sailors!"

"Sailors!" they protested.

"Silence. We don't have a flogger at hand, but if you continue, I'll have you given twenty blows with a stick."

"Ah, well! You are very gallant," stammered Wilhelmina, exasperated.

"I am gallant with ladies... But with sailors, that would be ridiculous... Be silent, or you will get the stick."

No one breathed a word, but the girls, Wilhelmina and Jeroboam exchanged a look which meant: "Than man is mad! He's insane!"

Then they looked at the servicemen and their faces expressed stupor.

"A madman... Why have they put him in charge of soldiers... Nepotism, probably, always bureaucracy... And the Director of the Electric Hotel, where is he right now? Just a word from him and everything would be cleared up."

Seriously, Ellick repeated:

"I ask you to not interrupt me again. I stated that your goal was to break the power of the Brahmins."

As Jeroboam made a movement, the Commissioner called one of the soldiers.

"My boy, take the butt of your pistol, stand beside the prisoner, and if he dares to speak or make a move, hit him with it."

Sanders' teeth began to chatter in terror and his questioner was able to continue without fear of being interrupted.

"You arrived in Mumbai with your crew of devoted sailors..."

"Sailors!" shouted the young girls, incapable of remaining silent after those outrageous words were used again to describe their charms.

But at a sign from the Commissioner, thirteen soldiers menaced the recalcitrant group with the steel butts of their guns. There are some forces against which it is useless to fight. The young ladies understood that, and silence was reestablished. Ellick continued.

"Near Bombay, in a property rented in advance, you built this aluminum house. Then you traveled to Aurangabad. There, with a courage that pleases me to recognize, you stopped the Chariot of Jagannath, and you won. Can you tell me why you did this, and for what purpose?"

Desperately, Sanders took his head in his hands.

"Can you do that?" insisted Glass.

"Ah! I would like to," mumbled the unfortunate Jeroboam, "but I have no memory of that. If I showed disrespect toward that chariot—and I say this just s because you say that I did—I was probably sleepwalking."

The faces of Ellick, Loo, the Officers and the soldiers broke in a disdainful expression.

"Ha!" Ellick laughed. "You are refusing to answer, my brave gentleman-bandit. But I bet your accomplices will be less discreet than you."

He pointed his index finger at Wilhelmina.

"You, the old sailor, come forward."

The Dutch woman was stupefied.

"Me...?"

"Yes, you. Despite your Hindu attire, it is easy to recognize in you an old seadog: your square frame, your moustache, your features discolored by gin, everything matches the description from the police report."

"You rogue! You boor! You rascal! You coward! You wretch..."

For two full minutes, Wilhelmina, terrified by the Commissioner, continued to bombard him with a wide variety of epithets.

"Those sailors are rude," remarked Loo.

"What do you expect, candy of my heart?" said Ellick. "You must pardon them. People who spend their life with sharks, whales and cod fish can't have beautiful salon manners." And in a fatherly voice, he added: "Come now, old sea dog, you have vented your bile; now, let's talk seriously."

"You are mad," continued the Dutch woman, increasingly furious. "You can't see more clearly than a mere conscript. And if you had a weapon on your shoulder strap, you would shoot yourself in the eye."

Military memories had come back to the ex-widow.

"He speaks nonsense," said Loo.

She pulled her handkerchief, soaked in pleasant- perfume; and daubed her big nose with it.

"That makes me sick."

"You see, boy," growled the Commissioner. "You're making my lady nauseous. Try to put moderate your language."

Wilhelmina puffed out her cheeks in rage, and replied:

"You first!"

"What, me first?"

"When you speak to a weak woman..."

"Where do you see a weak woman? My lady is strong, very strong."

"Not her—me!"

"You? A woman?"

Despite the gravity of the situation, Ellick burst out laughing. Loo imitated him, and the Sepoy followed suit.

"Yes, I'm a woman—Mistress Wilhelmina Sanders, née van Stoon—who is due respect! I, who has been called the candlestick with seven branches, because I have seven daughters."

Hilarity became general.

"Oh! The candlestick…" laughed all those present… "Mistress Sanders!"

Then, Ellick, with much effort, regained control of himself. He stomped his feet, and in a doctorial tone, he said:

"Enough of this joking. You don't fool us in trying to disguise yourselves. The police bulletin which instructed us to arrest you here said, in capital letters, that Doctor Mystery is accompanied by sailors."

"But I am not Doctor Mystery!" shouted Jeroboam.

"And we are not sailors," cried out the girls and their mother.

"Silence!" shouted Ellick. "The police bulletin is formal. You should realize that, between you claims and a bulletin from my superiors, there is no hesitation as to what I must believe. You are, and will remain, sailors. Whatever you say, you will be tried as such."

And as the feminine chorus protested, the Commissioner covered his ears and ordered:

"Handcuff these scoundrels! Silence them! They are breaking my eardrums!"

The soldiers came forward, but the prisoners would not allow themselves to be touched.

Suddenly, a new man entered the room.

"Those in ranks, fix bayonets!" commanded Sargent Barnes.

The newcomer was tall and lean. Blond sideburns surrounded his thin face. Completely dressed in white, he carried on his shoulder the insignia of a Lieutenant.

"Thar's Lieutenant Bull," whispered Barnes to the Commissioner.

Ellick immediately stood up.

"Are you the one, Lieutenant, who is supposed to take this rolling house away?"

"I am. I beg your pardon for interrupting your interrogation."

"Oh! I had finished. We're going to take our prisoners to the jail at Churu."

The officer held out his hand, saying:

"Just a moment! First of all, I want to share some information that will please every good Englishman. This morning, the cables have brought us this news…"

"News?"

"Yes. From Transvaal."

That word provoked some commotion. Soldiers, prisoners, all of them looked at Lieutenant Bull.

"You know," he said, "how difficult this war with the Boers has been… Well, our Generals Roberts and Kitchener have just reported a great victory at

Paardeberg.[79] They have captured the Boer General Cronjé with three thousand of his soldiers and six cannons. That's the beginning of our victorious march towards Bloemfontein and Pretoria."

"Hurrah!" shouted the soldiers.

Taller than all the others, carried away by his patriotic joy, Jeroboam also shouted "Hurrah for England!" But his cry strangled in his throat. He had forgotten Wilhelmina. The Dutch woman had heard angrily the report from Lieutenant Bull. Her husband's exclamation set off a storm. She jumped on him and exclaimed:

"Scoundrel! You married me, the widow of a brave office of the Dutch army, and now you are rejoicing at the losses of the Boers, the descendants of the free people from Holland. Damn you!"

"But I am English, my dear."

"English! You coward! You remind me of my shame! To be manacled to an Englishman!"

On the point of finding herself ill, Wilhelmina beat the air with her hands. Unfortunately, two vigorous slaps landed on the round cheeks of the unfortunate Jeroboam.

"Oh!" he shouted, "that's too much!"

And she, in a dying voice, replied:

"No, not enough for your insult!"

They separated them. And this time, they were all handcuffed and taken outside. Ellick remained behind with Loo.

"My dear," he said, "note that that sailor has claimed to be from Holland and holds hostile sentiments towards England. That may be important in the trial of these scoundrels."

Then the two left the aluminum house, painfully mounted their donkeys, and following the prisoners that the soldiers were herding away, headed down the road towards Churu.

Lieutenant Bull and four soldiers remained alone at the vehicle. The twenty horses that they had brought with them to pull the enormous machine brayed in a melancholy way on the edge of the road.

---

[79] 18-27 February 1900.

CHAPTER XI
Cicada Becomes a Mechanic and a Diplomat

Lieutenant Bull was a good officer. He had at his disposal everything that a Lieutenant of the Corps of Engineers should have. However, he had attached his twenty horses to the aluminum house and hadn't succeeded in moving it an inch. Its wheels, electrically locked, refused to turn. In vain, he attached the quadrupeds by two, by four, by eight, to the front. The horses, pulling, sweating, whipped, couldn't budge the vehicle.

Also in vain did the Lieutenant go through different rooms looking for a lever or a handle, any kind of mechanism capable of making the heavy machine that, only the evening before, was still rolling rapidly on the road to Churu, move.

Nothing!

Let us state right now that there were such mechanisms, but they were hidden inside the double metallic walls that formed the shell of the aluminum house.

Tired of this struggle, Lieutenant Bull finally had to give up. So, at the end of the day, his "study" of the vehicle had to be postponed until the following day. He sent his men and the horses back to the village to be fed. Finally, he decided to spend the night the strange machine, telling his subordinates to come and wake him at dawn.

But he barely slept a wink. Like all true engineers, he was frustrated by not being able to find a way to start the house. If he had had to explain that vehicle to an assembly of scientists, he would have declared, with the unsufferable arrogance of a polytechnician, that it *couldn't* move.

Unfortunately, he was a military man. He was not asked to prove that the vehicle could or could not move. His personal convictions mattered little in this mission. Under pain of discrediting himself, he had to make that machine move. So, by shutting himself up in the mysterious dwelling, his only goal was to continue his research without being watched by his subordinates.

He began to work, with no more success than he had had during the interminable day that had just ended. Towards midnight, still frustrated, worn out, the Lieutenant let himself fall into a chair.

"I can't do anything else now," he groaned. "I will be the laughing stock of the Engineer Corps. I will be the Lieutenant who could not make the wheels of a vehicle turn—that is pitiable. I don't know what's stopping me from smashing everything up."

Suddenly, he lifted his head, that he had held lowered in the classic attitude of a man crushed by fate. He had just heard a slight noise. It sounded like a person who was trying to approach without drawing any attention.

Lieutenant Bull jumped to his feet, drew his sword, and walked towards the door that connected the salon to the vestibule. But before he had reached it, the newcomer had rapidly turned the handle, and a boy of some fifteen years, clothed in green like the prisoners, appeared on the threshold.

He introduced himself:

"Good evening, Sir," he said. "I am happy to see you're still awake; that will spare me the trouble of having to wake you."

It was Cicada in flesh and blood.

Instantly questioning his casual way of entering the vehicle, the officer asked in a rogue voice:

"What do you mean? I don't know who you are. I should arrest you for coming in like a thief in a house that is not your own."

The Parisian boy shrugged.

"You're a real Englishman, aren't you? Friendly like a brick thrown at you."

"How dare you..." began the Lieutenant.

"Come now," interrupted Cicada, with a laugh. "You should be more polite. This isn't your own house, but mine, and I didn't ask you to come here. You're the intruder."

"Ah!"

"Let's close the door," continued the boy. "You have a very loud mouth, like all British. Plus it lets in a a cold draft that cuts like a sword." Then he continued in a more serious voice: "I have come here to get you out of trouble."

Hearing that, the officer stood up to his full height:

"A Lieutenant of the English Corps of Engineers is never in trouble."

"Really?" Cicada said calmly. "Then it seems I made a mistake."

"Assuredly!"

"In that case, I apologize. I guess you know how to drive that vehicle away. So I have nothing more to say to you. Good night, Sir. No need to show me out, I know the way."

The young Parisian had already put his hand on the doorknob, but his last words had made Bull's arrogance melt away.

"Wait, wait!" shouted the Lieutenant. "You're telling me that you know how to operate this house?"

"Of course!"

"How did you discover that?"

The boy scratched his head and replied:

"Ah, I'd like to tell you, but if I do, in exchange, you must swear to not arrest me."

"Conditions?"

"Yes, but only one—a very small one. After all, my arrest shouldn't matter that much to you. What would you stand to gain by throwing me on the damp straw of one of your cells? Promise me that I will remain free, and I will tell you what I know."

It was annoying to have to give in, but Lieutenant Bull has just lived through hours of agony, and so did not hesitate. Between two wounds to his self-esteem, he chose the least.

"Agreed," he promised. "If you tell me how to operate this vehicle, you will be free to go and get lost."

Cicada was careful not to show any resentment at the rather dismissive tone of the reply, but his eyes shone with malice. He said:

"I thank you for your courtesy. Now, let us get down to the basics. I am Doctor Mystere's mechanic. The engines were undergoing a general revision, but in a quarter of an hour, we can start moving. Please follow me..."

Saying that, he took the Lieutenant into the vestibule, and showed him some moveable panels which gave way under pressure from his thumb.

"There," he continued. "As you can see, the engines are almost ready. The indicators are in the other room."

Bull went into the neighboring compartment to check on what the young Parisian had just revealed. With exclamations of joy, he now saw various electrical equipment that his prior investigation had failed to discover.

"All right!" he shouted. "Now it's a question of making all that work together."

"The controls are on the second floor."

"Let's go there."

Both of them got into the wicker basket and were carried to the control room. Hidden behind other moving panels, the controls appeared under Cicada's fingers.

"There you are," said the boy. "Would you like to start?"

"Yes!"

"In that case, push that little knob."

The Lieutenant obeyed. Immediately, there was some shaking, followed by a hardly noticeable trepidation.

"We are moving," said the Parisian.

"Are we?"

"Look for yourself."

Making one of the wall panels slide away, Cicada made it possible for them to look out onto the road and the countryside. Bull put his nose out and made a delighted exclamation. The rolling house was moving at a moderate pace on the road under the light of the Moon.

"Hip! Hip! Hurrah!" cried out the Officer enthusiastically. "We are moving! I have only one thing to say, my young friend. You are indeed free to go, but before you do, could I ask you to give me a few more moments to explain to me the details of that admirable machine."

His initial stiffness and native phlegm were now a thing of the past.

"Gladly," answered Cicada. "I'll spend an hour on that; that should be enough."

His hand hit a button and the aluminum house stopped.

"If it pleases you, Sir, let's go down to the salon. That's where the greatest surprise awaits."

The joking tone of the boy escaped the Lieutenant, who was completely satisfied with having made the vehicle move.

"OK," he said complacently. "I can't wait to see that surprise you are talking about."

"You won't have to wait long."

Cicada got inside the wicker basket, the Englishman got in beside him, and they began their decent.

But the bottom of the basket had not yet touched the floor of the salon before Bull, surprised, was lifted out of it by strong hands; gagged, handcuffed, and deposited on the little couch formerly occupied by the traitor, Arkabad.

Around him were uniformed men clothed in green with darkened faces. Then a shaking confirmed that the rolling house had started to move again. Who were these men? Where were they going? What fate was in store for him? These momentous questions remained unanswered.

Cicada had disappeared. The Lieutenant, powerless, had to admit with rage that the boy had successfully tricked him. An hour went by. Suddenly, the vehicle halted, and almost immediately, the Parisian boy reappeared. He asked one of the men:

"We're twenty-five miles from Churu, Boss."

"Good."

The man then looked at his companions and said just one thing:

"Go!"

His assistants approached the Lieutenant, seized him without brutality, some by the shoulders, others by the feet, and carried him away. Going across the vestibule and the back terrasse, they carried their burden down to the road.

Once the Englishman had been deposited on the side of a ditch, the silent men took his revolver and removed the bullets. They then took the gag out of his mouth, and removed the handcuffs from his wrists, leaving his ankles bound.

Then, like a flock of birds, surprised by a hunter, they ran towards the rolling house which was moving away at full speed.

When Lieutenant Bull, completely confused by the adventure, finally succeeded in untying the complicated knots around his legs, the aluminum house was already far away.

Swearing, the British officer had to resign himself to walk back to Churu. Once back there, he could use the telegraph to contact his superiors and tell them the unbelievable situation of which he had been the victim. All the police forces would be sent to chase the electric house. It would surely be found again because a two-story house on wheels couldn't be hidden. The hope of retaliation gave him energy, and he walked with a light step.

Meanwhile, the rolling house continued its journey towards the west. It had gone over a range of small hills and found itself in the middle of the desert.

Doctor Mystery had sent Cicada ahead to distract Lieutenant Bull under the pretense of explaining the house's mechanisms to him, then had seized the opportunity, and, with the help of Kéradec and his sailors, had captured the hapless officer.

Now, the Doctor ordered a halt. Some tents were set up on the ground. Cicada and Anoor, tired out by the emotions of the day, were not long in falling to sleep.

When they again opened their eyes, the sun was already high on the horizon. Having left their canvas shelters, they let out a cry of surprise. The aluminum automobile was no longer there. In its place was a big wagon with panels of wood painted grey, covered with a heavy tarpaulin.

"What on Earth is that?" asked the Parisian boy.

The Doctor, standing nearby, answered him while smiling:

"Don't you recognize it, Cicada? It's the same which we have used since Bombay."

"It is?"

"Yes. The wall panels are entirely removeable. The aluminum plates are applied to a chassis of wood to stop the vibrations, and if we remove them in the appropriate fashion, this is what we get."

"Fantastic!" shouted the young man, whose admiration was always expressed by that word. "I get it. After yesterday's operations, we're going to have all the police after us. Only now, they could pass by near us without suspecting that this wooden chariot is the metal house that they're searching for."

"Indeed!"

"But there's one thing bothers me..."

"Which is?"

"I wonder why you didn't make that transformation earlier. That would have been simpler..."

"Than what I did?"

"Well, yes! We had to take in the Sanders, have them join us, get them arrested, and then retake the automobile."

The Doctor shook his head.

"You don't understand?"

"No. It just seems to me that..."

"That you are not thinking!"

"What?"

The boy frowned, indignant. The Doctor continued:

"I'm, going to help you. In order that everyone believes that the aluminum house is still there somewhere, it is necessary that no one else but us know about its transformation."

"Of course!"

"Now, this transformation requires five or six hours of work. Could we have done it with the certainty of not being disturbed in the middle of a populated place like Delhi?"

"I get it now! That's enough, Boss! You needed a deserted place..."

"Yes, my friend. Now we have nothing more to do but change costumes, and no one will recognize us as the infamous Doctor Mystery and his gang of rogue sailors, as the British papers are certainly going to call us."

Half an hour later, the two young people, who, on the Doctor's order had returned to their tents, reappeared, transformed. Thanks to a mixture of dyes, their faces, like the sailors', had been darkened, and their green uniforms replaced by crimson ones, decorated with pearl embroideries.

Anoor was now dressed like a girl, with her hair cut flat, and her body squeezed into embroidered vest that fell on a short dress with a million pleats. She wore large pantaloons tied at the ankles, and a gauze veil thrown over her head and shoulders. She was very pretty and Cicada murmured:

"You're like a love sugar rolled into a silk pastry."

That, without a doubt, in the mind of the young man, represented the feminine ideal. And such is the power of a sincere impression, even if expressed in a rather funny fashion, that the young girl blushed and lowered her long eye lashes.

For the first time, the boy from Paris and the little Hindu girl felt embarrassed when facing each other. The Doctor, who had not lost sight of them, did not seem to notice the problem.

"Let's go," he said. "Our brave sailors and I have become Parsee merchants. Get back into our vehicle, children, and let's get on the road to Lahore, where the traitor, Arkabad, and the devoted Dhaliwal, will help us find the sister of whom Anoor has kept a sweet memory.

They all got into the chariot, which started with vertiginous speed moving North, where, beyond the sandy plains of the Thar Desert, lay Lahore, the great capital of Punjab. It was there that Doctor Mystery had a rendezvous with the Leader of the Companions of Shiva and Kali.

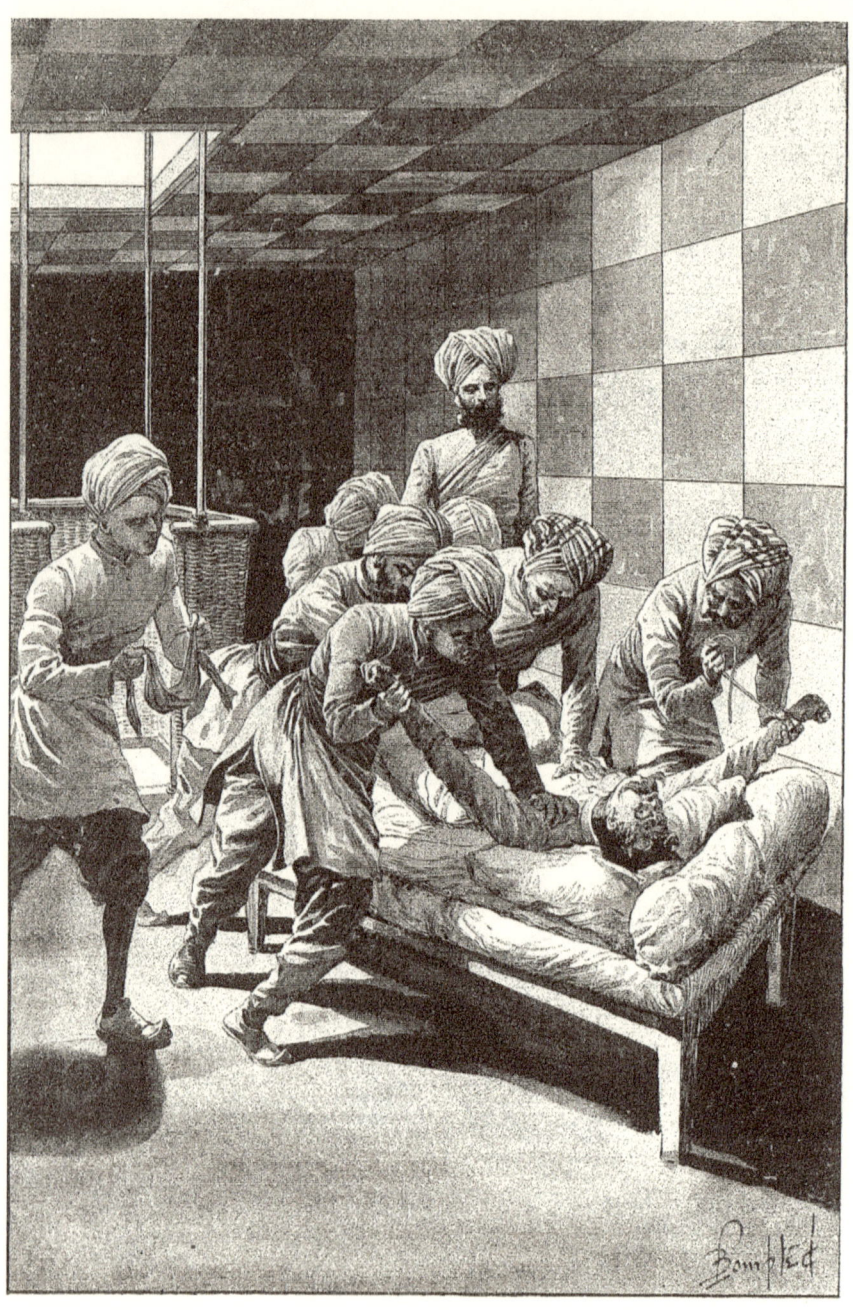

CHAPTER XII
The Mindless One

Unrecognizable, seemingly drawn by eight horses bought from a nearby villager, Doctor Mystery's vehicle entered Lahore through the *Achtat-Khan* gate.[80] Looking like a heavy and slow farm wagon, it went through the neighborhoods of Mozang and Ichra, crossed the outer boulevard, which occupied the emplacement of the former ramparts, and went through one of the crenelated brick gates.

---

[80] Lahore has (or had) 13 fates, none of which were named "Achtat Khan." They are the Delhi Gate (built by the Emperor Akbar), the Roshnai Gate (gate of light), the Akbari Gate, the Yakki Gate (originally named Zaki), the Bhati Gate, the Khizri, or Sheran Wala Gate, the Lohari Gate, the Kashmiri Gate, the Mori Gate, the Masti Gate (originally named Masjidi), the Shah Alam Gate, the Texali Gate, and the Mochi Gate.

Avoiding the winding little streets, the vehicle followed the long *Wales Avenue*,[81] whose gentle slope led to the granite plateau, the natural base of the Citadel. Thus, it passed in front of the Citadel and the Moti Masjid Mosque (Mosque of Pearls), the Aurangzeb Mosque,[82] and the Oriental College on Shish Mahal Road[83] the Mayo Hospital, and the Governor's Palace, established in an admirable building constructed in the Mongol era. Then, turning to the right, in *Strangers Street*, it arrived at a hotel recommended by all the Pocket Guides as "*Unique and Peerless*," managed by a Parsee named Beïrali.[84] That establishment merits further description.

The Lucknow & Patna Hotel [85] is an immense caravanserai formed of several interlocked buildings. There is a three-floor pavilion with tapered little columns, gothic crosses, and clover-leaf crosses, adjacent to a low stable, whose grass-thatched roof and cracked walls clash with the superb appearance of its neighbor.

Courtyards and narrow passages connect the various sections of the hotel and are decorated with pretentious names, just like the streets of a city. The main courtyard communicates by way of the *Allée Verte* with the Brahmaputra Square. From it spring two small alleys named Ellis and Jabbotah. The first leads to another courtyard named Mitri, the second to a square named Victoria. These buildings, these names, part Hindu, part English, make the strangest mixture, the most bizarre cacophony, and, to tell the truth, give the impression of British domination badly applied to a Hindu civilization made of half-forgotten dreams.

Whoever enters that enormous agglomeration is certain never to be found again. The individual is lost, leaving no trace in the swarming mass. It is constantly renewed with clients passing through. Men, women, children, horses, mules, camels, elephants, carts, work oxen, all cry out, weep, neigh, bark, bellow, obstruct the passages, hit each other in the courtyards, make the bells jingle, shout out the windows, cross each other between private carriages, cars, rental carriages, under the verandas, while servants circulate in the middle of

---

[81] Every British-era road in Lahore has since been renamed which makes following the characters' journey difficult. I could not find any trace of a "*Wales Avenue*" in Lahore. Ditto for "*Strangers' Street.*"

[82] The Badsahi Imperial Mosque, built by Mughal Emperor Aurangzeb.

[83] Punjab University.

[84] Parsis or Parsees are an ethnoreligious group of the Indian subcontinent whose religion is Zoroastrianism. Their ancestors migrated to the region from Sassanid Iran following its conquest by Arab Muslims under the Rashidun Caliphate in the 7th century AD.

[85] Lucknow is the capital of the state of Uttar Pradesh. Patna is an ancient city that sprawls along the south bank of the Ganges River in Bihar.

this chaos, indifferent to shouts and insults, carrying a procession of platters of food, pressed clothes or shaving implements.

One should deem oneself lucky when they don't give the kind of sarcastic reply that's heard the world over:

"I can't hitch up the Sahib's horse because I'm only the guardian of the stable."

Or:

"I wouldn't know how to serve the gentleman's steak because I can only serve deserts."

Because, in India, the multiplication of castes has entered the world of servants. When in Europe, a rich man may be content with a single butler, a man of the same social stature in India must have three servants. The job of one is to take care of his hair, the second is in charge of clothing, and the third of his shoes. If you go out, you must be accompanied by a parasol-carrier, a hookah-carrier, and a fan carrier.

A Hindu wetnurse gives her milk to a nursing child, but another servant washes, dresses, and puts the baby to bed. In addition, a male servant carries the child when they go out. A total of three servants for a three-month-old baby, and the number of these increases with the age of their charge, so that at five years, it takes a small battalion of people to serve that child.

Clearing out a passage through the crowd with great trouble, the wagon of Doctor Mystery finally stopped at Annex 28 of the caravanserai. It was parked under a hangar. While Kéradec and his sailors remained on board, the Doctor, Anoor, and Cicada, followed by Ludovic, went out and were served refreshments.

Seated in the shadow of a parasol, all three were watching the comings and goings of the travelers, when their attention was drawn to a person who, standing a few feet from them, remained immobile in the midst of the general confusion. His silk turban, his long brown caftan, his wrists surrounded by valuable jewels, identified him as a wealthy merchant. His black eyes, with a clear and frank look, said that he was an energetic and courageous man. He seemed to look at Anoor with sustained attention. Bothered by that prolonged examination, the Doctor was about to go out to question him, when the man approached them slowly.

"Do you know the village of Churu, at the other end of the Thar dessert?" he asked in a curious and ceremonious tone.

And as the Doctor was not answering, he continued:

"They say that some extraordinary things have happened there. The dreaded Companions of Shiva and Kali are said to have found a new leader, sent by Vishnu himself... He is called the Golden Tiger."

"Well," replied the Doctor, adopting the prudent circumlocutions of the person he was speaking to, "that is not the name that I heard."

"Is that right?"

"Yes. I was told Dhaliwar was their leader."

"No. Dhaliwar has left them."

"In order to come to Lahore, perhaps?"

The Parsee merchant crossed his arms over his chest and lowered his voice.

"It was you that I was expecting, Master. I thought I recognized the girl you protect, but resemblances may be deceptive, and I must be sure that our Brothers are not strangers to you."

The Doctor nodded.

"What do you want to tell me?"

After being sure that no spy was listening, the Parsee continued:

"Since yesterday, Dhaliwar is in the walls of the Ranjit Singh Convent, where he has met the Brahmin Arkabad, as you instructed him."

"How do you know that?" asked the Doctor, always suspicious.

"I took him right up to the doors of that Holy Place. There, he told me to go to the caravanserai and watch for the arrival of the Master. I am then to go back right after I have talked to you."

"He didn't confine anything else?"

"No, but if you will permit it, I will now return to see him. Since yesterday, he has undoubtedly found the secret you want to know."

A rose blush came to Anoor's cheeks. She whispered:

"My sister."

"No, *our* sister," Cicada corrected her, "because she will be my sister just as much as yours, and I will love her very much. Not as much as you, of course, but very much nevertheless."

"Well, well," said The Doctor, smiling, "so you love our little friend?"

The boy blushed.

"Er, yes," he said, embarrassed. "But like a sister, of course! And she's too grown up now..."

The Doctor smiled even more.

"The fact is," he declared in an enigmatic tone, "that she has grown up a great deal in a week... at least in your esteem."

Then without giving the Parisian the time to respond, he spoke to the Parsee:

"Go see Dhaliwar. I must reach the woman the Brahmin Arkabad seeks before he does. He wants to make a moral martyr out of her, after having already imposed the cruelest physical tortures. If the Mindless One ever recovers her reason, it will be because of the favor of Vishnu in the cause of freedom. Go and tell him that, then come back."

"I obey, O Master of the Golden Tiger."

After those words had been pronounced with the mystic fervor that only devout Hindus are capable of, the merchant pulled out of his kaftan a sheet of paper covered with Sanskrit characters.

"This," he explained, "is a statement that Dhaliwar has ordered to be given to all the sections of the Companions of Shiva and Kali in Punjab. It was given to me to give to the girl who has the eyes of a gazelle…" He pointed at Anoor. "This is to inform her of what she should fear."

The Doctor took the parchment. He glanced over it, then with a gesture, he said to the Parsee:

"Hurry up. On your return, the child will have read it."

Immediately, the Hindu started away and disappeared into a neighboring building. Then the Doctor leaned towards Anoor.

"Child, whom I have called daughter, listen to what Dhaliwar has deemed necessary to tell his faithful. You will understand what dangers surround us, and how much I need you to have confidence in me."

"Oh, father!" she said. "I believe in you, as if you were Brahma himself."

"It's not enough to believe. You must obey me."

"I am your servant."

"Don't make a gesture, don't say a word, that I haven't told you to do."

"My arm will be still; my mouth mute."

She was telling the truth. Her big eyes expressed faith and devotion. The Doctor considered her for a moment in silence. A damp fog had now fallen and was obscuring his view. Finally, he drew her to his chest, kissed her forehead, and said briskly:

"Listen, Anoor, and you too, Cicada, since you have sworn to defend that oppressed girl. Listen…"

And here is what he read slowly:

"Watch, Brothers, watch!

"In the past, the people of Sindh and Punjab dreamed of their freedom. They had no guns, powder, or ammunition. Only gold would allow them to purchase any, but they did not have gold either. So they decided that every day, each person would pay a tax for their country. The rich were to give a rupee, and the poor only a copper coin. Warriors, Merchants, Workers, and Farmers, all paid gladly. Only the Brahmins abstained. Despite that, the Treasure grew and became immense. A man, wisest among the wise, the most honest of all, was placed in charge of it. He buried it in a hidden location. Only he and his eldest daughter knew the place where the millions were hidden. But the man was taken by the Brahmins, who sought to steal the Treasure. Despite being tortured, he kept his secret and died without revealing its location.

"Watch, Brothers, watch!

"The Martyr's two daughters are still alive. One was four; the other, eight. The oldest one, who, despite her young age, had proved to have unbelievable firmness of character, had been taken by her father to the place where the Treasure was hidden. She had seen the millions, she had touched them, and the word FREEDOM had brought into her heart the devotion of the martyrs.

"On her blood, her life, and her repose in Brahma—the three most sacred oaths a Hindu can pronounce—the child swore to her father that she would never reveal to the enemies of freedom the hidden place of the gold.

"After her father died, she was subjected to all of the ruses and artifices of the Brahmins. They threatened to separate her from her younger sister, Anoor, for whom she felt the greatest affection. The girl cried, but didn't talk. The Brahmins were angered by her resistance. One dark night, they kidnapped Anoor. The elder sister felt overwhelming despair, but still did not talk. She then contracted an illness which led to a high fever. For weeks, she was delirious, between life and death. But the protection of Vishnu was over her. When she recovered, the god had taken away her mind, thus making her, according to our religion, a sacred being, whose existence all must respect, under pain of incurring the wrath of the Preserver.

"Since that time, she has lived in her palace, without memories, gentle, watched by the spies of the Brahmins and those of the English, who record her every gesture, her words, in the hope that the Mindless One shall betray the secret that is locked away inside her mind. She is seventeen today, but has never talked.

"Watch, Brothers, watch!

"The enemy is watching. He schemes to brutally shock the Mindless One back to reality. Then he will torture her again in order to learn from her the hidden location of the Treasure of Freedom.

"Watch!"

The Doctor fell silent. Suddenly, Anoor hid her face in her hands and burst out in sobs.

"My sister," she said in a trembling voice. "My sister!"

"Oh!" growled Cicada, overcome at the sight of her tears. "Don't worry, little sister. The first Brahmin that I catch, I will make mincemeat out of him."

The Doctor himself took the little girl in his arms.

"Don't cry, Anoor. We will find your sister and we will give her back her mind."

The sobs of the child stopped. She looked at the Doctor with her big, tear-filled eyes.

"You could accomplish that miracle, father?" she asked in an anxious voice.

"Yes, my child... Yes, my daughter."

Anoor's face became calm.

"Then, let's search for her, father. Find her, you who are so powerful... Me, I am afraid of the Brahmins... If we arrive too late..."

Suddenly, she stopped. The merchant wearing a brown caftan had just returned. He stopped near them, breathing as if he had just finished a long race.

All of his body expressed agony; his hands trembled and contractions tightened his discolored face.

"What's wrong?" asked the Doctor, worried.

"I can't reach Dhaliwar."

"You can't? Were the Brahmins from the Ranjit Singh Convent bold enough take him prisoner?"

The Parsee held out his arms in a discouraged gesture.

"A prisoner! I wish it were that! A prisoner can be freed..."

"Spea, then! What has happened?"

The man lowered his head and said:

"Following your orders, Master, O Chosen of Vishnu, I went to the Convent. There, I asked for Dhaliwar."

"And?"

"They told me that Dhaliwar had never come to that place. But I knew otherwise, since I had accompanied him there and seen the heavy bronze door close behind him."

"Then?" questioned the Doctor, whose face was growing dark.

"Then, I asked the favor of talking to the Brahmin Arkabad."

"Ah!"

"It was useless. I was told Arkabad was in Ellora. He never came to Ranjit Singh."

"So he wouldn't have come to a rendezvous that he himself had set up?"

The Parsee made a violent gesture:

"The Brahmins lied! Arkabad did come to the convent. He picked up the cloth stained with blood that Dhaliwar had brought and then fled without leaving any traces because he wants to be the only one to learn the location of the hidden Treasure."

"And Dhaliwar—what has happened to him?"

A savage smile formed on the man's lips.

"They have some deep *selavos* [86] at Ranjit Singh."

The Doctor trembled.

"You think that they...?"

"Our leader is dead, yes! Traitorously thrown into an abyss! He no longer presides over the Companions of Shiva and Kali."

Cicada, and Anoor had stood up, very pale, impressed by the words of the merchant. Suddenly, the Parisian boy had a light in his eyes:

"If you want me to, Boss, I will go and talk to those Priests of Brahma, and I'll see through their lies."

The Doctor shook his head.

"No, you don't know the wiles of these beings whose hearts are truly dead."

---

[86] A dungeon with an opening only at the top.

"They can't be more wicked than the beggars from Paris."

"They would kill you without a thought."

"If I put myself in harm's way, but I'm slippery like an eel. They won't be able to lay a finger on me!"

Sensing the refusal almost ready to escape from the Doctor's lips, he persevered:

"There is no real danger, or so little that you shouldn't be worried... Besides, I've appointed myself to be Anoor's minder, and, well, in that business, you know that you're occasionally going to have to risk your skin... But all things considered, it's better to do that than to grow fat doing nothing."

Anoor, with moist eyes, listened to her young companion being so simply heroic.

"Anyway," finished the young man, "I got it into my head to break into that convent. If you don't take me there, I'll do it alone. I'm sure I can find my way there. I have a tongue, and I know how to use it."

His resolve was so strong that the Doctor let himself be convinced. After all, something had to be attempted. Arkabad's disappearance put everything back in play. The painful trail they had followed since Audierne was in danger of being lost. It was important to not lose it again, at any price.

Ten minutes later, the Doctor, after having given his orders to Kéradec, left the Caravanserai with Cicada and Anoor. Behind them, Ludovic walked along gravely. The little bear had judged it good to join the expedition. All four went across the narrow little streets, bordered with tall houses showing the most complete carelessness of their alignment.

Some half-naked, dirty children were playing in the gutter. A little further off, there was a beggar sitting in a doorway, his legs crossed, his face immobile, his look vague, mumbling a vague incantation addressed to a small idol made of gold-plated wood. On a little table there were yellow wax candles burning.

Then, suddenly, they crossed English avenues with rickshaws pulled by natives, bordered by white stucco villas separated by attractive little fences, before entering again the Hindu parts of the city, with its children, beggars and narrow little streets. Sometimes, they saw a Tibetan Lama chanting while turning a prayer wheel, or a Hindu woman gracefully wrapped in veils, leaving in her trail the heavy smell of the benzoin perfume that Punjab women prefer to any other. Curious, they uncovered their dark eyes to look at the foreigners; then continued on their way.

The Doctor and his companions were still walking.

Some police guards, armed with long steel batons, stood at the crossroads, still like statues, waiting for a fight, an uprising, or a theft that might call for their intervention. If such an incident happened, they suddenly came to life and fell on the crowd, their arms outstretched, eager to reestablish order by striking the guilty as well as the innocent.

Finally, at the top of a street with a steep slope, the Nicha Chaitram Road, a spacious square opened up in front of the walkers. In front of them was the sculptured and crenelated wall of the Brahmin Convent of Ranjit Singh, inside of which was the mausoleum which gave it its name.

"Whew!" said Cicada, making a face. "It doesn't look like it's easy to get inside." But he shrugged and added: "But I see a door and some windows. With that, the Brahmin who could keep me out isn't born yet."

The young suddenly stopped talking. Ludovic, who, until then, had followed them like a well-behaved bear, had just gone past them. He placed himself in front of them, with the obvious intention of keeping them from going any further. And, as his attitude astonished them, the animal bounded toward Anoor, seized between his teeth the bottom of the girl's skirt, and tried to pull her toward one of the avenues that was bordering on the square.

"Down, Ludovic!" shouted the Doctor.

That was a useless order. The bear, ordinarily so calm, so obedient, seemed to be the prey of an unusual excitement. He was still pulling Anoor towards the avenue when the Doctor tried to make him let go. Ludovic showed his teeth and put out his claws. Then he went back to the girl and continued what he had been doing.

"It looks like as if he wants you to go down that avenue to the left" exclaimed Cicada.

"Yes," Anoor said, and, with naïve belief, she added: "He probably has a good reason for that. Brahma sometimes makes the animals very wise."

"Amritsar Road," said the Parisian boy, who during that time had consulted a road sign put up at an angle of the road. "Does that ring any kind of bell, Anoor?"

She shook her head:

"No... However," she said, talking to the Doctor, "I would like to follow the inspiration of that bear. He wants to take me to that side. Why not do it?"

Her soft voice was begging. The Doctor replied:

"Go then, child... Perhaps you are right to have confidence in that good and loyal creature, who has recognized you from the other side of the world."

With that, everybody started down the avenue. Ludovic understood that they had given in, and, with happy bounds, took the lead. He went ahead of his friends, and, after a few yards, he stopped to let then catch up, then started again. His muzzle in the air, smelling the wind, one might have said that he seemed to be following a trail. He didn't show any hesitation. On the contrary, his movements showed satisfaction.

On the dusty road, which sometimes paralleled the tracks of the railway line going from Lahore to Amritsar and Batala, sometimes moving away from it, the walkers continued to follow the bear, who seemed increasingly happier. He cavorted, made unexplained bounds.

Suddenly the road entered the shadow of a little wood. Then the animal started at a gallop and disappeared into the trees.

The young people looked at each other, indecisive, but the Doctor said:

"Let's keep going. Ludovic's behavior is strange, but everything leads me to believe that he has lived in this country... So let's follow him... Perhaps he will lead us toward the dwelling where he knew you as a child, my sweet Anoor."

The girl took his hand and carried it to her lips; then, without a word, they started on their way again.

Multicolored birds were singing in the branches. Delicate perfume came from the roadside bushes with which the soil was covered; the trunks of trees, standing up like the columns of a temple, with their canopies of leaves at the top, were like cathedrals inviting the passers-by to pray.

Feeling an emotion that was almost religious, the Doctor and his companions walked faster. The road made a sudden turn, coming out of the woods under a green arch. The walkers stopped, stupefied by the magic sight which they saw ahead. A lake bordered by white marble quays extended placidly in front of them. An island connected to the shore by a narrow pathway lined with by alabaster columns topped with gold candelabras lay in its center. On it was a white marble temple with a dome and gold bell towers shining in the sun.

Anoor shivered. She exclaimed:

"Ah!"

Then, she covered her eyes.

"What's wrong, child," demanded the Doctor, surprised by her sudden emotion.

"Yes, little sister, what's wrong?" repeated Cicada.

She shook her head and stammered:

"I... I know that's not possible... I am dreaming... Yet..."

"Yet, what?"

She gestured with strange authority.

"Be quiet! In the depth of my being, once forgotten memories are back. The shadowy veil thrown over my view is lifting... Ah! This lake... This lake... That sanctuary..."

Her whole being trembled. Her adorable face wrinkled under the effort of remembering. Suddenly she let out a loud cry, fell on her knees, and her arms extended as if she wanted to hug the countryside.

"I see... I remember... It is the Amrita Sara, the Lake of Immortality... It is the golden temple of Mahadeva...[87] I have prayed to Brahma on its marble tiles..."

---

[87] Shiva.

She was trembling; the Doctor took her in his arms. He was as emotional as she was; his heart beat with joy; he had accomplished his task and brought back the orphaned girl to her country.

He thought about the capricious nature of fate. It was Ludovic, the poor little bear, who had just guided them towards their goal. The animal's instinct had done more than all the complex schemes of human intelligence.

As if he were echoing his thoughts, the animal reappeared and ran at top speed to rejoin his friends; he began jumping around in joy, licking Anoor's hands and standing up on his hind legs to lick her face.

Immobile, her eyes looking into the distance, big tears flowing down her cheeks, Anoor seemed to have forgotten the presence of her companions.

"Let's go into this temple, where, when you were little, you prayed to Brahma," the Doctor suggested to her softly.

At the sound of his voice, she trembled. She took her two friend's hands and went down the passageway.

"Yes, come, may Brahma be glorified on this day."

Her steps reverberated on the tiles.

"Ah!" she continued. "I remember the temple of Mahadeva, its white wall covered with arabesques and precious stones… It was the pride of Punjab! Emeralds were used to represent the leaves of the trees, enchanted by flowers made of turquoise, garnet, lapis, and sapphires. Constructed by Guru Govind-Singh, the wisest of the Sikhs, it was venerated even by the barbaric Mongols, Afghans, and Persians, who, during their invasions, didn't lift their profane hands to loot the riches it contained.[88] My sister told me about the beautiful legends of past times, which our father had told her, and through her, I thought I could hear the voice of the martyr."

She was speaking as if in a dream, without talking directly to anyone, and her friends, understanding that that pause was useful and necessary, didn't interrupt her.

Cicada, always a keen observer, could see that the decoration of the wall, which he had thought were frescoes, were actually a mosaic of small precious stones. The cupola and the towers were made of massive gold, weighing over 300,000 pounds, with a value of 450 million francs.[89] Those simple numbers made any commentary unnecessary.

Inside the temple, stained glass windows let in a pale blue, highlighting unexpected nuances on the stones, or the tiles of gold and silver that covered the

---

[88] The Kandariya Mahadeva Temple is the largest and most ornate Hindu temple in the medieval temple group found at Khajuraho in Madhya Pradesh. It was built during the reign of Vidyadhara (r. c. 1003-1035 AD), not by Guru Gobind Singh (1666-1708), a spiritual master, warrior, poet and philosopher who was the tenth and final Guru of the Sikhs.

[89] About $6.6 billion.

walls and columns. Anoor went in. The Doctor and Cicada followed her and Ludovic moved about in a reserved way, seeming to sense the sanctity of the place.

At a marble niche, against which her fine silhouette detached like that of an icon of the Virgin Mary, Anoor prostrated herself and her companions, standing behind her, respected the meditation of the girl who had been exiled and was now returning to the land of her ancestors.

Some cadenced steps resounded on the dike. They stopped on the threshold. Cicada turned around and looked. A litter with purple drapes was put down on the ground by several porters draped in a red and white cloth.

Two women got out. One of them was old and ugly, with a devious expression on a face wrinkled like parchment; she wore big gold earrings. The other was young, shining with beauty, but with a strange expression of concern, as if she were distraught.

Both went through the portal. In the nave, they went forward and went past the group. At that moment, Anoor lifted her head. Her eyes became fixed on the newcomer, and reflected her astonishment.

"She!" she murmured with a strangled voice.

The Doctor had heard. He quickly leaned towards his protégé:

"Is it… her?"

"The one for whom I wept for such a long time," answered the girl with a voice as soft as a breath.

"Your sister?"

"Yes. My older sister."

"What is her name?"

"It is…"

Anoor hesitated, searching, and tears came to her eyes.

"I don't remember anymore… The name of my dear sister is no longer in my memory."

She trembled, incapable of moving towards the girl who was holding out her arms to her. And the Mindless One—for it was she—the victim of the Brahmins, the one whom Dhaliwar had mentioned, whose unconscious mind held the secret of the location of the Treasure of Freedom, went away slowly.

Was she going to disappear before Anoor could bring the consolation of her kisses to that pure forehead, the insensible shell of a sleeping brain?

No, that couldn't be! Anoor made a superhuman effort; she succeeded in standing up... She was going to jump, call out... But she didn't have time...

A man came out from behind the shadow of a column, blocking the way to the one she wanted to rejoin.

The Doctor, Cicada and Anoor recognized him. It was Arkabad! Arkabad who had come to fulfill the cruel mission that had been assigned to him.

In his hand, the traitor brandished a piece of linen on which there were dark stains of blood.

"Na-Indra," he said, "do you hear me?"

"Na-Indra," repeated Anoor. "Na-Indra... That was her name, a well-deserved name—the kiss of Heaven!"

However, the woman stopped. She looked at the Brahmin for an instant, then rummaged in a silk pocket fixed to her belt.

"A beggar," she pronounced in a soft monotone. "It's charity that you are asking for. It will be given to you..."

But Arkabad pushed the charitable hand away.

"No, I am a messenger that brings you a precious token. Look at that piece of cloth. It is stained with blood. It is the blood of Anoor, your sister, slaughtered on the altar of Shiva."

An inner confusion made fugitive wrinkles on the face of Na-Indra; then every trace of emotion disappeared. Her face became calm and placid.

"The dead return back to life in Brahma. May the Creator be praised."

She passed, slow and cold, in front of the disconcerted Arkabad, who exchanged a rapid sign with the older servant and rushed outside.

Thus, Anoor remained fixed in place like a statue. What a horrible nightmare she had just lived through! Alive, she heard her death proclaimed to the one she loved, and she had not had the strength to cry out that it was a lie. What's more, she had seen her dear sister, whose memory had lived in her heart like a perfumed flower; she saw her listen to the cruel news, and remain inert, insensible.

It was therefore a body without a soul that was moving in front of her in the blue clarity of the sanctuary. The one that she saw had the features, the form, the appearance of her regretted sister, but she no longer had her heart; she no longer had her mind. The bitterness of the disillusion rose to her lips... It seemed to her that, right now, she was further from Na-Indra than she had ever been, when she didn't know where she was.

Without strength, without will, she let herself be led toward the exit. Calmly, she stopped with her friends near the litter that was stationed on the dike.

What plan had Doctor Mystery conjured up?

The minutes passed. Na-Indra reappeared, still escorted by her servant.

"Anoor, embrace your sister," murmured the Doctor.

He pushed the young girl forward. She was lost. Her heart, beating in her breast, she embraced the inert woman. In order that her thought, her will, would not be wasted, a cry of sadness and tenderness came out of her pale lips.

"I am Anoor, your sister, who loves you, and wants to call your mind back to your soul."

The Mindless One trembled; her eyelashes batted several times. It seemed that Anoor's words had awakened a far-away echo in her mind. But that passing trouble was wiped out and disappeared. With an automatic movement, Na-Indra carried her hand to her little pocket, and said again in her melodic monotone voice:

169

"It's charity that you are asking for. It will be given to you..."

Anoor made a piercing cry.

"Charity, no! It is I who give to you the charity of my tenderness; I, who does not wish to leave you, who wishes to attach myself to your steps, to take care of you, to cherish you, to make you be reborn out of the night where you are struggling..."

The servant approached. She made a sign to the porters, ordering them to remove that stranger who was slowing the departure of Na-Indra, who suddenly held out her hand and said:

"To not ever leave me again... May that also be granted to you..."

The porters stopped. The Mindless One had spoken. No one could do anything other than what she ordered. So said the law of Brahma:

You will obey the mindless ones and you will venerate them just as you would me. Whoever transgresses that order will be excluded from heavenly graces; he will be cursed in his person as well as in his descendants...

As the old servant was going to try one last time, Na-Indra continued:

"Join me here in the litter. Your companions and mine will walk together. My dwelling is near. It is large enough to host those who would appeal to the hospitality of Na-Indra."

She drew Anoor towards the vehicle. Both sat down side-by-side. The purple drapes fell down again, hiding those inside. With the same smooth movement, the porters lifted the chair and carried it away with a supple and cadent step.

The Doctor and Cicada, and the old servant who examined them with a defiant eye, followed, hoping to hear what was said behind the closed curtains. But no sound came out.

Inside, Anoor, embracing Na-Indra, was weeping softly. Suddenly, she trembled from head to feet. A burning drop had just fallen on her forehead. She lifted her eyes to look at her sister. The Mindless One was also crying.

PART TWO: THE ROAD TO THE FUTURE

CHAPTER I
Conspiracy

"What! Garieba, you let strangers come into the palace of Na-Indra?"

"How could that be prevented, O Arkabad?"

A silence followed those words. The old servant of Na-Indra was standing in front of three men. One, with a fierce face and dark eyes, was the Brahmin Arkabad, whom we have already met. The other two were tall, blond, with a rosy complexion, and listened attentively.

They were Lord Farren, Governor of Punjab, and his son, Theobald, and they appeared to be concerned.

An hour earlier, both of them had been stretched out on a lawn chair in the shadow of the veranda of their splendid habitation, located on the hill of Varloor which overlooks the city of Amritsar. Both were discussing a matrimonial project.[90]

Vanilla plants and odorous sweet peas encircled the gold-tipped columns that held up the light roof of the veranda with their climbing leaves, filling the mid-afternoon air with their scents, easing the siesta of the British Administrator and his heir.

Half-asleep, the two men rarely talked except when separated by long pauses, as if the heat of the climate did not allow them the effort of continuous conversation.

"Na-Indra is beautiful," murmured Farren.

After a wink and a lazy yawn, Theobald replied:

"Undoubtedly, but deprived of any intellectual facility."

"But that's wonderful, Theobald. It is the dream of every man to have a mindless wife. That suppresses all arguments in his household. Think about that for a minute. The dream of a gentleman is a home that is comfortable and peaceful. Na-Indra would make you sure of one and the other."

The young man shrugged, took a breath, then in a conciliatory tone, replied:

"You're probably right, father; so I should marry that stupid goose who's going to lay golden eggs?"

"You should," concluded the Governor. "Riches and tranquility! You would kill two birds with one stone!"

Both of them had closed their eyes, worn out by the energy used to exchange those replies, when Arkabad had walked in, still irritated by his failure at the Temple of Gold.

He wanted to obtain from the Governor papers in good order to present himself at the palace of the Mindless One as a servant. In this way, he thought to find an opportunity to take his revenge.

Farren grumbled about the intruder who was troubling his siesta, but he could not send away a personage as important as Arkabad.

His orders were strict. Every administrator, from the Viceroy down to the least important agent of the British Crown, must help protect, and assist the venerated caste of the Brahmins.

Striking a gong, the resounding vibration of which brought his own servants running, the Governor was given everything he needed to write and created

---

[90] Considering that the distance between Lahore and Amritsar is about 30 miles, the travels on foot of the various characters between these two locations seem rather unbelievable.

all the necessary certificates and references, applied an official stamp, and stretched back on his chaise longue, hoping to return to his well-deserved rest.

But it was written that, on that day, he would not rest. A merchant from Amritsar followed the Brahmin. That man brought a double barrel full of honey.

The exquisite taste of that honey, stolen by hard-working bees from the local flowers, played a great role in the nourishment of the Westerners in India. It was transformed into a refreshing jelly, which, according to those who ate it, helped digestion, cleared the liver, regulated bodily functions, and so forth. The newspapers are full of stories about it. To tell the truth, it makes for a pleasant meal.

Its mode of preparation is singular. You take a barrel that you put in the ground just as one does with the watering cans in the garden. You fill it with honey, then you add some ginger, shelled coconut kernels, rum, and lemon juice. On the open top, you place a light trellis to stop the dust while leaving the mixture in contact with the air. It then ferments, hardens and takes the consistency of jelly, with a mahogany color. The product is ready. To serve it, you put it in a portable ice chest, and if one isn't cured of all the ills of the world, at least one has enjoyed a delicious sugary drink.

So, the merchant disposed of his product according to the rules of the art, leaving his samples on the edge of central walkway of the shadowy garden, which extended from the covered terrace on which the Governor and his son were vainly trying to sleep.

After he had gone, Arkabad returned because one of his documents had not filled out properly. Farren corrected the mistake. He was finally going to return to his nap when Garieba, the old servant, brought the news of the strange encounter between Na-Indra and the three strangers at the Temple of Gold. She said that the Mindless One appeared to have become attached to the newcomers.

Arkabad, Farren, and Theobald were thunderstruck. Someone unknown to them had seized the trust of the girl, in whose brain was hidden the secret of the location of the Treasure that they coveted. They understood each other without saying a word. Just a look was enough. Those strangers had to be chased away. The Brahmin, echoing his most intimate thoughts, murmured:

"This evening, I will be part of Na-Indra's household, then I will act. Come, Garieba, faithful ally of the Brahmins. The audacity of these strangers who alarmed your devotion will be punished."

And the two of them left the Governor, now definitely awake, employ the rich vocabulary of the British when it comes to profanities.

Arkabad, his forehead bowed, absorbed by his thoughts, went down the gentle slope of the Varloor hill, went around the Sacred Lake at the center of which was the Golden Temple, then turning toward Amritsar, he soon reached the thorny hedges that surrounded Na-Indra-Pur, the Palace of the Heavenly Graces, the name which the locals had given to the magnificent habitation occupied by the Mindless One.

Through the leaves one could see the façade, the terraces, the stone statues lined up on each side of a Court of Honor. A little to one side, there was a strange construction resembling a cage for wild animals or an aviary. Behind its bars, there were brown forms moving.

"The Bears of Shiva," mumbled the old servant.

Arkabad shook his head. What was the use in her telling him that? Didn't he know that one of the customs of the noble families of the region was to keep some bears, symbols of liberty, in their household?

"The strangers," Garieba continued, "those who gained the confidence of my mistress..."

"Yes?"

"They had a Bear of Shiva with them."

Suddenly, the Brahmin trembled.

"A bear! And there are three of them?"

"Yes. A man in the prime of life, an adolescent boy, and a young girl... The last one was wearing men's clothes, but that did not deceive me."

Arkabad's face turned dark.

"Then it is again Doctor Mystery, who, since Ellora, has constantly crossed my path." He grew more excited. "That is a second time that he has saved Anoor! Ah! He is like a living Sphinx, but I must destroy him!"

Garieba bowed her head, and, in that humble attitude, waited until it pleased her powerful companion to explain himself further. Arkabad seemed to have forgotten her presence. His eyebrows frowning, he was thinking aloud:

"And now," he continued after a moment, "they are under the protection of that Mindless One..."

The servant nodded.

"No one in this country, where they stupidly respect the mad, would dare make an attempt on their life. Even I, a Brahman, despite all my power, would be imprudent if I attempted any violence."

He stamped the ground violently.

"Still, they must die! I swore before the Brahmin College of Ellora, to crush those enemies, and I shall keep my word."

Suddenly, Arkabad seized the wrist of the old servant:

"Listen to me."

"My ears are open."

"You see Na-Indra every day?"

"I never leave her side."

"Good. Have you ever noticed in her some lights of reason? Has she ever seemed to appear to understand...nor, at least, to try to understand, what is happening around her?"

The servant shrugged, looking embarrassed.

"You are not saying no," Arkabad continued. "Then, you are not certain of her dementia?"

"I wouldn't dare confirm anything, O Lord, but…"

"But?"

"I often asked myself the same question your holy mouth has just asked."

A light passed in the eyes of the Brahmin.

"You have asked yourself that very question, Garieba?"

"Yes."

"Why?"

The old woman passed her hand over her forehead, seeming to be searching her memories, and finally answered:

"I am going to tell you all the truth, Lord. Perhaps my notions are those of an old woman, whose eyes and mind are growing weaker every day. You will decide what to do with this, but I do recall a few occasions, very rarely, I must say, when Na-Indra sometimes reacted when certain words were said in her presence…"

He was looking for her words carefully, like all those who are not used to public speaking, but nevertheless desire to convince their interlocutors.

"I cannot confirm it, you understand… I believe her eyes sometimes come alive… It has even seemed to me that, on rare occasions, her eyes positively laughed. It never last long. It's as fast as the light appearing behind a cloud, then vanishing away. But, in those moments, you would swear that she was making fun of me."

Arkabad quickly came forward:

"Making fun of you? How is that even possible?"

"Perhaps I am mistaken, Lord, and yet…"

"Continue."

"Here it is," continued the servant. "There are some things that I see, that I feel, but that I do not know how to explain. For example, last week you sent me a message."

"That's true."

"Ordering me to speak to my Mistress about her sister Anoor, who has disappeared."

"Yes, and then?"

The old woman lowered her voice, as if she feared a low breeze would carry her words to an invisible spy.

"Well, I obeyed. Then, the next day, I took Na-Indra to the park. She was singing a monotonous melody, like the ones mothers use to rock their children to sleep. I was walking besides her. Without seeming to pay attention to her, I murmured: 'Anoor! Anoor!'"

"Yes, and…?" the Brahmin asked avidly.

"Wait, Lord, wait. At first, she didn't seem to hear me. Her face remained calm, her eyes distracted, but her foot suddenly began to move, and she bent over to pick a flower."

Arkabad made a violent gesture.

"If that's the only evidence you have..." he began.

She interrupted him:

"I know I'm not educated, and I have always been a servant. The words I use do not always exactly match what I think, but I have lived for many years, envying the riches of my masters. I have picked up the habit of watching them closely, in order to divine their thoughts. So I swear to you that when I said the name 'Anoor,' it reached her innermost mind."

She spoke with such conviction that the Brahmin was impressed.

"Don't be irritated, Garieba. You are loyal, and I have every confidence in you."

"Thank you, O Lord."

"I have promised you that if we succeed in getting the location of the Treasure from Na-Indra, the Brahmins will make you rich. You will command, in your turn, many servants."

The parchment face of the old woman turned slightly colored.

"I have faith in the word of the Brahmins."

"Of that, I am certain. Keep looking into your memories; search them... Success may depend on a forgotten detail, almost nothing..."

"Then, believe old Garieba, Lord. I shall continue with my story. We were walking when, suddenly, I seized Na-Indra's hand and carried it to my lips, as if I were not in control of that movement of affection."

A smile passed over the Brahmin's dark face.

"Well done! The comedy of the devoted servant."

"Yes, Lord. And I said: 'Oh, my dear mistress, you who can't understand my affection, may you see better and happier days.'"

"Perfect!"

"Then I began to recount a dream, totally made up, of course," cackled the old woman. "A dream in which Anoor, alive, reappeared at Na-Indra-Pur."

Arkabad ground his teeth and said:

"That dream has come true."

"What?"

"Anoor is the girl with the strangers."

"Then, she has escaped you, master?"

Tightening his fists, the Brahmin growled:

"Yes! The one who protects her is a terrible adversary. He snatched her out of the waves. He turned aside the dagger of the Companions of Shiva and Kali."

As Garieba shivered, Arkabad changed his tone.

"But we will destroy him, no matter what. Continue with your story."

"While I was talking—this is that I wanted you to hear, Lord—Na-Indra was looking at me. Her eyes were not vague; one might have believed that she was laughing inwardly, thinking: 'Stupid servant girl, your story is ridiculous.'"

The old woman became excited.

178

"I certainly recognized that disdainful look which I had often seen on the faces of my previous masters. I am not mistaken, Lord, believe me. The Mindless One is having fun at our expense. Once again, one of those arrogant beings to whom Brahma has given riches was thinking. 'Old Garieba is stupid.'"

Arkabad was now listening attentively.

"Yes," he finally said, "everything you said is possible, but those slight clues are not enough. Na-Indra, if she is mindless, is sacred in everyone's eyes. Whoever lifts his hand against her or those surrounding her, even if it were Brahma himself, would be torn apart by the crowd. She must be led to betray herself in a way that is so clear, so convincing, that no one shall believe in her madness any longer."

As Garieba shook her head with an expression of doubt, he ordered:

"Let's go our separate ways from here, old woman."

The old woman bowed.

"As you wish, O Lord."

"I will rejoin you later. At the evening meal, I want to serve at the table."

"You, serve, like a domestic?"

"I will be a domestic. There is no task that is too low for someone fighting in the name of the All-Father... Is what I ask possible?"

"Of course! I'm in charge of all the hiring and firing. Na-Indra doesn't even notice the changes in her staff."

Arkabad smiled.

"Are you sure of that, Garieba?"

Then, stopping the answer on the lip of the old servant, he added:

"Go now! You will see me again soon."

She did not insist. She crossed the door to the park and her silhouette was soon lost behind the trees.

Then the Brahmin, in his turn, entered the property. Slowly, as softly as a cat, he moved towards the habitation whose façade appeared in the middle of the greenery. It had once been the country house of a rich Nabab. It was constructed of stone, and its wall had the thickness of a fortress, like many of the Punjabi residences, where Afghan incursions had made the owners build their houses like fortresses.

But the solidity of the edifice did not exclude either lightness or grace. Sculptures were carved into the massive pillars. On the openwork cornices ran airy balconies, whose fine balustrades of sandalwood were cut into laces. The conical wooden roof was supported by several rows of small columns which separated it from the main building. It stood like a giant parasol under the shelter of which shade and coolness prevailed. In the apartments, springs of cold water flowed in marble basins.

At the top of the twelve-step stairway, at an angle where they were aligned like ever-vigilant guards, there were stucco figures representing the Bears of Shiva. A veranda with tall columns, blue and gold, occupied all the façade.

There, sitting in curved chairs made of wood from the branches of the aromatic nauclea, Na-Indra and her guests reveled in the shadows, enjoying the sight of the park, which the sun filled with golden sparkles.

Anoor never stopped looking at her sister, whom she had finally found. Out of her mouth came caressing words, a song of tenderness with which she rocked the mindless girl, her eyes half-closed.

"My dear sister... The Master had promised it... Reason has come back inside your pure forehead... Your eyes, velvety as the blooming flowers, have recognized me. You will love Anoor as she loves you, and your heart will also go out to those who have risked their lives in order to reunite two orphans. You will come to cherish Cicada, the French boy who always laughs... He comes from a far away country where they are happy and they do not know the Brahmins... Your affection will also go to the Doctor, the one whom I call father... Your heart will feel a single love, because if you are Na-Indra, the Grace of Heaven, he himself is certainly Ob-Indra, the Kindness of Heaven."

"That's well said," interrupted the Parisian boy, "but, God's blood, what funny names! Ob-Indra... Now, that's not ordinary!"

The Doctor was listening to her words, and Ludovic, stretched at the feet of Na-Indra, remained without moving like a bear rug.

No one suspected the presence of Arkabad.

Twenty feet from there, hidden behind a tree, the Brahmin was watching. For half an hour, he remained still as a statue, scrutinizing the features of his enemies, taking down their words. Then, with a gesture of impatience, he slowly withdrew. Still hidden by the reddish trunks of the trees, he went back into the bushes, and making a big detour, went the commons.

The night was about to fall.

In the confines of the horizon, the sunset created an infinite canopy of scarlet clouds, like fireworks at the end of a banquet. The stars darted rays of rubies, filling the firmament with purple light that the shadow of the trees, constantly elongated, striated with bands of deep scarlet.

On the covered terrace, the silent servants had set up a table. They had hung lanterns made in the shape of flowers to the columns, and their rows of pink-colored glass filtered the light of the descending night, giving everything a dream-like tint. There were no protective nets against mosquitoes because, already circulating in the air, a flock of Bengali birds, clothed in an azure and black plumage as soft as velvet, took care of any marauding insects with their avid, wide-open beaks.

The sun eventually set. Its orb ceased to be visible; where it had been, a last rutilant arc appeared, like the open mouth of an oven, drawing its line of fire against the horizon, and, little by little, making the violet, lilac, blue, and indigo colors disappear. The dark firmament then revealed its river of diamond-like stars, and the Moon, like a silver medallion, whose face seemed to smile on all Earthly things.

Strange sounds filled the nocturnal air as the diurnal world was going to sleep. The trees, the bushes, the grass, all made sounds... They seemed to be stretching their branches, or their twigs, before going to sleep after the fatigues of the day. With trembling cries, the birds of prey called to each other; the insects flew in thick clouds, each time bringing a momentary silence to the frightened landscape. Then, the low deep grown of a tiger hunting resonated like a song of death in the night.

"Na-Indra, Grace of Heaven, Smile of Creation, beloved mistress of her adoring servants, your table is served for the meal of your beauty."

Thus Garieba, bent double, her hands crossed on her chest, announced that dinner was served.

The young girl let herself be conducted to her place, and around the table, covered with a cloth of transparent silk, with blue edges embroidered with white bouquets, the Doctor, Cicada, and Anoor sat down in silence.

Standing, two steps from them, wearing the white and red colors of the household, a native servant stood ready to obey at the slightest sign. Na-Indra looked at him for an instant with her vague eyes, then she turned away and began to eat mechanically. The Doctor also had examined the servant. A smile passed over his lips and then, he appeared to no longer pay any attention to the man

Cicada was chatting away:

"Say what you will," he declared with his mouth full, "but a country house like this outside of Paris would cost well over a hundred thousand francs to rent. That would be quite a *barda*."

He corrected himself quickly.

"Sorry, I always forget that you don't understand Parisian slang. I would register Anoor at a secondary school so that she can become a true Frenchwoman... I would take her there in the morning and pick her up in the evening... And at the end of the year, she would take her exams, and that would be that."

"Very good," the Doctor approved, "but afterward?"

"After what?"

"After her studies are finished, what would Anoor do?"

"What would she do? Nothing at all. That's the nicest of jobs. It doesn't require any learning."

"She would soon be bored."

"No, she wouldn't. We could go on walks, shopping, to the theater, the opera; we could dine with the upper-crust bourgeoisie, and discuss the affairs of the world at dessert... How could one ever tire of such life? Isn't it true, Mademoiselle Anoor, that you wouldn't be bored?"

The young girl smiled sweetly.

"I don't think so... but I don't dare say anything definitive, because..." She fixed her velvet eyes on him, and finished: "...because father thinks otherwise."

As the Parisian boy made a face, the Doctor explained:

"You see, Cicada, our young friend talks like the angel that she is. And I believe that you would spoil her nature by trying to turn her into a Parisian."

Cicada suddenly jumped up:

"Spoil her nature? Now, there's a joke! A Parisian woman is the most wonderful thing in the world... The prettiest woman in the best city ever... How would that spoil her nature?"

The Doctor, and Anoor burst out laughing.

"Don't get upset," said the Doctor. "I'll gladly admit that the great wickedness of Creation is to have placed a world around Paris for her to be admired... Are you happy now?"

"Yes and no."

"Why?"

"Yes, because you've told the truth. No, because you're pulling my leg."

With a movement of impatience, the Parisian boy grimaced.

"More slang! I'll never get rid of it. I meant, you're making fun of me."

"You're wrong, Cicada, I'm not. You are good, devoted, happy, and seeing that, I am completely disposed to think of Paris as an admirable and unique city. But let's drop that. We were discussing Anoor's future..."

"Yes," agreed Cicada, delighted by the words the Doctor had just spoken.

"Well, the goal of life for a young woman isn't to go to the theater."

"That's true."

"As for her education, you spoke as if you were her tutor."

"Yes, something like that."

"Good, then let's continue. If you are her tutor, you have to think about getting your pupil settled."

"Settled?" protested the young man. "But I don't want her to become a shopkeeper!"

"That's not at all what I meant. Settled means getting her married."

"Married?"

Cicada remained with an open mouth; his face turned pale.

"Married?" he repeated.

"Of course!" continued the Doctor, pretending not to notice that Cicada was upset. "Such is your duty as her tutor. And you must guide her choice among those who will aspire for her hand..."

"Must I?" stammered Cicada, with a trembling voice.

"Absolutely! And to begin with, let me know what qualities you would require of the candidate who will meet with your approval."

"My approval..." said the young Parisian with dull anger. Then sadly he continued: "Of course, she shouldn't marry a poor devil; she shouldn't do that, even if he loves her like the apple of his eye…"

"In fact," the Doctor said casually, "she needs a gentleman."

"Yes, a gentleman," growled Cicada, letting loose his bad temper. "Let's talk a little about these gentlemen; they're all phonies, selfish, pretentious and ridiculous. After they've waxed their mustaches and hung flowers in their boutonnière, they think no one should ask anything more of them... Anoor would die of sorrow with a husband like that... And if he made her die, I'd kill him!"

There were tears in his eyes; his face was scarlet with determination and anger. Suddenly, he shut his eyelids and remained that way, his lips slightly trembling. That was because his eyes had met those of Anoor. An electric shock had shaken the young couple, and while she was blushing, persistently fixing her dark eyes on one of the canopy trusses, he felt his heart beat from the depth of his being. It seemed to him he was going to fall over because of the depth of his feelings.

A revelation had just occurred. At last, Anoor, and Cicada had understood each other. For months, they had lived side by side, exposed to the same dangers, their minds working towards the same end. At the contact of the graceful young girl, the Parisian boy had become refined and his protective instinct had grown greater. Anoor, for her part, had become accustomed to drawing confidence from her companion. At the Temple of Ellora, it was his arm which she had grabbed when the tigers had appeared. When she had been prisoner of the Companions of Shiva and Kali, it was Cicada whom she had called for help.

After this exchange, cleverly directed by the Doctor, both of them, without being prepared, had suddenly gained the clear perception that they could not live apart.

Like an incense holder suddenly opened before an altar causes the balsamic fumes of myrrh and frankincense to rise and fuse together, their hearts had become united by the song of pure love, a poetic and mysterious treasure. Nature, the careful mother of the future destinies of humanity, appears without being invited, a thousand times more generous than the fairy godmother of our fairy tales, and slides into the souls of the just-born child.

What is the value of this gift that has no commercial value? ask the stupid people that, in our modern societies, bowing before the power of gold, and like to call themselves "practical" or "serious"? What is its value? I am going to tell you: it is to recompense the true heroes, acclaimed or obscure, to give them that bright inner superiority which leads them to disdain the vain palaces and artificial opulence of the "practical" people. It leads them to pity them, those who have gathered millions, but whose hearts and should are truly indigent.

This gift, it was Heaven opening into the hearts of Cicada and Anoor, because, without transition, their love, like a divine eruption, had projected them into the skied.

At that moment, a servant wearing a turban came forward carrying a golden basket full of fruit. The pineapples, the guavas, the bananas, were mingled with berries from European vineyards, apples, pears, and peaches. White raisins fell in delicious cascades on its sides.

The servant passed the basket around.

"Some fruit, Sahib?" he murmured, coming to Cicada.

His features were directly across from the rays of a lantern; his face was fully lit. The Parisian boy made a stifled cry.

"What's the matter?" asked the Doctor

"Nothing," replied Cicada, who had become calm again. "I bit my tongue."

He took a peach, but as the servant was going away, carrying the basket, the young man leaned quickly toward the Doctor and said:

"That man, did you recognize him?"

"Yes."

"It's Arkabad, the Brahmin, Anoor's enemy."

"Quiet!"

It seemed that Na-Indra might have perceived the sense of this rapid exchange because her eyelashes batted slightly. The corners of her lips lifted with a smile, which soon vanished. That was all. Anoor herself had seen nothing. As a gourmand, she tasted one of the little blood-red apples that had a citrus taste and which were produced by the manchineel tree.[91] The poisonous tree had been changed by the cultivators and its fruit had become without danger. Nevertheless, accidents sometimes happened. Since nothing was apparent to the eye, nor to the palate, it was not apparent whether or not the helpful graft had been applied. So, some cases of poison happened each year and were reported in the scientific annals of Bengal.

Suddenly, Arkabad came back into the room. The deceitful man had assumed a very upset expression.

"Have any of you, Lords, eaten any of the red apples?"

"Why?" questioned the Doctor.

"There's been a mistake. A new servant has cut some fruit from a tree that has not yet been grafted."

"And?" questioned Anoor.

"That fruit is a violent poison. If it is ingested, it can cause death."

The young girl let out a cry of terror.

"Father, father, I ate some of that poisoned fruit. Save your little Anoor!"

But the Doctor reassured her with a smile.

---

[91] The manchineel tree (*hippomane mancinella*) is a species of flowering plant in the spurge family. Its name comes from the Spanish *manzanilla* (little apple), from the superficial resemblance of its fruit and leaves to those of an apple tree. The manchineel is one of the most toxic trees in the world: the tree has milky-white sap which contains numerous toxins and can cause blistering. However, its native range stretches from tropical southern North America to northern South America—but not India.

184

"Coffee is an antidote for that venom."

And filling a transparent porcelain cup decorated with delightful colors, he handed it to Anoor.

"Drink, child, and don't worry."

During that rapid scene, the Doctor hadn't stopped watching Arkabad, who was looking at Na-Indra, with an ardent light in his eyes. The unconscious woman had not made a movement. Suddenly, her nostrils became pinched. A pale blush had covered her cheeks, but no gesture had shown that she had paid any attention to what was happening around her.

Arkabad frowned and went away with the slow steps of a fatigued servant. The meal was finished. With affection, the Doctor took Cicada by the arm. The young man wanted to talk, but a brusque tug that his companion gave him, warned him of the necessity of remaining quiet. Both of them went down the steps and reached the garden as if they sought to take a little exercise after dinner. They continued until they reached an open space. Then, with a voice, soft as a breath, the Doctor murmured:

"Don't make any gesture of surprise. In the darkness, there are eyes spying on us. Look at the sky; I am pretending to talk to you about the stars."

And while his raised hand seemed to point at the constellations, the Doctor continued:

"You recognized Arkabad?"

"Yes. I almost said so out loud."

"He is here to continue his wicked work."

"Of course!"

"Tonight, you must not sleep."

"I will not."

"Watch over Anoor."

"You can count on me."

"As for me, I have to go away, but I'll return before dawn."

"Very well."

The Doctor made a satisfied sigh:

"You are not going to ask me where I am going?"

"No. At this hour, we are at war with the enemies of those two angels who are named Anoor and Na-Indra. You are the General; I am the soldier. You command; I obey."

"God's blood! You are becoming disciplined!"

"Not really. A Frenchman may be turbulent during peacetime, but he always follows the strictest discipline in time of war."

Two yards from the two men, to their right, a huge tree was moving slightly, although there was no breeze. The Doctor was watching it out of the corner of his eye.

"A spy is hiding over there," he murmured. Then, raising his voice, he said: "Let's go in. I am exhausted; I would give ten years of my life to already be in my bed."

"Me, too," said Cicada, instinctively guessing that invisible ears were hearing the words they pronounced. "Let's go back."

He seemed to stifle a yawn with some trouble and, with a heavy step, he followed the Doctor who directed him towards the house. Behind them, in the bushes, there was like an almost invisible ruffle. The young man noticed it at once.

"Ah! Now, I get it!" He continued walking and then said loudly: "All right, so there were some *snoops* in them bushes... Damn! I'm using slang again..." But shrugging, he added: "Bah! I am talking just to myself, so it doesn't matter!"

Five minutes later, the Doctor and his young companions were lodged in the apartments put at their disposal in one of the wings of the villa. Anoor retired into her bedroom, and, confident in the vigilance of her friends, was not long in falling asleep.

Then, Cicada opened his door, slid a chair into the hallway and sat down, his eyes on watch. His hands crossed on his knees, held a revolver. Ludovic was stretched out at his feet.

As for the Doctor, he proceeded to get ready for bed in an unusual way. Taking off his clothes, keeping only a dark-colored loincloth, he anointed his body with a brown substance similar to walnut, extracted from the bark of a palm tree. It took him more than an hour to complete that operation. But he had become unrecognizable. He looked like a Hindu from the poorer classes. His black turban, his dagger hung around his neck by a thong, the dark color of his skin, everything worked together to complete the illusion.

Once he was ready, he approached Cicada and repeated:

"Keep watch."

"Don't worry," replied the young man. "With Ludovic and me, Anoor has nothing to fear."

The Doctor nodded. He took the silk belt which was a part of his abandoned costume, and silently, he went towards the window which was at an angle of the house. He leaned in from outside, inspecting the inside.

"Everybody is asleep," he said, as if talking to himself. "Master and servants have closed their eyes. I can leave."

And saying those words, he tied one of the ends of his belt solidly to the balustrade and threw the fine silk cloth outside. Those belts, several meters long, have fabric so light that it can pass through a ring, yet have extraordinary strength. Without tearing, they support the weight of a man, and they are used constantly to climb palm trees, or cross ravines. At rest, the light fabric becomes a belt and can hold weapons.

After a last signal to Cicada, the Doctor climbed through the window. The young man saw him glide right down to the ground with an agility which indicated a long practice. Then the Doctor scampered through the grass like a giant lizard, reached the massive shadows made on the earth by the silver moon, and disappeared. Where was he going in this fashion in a night inhabited by spies and tigers?

Some faraway noises made the question come to Cicada's lips, but he didn't have time to consider suppositions. A hardly perceptible brushing sound caught his attention. What was it?

A shadow was balanced on the white façade. Like an enormous spider at the end of its web, it came down. It jumped to the ground... It was a man! A spy! It followed the traces of the Doctor, and, like him, soon got lost in the bushes.

Cicada's heart skipped a beat. He had no way to warn his master that his departure had been noticed. For a moment, he thought of following the spy, but the sleeping Anoor made a movement. He could not desert the post that had been entrusted to him. He had to keep watch over the girl. Full of agony, trembling, his fingers tightened on his chest. He remained at the window, his neck extended, trying to peer through the shadows.

Suddenly, he heard a sharp piercing noise cutting through the night. At first, he thought it might be the cry of a vulture snatching its prey; but no, that strange clamor came from the house itself.

Cicada leaned over, looking in every direction. He didn't see anything but grass. Where the moon rays played, there was nothing but trees casting their dark shadows against the scintillating stars. The mystery of the night surrounded him and oppressed him. Everything seemed to be at rest; yet, there were a thousand clues testifying to the fact that there was agitated life everywhere. In the darkness, one could only guess at the hungry activity of the big cats and the pursuit of the bronze men. There was terror in that silence and fright in every movement of the branches.

Meanwhile, the Doctor had reached the edge of the park. With one jump, he crossed it. He was on the desert road, a clear ribbon in the middle of the blue-green countryside that had scattered rocks and some copses of trees.

At that moment, he heard the same cry that had caught Cicada's attention. He stopped for a moment, surprised.

"That's the signal warning me there's a spy on my heels," he growled. "But who could be warning me? It must be Cicada! That boy sees everything and he must have noticed it, as he had done with a lot of other things in the past."

As we know, Doctor Mystery was wrong. However, he had been warned that an enemy was on his trail.

"It must be Arkabad," he continued. "He is the only one who would spy on me."

He jumped quickly behind a formation of rocks.

"I am going to let him pass me."

But he waited in vain. One, then two minutes, but no one appeared.

"The Devil! He must be tracking me by sight; my movements betray me, and he is waiting for me to move again."

The Doctor considered the situation. Obviously, he did not like it. Finally, he made a decision.

"After all, happen what will! If the final battle must be fought tonight, I'll be ready!"

Jumping out of his hiding place without any further thought, the Doctor started running across the wide fields as fast as an antelope. Soon, a shadow jumped out of a ditch located a few meters away, crossed the road in two leaps, and started quickly on the same path.

The Doctor did not look behind him. He went straight in front of him, scaling the rocks, jumping over some. No one would have recognized in him the perfect and smiling gentleman known as Doctor Mystery.

Like a wild man, he ran without hesitation through the night with the supple quickness of a tiger. Obviously, he had once lived a free life with the wild beasts of the jungle. The spring in his feet, his resistance to fatigue, everything indicated that. He had already run a mile and yet, his breathing remained calm and his skin dry. His steel muscles supported him without effort.

The Doctor had crossed the plains. Now he was climbing the foothills of the mountains above Amritsar. There, a tangled area of boulders and spindly bushes slowed him down; nevertheless, his speed remained prodigious. He was still running as easily as if he were on a road in perfect condition. His eyes could see free passages through which he could slide.

Suddenly, a shadow stood up from behind a bush.

"The Red Queen[92] forbids entry into her territory," chanted the newcomer.

"The Golden Tiger stops for no one," replied the Doctor without showing the least surprise.

And his open hand, stretched out towards the stranger, showed the golden figurine on which a ray of light picked up brilliant sparkles. The man bowed and said:

"Come, O Lord. The Master is at home everywhere on his domain."

But the Doctor didn't take advantage of that permission. He leaned over towards the man and said in a ushed murmur:

"A spy is following me."

"I will stop him."

"It might be Arkabad, the henchman of the Ellora Brahmins."

"I can't strike him without a formal order from the Golden Tiger."

---

[92] Note from Paul d'Ivoi: *Kali.*

"I know. Yet, the time hasn't come for the avenging steel. What I want is for you to detain him for a few minutes so that he will lose my trace."

"You will be obeyed, Lord!"

Without another word, the Doctor continued his run.

A minute had hardly elapsed when Arkabad appeared. It was indeed he, as the Doctor had guessed. The Companion of Shiva and Kali stopped him, saying:

"The Red Queen forbids entry into her territory."

The Brahmin laughed.

"Not to me. I am the high executioner of Ellora."

"The interdiction applies to every man, high or low."

"I must come through!"

"Pardon me, Brahmin, but I cannot disobey the order."

Arkabad ground his teeth. Each passing second added to the advance of the man he had been following. In a menacing tone, he growled:

"Be careful!"

But the Companion remained immobile, his arms held out.

"You can kill me, Brahmin, but I cannot let you through. If you do, the Companions will avenge my death, because you yourself will have broken the treaty between the worshipers of Brahma and those of Shiva and Kali."

Arkabad's hand, which had already grabbed the handle of his sword, dropped. That was true. The murder of a Companion would make the College of Brahmins open to the vengeance of the dreaded Companions. The situation was already complicated enough without creating new problems. He gave in and he said:

"So be it! You will tell your people that I have respected the orders they gave you."

"I will do so, Brahmin."

"Good-bye!"

And the spy went back the way he had come. The fugitive had escaped him, but now, he was certain that the Doctor was, if not affiliated with, but at least in contact with the Companions of Shiva and Kali.

"All right," he said to himself after a moment of silence. "I have only one resource. The Companions of Shiva and Kali are obviously allied to that Doctor Mystery... So I am going to pit the fanatic worshippers of Dheera [93] against him. After all, those people fear nothing, not even the wrath of the gods, and I could also use them against that madwoman, Na-Indra..."

---

[93] Dheera generally means "courageous" and is associated with the worship of the god Hanuman. There follows a couple of paragraphs in which D'Ivoi gives some basically inaccurate information about the Hindu epics, claiming for example that Dheera is Hanuman's mother (whereas it should be Anjana). Rather than trying to correct his mistakes, we have chosen to delete them.

Practicing the rule of the Brahmins, "Divide and Conquer," Arkabad was going to pit the Companions of Shiva and Kali against the Sons of Dheera.

Meanwhile, the Doctor, certain of no longer being followed, was progressing more slowly in the middle of the chaos of stones, which looked like the battlefield of two armies of titans. From time to time, a man came out from behind a boulder, but the Doctor murmured:

"The Golden Tiger!"

His open hand showed the metal figurine, and the guard returned to his hiding place without stopping him.

Thus, he arrived on the plateau, scattered with huge boulders not unlike the standing stones from England and Brittany. He slid between those massive granite stones and came to a giant cromlech.[94] Three men were seated in the center. With a guttural exclamation, they stood up at his approach. He extended his arms vertically, brought them up to his eyes and then crossed them over his chest. And in that last posture, he went to sit down near the unknown strangers, who went back to their places.

There was a long silence, then the Doctor spoke:

"Great is Shiva," he said.

"All freedom comes from him," responded the others.

"From Death comes Life."

"And life has no value except for the free man who has shaken off his yoke."

After those words of acknowledgement, there was a new silence that the Doctor again interrupted:

"Brothers, I am close to Na-Indra, the faithful guardian of the Secret Treasure of Freedom."

A murmur of agreement greeted those words.

"But the enemy is encroaching all around her. Arkabad, the Brahmin from Ellora, has inserted himself among her servants. He is the one who murdered your leader, Dhaliwar."

"Arkabad whom you protected, Master, by telling us to defer our vengeance."

"That is what I still ask of you, because the hour of battle has not yet struck on the clock of infinity."

"Then, what do you want?"

"Two things. I must stay here, in this country, because I must find the Treasure that will make us all independent, but I also want to protect my companions from the dangers that only I should face."

"Yes, Lord."

---

[94] Note from Paul d'Ivoi: *Stone circle.*

"Have one of your people go tomorrow to the caravanserai of Lahore; have him give this paper to my men who have remained there with my magic chariot. Here is a ring that will make Kéradec, their chief, trust him."

He held out to a gold signet ring which bore the head of a tiger and gave it to his listeners. One of them took it, and, with marks of the most profound respect, asked humbly:

"What words should I carry to your friends?"

"These: '*Leave immediately with the Chariot. Go South as far as Multan. There, you will cross into Balochistan and, by way of Quetta, you will reach the city of Kandahar in Afghanistan, where you will wait for me. On the way, you will survey, with the apparatus that you know, the lay of the land. If after three months, I have not returned, open the sealed envelope in compartment 21 and carry out to the letter the instructions that it contains.*'"

The three men repeated word for word the Doctor's orders.

"That's all," continued the Doctor. "My friends will leave Lahore at about four in the afternoon. I want them to take with them Anoor and Cicada, the young boy who is accompanying me. Tomorrow, after lunch, I will go out with them. Stay near the area and I will hand them to you, and you will take them to my chariot. They will likely protest, but do not pay any attention to their recriminations..."

"You will be obeyed."

Then, the Doctor gave a signal. Those present leaned towards him in such a way that their heads touched each other. He talked to them for a long time in a very low voice. Quick shivers crossed their bronzed faces, their dark eyes casting bright looks suddenly veiled by lowered eyelashes. Without any doubt, his words caused great joy in the Companions of Shiva.

The conference came to an end.

The Doctor stood up. He was preparing to return to the dwellings of Na-Indra, when there was a sharp cry in the distance. It sounded like a Heron surprised by a wildcat. Everybody stirred, then remained immobile, waiting. The pause was not very long. Bounding from the behind the rocks, a man, semi-naked, his loincloth soiled with blood, came inside the cromlech.

His breath was halting. Sweat like pearls ran down his torso. Under the pale light of the Moon, it looked like silver streaks, an indication that he had run a long distance very quickly. He stopped three steps away from the Leader, bowed, and standing up again, he looked at the Companions of Shiva, seeming to dare them to question him.

One of the men started to talk:

"I recognize you, Brother Fendit."

"Yes, Lord of Nights.[95] Your eyes are not mistaken."

---

[95] Note from Paul d'Ivoi: *A title given by its members to the Leaders of the Companions of Shiva.*

191

"You seem tired."

"I am tired, O Lord."

"The road was difficult?"

"Difficult and also very long. But my run was, most of all, quick, because I was afraid of arriving too late to meet with you and the Golden Tiger."

The Leader could not help being surprised.

"Who told you that the Golden Tiger was among us?"

"The echoes from the Temple of Nurabad are gossipy, and my ears are open."

"What? You come from the Temple of Nurabad?"

"Yes."

"From the same Temple where fools worship Dheera, who dares defy Great Shiva?"

"The same Temple."

The Doctor, his eyes riveted on those of Fendit, was listening.

"What were you doing in that place?" the Doctor asked him.

"O Son of Vishnu, Master of the Tiger, dear to Shiva, I was watching our enemies. They have increased to the number of three hundred. In order to practice their ridiculous cult, they slaughter victims on the altar of their goddess. These are fanatics who do not work, as we do, at the deliverance of India. I was there to learn the names of those who were going to die, in order to testify if we are accused of these murders."

"Good. Continue."

"You know this. The shapeless statue of Dheera with its crocodile face stands on a pedestal reddened by blood. On the right and the left, two giant bas-reliefs cover the wall. One of them represents the terrible fight of the hero Arna against the giant Lchamsor. The other tells of the death of Typhum, who had kidnapped Miria, daughter of Dheera,[96] who, in order to escape her ravisher, jumped into the waters of the Indus, which closed over her. It is said that the statue of Typhum sometimes comes alive and proclaims oracles when grave events are about to happen. I don't know if that is true, but what I am certain of, is that between it and the wall, there exists an empty space, big enough to hide a man. That is my observation post."

"To the point, Fendit!"

"I was hiding there when a Brahmin from Ellora..."

"Arkabad?"

"That was his name."

"That person came to ask for help from the Sons of Dheera against you."

"Against me?"

"Yes, and against a boy and a young girl who are presently asleep in the palace of Na-Indra."

---

[96] I couldn't identify any of the names mentioned in this paragraph.

The Doctor trembled violently.

"Are they supposed to act tonight?" he asked in a shaking voice.

"No, because the Sons of Dheera will only be gathered together tomorrow."

"Tomorrow!" the Doctor exclaimed with joy. "Then everything is saved. What do they intend to do?"

Fendit moved his arms to the right and left in a sign of ignorance.

"The Brahmin drew the High Priest and the Chief of Sacrifice into a tiny room where no one can go except them; it was impossible for me to hear their words."

"Then how did you find out the time for their gathering?"

"When the High Priest returned, they told those present that Dheera would be asking for their devotion tomorrow."

The courier fell silent.

"Thank you, Fendit. The Golden Tiger will learn of your name and will inscribe it among his favored children," declared the Doctor gravely. "Now, go in peace. The gods are happy with you."

The man prostrated himself, and then in two bounds, jumped outside of the cromlech and disappeared.

Then the Doctor held out his hand toward the Leaders of the Companions of Shiva and said:

"You have heard?"

"Yes, O Lord."

"Let my instructions be followed to the letter."

"They will be."

"Good. The time of freedom is approaching and no obstacle will be able to stop it."

In his turn, the Doctor left the circular enclosure, and started again in the opposite direction—the road that he had taken to get there. Without encountering any obstacles, he eventually returned to the gardens of Na-Indra. He went through them and reached the house. His silk belt was still floating at the corner window. With the nimbleness of an acrobat, he climbed right up to the frame, but just as he was going to jump inside, the end of a revolver was placed against his forehead, while the voice of Cicada spoke this bizarre warning:

"No one can come in. The box office is closed."

"It's me, Cicada," murmured the Doctor, without showing the least emotion.

"Ah! Sorry! Then, please come in and sit down."

The Doctor did not take advantage of that second part of the invitation. He said:

"First, I should clean myself and put my clothes back on, then we will talk. But I don't want to postpone my complements. You imitate the call of the vulture marvelously."

"The call of the vulture?" repeated Cicada stupefied.

Then he remembered and struck his forehead. That cry through the night just as a mysterious spy had started to follow the Doctor... That's what it was!

"Ah!" he said, "so you heard it... But it wasn't me who made it."

"Not you?"

"Of course not. Where do you think I would have gotten the idea to warn you in that fashion?"

The Doctor was no longer listening.

"So that wasn't him..." he said in a monologue. "Anoor perhaps?"

"Anoor? Not a chance! She is sleeping like a little lamb. She has not opened her eyes for an instant."

"Who, then, warned me about the spy?" the Doctor asked. "Who knew of that signal?"

"That," declared Cicada, "I can't tell you, because tried as hard as I could, I couldn't see the person who uttered that cry. I was at the window; I watched you run away. Suddenly, I saw a man getting down and running after you. I was confused. How could I warn you? Suddenly, I heard that cry of the vulture. But there was no one there."

Giving up trying to discover the answer to this puzzle, the Doctor shrugged and went into his bedroom. He soon returned, looking like his old self again. No one would have believed that this elegant man and the wild creature who had run across the hills an hour earlier could be the same person.

He told Cicada about his adventure, omitting, however, to tell him that he intended to separate himself from Anoor and him the next day. That omission kept him from hearing recriminations from the Parisian boy. Cicada laughed at the notion of Fendit hiding himself behind the statue of Typhum in order to spy on the Sons of Dheera.

"You see," concluded the Doctor, "that we have nothing to fear tonight. So, go to bed."

"What about you?"

"I will do the same, and I will sleep well, although there is one thing that still bothers me a great deal."

"What is that?"

"To know who uttered the cry of the vulture came to warn me about the spy."

"I bet that spy must be asking himself the same question."

"Very likely. Everything will eventually be clear, I suppose. Goodnight, Cicada."

"Goodnight, Master."

Like Anoor, Cicada had come to call the Doctor Master.

When Anoor woke up, fresh and rosy after a night of good repose, she found the Doctor and Cicada looking happy, and she did not suspect that her friends had stood watch through most of the night.

CHAPTER II
The Heroism of a Young Girl

Arkabad did not appear in the morning.

Worried about his absence, the Doctor looked throughout the house, asking himself where the Brahmin could be hiding. After the house had been searched, he went down to the park and searched it carefully in every direction. But in vain.

He eventually stopped near the wooden door in front of which Arkabad had, the evening before, given his last instructions to old Garieba. From that spot, he could see the veranda where Anoor and Cicada were playing with Ludovic, and Garieba was slowly waving a great fan of plumes before Na-Indra, stretched out on a chaise lounge.

Absorbed in appearance, he was following all the movements of the servants, with the vain hope that a gesture, a look, would show him a clue about the whereabouts of his enemy. Suddenly, his body was shaken because, behind him, a nasal voice pronounced these words:

"Oh, you, whom Brahma has showered with his blessings, take a portion of what you do not need and let it fall into the hands of a poor fakir, slave to his vow of poverty."

The Doctor turned around.

From the other side of the gate, a man with skin like parchment was bowing in a begging posture.

"Ah! You are a begging fakir?" asked the Doctor.

"Yes, Lord. Vishnu, who takes care of the wise, has given me the strength to reject work, that leads to wealth. Willingly poor, I hold out my hand and only charity enables me to live."

His tone was haughty with pride. He expressed the philosophy of his caste: rejection of all work, glorification of Nirvana.

The Doctor smiled. From his pocket he took a coin and approached the gate. He passed his offering to the fakir, who grabbed it with an eager hand. But while he was bent over, giving the appearance, to any faraway spectator, to be only a poor man expressing his gratitude, his mouth murmured:

"The Companions of Shiva and Kali have carried out your orders. Your friends at the Lahore Caravanserai have been informed. They will leave the city in your magic chariot this evening."

The Doctor had not made a movement. His face had not expressed any surprise. Looking around, he had made sure that there were no indiscreet persons wandering about. He leaned lazily on the gate and replied in similar fashion:

"Good. Tell your Leaders that I am pleased."

"I shall do so, O Lord; but danger still surrounds you."

"I know that."

"Do you know where the Brahmin Arkabad is at this moment?" asked the fakir.

The Doctor, still preoccupied by the Brahmin's absence, paid renewed attention.

"I do not. Can you inform me on that point?"

"Yes."

"Speak, then."

"Arkabad left the villa at dawn. He went to the residence of Governor Farren."

A shadow passed over the Doctor's features.

"Finish," he said.

"He informed him of your presence here. He also told him of your exploits at Ellora, Delhi, and Churu. The Governor has now cabled the Vice-Roy and is waiting for his response before arresting you."

The Doctor bit his lips.

"Should I be forced to flee with Anoor and Cicada, and abandon Na-Indra?"

Still in his humble attitude, the beggar replied:

"Alas, flight is no longer possible."

"Why?"

"The Sons of Dheera have spread throughout the countryside; they're lying in wait behind every bush, rock, tree, their eyes open, watching. All of their attention is focused on this palace. If you only cross the threshold to walk away, the hiss of the Naja serpent will come from every direction and death will follow. Vishnu, of whom you are the Beloved, must make you invisible, since you do not permit the Companions of Shiva and Kali to shed the blood of your enemies."

The fakir stopped talking, and with dragging steps, went away, shaking from his feet the dust of the road. The Doctor's head remained lowered. He was thinking. The situation was perilous indeed. The Sons of Dheera were encircling the palace, rendering any flight impossible. Before the evening, English soldiers would come and arrest him, and do the same to his young friends. If that should happen, Anoor and Na-Indra, without any defense, would fall into the hands of the Brahmins. All that had been planned by that scoundrel, Arkabad, and there was no way to prevent it from happening. It was necessary to become invisible, according to the fakir's suggestion, to go through the circle of spies spread throughout the countryside.

That misfortune could not happen. Certainly, a disguise would be enough to deceive the English soldiers, but the sharper eyes of the Sons of Dheera would not be fooled. Under whatever clothing, they would recognize the targets named by Arkabad.

What was to be done?

Walking slowly, the Doctor returned to the house.

On the veranda, Garieba was still fanning her mistress. Cicada and Anoor, leaning against the balustrade, were talking softly, with bursts of laughter. Ludovic, unleashed, was stretched out, yawning with a bored air. The Doctor casually strolled towards them.

"Doctor!" shouted Cicada, "do you know what Anoor has been saying?"

"No."

"She was looking at the pond down there, behind the cage of the Shiva bears—the pond whose water is hidden by the green leaves of the plants, the Nenuphars and the Nympheas..."

"And," interrupted the young girl, "I saw a dark head lifted above the leaves, and then disappear. An instant later, the high grass which borders the pond became agitated, even though there was no breeze. There was a man there, watching us, and seeing that he had been discovered, he took flight."

"The dreams of a little girl!" Cicada began.

But the joke died in his throat. The Doctor had shaken his head with a worried expression, and from his lips these words fell:

"Anoor was right. She saw correctly."

"What! You believe that...?"

"I believe that we have never been as close to danger as we are right now." Then he added rapidly: "There are things that Anoor, my little daughter, does not know. She is courageous and trusting. She deserves to know everything."

The Doctor drew the pretty girl closer to him. In short phrases, he told her of the events of the night, his morning walk, and the warning of the fakir.

"And now," he concluded, "each minute increases the chances of our enemies striking. We must act, and quickly, but there is a veil over my mind. I am undecided. I cannot settle on a way to escape this trap."

With a touching sadness, he added, while his listeners remained still, their chests contracted by emotion:

"Am I doomed to fail so close to my goal? I had lost all hope about humanity, then fate threw you across my path, my sad convictions, Anoor, my child. Your sweetness, your tenderness, your goodness revived my heart that I had thought dead. You conquered me completely, like all children do, and my desire for your happiness has become my overriding motivation. Is it because of that I now struggle in the darkness without a clear plan? I don't know. But in thinking that I might fail to save you, madness threatens to submerge me. Its steel claws gnaw at my brain."

Tears rolled down his cheeks. Anoor hugged him and said:

"Father, don't cry! There is always a way to escape the wicked."

"A way, you say. But which one?"

She had an adorable smile, and, with heroic indifference, she answered:

"Death, father, which will reunite us eternally in the country of Nirvana"

And Cicada, overcome, stammered in a rush of comic despair.

"And if you go to Nirvana, I will also buy my own ticket... A first-class one-way trip to Nirvana. I don't want to remain all alone at the station."

The Doctor did not answer, but his wet eyes stayed on the young people with a proud look. How he loved them, these young adults whom he had brought together in the furthest reaches of Europe. How they followed him, ready to abandon life to serve him! At the same time, his sadness became more encompassing. His duty to save them became more commanding.

"Garieba, like Tainareïa, daughter of Arçoli, trembling near the pyre of the hero Rama, thirst consumes my lips."[97]

Everybody turned around. It was Na-Indra who had just spoken. The mindless woman continued:

"Crush the ripe lemons in a cup with sugar. Pour in some fresh water and immediately present that drink to my mouth."

---

[97] I couldn't identify any of the names mentioned in this paragraph, except, of course, for Rama, a major deity and the seventh and one of the most popular avatars of Vishnu.

Without hesitation, the old woman put down her fan on a chair and rushed inside the house.

She had hardly disappeared when the Mindless One got up quickly. She went to the Doctor, grabbed his wrists, and, without looking at him, murmured:

"Come." Then, in a more begging tone: "Follow me! To disobey those whose mind floats around the chalice of flowers is to outrage Brahma."

That was a strange comment. Was Na-Indra aware of her condition, or did she merely repeat a sentence she had often heard?

The Doctor didn't have the leisure to solve that riddle. The young girl was drawing him along and he followed her. Cicada, Anoor, and Ludovic did the same. Na-Indra, undoubtedly satisfied by their obedience, had let go of the Doctor's hand.

She was walking with a light and rapid step that contrasted with her usual walk. You would have said that she was hurrying towards a mysterious destination. Eventually, they arrived at the entrance of the underground cellars, crypts dug deeply into the rocks in order to keep the food fresh and the drinks cool.

She went down a stairway, after having repeated:

"Follow me!"

As in all the palaces, the cellars were subdivided into two levels. Na-Indra went through the first one without stopping. Another stairway went to the lower level. She took that one. There were dark corridors, lit from place to place by crisscrossed lanterns. But the Mindless One was undoubtedly familiar with thei place because she went forward without hesitations, without slowing down an instant. Finally, she pushed on a door and went into a cellar shaped in the form of an octagon.

"Why did she take us here?" asked Cicada, noticing that the room had no other exit except for the door that they had just used.

The Doctor shrugged. Having followed a mad woman, he wasn't hoping for anything in particular, but had not wanted to upset the poor child further.

Na-Indra then began a strange dance. She leaned against one of the walls; then took three steps forward, then stopped. She pivoted on her heels to face the wall perpendicular to the one she had just left, then she went back to that wall. Now, her face against the stones, her arm extended in a cross, she passed her hand slowly on the plaster and said:

"Na-Indra, dearest sister, what are you doing?" asked Anoor.

But the Mindless One paid no attention to that prayer. She continued her inexplicable behavior. Suddenly another cry rang out from a distance:

"Na-Indra, beloved mistress, where are you?"

That was Garieba, who had returned to the terrace. She was worried about the disappearance of the young girl whom Arkabad had ordered her to guard.

"The servant is going to rejoin us here," grumbled Cicada.

"Obviously."

"Na-Indra…" Anoor repeated in a begging tone.

But she didn't finish. A noise like that of a badly oiled hinge was heard and under the stupefied looks of all those present, the section connecting the two walls together, the one touched by the Mindless One, slid slowly back, revealing a wide opening.

Then Na-Indra turned around. Her face was transfigured; her eyes were shining.

"Come!" she said. "This way, you will remain invisible to the eyes of the spies of the Brahmin Arkabad."

A veritable howling escaped from the lips of Doctor Mystery, Cicada, and Anoor. All three of them ran forward, eager to question Na-Indra. But she slid through the opening. They entered, following her, pushed a little by Ludovic, who did not want to be left behind.

There was a grinding noise and the stone panel closed behind them. Everyone now stood inside a narrow cave; their outstretched hands touched the walls; opaque shadows surrounded them. Suddenly, there was a faint light in front of them. Na-Indra had just lit a candle of that perfumed wax that is commonly used in Punjab.

With a gesture, she silenced the questions about to erupt:

"Let's not waste any time in useless chatter. The next hours are important. We must start walking... There is no obstacle in front of us."

Obeying her own recommendation, she lifted the rose-colored candle above her head with a gracious gesture and started walking. Her companions were forced to imitate her. The underground passage went forward in a straight line, and the Doctor calculated that it extended well beyond the limits of the property. It certainly went under the countryside, under the rocks, under the massive trees that sheltered the spies of Dheera.

The Mindless One had told the truth; the fugitives had become invisible. The wish of the fakir had come true. Vishnu was permitting the miracle, and to do that—divine irony!—he had inspired a madwoman.

But was she? Yes, she was out of her mind, but at the moment when the wise Doctor Mystery had not known what to do, the light of intelligence had returned in her in order to arrange for their common safety

The Doctor was still mulling those thoughts over in his mind. He followed Na-Indra, who walked with her head high, sliding over the ground without saying a word or looking back at her companions. How long did that underground walk last? Neither he nor his two young friends would have been able to say. But as a guess, they estimated that they had been gone from the palace for about a half hour when Na-Indra stopped at the foot of a granite stairway with steep steps which seemed to go back up to the surface.

The young girl put the candle on a step, and then looked at those who were near her. Finally, she said in a soft voice:

"Before going any further, I will explain to you what might have seemed incomprehensible. Later, we may not be able to talk in total safety."

They all looked at each other, stupefied. Nothing in her showed any traces of madness. Her voice was clear, controlled; intelligence was shining in her big eyes.

"First of all," she continued, "Anoor, my dearest sister, come into my arms so that I can shower you with the kisses that it was forbidden for me to give you under the threat of losing you, while spies were watching everywhere."

Anoor cried out.

"Na-Indra, my sister, you have recovered your mind!"

"I never lost it." Na-Indra replied.

"Never? But when I met you only yesterday..."

"When you met me at the Temple of Gold, I thought I was going to die of happiness. My heart was beating so hard that I thought I was going to die. My head was boiling like a cauldron."

"You recognized me?"

"Your image was ever engraved upon my heart!"

Weeping and laughing, the two-sisters hugged each other. The Doctor and Cicada watched them, stunned by the resurrection of the intelligence that they believed had been lost forever.

After this emotional outburst, the Doctor approached the young girls.

"So was your madness faked?"

Na-Indra laughed happily.

"Yes."

"Why?"

"That's what I want to tell you, but before doing that, let me tell you how grateful I am to you two. You have saved Anoor. the child whom my dying father had given me to protect, and you, Doctor, are the one that the oppressed people of India have been waiting for. From this day, you have one more ally—myself!"

And with touching simplicity, she added:

"This ally may look weak to you, but despite appearances, I can give strength to the warriors of Punjab, and all those of Rajputs who are now under British rule. The Treasure of Freedom exists. I know where my father buried it, and I can lead you to it. In that way, I can be sure of guaranteeing the success of the vast designs that you have dreamed."

The Doctor took her hands.

"Thank you, Na-Indra. Your confidence makes up for all that I have suffered in this land."

She shook her head:

"I am only obeying the wishes of those who no longer live, whose souls wander around our countryside, shivering across our enslaved land."

But suddenly changing her tone, she said:

"I want to tell you about my life. I want you to feel that I am worthy to share your dangers."

There was silence. In the crypt, one could hear nothing but the regular sounds of drops of water falling from the ceiling.

"Ten years ago," Na-Indra began in a dull voice, "all of Brahma's graces fell like a shower of rose petals upon our household. I was seven years-old; Anoor was three years-old... Our father, an honored descendent of the warriors who, in the past, had colonized Punjab, was at the height of his glory. For his courage and his noble character, the people of India, from Sindhi to the Himalayas, had conferred upon him the highest honor by making him the guardian of the Treasure of Freedom. In vain, the Brahmins surrounded him with spies. In vain, they used the most unexpected ruses to get from him information about where he had hidden it. They could learn nothing. The tribute paid by the patriots was brought to our city and was stored in our cellars. From there, it disappeared without leaving any trace, and without the greedy Brahmins being able to guess how. Oh, they tried everything. These wicked people went as far as that supreme cowardice of trying to get a child to spy upon her own father! Yes! I was only seven, but they dared to suggest that I tell them the secret. How did I not let their promises deceive me? I don't know. Undoubtably Brahma had resolved to deliver his faithful from the foreign tyranny and inspired me. I told my father. Then, there was a scene that has dominated all my existence. My father took me in his arms, and said:

" 'Na-Indra, nobody knows the hiding place of the Treasure of Freedom. What you have just told me shows that our enemies are becoming impatient. I feel a threat hanging over my head. I may suddenly die, and yet, someone must return that gold to our patriots at the beginning of their fight so that they can turn it into weapons. Only you can do that. I will deliver the Treasure to you, but remember, child, that the secret may not be revealed to anyone, except the warriors who have revolted against our oppressors. Only to them! And you must die rather than allow the Brahmins to get their hands on it.'

"One does not ordinarily speak like this to children, but did I still have the carefree nature of a child? Each day, I heard stories of the misdeeds of the Brahmins, and of their vain attempts of corruption. My young mind thought about becoming a martyr for the cause of oppressed India..."

" 'You are now seven,' continued my father.

" 'Yes.'

" 'Perhaps soon, you and Anoor will become orphans...' And with a sad smile, he added: 'You are the oldest. You will watch over her. I am leaving her in your care.'

" 'I will take care of my sister,' I promised gravely.

" 'But, dear little one, not even to her will you reveal the secret of the Treasure.'

" 'No, father, not even to her. I swear it upon Brahma.'

"Was there in my voice a power which my father understood? Did he recognize in me that unconquerable stubbornness that later circumstances were going to require me? He didn't reply, but what is certain is that he didn't insist. But the following night, my father entered my bedroom. I was asleep. He woke me.

" 'Come,' he ordered.

"I got up. I threw a shawl over my shoulders. I put my naked feet into my slippers. Dressed this way, I followed him. We went through the house, where everyone was asleep. We went down to the cellars. My father walked in front of me, and eventually, he showed me the secret underground passage through which the patriots of Punjab carried the gold out of the city—that very same passage that has led us to safety."

"But where did they take the gold?" the Doctor asked.

"That, I cannot tell you, because my oath forbids it. My mouth cannot tell the hiding place to anyone."

"Nevertheless, you do trust me?"

"Blindly. So, instead of telling you, I shall take you there, where the accumulated riches are waiting for liberation. But you must wait. Do not insist that I do it right now. Perhaps my scruples are exaggerated? But I have sworn on my life, on my blood, on my rest in Brahma, to never say the words indicating the hidden location of the Treasure, and it seems to me that I would be wrong to speak."

She shook her head gently, and continued:

"In making me take that oath, my father had a hidden motive. He wanted me to never be able to give that information in a careless moment. Speech is quick and it comes out one's mouth dangerously. By conferring upon me the obligation of taking those I trust to the hiding place myself, that wise man gave me the time to reflect upon my decision."

Then, taking up again her story, Na-Indra continued:

"No one suspected our night walk. How did the Brahmins come to guess that my father's secret had been passed on to me? That, I never learned. What is certain is that, a week later, my beloved father disappeared on a trip to the mountains. The truth was only discovered a great deal later. He was taken by ambush by the Brahmins and led to the Temple of Nurabad, situated in the mountainous region of Pind Dadan Khan, between the Jhelum River and the Indus. For five days, he underwent every torture known to man. Hunger, thirst made his throat contract, steel swords glowing red by fire tore into his flesh. On his bleeding wounds they poured boiling sap. After every suffering a Brahmin presented himself, and asked:

" 'Have you decided to give us the Treasure of Freedom?'

"And my father, panting, choking, gathered together his last strength in order to look at his torturer, who was tearing him apart, in the face, and responded in a firm voice:

" 'No!' "

It was with that same fierce energy that Na-Indra was expressing herself now. Her supple form had straightened up and in her dark eyes shone the mystic flame of those who are called to martyrdom.

"That atrocious torture lasted one hundred and twenty hours. Then, Vishnu the Preserver took pity on him and allowed him to enter the realm of death. His heart and flesh were fed to the dogs. His bones were calcinated on a pyre and their dust mingled with the cinders of the wood. As a last profanation, these ashes were then thrown to the wind. The Brahmins did not want those pious hands preserve the tomb of their victim."

She stopped, as if oppressed by those cruel memories. Neither the Doctor nor Cicada found a word to say. Anoor was weeping softly at the sad story by which she had learned of the end of the hero of the Independence of Punjab.

Then, once more, the voice of Na-Indra was heard, dull, stifled, broken by sudden pauses which betrayed the uncontrolled beating of her heart.

"The first part of the drama was finished. After eliminating my father, the self-serving Priests of Brahma believed that they would make fast work of me. I would no longer have any support, any protector against my own weaknesses; that fearless warrior, to whom this implacable duty had been his only joy, was now gone. You know what followed. Constant threats rang in my ears like annoying mosquitoes. As a child, I didn't suspect the cruelty of men who had such a thirst for gold. As I remained silent, they decided to take Anoor."

"Sister, my dear sister!" stammered the young girl as she threw her arms around Na-Indra, then kissed her forehead. But her sister tenderly pushed her away and said:

"Time passes quickly. Let me finish my story," and pointing to the Doctor, she added: "He must be told everything, because he has devoted his life to help the weak and the oppressed."

Her big velvety eyes looked at the Doctor, and with a firm voice, she continued:

"My sister's disappearance tore me apart. If my soul, inspired by the memory of my dear departed father, remained unshakeable, my body was trembling. A high fever forced me to take to my bed, and I was delirious, unconscious. I remained in that state for weeks, in a coma, with vague knowledge of my suffering. That wasn't life, and yet that wasn't death. Then, one day, I woke up without any strength, but also without any fever. My blood was flowing, refreshed, in my veins. The iron circle around my brain had been released, had disappeared. The sickness had been vanquished. I had returned from the dead. It was like coming out from the shadows; my eyes, unaccustomed to seeing, were shocked by the light.

"The sad memories no longer haunted me, and I was enjoying my good health after being reborn into life. Then, the sound of conversations came to my ears, the half-heard voices of those seated at the foot of my bed. A careful glance through my lowered eyelashes let me recognize Garieba, my servant, who was then talking with the Brahmin Aïtar from Ellora, and Lord Farren, the Governor of Lahore.

"What instinct warned me not to talk, not to make any movement? That's impossible to explain. Perhaps Brahma himself, in his supreme wisdom, had decided that this was how it should be in order to work together for the deliverance of his people. This is what I heard:

" 'The doctor has declared that her healing is going well,' said Garieba, 'and that she should recover in three days. Na-Indra will return to consciousness and in a month, six weeks at the most, with her youth aiding her, she will be as strong she was before.'

" 'Six weeks more to wait!' grumbled Lord Farren. 'Six more weeks during which a thief might discover where the Treasure is hidden!'

"The eyes of the Englishman were shining with greed.

" 'So much gold," he continued, "millions sleeping underground, when they could be ours, turned into palaces and pleasures of every type. That is mighty irritating.'

The Brahmin smiled ironically and said:

" 'Bah! Those riches will reappear someday.'

" 'Are you certain?' asked the Lord.

" 'Yes, I am. The father had the courage to endure all the tortures without betraying his secret, but his little daughter will talk. At the first stream of blood flowing over her skin, she will lose her head with fear and obey our very words. She will tell us everything that she knows.'

"In my bed, I trembled. Yes, the Brahmin was right. I was only a child and afraid of suffering. I knew that, in the hands of the torturer, in front of the sinister instruments of torture, I would betray the hope of our patriots.

" 'Ah!' murmured the Governor with a quiet ferocity, 'I would like to see her tortured.'

" 'Don't be impatient,' said the Brahmin. "That desired moment will come soon enough.'

" 'But why wait for her to get well?'

" 'Why, you ask?'

" 'Yes.'

" 'To keep the stupid people in the country at peace, and not provoke one of those insurrections that the British try to avoid at any cost.'"

Melancholy and sad, Na-Indra's voice resonated in the crypt. Under the trembling light of the rose-colored candles, her charming face, to which the remembrance of a past tragedy gave an impressive gravity, enforced by the play of light and shadows, took on superhuman characteristics. She was no longer herself, a young girl, but an incarnation of the agonizing enslavement of India.

The listeners heard without a gesture, without their lips saying a word. What would have been the purpose of interrupting her anyway; what words would have expressed the horror and pity with which their hearts were beating?

She continued softly:

"The response of the Brahmin Aïtar had surprised me. Why had he mentioned the people of the country? A vague hope had just come to me. During a few weeks, I would be protected by an unknown thing. Why would that protection stop? Probably Lord Farren had made a similar reflection because he asked:

" 'Let's see… Let's understand each other…'

" 'It seems to me that we are in agreement,' began the Brahmin.

"But the Englishman interrupted him:

" 'Without a doubt, but I don't see why we should have to wait when there is great interest in bringing that business to a close quickly.'

"That business! That was the way that he used to describe my forthcoming torture!

" 'Ah, my Lord,' said the Brahmin jokingly, 'you don't know the people of your province.'

" 'They have only to obey.'

" 'Yes indeed, but you must take into account their religious scruples. The Vedas are unambiguous.'

" 'The Vedas have nothing to do with Na-Indra!'

"I think," added the young girl, "that Aïtar was making fun of the Governor because his tone was unusual when he explained:

" 'I see that I will have to fill you in, my Lord. Look at old Garieba who is listening to us. You don't have any doubt about her loyalty, I think?'

" 'None certainly.'

" 'Well then, ask her, who betrayed her master, who turned over Anoor to us, who hates Na-Indra, ask her if she wouldn't defend she who is lying there on the bed with her last breath.'

"He pointed out to me.

"The Englishman seemed astonished. He turned around towards my servant, and said dryly:

" 'Explain!'

"And Garieba murmured:

" 'Brahma curses until the furthest generation the family who harms a Mindless One.'

" 'Ah!' exclaimed the Governor, 'I understand now, but how does that affect my plans? Na-Indra is not insane.'

" 'No,' replied the Brahmin, 'but during her sickness, she was delirious. She was for a moment deprived of her reason. That's what all those around her said.'

" 'And now?'

" 'Now? She must go out so that everyone can be sure of the return of her sanity, and that she is completely well. After that, we shall be free to do whatever we like. But if we act before that, we would trigger general reprobation and perhaps a revolt.' And he concluded: 'It would be imprudent to put in motion

206

anything that might create public outrage. Let us not forget that this province is named Punjab, and that the neighboring provinces are Sindh and Rajputana, the birthplace of rebellion…'

"He spoke a long time," continued Na-Indra in a toneless voice, "and implanted in my mind, unknowingly, the resolution which would permit me to keep my secret. No one dared torture a madwoman! Then, I would become one for everybody, in appearance at least. I would stay there, faithful guardian of the Treasure of Freedom, until the day when the clock of Eternal Justice would ring out the blessed hour of freedom.

"That same evening, I pretended to wake up.

"Informed of this, the Brahmin and the Governor came running, but their disillusionment was cruel.

"I uttered incoherent words; I had become the Mindless One! And I played that comedy for nine years."

A silence followed those last words. The Doctor, Cicada, and Anoor had listened with astonishment to that young girl who had had the bold and admirable courage to simulate insanity for so long.

For an instant, the Doctor kneeled. One would have thought that he wanted to kneel in front of that victim of the holy cause of liberty. What suffering, what abnegation, were comparable to that complete forgetfulness of self that Na-Indra had expressed so simply?

She, pensive, finished by saying:

"Now you know my story; only, do not tell it. I still have to pretend to be mindless to protect you, in order to lead you safely where my father has securely hidden the Treasure."

Without leaving her companions the time to answer, she replaced the half-consumed candle and started up the stairway.

"Come," she said, "and be quiet, because now, we are going to walk within the thick walls of an inhabited house."

"Inside a house?" exclaimed Cicada.

"Yes."

"Inhabited by whom?"

"By Lord Farren, Governor of Punjab, and his son Theobald."

The travelers followed her. Na-Indra had taken them from one surprise to another. She was fully sane and had saved them at the exact time when they thought themselves irrevocably lost. And now, she was going to take them to the hiding place where no one would think of looking for them: the very house of their enemy.

CHAPTER III
A Change of Government

"Theobald!"

"Yes, my Lord Governor and father?"

"You sent a telegram...?"

"Just as the Brahmin Arkabad had asked, yes."

"And?"

"I thought that the fifty men sent by the Amritsar garrison should be searching Na-Indra's estate as we speak."

Lord Farren and his son conversed lazily in the sumptuous first floor of their palace. Reclined in wicker armchairs, they looked at the countryside bathed in sunlight while an electric fan provided a soothing breeze over their heads. Above the window, the ceiling went forward, letting only a soft light into the room.

"Who's in command of the search?" asked Farren.

"Captain Roberts."

"A good officer?"

"Excellent, they say."

"He is to arrest those travelers who are bothering Arkabad so much and leave us in peace."

Theobald shrugged.

"An annoying man, that Arkabad."

"Hush!" said the Governor quickly. "The Brahmins are faithful allies of England. Don't say anything bad about them... At least not aloud," he finished softly.

Then the conversation became low, and the two men remained immobile, sleepy, their eyes lost in the distance. They certainly were not aware that, behind them, listening from the secret tunnel built inside their walls, Doctor Mystery and his companions had not lost any of their conversation. A little hole had allowed the fugitives to see and hear what was happening.

After they had moved away, Na-Indra resumed talking:

"The neighborhood must be full of spies from the Sons of Dheera."

"Very likely," replied the Doctor.

"It is then impossible for us to leave. We will have to spend two or three days here, so that Arkabad and his accomplices come to believe that we have left the region."

"Yes, but..."

"I know what you are going to say. I shall answer you. The house where we are now was built by the Begum Reesit, a noble Sindh who was a friend of our family. At that time, our country was in turmoil, so this secret passage was built in order to create a hiding place for our ancestors, as well as for the Begum."

"That's all good," interrupted Cicada, "but if we stay here three more days, we're going to need some food."

"There are other tunnels, just like this one, with trap doors opening into all the rooms. It will be easy to steal what we need without danger."

"Ah! That will be fun! It reminds me of *Pierrot the Thief*."[98]

"Talk lower," commanded the young girl. "The people we are listening to can also hear us."

In fact, the Governor and Theobald had stood up. Leaning forward, they seemed to be listening. Evidently, they had heard something.

"Did you hear something, Theobald?" asked Lord Farren.

"Yes, I thought I heard..."

"Something like a distant conversation?"

"Exactly!"

The Governor sat down again.

---

[98] A popular comedy by Georges Lorin staged in 1876.

"Perhaps one of the gardeners?"

"That's probable," agreed Theobald. "Those fellows laugh about the heat and they chat as comfortably as if they were playing a game of cricket on the banks of the Thames." Then, he added in an engaging air: "Don't you believe, dear Father, that some *refreshment* would do us some good?"

A *refreshment* in India is not what we, in France, would call refreshment. It is a light lunch made up of roast beef, eggs, and smoked fish, served with abundant beer and port.

What they had just said tickled the ears of those unseen listeners in the wall. None of them had eaten, and for Cicada, most of all, hunger was translated into a disturbing impatience.

The eyes of the boy were shining:

"They're about to eat while we..."

He stopped talking because Na-Indra had just put her hand on his arm.

"We will too, but remember to be quiet, please."

At that same instant, Lord Farren told his son:

"My word, Theobald, despite your young age, you often have smart ideas. Please ring the bell. I will enjoy a snack, because, really, this temperature is the most tiring that I could imagine."

The young man took advantage of that permission. A servant, called by the sound of an electric bell, soon brought a large plater on which there were cold cuts, varied *hors d'oeuvres* and bottles of beer.

From his hiding place, Cicada devoured those vittles with his eyes. Na-Indra took his hand and pressed it against the wall.

"Do you feel the angle of the stone here?"

"Yes. It's pressing into my hand."

"Well, in an instant, the Governor and his son are going to get up and go out onto the balcony."

"How do you know that?"

"That doesn't matter. Then, press on that rough edge, a panel of the wall will slide in front of you. Jump out, grab the platter, come back here and close the panel in the same manner as you opened it."

"All right!" said the Parisian boy, still obstinate in his curiosity. "But what if it doesn't move?"

Na-Indra smiled:

"Everything will happen just as I told you."

Then she spoke several words in Hindi to the Doctor, and, sliding into the shadows of the corridor, she disappeared.

Meanwhile, Cicada, his eyes glued to the narrow slit that allowed him to look inside the house, saw the Governor and his son approach the table and look with a bored expression at the different treats stacked on the platter.

"Good," grumbled Theobald, "a slice of beef and curry, will do for me."

The hungry Parisian boy saw him point a fork at the plate where the roast-beef was surrounded by dressing.

But, suddenly, the Englishman made a gesture of indignant surprise. From the garden came a piercing voice, shouting:

"Death to the Brahmins and their English lackeys!"

"What is that?" stammered the Governor.

"What impudent fellow dare shout like this?" exclaimed Theobald.

The voice continued:

"India for the Hindus! The rope for their oppressors!"

Suddenly, father and son, forgetting their gastronomical endeavor, ran to the window and rushed out onto the balcony.

"Quickly," the Doctor ordered. "I recognized Na-Indra's voice. She made up that ruse to distract our enemies."

Cicada needed no other explanation. With one strong push, he pressed on the spot indicated by the young girl and a panel of the wall slid back. It uncovered a rectangular opening.

The way was clear!

In three leaps, the Parisian boy was near the table, but he had miscalculated his jump. He hit the back side of an armchair and fell on the floor, making an infernal racket.

With a quick movement, he got himself upright. Unfortunately, it was too late. Drawn by the noise, Farren, and Theobald burst into the office.

A minute of indecision would mean that the fugitives were lost. If the Governor called his servants, Na-Indra, and Anoor would fall back into the hands of their persecutors. In a flash, those thoughts went through Cicada's mind. At any cost, the English had to be kept from summoning their servants.

Quickly, the Parisian boy ran towards Theobald, and hit him in the middle of his stomach with his head, knocking him to the ground, breathless.

Farren opened his mouth to cry for help, but no sound left his lips. A handkerchief was put roughly over his face and drawn tight.

The Doctor had come out to help his young companion!

In an instant, the two Englishmen were tied up and carried inside the secret tunnel, the wall closing behind them.

"Whew!" exclaimed Cicada. "That was a narrow escape!"

"I am frightened," murmured Anoor, trembling.

Na-Indra, who had come back without making any noise to be near her friends, said sadly:

"This might compromise all our plans."

Everybody looked at her in surprise.

"What do you mean?" asked the Doctor.

She shook her head.

"I mean this: Within the hour, the servants will return to clear away the dishes."

"Obviously."

"Then they will notice the disappearance of the Governor and his son. They will look for them."

"But they won't find them," laughed Cicada.

His joke didn't amuse the girl.

"The Governor of Punjab is a powerful man," she continued. "The news will spread quickly. It will come to the ears of Arkabad."

"So?"

"That unworthy priest of Brahma knows all the tricks of the temples, with their secret passages and moving walls. He will guess how we escaped his trap. We vanished from my palace and an hour later, the Governor disappears from his. Arkabad is cunning. He will connect these two events. From that to the discovery of the truth, it is only one small step."

Everybody frowned. Obviously, Na-Indra was right.

"Are you afraid that he will find this secret passage?" the Doctor asked after a silence.

"No. For that, he would have to tear down my house one stone at a time." And she added with a sad smile: "And the house of a madwoman is sacred."

"Then, why should it matter?"

"For us to flee safely, we need for the Sons of Dheera, who are watching, to leave. But if Arkabad suspects the truth, his spies will remain here, and we will have simply changed prisons."

No one dreamed of challenging Na-Indra's conclusions. So, after having dreamed of escaping safely, were the fugitives now going to be trapped in an even more difficult situation, stopped by even greater difficulties?

Suddenly, Cicada burst out laughing.

"It's just like in the theater," he said.

He laughed even louder. As his friends questioned him with a look, amazed by that explosion of laughter, not justified by their predicament, the young man explained:

"The Governor and his son are prisoners here. Nevertheless, they must be seen to be moving freely in their house. Well, there is a way..."

"A way?" repeated all those present.

"Of course! They do it all the time in the theater. I myself saw it when I was selling peanuts at the Ambigu Theater."

"How?"

"Very simple. We'll take their place."

"But how...? Who...?"

"Just us. You, boss, will be the Governor; and I'll be your son and I'll call you Papa, but in English."

At that fanciful proposition, that Cicada, a true child of the Parisian streets, had announced as if it were the most natural thing in the world, smiles returned to all their faces.

"That's crazy…" began the Doctor.

But the young man did not let him continue.

"Not at all! First, we will put on the clothes of our prisoners. There won't be anything but our faces to betray us. We shall cover these with a veil using the pretext that a swarm of mosquitoes invaded the house and stung us. Then, we would be impossible to identify, am I right or not?"

"On my word," murmured the Doctor, stunned by his young friend's reasoning, "this seems less crazy than it sounded minutes ago."

"There, you see!"

"But what if Arkabad should come?"

"We won't let him in."

"The Governor can't shut his door to him."

"Oh, yes, he can! It's just a matter of knowing how to do it. 'It doesn't matter what's inside the store if the windows look good,' as we say in Paris— and they are right. Consider this: eaten up by mosquitoes, our faces covered behind veils, we will tell them that we have caught a fever and are forced to stay in our rooms. Arkabad, just like everybody else, can't see us. Only one servant will be allowed to see us, one easy to trick, and we will speak to him just enough to carry out indispensable orders."

Since no one else around him was protesting, Cicada exclaimed:

"Then, it's settled! Let's go quickly, get dressed, and eat our lunch. I am starving!"

A moment later, Na-Indra and Anoor, holding hands, withdrew into the shadow of the tunnel.

The Doctor and Cicada swapped their clothes for those of their captives, who did not understand anything that had happened. Finally, ready to play the audacious comedy imagined by the young Parisian, they called back their companions.

"Na-Indra, Anoor," said the Doctor in a grave tone, "guarding the prisoners will be your task. Remember that our existence depends on your vigilance."

They nodded with the same gracious movement.

"They will stay like that, silent and docile, or they will die," stated Na-Indra.

For these two young girls, death was not the terrifying idea that it is in Europe. They could die without complaining and kill without remorse if the existence of those dear to them required it. The Doctor knew this and showed no surprise.

"I am counting on you," he repeated.

Then, making the moveable panel glide again, he went into the Governor's salon, followed by Cicada, enchanted by the idea that his plan had made it all happen.

The first thing the Doctor did was to lock the door.

"Now," he said with sigh of satisfaction, "we are secure. Let's eat."

The food laid out was abundant, so everyone had a share. Even the two prisoners were given a slice of curried beef, which they had expected to eat under different conditions.

Cicada, delighted to have satisfied his hunger, had almost forgotten the nature of their predicament, when someone knocked at the door. Everybody remained fixed where they were. The critical moment had come. They were going to have to put in practice his crazy scheme.

Someone knocked again.

"Who is it?" asked the Doctor in English, raising his voice.

Outside, a respectful voice answered:

"Captain Roberts is back from his expedition to the residence of Na-Indra and wants to report to his Excellency."

"Ah!" murmured, Cicada, "the one who was supposed to arrest us... We've got to see his face."

Carried away by his nature, and because everything about the situation was somehow comical, the young man replied:

"Ask him to wait. I will ring for him."

"Cicada!" whispered the Doctor in a tone of reproach.

"Bah! Sooner or later, we would have had to show ourselves, but don't be upset, we'll wear our masks."

While talking, Cicada looked around. He saw half curtains at the window, pulled them down, took off the gold rods, and then, giving one of the two pieces of cloth to the Doctor, he said:

"Wrap your head in this, and I will do the same."

With rare dexterity, he put it around his head, leaving only a narrow opening around his eyes.

Cicada put so much comedy into that masquerade that the Doctor found it contagious. With a gesture, he ordered Na-Indra to close the entrance to the secret tunnel. After she had, he did the same as the boy. He then unlocked the door and rang the electric bell.

After a minute, heavy steps sounded, striking the floor; the door opened. Captain Roberts appeared on the threshold. Stiff, phlegmatic, extravagantly dressed in his military uniform, he lifted his hand to his colonial helmet, and. with an impeccable military salute, he started to talk in a respectful voice:

"Governor..."

Suddenly, he stopped, out of breath, staring intently. The two people that he saw before him were like strangers. He recognized their clothing, and the insignias marking their ranks, but why were they wearing turbans around their head? They looked like Dutch cheeses that a careful grocer wraps in cheesecloth to protect them from the heat.

The Captain felt like laughing, but realized that any hilarity would be out of place and disrespectful. So, he bit his lips and chewed his mustache, offering Cicada the most amusing sight imaginable.

The Doctor, however, remained impassible.

"You are surprised by our dress, Captain?" he asked, disguising his voice.

The office bowed:

"Well, yes, sir, I am quite astonished... if Your Excellency doesn't mind my saying it..."

"I don't mind at all, and what's more, I'm going to explain it to you. A flight of mosquitos assaulted us, me and my son, and almost disfigured us. That means that we will have a fever for maybe two or three days. We will not receive any visitors during that time... Only the seriousness of the circumstances let us make an exception in your favor."

Once more, Roberts bowed.

"Circumstances are, in fact, serious, sir," he said, becoming grave again at the thought of his failure to locate Na-Indra.

"What do you mean, Captain?"

"That I have failed in the mission you gave me."

The Doctor and Cicada pretended to be surprised.

"Failed? Do you mean to say that the strangers that took refuge in the house of that madwoman have escaped?"

"I'm not saying that, Your Excellency, because I don't know anything about them."

"Why?"

"Because I didn't see anyone there."

The expression on the face of the unfortunate Captain was so confused that Cicada and the Doctor had trouble keeping a straight face.

"Explain yourself," the Doctor managed to say.

"Gladly! On receiving your orders, I left my garrison with twenty-five men. I arrived exactly at noon at the palace of the mindless woman."

"Good."

"The Brahmin Arkabad then joined me and, together, we went into the dwelling where we found all of the servants upset, crying, kneeling, praying to the spirits of the earth, air, and water."

"What had happened?"

"That's what I wondered myself."

"And?"

"An old servant named Garieba, assigned to watch over Na-Indra, told me this: her young mistress had been seated on the terrace with the three strangers who had been designated as suspects. The madwoman asked her to go and get some lemonade. Without arguing, she obeyed. She had hardly been gone five minutes that, when she returned, she discovered that her mistress and the strangers had gone."

The Doctor raised his arms to the Heavens and, with perfectly acted disbelief, said:

"They couldn't have gone very far away, because the borders of the property are watched by people who let no one escape."

"That's what the Brahmin Arkabad said."

"He is right. So, what happened next?"

"We searched the villa, the basement, the park, everywhere..."

"Good."

"But," the Captain added, piteously, "it was all in vain. The fugitives had left no traces anywhere."

"That's impossible!"

"Certainly, sir, their disappearance cannot be explained. The Brahmin then called in some of the men posted throughout from the countryside—men, who, as an aside, seemed to me to be criminals. No one had seen the madwoman or the strangers. Arkabad sent them out in all directions. He hopes that those suspicious fellows will find some trace of them."

With an impeccable attitude, Captain Roberts, charged with a mission which had failed, was waiting for the pseudo-Governor to berate him with the usual reproaches. Certainly, the failure to apprehend the strangers was not his fault, but the mechanics of military command decreed that his chief should give him a reprimand. So, it was with real surprise that he heard the man that he mistook for the Governor say to him in a friendly voice:

"I suppose you did the best you could, Captain. You cannot be blamed for the situation. Take your men back to your garrison. Perhaps you will be more successful another time."

Roberts stammered some thanks that the Doctor interrupted:

"Also, give your men an extra ration of wine and ale; the day has been hard for them. And ask the garrison treasurer to count out a gratuity of twenty pounds sterling for you."

"Ah! Governor!" the officer stammered, very emotional about receiving a gratuity when he had been expecting a disagreeable tongue-lashing.

"Go, and remember that Lord Farren judges the conduct of his subordinates not according to the results, but according to the effort."

Then, in a gentlemanly voice, he added:

"And tell my servants that I am not to be seen by anyone until I feel ready again. I must first repair the damage done to my face by those dreadful mosquitoes."

After a formal military salute, Captain Roberts left the office. When the door closed after him, Cicada reclined in an armchair, his whole body shaken by irresistible hilarity.

"That was the best!" he said. "What a superb idea! A gratuity to the good Captain because he didn't arrest us... That's too funny! And the look on his face... Ah! ah! ah!"

Suddenly, he stood up, ran to relock the door, then went to shout at the wall:

"Mademoiselle Na-Indra, Mademoiselle Anoor, open the panel."

The wall slid back immediately, revealing the two young girls and their prisoners. They were laughing whole-heartedly, while the Englishmen were making faces of anger and stupefaction at the same time.

"Ah!" growled Farren. "I shall not ratify that gratuity to Captain Roberts."

At that statement, the Parisian boy laughed even more, and said:

"If you knew how much I don't care about that, my good Governor!"

The Governor replied:

"I would rather that you didn't speak to me disrespectfully."

"I can't keep myself from doing that because I like you so much."

"And I ask you," continued the Governor, whose rage grew from minute to minute, "to release me at once."

"Not possible. You're not big enough to walk by yourself."

"You won't?"

"Nope."

"Then I'm going to call for help, and you will have to answer before British military justice."

Cicada stopped laughing.

"My fat Englishman," he said calmly, "if you have the bad idea to call for help, I'm going to kill you like a common rat, which will make it impossible for you to testify in front of any type of British tribunal. But if you behave nicely, in three days, you will be free. Choose."

Farren bowed his head. The dilemma posed by Cicada embarrassed him, and then, that devil of a Parisian had a look so fierce, a voice so rude, that it was clear that, at the least resistance, he would execute him.

"All right," the young man continued, "both of you give me your word as officers and gentlemen that for the next three days, you will remain obedient and silent. After that time, you can do whatever you like."

Farren and Theobald still hesitated a little, for appearances' sake, but the gun held by Cicada was a matchless argument. They agreed to their captor's demands.

"There," said Cicada. "Now, we have some time to rest and relax at the expense of England!"

The afternoon went by without any difficulty.

Helped by the young girls, Cicada succeeded in making cardboard masks covered with cloth which fit easily over their faces. Thus, the Doctor and him could easily hide their features if some indiscreet visitor showed up.

The dinner hour finally arrived. The young girls hid inside the tunnel, while the Doctor and Cicada, wearing their masks, called the servants, and had the table set.

However phlegmatic the servants were, they could not hide their astonishment at hearing the menu that the false Governor ordered. The English are generally endowed with a hearty appetite, and Lord Farren was no exception, but never had the gentleman eaten such a quantity of food!

Little did they know that they had six mouths to fill—not two!

The meal went on, however, without incident. The Doctor and his friends, still locked in the salon, saw with satisfaction the evening descend on the countryside. The night meant hours of rest from their worries. Therefore, standing in front of the large open window, everyone was breathing, with delight, the cool evening breeze.

Suddenly, they heard the sounds of a galloping horse.

In their situation, the slightest incident might become important. They listened. The shock of steel on the ground became louder. There was no doubt. A horseman was riding at full speed towards the Governor's residence.

Then, Anoor, Na-Indra, and their companions heard the noise of wooden shoes on the tiles of the Court of Honor, the sounds of a quick conversation, then nothing more.

After one more minute of waiting, there was a knock on the door. The young girls took refuge in the secret tunnel, and the two men put on their masks. It was a servant. On a platter, he was bringing a letter that a messenger had just brought to Lord Farren.

The servant went away and the Doctor again called Na-Indra and Anoor and read aloud the following letter:

Lahore, 6 p.m.
Your Excellency,
Your impeccable memory must still remember the Honorable Jeroboam Sanders, formally a representative in the House of Commons, now a free citizen and local tourist.

It is I, Jeroboam Sanders, who am writing these lines.

Looking forward to seeing you again, you who have done so much in the service of England, to shake your loyal hand, and to meet the noble and charming Theobald, your worthy son and heir, who went away at the tender age of three, I left the soil of virtuous England with my five daughters, one of whom, a treasure of grace and good behavior, has never forgotten the rosy chain of engagement that formerly tied her together with the charming and noble Theobald.

Certainly, I don't doubt the pleasure that the coming of our family, arriving from such a long trip, will bring to you. And if my five delightful daughters accompanied me alone, I would have knocked on your door without warning you, in order to give you the surprise and joy that the appearance of visitors who are worth 500,000 pounds sterling.

But, the pixies of Hymen have assaulted my heart during the crossing, and I have surrendered my freedom to the virtuous Wilhelmina van Stoon, who has increased my household with her own seven daughters.

That would still not be much for me to worry about, because if a friend can open his house to six persons, he can just as well accommodate fourteen. It's only the first invitation that counts.

But there is something else: a strange intellectual heresy afflicting my wife, atrocious and phenomenal, capable of tearing apart your soul if you have not been warned in advance. Wilhelmina is Dutch, Your Excellency, Dutch like the thieving Boers who, in their Transvaal Mountains, dare to resist the troops of our gracious Queen. And despite our affection, she refuses to join in the normal feelings that any English person should feel when I tell her that the world must belong to the English. Then, she protests vehemently. She is a very honorable woman, and yet, remains unretractable on the subject.

Since our troops have entered Bloemfontein, Capital of the Orange Rebellion, she spends her days in constant anger. The least success of the Boers, the robing of a convoy, the seizing of a canon, makes her exult with joy. Lastly, when the newspapers publish the number of our deaths and wounded, do you know what she says to me, instead of weeping for all those cruel losses? She says that the Boers are still about thirty thousand men strong at this time, that the war has just begun, and that Transvaal will be the burial ground of the arrogant English.

Such is the sickness from which my respectable spouse suffers. I wouldn't have wanted to introduce her to you without bringing you this information. That duty fulfilled, since this letter is traveling only two hours ahead of us, I will have the great honor of shaking hands with you this very evening.

Yours truly,

Jeroboam Sanders

After the reading, the Doctor and his friends looked at each other.

So, Sanders, his wife, and his daughters, left inside the aluminum house, were going to arrive at the Governor's residence! It would be impossible to remain incognito in front of that encumbering, curious, and noisy family. What's more, if those angry people recognized the "manager" of the Electric Hotel, many complications were to be feared.

Cicada, translated the thought of everybody when he cried out:

"Why did the stupid soldiers who arrested them not keep them in prison?"

To that question, the answer was simple.

The Lieutenant of the Engineering Corps once kidnapped by the young Parisian had finally returned to Churu after a long and painful march. There, burning with vengeance, he had reported his misadventure, leaving out the details unflattering to himself.

Once told, Ellick and Loo felt themselves invaded by doubt. Could they have put innocent people in jail? Those people who had defended themselves from being either Doctor Mystery or his sailors had perhaps told them the truth.

From that point on, there was a new investigation, followed by more explanations, from which the conclusion were the remarks made by Loo:

"Mrs. Sanders, young ladies, we regret this misadventure, but you must admit that being so thin, so elegant, one might have hesitated to recognize in you the sex to which you rightly belong."

After that, the Sander-van Stoon family was united in freedom. Naturally, Jeroboam had gone to look for the interpreter, the first cause of their tribulations, but that person had disappeared.

It was with some difficulty that the Anglo-Dutch family got back to Delhi, where they learned with consternation that there had been a railway accident on the Lahore line. Cursing and grumbling, they had taken the train after a week's rest, which had been well earned. They had arrived in Lahore, and there, they had hired several cars to take them to Amritsar. Before that, they had sent a courier ahead with the letter.

"What are we going to do?" asked Anoor sadly.

Everybody looked at each other, not daring to answer. Then Na-Indra spoke:

"We must leave this house as quickly as possible."

"But what about the Sons of Dheera, spread throughout the countryside?" said Anoor. "They will recognize us. Arkabad will be warned."

"Yes."

"And we will be attacked by numerous enemies."

Na-Indra shook her head negatively.

"No, they will follow us; they will try to slow us down, but no one will resort to violence."

"Why?"

"Because I am the Mindless One."

"But you're not insane!"

She smiled delightfully.

"They don't know that. Mindless ones are venerated. Whoever causes them harm is made to suffer by divine wrath. I was lucky to escape torture. I still will be, in order to save you and lead you towards to Treasure of Freedom."

Holding her hands to the Doctor and looking into his dark eyes, Na-Indra added:

"Believe me. Trust this frail creature upheld by Brahma in order to help you in your task of liberation."

The Doctor was still hesitating; Na-Indra bowed in front of him:

"I sense it; we will escape from our enemies. The journey will be long, filled with danger, but destiny has reunited us: you who speak about freedom, and I who have had the good fortune to preserve the wealth accumulated for years to fund the supreme fight for independence... From our encounter, there shall be born something fortunate for the cause that we have both embraced."

Then, taking command in some fashion, without anyone objecting, she told the Doctor:

"My friend, call a servant. Give the necessary orders for the Sanders family to be received properly. Tell them that you are sick, not able to appear in front of the ladies. You are indisposed for this evening, but you believe you will offer them explanations and excuses tomorrow."

"Tomorrow?" asked the Doctor.

"Yes, because tomorrow, we will be far away."

With her soft voice and her calm energy, Na-Indra exercised an irresistible influence over her listeners. They felt an overflowing respect for the gracious child, and they themselves now understood something that had been inexplicable until then: the patient courage that had allowed her until she reached maturity to pass for a madwoman for nine years!

Na-Indra was certainly one of these heroic women from Punjab, who, from the height of the terraces of their houses, had followed the ups and downs of the battles in their cities, and who, when fate had turned against them, had not hesitated to plunge a knife in their own bellies, still smiling, leaving only a city full of corpses to their enemies.

While circumstances changed, when Doctor Mystery himself hesitated, Na-Indra remained calm, and considered the dangers without emotion. She knew very well the ruses employed by their foes. She understood that each steep on the journey that followed would be marked by ambush and betrayal. Powerless before her supposed madness, their enemies would attempt the impossible in order to force her to betray herself—to show that she was sane. However, she showed no such emotion now, and her voice kept its monotone in order to repeat:

"Tomorrow, we will be far away."

Far from this shelter that presently guaranteed them us protection against all attacks.

What she had decided was done. The servants received the Doctor's instructions. Locked inside the salon with their two prisoners, that Ludovic never took his eyes off of—it seemed that the little bear had given himself the mission of guarding them—they heard the brouhaha caused by the arrival ot the Sanders-van Stoon family, the sounds of steps, doors opened and closed, laughter indicating the difficulty of installing the tourists. Then, silence returned, little by little. The guests had probably gone to bed. The hour to leave had come.

Farren and Theobald were taken out of the secret tunnel.

"Gentlemen," the Doctor said to them, "I am going to set you free sooner than I thought."

"Ah!" growled with satisfaction father and son.

"But I will need four horses."

The Governor's face clouded over.

"Four?"

"Oh, don't be afraid. This is not a theft. Just say your price for your best mounts and I will pay it immediately."

At the bottom of every good Englishman's heart, there sleeps a business-man. The Doctor's proposition brought back a smile to Farren's lips.

"Fifty pounds for each," he replied after a rapid calculation.

He was asking twice as much as they were worth, because in India, the price of horses was far from reaching the exorbitant amounts that are quoted in Europe. But the Doctor did not to appear to notice.

"Then I owe you two hundred pounds?"

"Exactly."

"Here they are."

The Doctor took out of his billfold and counted ten bank notes that he gave to the Governor. The man examined them carefully, and after making sure of their authenticity, put them in a drawer. After that, he held out his hand to the Doctor and said:

"Deal concluded."

In truth, Lord Farren no longer resented the man who had momentarily taken over his house. At such a price, he would have gladly offered him hospi-tality again, even if he'd been his government's worst enemy. Imagine: two hundred pounds, one hundred for each day of captivity! That was a profit which would have any noble scion of Great Britain fall in love with the notion of enter-taining mysterious strangers.

The Doctor took advantage of his host's good disposition.

"I have a last question."

"Speak, honorable gentleman."

Farren bit his lips. In his satisfaction, he had perhaps gone slightly over-board, but the Doctor did not take advantage of his confusion.

"We are going to leave this room and leave you alone. I ask you to give me your word that you will not cry out or try to cross the threshold for forty-five minutes."

"What if we refuse?" asked Theobald, trying to regain some dignity.

"In that case," the Doctor calmly explained, "for our safety, I shall have to insure your discretion."

"Meaning?"

"That the dead are the most discreet of people."

The two Englishmen felt a little shiver go down their spine, and the Gover-nor, not without some sweating, stammered:

"After forty-five minutes have gone by, we will be free to do whatever we like?"

"Absolutely."

"Then you have my word."

"And mine," Theobald finished.

"Good."

The Doctor put his hand on the shoulder of Cicada, who had been listening intently, and said:

"Go down to the stables, child, saddle four horses and bring them to the courtyard."

In one leap, Cicada ran out.

Then the Doctor approached the girls and talked to them in a low voice.

"Go wait for me in the next room."

They both obeyed without asking for an explanation.

Remaining alone, facing his prisoners, the Doctor placed his hand on the handle of the revolver he kept in its holster.

"One last formality, Gentlemen. Please take off the clothes we loaned you in exchange for ours and put them in a package. We'll keep your uniforms which may come in handy in order to leave your house safely."

His accent was so clear, his gesture so expressive, that the Englishmen didn't even think of resisting. The father and his son began to disrobe.

CHAPTER IV
Despondent Maud

Jeroboam Sanders, Wilhelmina van Stoon, and their dozen charming daughters had been disagreeably impressed upon their arrival. Neither Lord Farren, nor Theobald, were there to receive them. If we know the cause of their absence, the newcomers did not. Wilhelmina had taken advantage of that opportunity to launch herself into a full charge against British manners. Then, she had continued with an exposé contrasting the former with the perfect Dutch customs, which made Jeroboam angry. The inevitable discussion about the war in the Transvaal had begun again, with him declaring that the British troops would soon be in Pretoria, and she holding onto the fact that no Englishman would ever come in sight of the capital. In short, everybody had gone to bed in a bad humor.

The girls, gathered together in three bedrooms transformed into a dormitory, had followed the rules set down by the ex-widow van Stoon: they had carefully brushed their hair and put on long night shirts, which made them look like angels without their wings. But instead of going to bed, they had gathered around Maud, who was truly melancholy and mournful.

Gentle Maud had been more affected than anyone by the cold reception at the Governor's mansion. How could she have crossed the Mediterranean Sea, the Red Sea, the Indian Ocean, and the Ganges Valley, with her sisters and stepsisters, telling them:

"My fiancée, to whom my heart has been bound since age three, surely has some friends who are also of marriageable age. That means that marriage *en masse* will be available for all of us."

And yet, her fiancé had not been there to welcome her!

"But, Maud," the other girls repeated to her, "he's been devoured by mosquitoes. He is afraid to see you when he is so ugly. There's nothing wrong about that."

She shook her head stubbornly. The pretty blonde girl was being totally stubborn. She even went so far as to claim that, in such a case, she would have shown herself without hesitation. All the other young women affirmed that she was being unreasonable. What young girl would consent to show herself to her fiancé without hesitation with a face ravaged by the poison of the mosquitoes?

Therefore, she sat in the middle of her sisters, in front of a window which allowed her to look at the Court of Honor outside.

Suddenly, she put her head out and noticed something below.

"Horses!" she said. "Who could go out at such an hour?"

Soon, there were a dozen curious heads, grouped like a bouquet of youthful faces behind the windows.

Maud had not been mistaken. Four saddled horses, held in the hands of some person obscured by them, were stamping on the stones of the courtyard.

"She's right!" exclaimed Frijfine. "Is it true that one goes out at night like that in this country?"

"It could happen," replied another girl. "Look! Unless I'm mistaken, two of those horses are going to be ridden by ladies."

Maud was shaken with a tremor.

"Ladies?"

"Look for yourself."

"Why, that's true."

And, in fact, the observation was correct.

In the group of young ladies, there was a heavy silence. Lord Farren was, as the English say, in a state of widowhood; his son, Theobald, was in a state of celibacy. How could some persons of the weaker sex find themselves in their house and mysteriously leave it in the middle of the night?

"I think I understand," said one of the Dutch girls seriously.

Every look converged on her.

"You do?"

"Yes. I listened to the stories that our worthy mother told us about the customs of Sumatra."

"So?"

"It must be the same here."

"The same what?"

"I shall explain."

Meanwhile, Maud had said nothing. She remained silent, her forehead pressed against the glass window, absorbed by the view of the horses, whose elegant form were shown as dark silhouettes against the white background of the courtyard.

"In Malaysia and Java," continued the other girl, "a Westerner who desires to marry a native woman goes to see her parents and shower them with gifts."

"That's the same everywhere," interrupted Anneke, "even in Holland."

"Wait! The next day, the intended bride goes with her family to the home of her future family. She and her parents spend the day looking at the accommodations. Then, during the evening, at dinner, the woman is asked if she consents or not to the proposed union, and she replies that she can't because she cherishes her parents too much and can't leave them, unless forced to. All that, my dear sisters, is not a refusal; it is simply a necessary ceremony..."

"Go on!"

"Then the parents pretend to be angry. They lock the girl in a room, telling her that she will obey willingly or by force the will of her family, who has negotiated the most honorable and advantageous of marriages for her. Then, in the middle of the night, the mother, as if overcome with pity, comes to free her. Two horses are ready. The two women jump in a saddle and leave at a gallop. But the father and the fiancé, who have been spying on them, also jump on fast horses and pursue the fugitives. A frenetic chase takes place in the countryside. At the end, the girl lets herself be caught and the marriage can then take place, because all the conventions established by their ancestors have been respected."

Maud let out a long sigh and, in a voice that seemed to come from a cave, said:

"Then, are you saying that my Theobald, taking back his word given in the past, would be about to marry a native woman?"

"Alas, I fear so."

Maud hid her face in her hands:

"What humiliation!"

Sisters and sisters-in-law rushed over to console her. But suddenly, resounding steps were heard in the courtyard. They all ran to the windows and watched.

The two women, each mounted on a horse, were crossing the gate. A couple of yards behind them, two horsemen were following them. They were clothed in white, and on their sleeves, as light and clear as the Moon, were recognizable insignia.

"The Governor!" shouted eleven angry voices.

"Captain Theobald!" shouted Maud.

She fell back onto her seat, without any strength. There was no longer any doubt in their minds; they had watched a ceremony like that mentioned a moment before. The very evening of the arrival of his British fiancée, Theobald had chosen someone else to marry—and worse, a native woman!

227

Tears, cries, maledictions, all that a wounded ego could inspire in a spurned young woman, Maud sadly presented to her sisters. It didn't take less than thirty-five minutes for her to regain control. She then became calm and, after a quick discussion, the twelve Sanders-van Stoon heirs decided to take a well-earned rest.

However, a terrible racket made them put off that wise resolution again. Electric bells rang. There were many angry and frightened shouts. Heavy steps shook the floorboards. The girls thought there was a surprise invasion, a natives' revolt, or an attack from an enemy army.

Following the wise instinct of well-brought-up young ladies, they immediately looked for the protection of their venerable parents. They rushed towards the door in a tumultuous herd, and opened it... and were thrown backward, letting out, as a choir, a shocked exclamation.

In a neighboring room, they had seen two men dressed only in their underwear, shouting loudly in the midst of an army servants who stood transfixed.

The 45 minutes delay was over, and Lord Farren, and Theobald were trying in the coarsest language to send their servants after the fugitives.

A well-bred English girl could never tolerate such a breach in good behavior and this is how that unforgettable night had broken forever the marriage contract for which Jeroboam Sanders had traveled 3,500 leagues.

It was true, however, that the former Member of Parliament had himself married during that journey and didn't find himself any happier because of that. Such are the games of luck and the system of compensation designed by Fate.

Meanwhile, Doctor Mystery and his three companions galloped across the countryside. Cramped in the front part of Cicada's saddle, Ludovic raised his head in order to see in the distance between the ears of the horse running at full speed. Two or three times, the little plantigrade growled, which made his master scold him. However, the animal was, in his own way, signaling danger.

If the horsemen had thought of looking behind them, they would have seen some human shadows rise up from behind the bushes they had passed an instant earlier. Those dark silhouettes started running among the bushes, all of them going towards the north.

And the Doctor and Na-Indra would have recognized the savage followers of Dheera, to whom the Brahmin Arkabad had entrusted the task of watching over the region of Amritsar. But had these spies been deceived by the disguises of Cicada and the Doctor? The Sons of Dheera were silent and no sound betrayed their rapid dash in the night.

The fugitives, still running in the shadows, soon recognized the town of Bhera.[99] On a wooden bridge, they crossed the Jhelu River, which, sixty miles to the south, brought the tribute of its water to the Indus.

They traveled through the little populated districts located between the Jhelu and the Indus. There, rocky hills and thick woods forced them to make constant detours.

At dawn, their horses exhausted, they stopped some hundred meters from the village of Tsilahan.[100] Perched on a high escarpment, like the nest of an eagle, Tsilahan was surrounded by a crenelated enclosure. Some massive towers could be seen in the distance. Their dark mass gave away the hiding place of this fortress charged with stopping invaders which had come by way of the valley of the Indus, a large pathway designed by nature to facilitate invasions from the faraway mountains of Afghanistan.

After two more days of riding, the Doctor and his friends crossed the Afghan border. Without a doubt, the wrath of the Brahmins could still follow them beyond said frontier, but at least they wouldn't have to fear the English police and soldiers any longer. [101]

Thinking that, they forgot how tired they were. A smile lit up their faces, and, filled with new hope, their eyes became fixed on the western horizon, behind which lay he free land of the Afghans.

But, for the moment, it was a matter of giving the horses a well-deserved rest, as well as allowing the travelers a few hours of sleep. The girls, despite their courage, felt themselves broken by the rapid race, after a day of agony. So, taking after their mounts, which were running with sweat, everybody gravitated with slow steps to the sinuous road leading to the village. Already, the inhabitants were moving about. Men, women, children, were busy extracting the mineral copper which abounded in that place. Taking advantage of that natural resource was very simple. In the rock, open to the sky, they set up a furnace. The explosion produced pieces of copper rock that were then collected, and carts carried them to Valliyur, where a private rail line carried them to the station at Rawalpindi.[102]

Poor but generous, the inhabitants of Tsilahan greeted the newcomers with hospitality. The *Adji*, or head of the village, received them in his own home.

---

[99] While Amritsar is about 30 miles east of Lahore, Bhera is 100 miles west of Lahore. This seems rather complicated a journey.

[100] There are many fortified towns between Islamabad and Kabul, where this is obviously taking place, but none have names remotely close to "Tsilahan."

[101] The distance from Bhera to the Afghan border is about 230 miles.

[102] Rawalpindi station was opened in 1881 during construction of the Punjab Northern State Railway which began in 1870. The route was first surveyed in 1857 and aimed to connect Lahore with Peshawar. There is a Valliyur (or Vallioor) in Southern India but I couldn't find one in Pakistan.

Some millet cakes, honey, and fruits allowed them to lessen their hunger. After which, their host said goodnight and returned to work, leaving them masters of his house.

Na-Indra and Anoor threw themself immediately on the mattresses set up for them. Soon, their two companions did the same. Hours of sleep went by without the fugitives being aware of it. Only at the end of the day, did they pull out of the unconsciousness in which their extreme lassitude had plunged them.

They felt themselves rested, ready to continue the journey towards freedom. Big basins filled with water had been placed near their couches and they all used them to freshen up with great pleasure. Refreshed, they thought of taking leave of their host, but on the threshold, an unpleasant surprise was waiting for them.

The *Adji* stood there. He had changed from his ordinary clothes into his ceremonial attire. On his embroidered silk shirt, he wore his ammunition shoulder-strap. Seeing the fugitives, he bowed ceremoniously, and said:

"Greetings, Brother."

After the Doctor had answered with the same greeting, Adji continued:

"You are my guests. Under my roof, you are sacred, as are those who accompany you."

The tone of his voice bothered the Doctor.

"Why those words, *Adji*?"

The man smiled with embarrassment.

"It is the duty of the master of the house to warn his guests of the dangers which threaten them."

"Is there, then, any danger?"

"Perhaps."

There was silence. Anoor had approached quickly. As for Na-Indra, she had again taken on her distracted expression and seemed to pay no attention to the conversation.

After a pause, the Doctor asked again:

"What danger are you talking about?"

"The most dreadful of all."

"Please explain yourself more clearly."

"I will. The Brahmins are angry at you."

The Doctor shook his head. The Brahmins! Had their enemies picked up their trail? So it was with a heavy voice that he asked:

"Which of the Brahmins said that?"

"Arkabad of Ellora."

Arkabad! So, it was true. The miserable scoundrel had managed to track down his prey. However, the Doctor did not lose his confidence. He raised his head, and asked:

"Don't hide anything from me. What happened?"

The *Adji* looked straight at him, spread out his hands and slowly replied:

"I came back here to take a nap, at the hour when the sun's heat is such that believers wonder why the gods bothered to create Hell. You and your companions were sleeping. Certain that you didn't need anything, I was going to take my nap when Arkabad arrived, followed by several men who wore ornate emblems on their turbans. I recognized them as the Sons of Dheera..."

"I see4. Please continue," said the Doctor.

"Their horses were white with lather," said the *Adji*. "They must have galloped a long way.

" 'You are the *Adji* of Tsilahan,' the Brahmin said to me, 'and you are giving hospitality to the travelers who arrived this morning.'

"As I hesitated to answer, he continued:

" 'There are four of them. A gown man, two girls and a boy who has a Bear of Shiva on a leash.'

"Hearing him, I understood that he was well informed.

" 'That is true," I replied. 'Those are my guests.'

" 'You are going to turn them over to me,' he said haughtily.

"I shook my head to say no; I said: 'These are doubly protected; first, as guests, and also because one of the girls appears to be devoid of reason.'"

Here, the Doctor rapidly glanced at Na-Indra. She stood there, apparently indifferent, playing with the sequins embroidered on her clothing. Was the trial that she had predicted the evening before, in the mysterious tunnels dug under her palace, going to take place now? Would she be able to simulate madness in order to protect her friends?

"What did Arkabad reply?" asked the Doctor.

"He said this: '*Adji*, you are mistaken. She is not mindless. It is a role she is playing in order to keep those wicked people away from my wrath.' But I duid not yield despite his words."

"You were right, because—alas!—she is deprived of her mind," the Doctor confirmed.

"I believe so," the *Adji* agreed. "Then the Brahmin became angry, threatening. I limited myself to telling him the decree of Brahma, requesting men to honor the Mindless Ones under pain of incurring the god's anger. Then Arkabad was placated.

" 'You are right,' he said, 'but you won't refuse me the right to prove to you that that girl is not insane, as you believe her to be. My followers shall, remain in your village. You will take your guests and I, escorted by as many warriors as you desire, to the place where I can provide proof of what I say. If I am telling the truth, you will turn those guilty or afraid over to me. If not, they will be free to leave.'"

The Doctor was listening, his brow furrowed. Just a while before, he had feared this. What scheme had Arkabad devised to lead Na-Indra to betray herself?

Again, he looked at the young girl. She didn't seem to be aware of what was going on. Now, she gracefully lifted her long tunic and took a dancing step as if her mind was haunted by some long-lost vision.

However, it was necessary to respond. In an instant, the Doctor saw the situation. To refuse to submit to this test was to admit that Arkabad had told the truth, to condemn themselves to live as guests, prisoners in the house of the *Adji*. On the other hand, to accept the challenge of the Brahmin was full of danger. What devilish plan had he conceived? Could Na-Indra, a frail young girl, undo the schemes of her enemy? He hesitated.

Suddenly, Anoor's sister let out a little cry. She crossed the threshold, seeming to follow an invisible shape created by her imagination. She went towards the door opening onto the public square. The Doctor made a concerned gesture. It was clear that Na-Indra had chosen to accept the challenge. There was no longer enough time to step back; so, affirming her voice, he said:

"Lead us, O *Adji*. I have confidence in you."

A quarter of an hour later, escorted by fifty soldiers bearing arms, the travelers, Arkabad, and the *Adji*, left the village and started out towards one of the miners' sites, located not too far away. At Cicada's request, the horses, held by four young men, were following them, fully saddled. On the young man's horse sat Ludovic, his snout partly open. Looking closer, one might have believed the bear was laughing. Perhaps that was true. What human could ever know what thoughts dwelled in the mind of animals?

The Doctor had taken Na-Indra's arm. He seemed to be guiding the steps of the madwoman. She let him do it, but, with her incredible strength of wil, she kept her astonished look with barely any expression on her face. As close as he was, Arkabad scrutinized her visage, hoping to see the light of reason in her eyes, which would demonstrate the truth of his statements, but in vain; he saw nothing. In every way, the young girl did seem mindless.

The Doctor felt his worries diminish. He felt his respect for Na-Indra increase. He admired her energy. His mind went backward, thinking about the long years of fake dementia she had had to endure under the wicked eyes of the spies of the Brahmin and the British authorities. An almost mystic perception of her grew in his soul. Na-Indra assumed the role of the divine incarnation of Freedom, of that saintly cause for which both would suffer. In the hours of crisis, when nations are torn between life and death, destiny, wanting to inflame the hearts of warriors, to lift them to the level of the willing and necessary sacrifices required of them, brings forward such women which exalt the virtues of devotion. They seem frail, pretty, created only for love, smiling at worldly reunions, concentrating on their mundane tasks, but once inspired, the burst into existence suddenly. Their lips let flow out the music of their voices, the poetry of their thoughts, and at their call, the people rise up to throw off the oppressors, or give their gold, their very blood, in order to make grow the most beautiful of all flowers, the flower of liberty.

Na-Indra, walking with a peaceful expression, unconcerned, putting on her face the mark of insanity, created a moral dilemma for the Doctor. He had the impression that her pure forehead was surrounded by a halo of light. She appeared to him like one of those pure inspired virgins who, at the hour of liberation, guide enslaved peoples towards their independence, as if in their young bodies was enclosed a star of rare clarity snatched from the very Heavens.

Anoor, herself, was walking next to Cicada.

"My friend," she said suddenly, as if continuing an interior monologue, "I don't want to ever become Arkabad's slave again."

The Parisian boy shivered. He had just thought about that. He was trying to find a way to snatch his gentle companion from the jaws of the Brahmin. Here was something strange: she was answering his unvoiced thoughts.

"Neither do I," he said. "I don't want him to take you captive, to make a victim of you. But I have become a stupid as a sardine, because I can't seem to find a way to prevent it."

Despite the colorful turn of phrase, a very real emotion resonated in his voice. Anoor smiled with melancholy.

"I found one myself."

"You?"

"Yes."

"You have the spirit of an angel!"

The little girl shook her head.

"Oh! Don't praise me yet! I have found something that you would never have thought of—a desperate mean, nothing more."

Cicada, thoughtful, vaguely guessed what she was going to say and bowed his head. A silence followed and she repeated slowly:

"When life is too cruel, Brahma allows one to search for a refuge in annihilation."

"To die! You?"

"To be free," Anoor corrected. "To choose death, and the hand which must grant it, is a joy."

She looked toward the Heavens as if to take them as her witness; softly, she continued:

"Thus I require a promise from you."

"From me?"

"Yes. Over there, in your country, you saved my life. Here, you have faced a thousand dangers to reunite me with my beloved sister, Na-Indra. I belong to you, since I would not exist if it were not for you. But you also belong to me, because you couldn't abandon me without ceasing to be yourself."

"Oh! Mademoiselle," stammered Cicada.

She interrupted him:

"Coming from you, death will seem to me like a friend. Promise, then, that if our enemy triumphs..."

"I can't promise you that! I would never have the courage..."

"Would you prefer that he takes me away in chains, and that he tortures me in a thousand ways?"

A wave of blood rushed to the pale cheeks of the Parisian boy, and, with an angry tone, he replied:

"I understand! And I agree: I will kill you..."

"Thank you."

But then he added in a heart-rending fashion:

"And then, I'll kill myself afterwards. "Like that, we will continue together on our journey, except that we will have changed trains."

Tears welled up in Anoor's eyes, but she held them back and held out her hand to Cicada. He took it and did not let it go. Their fingers interlaced, they walked side by side without looking at each other, without speaking. What would they have said? Didn't they know, those sad children, that the thoughts of one were completed by the other's?

Meanwhile, the *Adji* and his warriors were descending the steep slopes of the hill, upon which the walls of Tsilahan had been erected. They came down into a narrow valley, whose rocks showed that the extraction of copper was in full activity. On the walls, caressed by the rays of the oblique sun, there were sparks of light. That was the raw copper uncovered by the work of the miners.

Everywhere, there were excavations, boulders, broken tools, crushed bushes, calcinated trees. Through its gashes, opened like sad mouths, the mountain seemed ready to weep because of the suffering imposed on it by the greed of men. And in that chaos, a great and sad field of industry, Arkabad, at the head of the little troop, advanced with a firm step.

Going around the obstacles, making a path across the undergrowth, he was walking without hesitation. To watch him, one could see that he had reconnoitered the land with some care before the battle. The Doctor's heart tightened at that realization. To what trial, set up by the perfidious Brahmin, was Na-Indra going to have to submit?

Arkabad finally stopped in front of an enormous block-shaped rock, which was like a promontory located at the highest point of the valley. On one of its sides, there was cut-out a space like a square opening. Arkabad pointed to it with a gesture:

"*Adji*, do you recognize this?"

"Yes, it's a mine," answered the chief of the village.

"Inside are two hundred pounds of gunpowder."

"As much as that?" murmured the Adji, surprised. "That entire stone block will be pulverized"

At that answer, the Brahmin gave Na-Indra a cruel look.

"Yes, that rock will be pulverized," he said, then adding: "And whoever remains close to that explosion will be in danger of death."[103]

"True. The danger will indeed be great. But I don't see the connection between that mine and the reason why you brought us here."

Arkabad had a loud burst of laughter:

"You will understand in a minute."

With a speed that proved that the villain was well prepared, he lit a match and brought it close to the wick.

"I am going to light this wick, and whoever can do so must now run to save himself."

He lit the wick and followed his example by running as fast as his legs could carry him, giving the signal for a general flight.

Cicada, one of the first to run away, lead Anoor away, but fifty feet away, the young girl pulled loose and went back.

"Look!" she said.

Cicada obeyed and remained stupefied, thunderstruck.

The Doctor and Na-Indra were standing immobile in the same place that they had occupied a moment before. The Doctor's first impulsion had been to jump towards the young girl, to move her quickly away from the explosion that was going to vomit a burst of flame, and a machine gun-like protection of rocks; but she had stopped him by these simple words:

"If I save myself, he will say that I am not insane."

In the space of a lightning bolt, the Doctor had understood Arkabad's devilish plan. The Brahmin, sensing the truth, had hoped to scare the young girl. He was thinking that, by obeying her instinct of self-preservation, she would start running. Then he could be sure of her sanity. If she understood the danger and ran to safety, her insanity was not real.

Without hesitation, with that strange clarity of mind that long practice and that the war of ruses had given her, Na-Indra had seen through her enemy's scheme. Now, she remained there, beside the mine, which was ready to explode, braving death to keep her secret.

An enormous admiration filled the Doctor's soul. A wave of words mounted to his lips without his being able to say them. The most he managed to do, with an immense effort, was to mutter:

"If you are staying, then so I am."

The cheeks of the young girl became like a rose-colored cloud. For an instant, her eyes lost her haggard expression, and fixed themselves with tender

---

[103] Note from Paul d'Ivoi: *A mine consists of two main parts: the chamber or furnace where the explosive material is stored; and the powder magazine which contains the stuffing and the wick that goes outside. Nowadays, the wick is replaced by an electrical circuit.*

gratitude on the man, unknown to her only three days before, who now was prepared to die with her.

Then, all traces of emotion went away. She looked at the fuse that was burning slowly. The outside part was going—gone.

Inside the chimney, like a fiery mosquito, the burning section went further, still sizzling.

A moment of horrible anxiety went by. Then, like the end of a bad dream, she heard these words articulated near her:

"You can see that Brahma himself has taken away her mind. She must be freed, along with her companions."

"Yes, *Adji*, I see that it is how it seems," replied Arkabad between gritted teeth.

The Doctor threw a surprised look around him. The *Adji*, Arkabad, and the warriors had again approached without their hearing them. The Brahmin was somber. A dull anger burned in his black eyes. The Doctor then guessed the truth: the mine inside the rock didn't exist. It was a fake designed by the cunning Brahmin who had counted on surprise and fear to make his victim expose herself. But he didn't have time for longer reflections. The *Adji* energetically shook his hand, saying:

"I am glad that my guests can continue their journey in freedom, under the protection of Brahma. Your horses are ready, so you may leave. I, whose house sheltered you, make vows for your good fortune."

He was sincere, and his whole body expressed his satisfaction. His guests were saved, and the representative of those Brahmins whom everyone secretly hated, had been defeated.

The Doctor and the *Adji* hugged each other. Then, he helped the young girls get into their saddles. He, himself, jumped on his horse. Cicada did the same.

"Good-bye," said the Doctor, waving his hand.

"Good-bye, indeed," replied the *Adji*, smiling.

And the Doctor added:

"Maybe soon."

Then he spurred his mount. Followed by his companions, he rode down the winding valley road. A rocky premonitory soon hid the group. Then he stood up on the stirrups and shouted:

"Start galloping! Our safety depends on how fast we flee!"

The four horses, spurred by their riders, bounded ahead and a dizzy ride began. The hooves hit the rocky ground, making sparks spray out. Their mane floated behind them like wings. Leaning over the shoulder of their mounts, their faces struck by the wind, Na-Indra, Cicada, Anoor, and the Doctor rode westward. It was the frantic riding of those pursued by death.

CHAPTER V
The Ferryman

The banks of the Indus River west of Rawalpindi were a magnificent and wild country.

On the left bank, there was a large plain, dotted with low bushes. On the right bank, there was a thick forest that the people of the country called the Balochistan Forest.[104] On that side, the banks were steep, with ravines. The ground had collapsed in some places, leaving some reddish gashes. They looked like streams of blood flowing under the dark green of the trees. The river itself, running over the last slopes of the Afghan Mountains, far cousins of the snowy hells of Pamir, rolled in violent, tumultuous waves, on which the foam looked like great, dead seagulls.

That was the preferred refuge for the Sons of Dheera. It was there that the bloody religion has been founded by the Baloch Armin Log. That fanatic who

---

[104] Considering that Balochistan is located about 700 miles to the south of Rawalpindi, this would make sense if our travelers were going towards Kandahar as opposed to westward towards Kabul. The juniper forests of Balochistan are some of the largest and oldest in the world. According to a report submitted in April 2016 at UNESCO by Pakistan's Directorate General of Archaeology, they are spread over nearly 110,000 hectares.

had refuge in the forest to which he gave its name,[105] claimed to have been favored by an appearance of the Goddess Dheera.

"Kill," she would have told him; "Death pleases me."

And the fanatics killed... In five years, they had slaughtered eleven thousand people: men, women, and infants. Everything is larger than life in India, even assassination. In our more temperate countries, those monsters would have passed for insane.

In Hindustan, where the sun seems made of fire and causes brains to boil. Aramin was made divine. He became the head of the school of a religion whose dedicated goal was murder. There were no Holy Books, no morality principles, just a single imperative, unique and disconcerting:

"Kill!"

Tigers must have shared a similar faith. It was the creed of wild animals. Now, in that place the river cut through the road from Jhelum to Kohat, the last town before the Afghan border. A ferryman had set up business there and, on a little motorized boat, carried the infrequent travelers and their merchandise across. Gakan was his name.

Now, the morning of the day when the Doctor and his friend were still asleep under the roof of the *Adji* of Tsilahan, Gakan had carried two travelers, one of whom was a woman. She was pretty and strong. She had dark hair, big eyes, white teeth, and a tanned complexion. All those attributes, taken together, made her very pleasant to look at. That charming woman had taken evident pleasure in crossing that difficult river.

The feeling of her companion, a young, frail, pale man, had been different. And the great "whew!" that he had not been able to hold back when putting his foot back on the bank, told a great deal about how much he feared being in a boat.

A small bag, with a portable tent, which each one carried, was their only luggage. Once back on solid ground, the young girl, with a contralto voice and a strong Italian accent said:

"Timoteo, will you please set up my beautiful tent?"

And the man replied:

"I obey, my dear Graziella, Queen of my soul."

On that, with a dexterity which proved a long habit of that exercise, the man had forced the stakes into the ground, spread out the canvas, adjusted the ropes, and soon a pretty, blue tent was upright on the ground like a giant flower.

Then Timoteo bowed in front of his companion.

"Signorina, the tent which the Marchesina asked for is ready for her."

She deigned to smile:

---

[105] There are many forests in Balochistan, but I couldn't find one whose name even approximated "Aramin Log."

238

"I am pleased to see you so attentive, dear Timoteo. I think more and more every day that a woman will be happy with you."

The young man clasped his hands.

"By the Holy Madonna, I am overcome with joy."

"You may, my friend," Graziella permitted. "As for me, I am going to sleep. I count on your vigilance so that nothing is going to disturb my rest."

"I will watch like an archangel over a treasure, I swear it."

The Italian woman made the gesture of a queen and disappeared into the blue tent. Her companion walked away, while at some distance, near his moored boat, the ferryman sat in the shadow of a bush, waiting for a new client.

The voice of Graziella could be heard, saying:

"You will stand watch, Timoteo?"

"I am watching over you, Star of the Morning."

"Then I am sleeping with confidence."

And silence returned, troubled only by the wind in the grass and the buzzing of the insects.

Stretched out in the narrow length of the shadow of the tent, the young Italian man was dreaming.

He remembered the situation that had led him, a student from Bologna, so far from his homeland, following the little Marchesiana Graziella—for the attractive woman was really a Marquise and, furthermore, something rare in Italy, very rich.

As memories flooded back into the young man's mind, he saw himself, Timoteo Galieri, a student, wandering the streets of Bologna. One day, he had seen Graziella pass by in a carriage pulled by white horses and, from that time, he had gravitated into her orbit. The University had seemed to him to be suddenly ridiculous, and his universe had become a glance of the Marchesina.

The model student became an idler. Every day at five o'clock, he went to the Salvedri ice cream parlor, frequented by the upper classes. At the theater, he applauded plays which bored him, because what he liked most was the intermission, during which he could turn his back to the stage, and remained delighted and ecstatic, his eyes fixed on the box where sat Graziella, enthroned and beautiful.

By encountering him everywhere, the little Marchesina noticed him. Italian, poetic, and romantic, she was touched by his silent admiration. In short, one Sunday, when she encountered him on the Corso, she made her carriage stop, and getting out, with the candid lack of decorum of women of her nation, she approached the student.

"Good morning, stranger," she said to him.

He stammered.

"Good morning, Queen of Beauty."

This was not a bad compliment for one so obviously taken by surprise.

She replied:

"I feel your eyes always on me."

"Pardon me..." he began.

She interrupted him quickly.

"Only insults need pardons, and you haven't insulted me. But I'd like to know the name of those eyes that never stop looking at me."

He blushed and turned pale; then in a hardly distinct voice, he answered:

"Timoteo Galieri... who was born for nothing in the world but to be your devoted servant."

"I accept. From this moment, you are my cavalier servant."

The Italian language allows a wide range of choices for the expression "cavalier servant." For example, it can mean one who is a companion on a walk, to the theater, on a trip, or one who holds the horses of a carriage, and holds places at the theater, or on the train, carries an umbrella, or lorgnettes, or checks the baggage. It defines, in a word, the position of one who willingly becomes the servant of the one who has chosen him. Almost always, the "cavalier servant" is eventually promoted to the more elevated rank of fiancé. The initiation had been painful for Timoteo, who had a gentle, almost timid, nature. More given to philosophical dreams than to the harshness of action, he had found Graziella a tyrant, gracious, but perpetually moving about.

The Marchesina was scatterbrained, adept at all sports. Running, automobile racing, swimming, and shooting, were all familiar to her, and Timoteo often turned pale, unused to violent exercises, which appeared to him as fighting.

She undertook to instruct him. Then there appeared, for the poor boy, the most agitated moments of existences. Horseback riding, bicycling, car racing, canoeing. He always had something in his hand, reins or oars. And when he was tired, his fiancée sent him to the shower, to a massage, in order to put him back in shape quickly, and make him able to take up again his sporting existence.

His days flowed by in a state of being constantly out of breath. In that condition, he grew thin, became a little paler, but the nerves of that dreamer acquired an unexpected vigor.

One afternoon when Graziella, despite his begging, wanted to jump a height of four meters onto a platform of rocks, the student rushed forward, took her into his arms and put her on the ground without having bent from the weight. The little Marchesina was astonished. She had become accustomed to considering her "cavalier servant" as a student; and now, suddenly, he proved to have a strength that she found herself impossible to ignore. That little imaginative head started to think. The results must have been bizarre.

A certain morning, at the time the student came to take orders from her, she called him, using these words:

"Timoteo, my devoted servant, I believe books have no secrets from you."

"They are friends that I understand," he replied.

"Good."

"Why do you ask me that?"

"Because I am thinking of going to India and I don't understand the language of the people of that country."

"I don't know anything about it at all."

"That's as clear as the sun. To travel, it is necessary to speak, to converse. Therefore, I count on you, my friend. to learn Hindustani. I am giving you six months to do so... Afterwards, we will leave."

"But my beautiful Graziella..."

She didn't allow him to finish.

"Six months, that's a lot of time," she said with a gentle smile, "but I wish you to speak it well. You're best in the world. I will allow you three hours of study every day. And because I'm good, I'll allow you to kiss my hand."

And Timoteo started to learn Hindustani. The semester flew by. The two fiancés eventually embarked at Brindisi. Wanting not to do anything like others, Graziella, instead of going to Mumbai, Madras, Colombo, or Calcutta, had wanted to start her journey at Karachi, a port situated near the mouth of the Indus River, not far from the border of Balochistan. Then, she had traveled up the right bank of the river, disdaining to use the railroad, which, by way of Khaipur and Multan, went to Lahore and the main Punjab-Bengal line.

Their luggage had been entrusted to the railway. From station to station, the stamps on it kept sending it north, followed step by step by the travelers. It was thus that Marchesina and her patient fiancé had reached the Baloch Forest and crossed the Indus.

Graziella was now sleeping under her blue tent. Outside, stretched out on the ground, Timoteo was dreaming. He wasn't complaining about his fate. To see her constantly, to be her servant, to hear her voice, what greater happiness could be hoped for? If she had wanted, he would have accompanied her to the Moon, to the Sun, to the stars. They were less brilliant, less luminous, than the eyes of the Marchesina.

But the student was tired. The sharp light which covered the ground was blinding him. Soon his eyelids started blinking, a veil covered his thoughts and he remained immobile, absorbed in a state that transitioned from awake to sleep. Suddenly, he felt a strange impression. It seemed to him that a man was slipping by near him, that his piercing looks were weighing down on his face. He could not succeed in shaking off the torpor, that had invaded him. Finally, after a tremendous effort of will, he managed to open his eyes. Was it his effort? Was it chance? Timoteo never dared to decide for himself. The young man did not move.

Looking around, he examined the area, and, suddenly, he jolted. Ten feet from him, hunched over on the ground, there was a man with a naked torso. He was walking carefully. Timoteo again closed his eyes, then looked once more. The apparition was still there. He looked towards the place where the ferryman was resting The Italian suddenly felt anxious. Without being very aware of his action, he got up slowly, and, after being sure that his darling Graziella was

241

sleeping peacefully, he began to follow in the steps of the other man. For the first time, he understood the usefulness of sports. His body had been made more flexible by all his strenuous exercises and was certainly the docile slave of his will.

Without making any sound, with the silent movement of a feline, he glided over the ground, going around the bushes. In front of him, he could still make out the silhouette of the Indian, who now was no longer taking any precautions. He had straightened up and was walking like a man sure that he has nothing to fear.

Suddenly, the man disappeared as if he had been swallowed up by the earth. But Timoteo did not believe for a second in a magical intervention. The riverbank in that place formed a kind of staircase. The walker had only to jump down to land near the ferryman who was still asleep. Increasing his caution, the student continued going forward and soon, hiding between the stems of rose bushes that decorated the bank, he saw his target.

The Hindu had shaken the ferryman, who got up painfully, rubbing his eyes with a startled look.

"C'mon, wake up, you lazy thing!" growled the newcomer in an authoritarian voice. "In your case, it's true, fortune comes to you when you're asleep."

"All right, all right," stammered the ferryman. "Brahma does not forbid his worshippers to rest when they have nothing better to do. And in this forest, consecrated to the divine Dheera, there are not that many travelers."

On that day, all of Graziella's crazy notions would finally prove their usefulness! The two natives were conversing in their native dialect, but Timoteo understood it and did not lose a single one of their words.

"Cara Mia," he murmured in a whisper. "I reproached her for making me study Hindu. I was wrong! I will beg for her forgiveness."

But he stopped himself from speaking in order to better listen to the conversation.

"Your boat is very small," remarked the person talking to the ferryman.

"The currents would swallow a larger boat."

"I see. How many persons can you take across at one time?"

"Two, plus me."

The questioner fell silent as if he was thinking, then suddenly in a harsh halting voice, he asked:

"That boat belongs to you?"

"Yes, *Sahib*."

"And you know this river well?"

"I have been a ferryman for twenty years."

"Don't brag. At the last fair at Rawalpindi, you bragged of being capable of swimming across it."

The sailor looked at his questioner with great surprise.

"How do you know that?"

"That doesn't matter. Did you say these words that I have just repeated to you—yes or no?"

"Yes."

"Were you telling the truth, or were you being vain?"

"I was telling the truth. The Indus seems terrible, but it's a good river for those who understand it. Its currents carry the swimmer without fatigue, without danger, and one can reach the other bank."

"And you would do that without any fear."

"Yes. Do you intend to test my talent as a swimmer?"

The other man didn't answer immediately.

"One more thing," he said. "You said you owned that boat?"

"Yes. It was made in Sialkot, a city whose inhabitants excel in the construction of boats. Last year, I paid off the last rupees that I still owed."

And with a feeling of pride, the ferryman added:

"It's now all mine! No one can claim even one plank, or one nail, of it!"

"How much did you pay for it?"

"Four guineas."

"I'll give you ten for it."

The thin face of the ferryman smiled.

"Ten guineas!"

And juggling the pieces of gold the other man had just given him in his hand, he added:

"I regret that I have but one boat to sell you."

The other man smiled

"For another ten guineas, will you agree to capsize your boat in the middle of the river?"

"Yes. Is it because you want to see me swim?"

"Not really..."

"Then I don't understand..."

Timoteo was still listening. He had the feeling that the unknown person, who was so generous, must have criminal intentions. Why? he couldn't explain it, but his mind was made up, and his heart was jumping at the thought of perhaps preventing the carrying out of some kind of murderous plan.

The newcomer did not answer the ferryman immediately. He appeared to be thinking. Finally, in a cutting tone, he asked:

"Are you a worshiper of Brahma?"

"Yes, *Sahib*," murmured the ferryman, bowing with respect.

"I am Arkabad, who carries out the Will of the Brotherhood of Ellora."

The ferryman bowed even more:

"Lord Arkabad, I need no more explanations. I will obey you blindly."

"Good."

Arkabad took some time before continuing.

"It is possible that this evening four persons will arrive here on horseback. There will be two men and two girls, and a Bear of Shiva will accompany them."

"Excellent, My Lord. If those people come here, I will recognize them easily."

"I'm counting on that. They will ask you to take them to the other side of the river. You will agree. Only your boat is small, and you can carry only two travelers at a time..."

"That is true."

"The boy, without any doubt, will take a place in the boat with the smallest of the two girls."

"As you say, *Sahib*."

"Those people have been condemned by the Priests of Ellora. When you reach the middle of the river, you will capsize your boat."

The ferryman did not raise his eyebrows. He didn't even think about arguing. The Brahmins ordered it, so it must be the will of the gods.

"You paid most generously for my boat," the ferryman said. "It is yours to do with as you will. I am your humble servant, *Sahib*, and promise you obedience."

"Good. Wait until this evening. If those I mentioned do not appear, it is because they will never cross the Indus again. Then, keep the gold and go on with your job. Forget that you ever saw me. Remember that the Brahmins, who are generous to their faithful, are merciless towards those who betray their secrets."

Again, Arkabad extended his hand towards the boatman:

"Here are the other ten guineas for the risk you will be taking."

"That makes twenty."

"Yes. Is that enough?"

"Yes, *Sahib*!"

"In that case, goodbye. And remember what I said..."

And with a jump, Arkabad left the hole where the conversation had taken place. Without seeing him, he almost bumped into Timoteo, who, with his rumpled hair, had witnessed the preparation of a crime, the reason for which escaped him. Then, he left rapidly across the plain, not feeling the heat from the sun, ignoring the thorns which scratched his skin as he ran.

Calmly, the ferryman went back to his interrupted sleep.

Then Timoteo slid out of his hiding place and went back to his post by the blue tent.

But the ex-student from Bologna no longer wanted to sleep. His eyes were fixed with a terrible intensity on the river and its foaming waves. Each movement seemed to him like a hungry mouth trying to swallow up the victims that the mysterious Brahmin had marked for death.

There were two men and two young girls, he had said.

Timoteo's tender eyes were directed towards the tent which sheltered the amazing Graziella. Under the blue material there rested another young girl, to whom he had given his heart. Those that the ferryman was waiting for were perhaps also dreamers, lor overs, who, without knowing it, were walking towards death.

No, they would not die! Fate, in its mysterious way, had willed that the fantastic Graziella would bring Timoteo to India, so that the modest and timid student would be able to thwart the unknown menace, shouting to its intended victims:

"Stop! You are going to be murdered!"

For a long time, he had dreamed of something like this. Transformed by circumstances, he was no longer was afraid of the unexplored countryside, or of the deserted fields, or of the danger posed by the thousand perils created by the wild terrain. The idea of devoting himself to a heroic cause became greater.

"Timoteo," called out a sad voice suddenly.

He rushed to the entrance of the tent where his fiancée had just appeared, refreshed, with a rosy appearance, well rested.

"Timoteo," she continued, "I don't see the fire for the tea?"

"Pardon me, *mia cara*, I forgot."

The pretty Italian girl lifted her arms towards Heaven, and said:

"You forgot! Holy Madonna! How unhappy I am to be thus neglected by my cavalier servant!"

But the student had already put down some wood that he had picked up from the neighboring bushes. A match showed its blue flame, and a nickel-plated tea kettle filled with water was soon placed over the nascent fire, Then Timoteo dropped with precaution a few pinches of the perfumed tea leaves from China in it.

Graziella, however, was not disarmed by his industriousness.

"All of that is too late. At what hour at night will I continue my journey!"

She stopped herself, stupefied because her fiancé had responded:

"We may not leave at all, dear one. We have to wait here until the arrival of travelers with whom I need to speak."

Graziella was stunned. Her slave was revolting. He claimed he needed to stay here, on that isolated stretch of land, far away from civilization!

"So, I shall leave alone," she declared with impatience. "And I will say to everyone that my cavalier servant as abandoned me."

There was a new surprise: Timoteo shook his head.

"You will not leave."

"I will not..."

"And you will approve of our staying."

"I will?"

"Because your heart, which is most excellent, will advise you to stay."

Out of breath by such audacity, the Marchesina couldn't say a word, and Timoteo cleverly took advantage of her temporary silence to tell her of his adventure.

As he spoke, the face of the gentle Italian woman became calm. She clasped her hands, saying this:

"The poor things!"

Finally, she took Timoteo in her arms, and placed a kiss on his forehead!

"What you did was heroic, *carissimo*. I am proud of you. Yes, you are right... We must save those signoritas and those signori that they want to kill. By Saint Beppo, they may be fiancé s too... That Brahmin Arkabad is an evil man. If I ever encounter him, I will not say hello to him."

All there was of goodness and nobility in the frivolous creature shone on her face.

"But," she said suddenly, "you must be tired, *mio caro*! No rest, no sleep this morning!"

"That's as true as the Holy Trinity," he answered.

Graziella clasped her hands:

"And he's still standing up... And he made tea! Heroic, I say, heroic!"

Then, with typical Italian exaggeration, going from her usual tyrannical habit to voluntary servitude, she said:

"Sit down, *mio dolce amico*, seat under the umbrella of my tent. I will prepare the tea... Rest yourself, my brave cavalier... I will keep watch."

Timoteo tried to resist, but in vain. His gracious companion put into serving him tea the same stubbornness that she had ordinarily used to order him around. Soon, stretched out in the shadow of the tent, his eyes half- closed, his heart delightfully full of emotion, he watched the comings and goings of his fiancée.

Without questioning the inversion of their roles, he thought he was dreaming. From his mouth escaped admiring exclamations:

"*Mia cara... Mia divina...*"

And she, turned rosy by her culinary ardor, turned around and, lowering her voice, replied:

"Sleep now... I want you to..."

The hours which followed were sweet. For the first time, the two fiancés understood each other. Graziella no longer wanted as her companion a docile toy, and she no longer appeared to Timoteo as a fantastic and disconcerting angel. Both of them declared that tea had never before been so perfumed, the mixture was so exquisite, the temperature so right.

After the nap that the Italian girl wanted her friend to take, she sat down near him, took his hand in hers and started humming one of those lullabies that Roman women chant near a cradle. And he, happy about that sudden tenderness, lost his thoughts, stammering:

"If this is a dream, may no one wake me."

A long moment passed by in that way; then suddenly Graziella leaned over, listening attentively. Finally, with her slender fingers she caressed the face of the sleeper.

"*Caro* Timoteo... *Caro* Timoteo!"

He opened his eyes. She said:

"I hear the sound of horses coming in at a gallop."

The Italian jumped to his feet and grabbed his carabine.

"Oh!" she said with admiration. "You are as courageous as the god Mars himself. I was afraid before; now I am reassured to be at your side."

Timoteo straightened up, delightfully caressed by the words of his companion. He made sure his gun was ready and listened in his turn.

"Yes, it is the sound of the horses' hooves."

"That must be the travelers that we are waiting for."

"We will know that soon."

The sound approached rapidly.

Soon, some galloping silhouettes appeared on the plain, and five minutes later, four horsemen placed their feet on the ground facing the Italian fiancés.

"Ah! The two Signori," exclaimed Graziella.

"And the two Signorinas." Timoteo said. And he added: "And the bear."

"That's them."

"No doubt."

Doctor Mystery and his friends—for it was them—looked at the two Italians with considerable surprise. They seemed drunk with joy to see them. The explanation did not have to wait long. Graziella ran to them, and accompanying her speech by wide gestures, she said:

"Travelers, listen to the voice of Providence. Do not cross the Indus."

And as they looked at her with astonishment, she finished by adding:

"Death is watching you and lies in wait in the turbulence of the river. It is the Brahmin Arkabad that has planned that fate for you."

Arkabad! At that name everyone trembled. The Doctor approached the Italian woman and asked:

"What are you saying"

"That the boat is going to capsize, and your little Signor and Signorina will be drowned in the furious waves. Timoteo has overheard the conspiracy. But you don't know Timoteo is... Let me introduce him to you..."

The pretty girl took the hand of her fiancé and said:

"Timoteo is my cavalier servant, my brave companion, my heroic fiancé whom I would marry happily. You don't seem to understand. Timoteo. Speak, explain to the Signor what your eyes have seen."

The intervention of the young Italian was necessary, because the travelers had begun to doubt Graziella's sanity.

In a more controlled voice, Timoteo told his adventure and the plan put together by Arkabad. At that recitation, the faces turned somber. However, the Doctor held out his hand and in a serious voice said:

"Thank you, who have not been afraid to stay here in order to keep some strangers from the danger with which they are threatened. Unfortunately, our enemies are pursuing us. We must cross the Indus... We must!"

The Italians kept silence, impressed by the Doctor tone. They felt chance had just embroiled them in a terrible drama, and they shivered. Suddenly Cicada spoke, mocking as always.

"Good, we're going to turn the tables on Arkabad!"

Everyone turned towards him.

"We must cross the Indus," he said calmly, "and we will if my dear little sister Anoor has enough confidence in me to trust me to protect her life."

The girl smiled delightfully.

"I believe you would give your life in order to save mine. I have confidence in you."

A dark blush spread over Cicada's cheeks and he stammered:

"Thank you, sister."

But his face, veiled with tears, gave much significance to these words; they were said with such tenderness that Na-Indra's sister lowered her long dark eyelashes. Meanwhile, the Parisian boy had already regained his composure.

"You, Doctor, you will cross first with Na-Indra; then, it will be our turn."

"What do you plan to do?"

Cicada shrugged.

"Do you really think that I'll meet my maker in a ferryboat?"

"No, of course, but..."

"Well, then, let me give you the pleasure of a surprise."

Without a doubt, the Doctor was going to insist on knowing his companion's pla, but Graziella, for an instant, was conferring in a low voice with Timoteo and did not allow him to do so.

"Signor," she said. "I have something to ask you."

"After the great service you have done us, Signorina," replied the Doctor, "these are no longer prayers, but orders, that you are in your right to give us."

She smiled pleasantly:

"No, no, no, not an order, but a prayer. Timoteo is as courageous as a lion. He shoots accurately, and his pistol is of the best quality. Please allow us to accompany you. We are traveling without a fixed goal. It would be pleasant for us to travel the same road as you."

A new fad, one that was generous, had germinated in the Marchesina's head. Because her fiancé and her had been able to render a valuable service to the fugitives, why not continue to do so? Because of that love of the *romanesque*, which never lost its hold on the Italian soul, the journey would be even more interesting. In vain, the Doctor talked about the many dangers which menaced them. She persisted so much and so well that it was necessary to consent. The order of those going on the journey was reorganized in this way: the Doctor and Na-Indra would use the boat first. Timoteo would join them next with Graziella. Finally, Cicada would embark with Anoor, and put into operation the plan which he had refused to share with his friends.

Everything was agreed; the blue tent was taken down and rolled up, and the little troop went down towards the river.

The ferryman had seen them coming. Standing up near his small boat, he put the oars in place. He seemed slightly surprised on seeing Timoteo and his companion, but probably told himself it was not up to him to discuss the fantasies of western travelers, and shrugging nonchalantly, he declared he was ready to depart.

However, his glance had looked at Ludovic who, totally happy at not being shaken anymore by the galloping of a horse, showed his joy by a mad run through the bushes.

The Doctor had noticed the ferryman's attention. He had observed the enigmatic smile which had contracted his face. The thought of the other man had been clearly revealed to him:

"I am not mistaken," he confirmed to himself. "This is the Bear of Shiva that was mentioned by the powerful Brahmin, Arkabad, and there are the two young people who must die."

But nothing betrayed the agony that was oppressing the Doctor. Supporting Na-Indra, he took his place in the boat with the young woman whose hand trembled in his.

The ferryman took his place at the oars and went across competently without any mistake. The same went for Timoteo and Graziella.

The Italian, so troubled by the sight of the foaming waves from their first crossing, seemed transfigured. The heroic fiber of the Latin people had been awakened in him, and his arms, in a protective gesture, went around the waist of Graziella, who had become timid.

Before, she had protected him; now, she made herself very small in his arms as if seeking refuge in the sudden courage revealed by her companion. And with a kind of respect for him, she felt herself pushed into an adorable feminine weakness she had not known about till then. It was with a look full of emotion that she considered the turbulent waters faraway and her big, soft eyes fixed with a tender gratitude on him when he said to reassure her:

"Don't be afraid, *cara mia*... This river, it's mostly noise. Its current flows towards the right bank and that ferryman will have almost nothing to do."

Finally, both of them jumped on the bank to stand beside the Doctor. whose arm Na-Indra was holding, trembling.

The branches of the great trees of the forest dropped down on their heads, casting a blueish shadow and highlighting the unusual paleness of Anoor's sister, Na-Indra was colored with nuances of azure, giving her face a supernatural appearance.

Graziella was struck by that. Born in the land of Fine Art, she strongly felt the emotions cast by shadow and of light. She grabbed Timoteo's arm and the four travelers silently stared with an agonizing look at the boat that was turning around to pick up Cicada and Anoor, who was busy petting Ludovic.

Little by little, the embarkation reached the middle of the Indus. With each stroke of the oars, it progressed towards the left bank.

"Another five minutes, and he'll be there," Na-Indra said, shivering.

The voice of the young girl echoed the Doctor's thoughts. The evil scheme, set up by the traitor Arkabad, was going to unfold in front of them. Powerless to be a part of it, they followed its slightest changes.

Could Cicada be outsmarted by the ferryman? Evidently, the Parisian boy had a plan. The Doctor knew him too well to doubt that. The young man had spoken with a calm confidence, in order to reassure his friends, but is anyone ever certain of success? The best laid plans could be unraveled by chance...

And what if the brave boy made a mistake... That would mean disaster in the bellowing waters, Anoor herself perishing in that white whirlpool...

At that moment, the Doctor reproached himself for not having forced his companion to speak.

By his gestures, they guessed that the ferryman was inviting the two young people to step into his boat. They didn't have to be asked twice. As light as a bird, Anoor went to sit at the back. Cicada took his place near her and, with a bound, Ludovic came to sit at their feet under the bench. Putting an oar on the shore, the ferryman pushed off the boat into the water, then sat on his bench and started to row vigorously towards the middle of the river.

The hour set for the crime had come. The attack and the defense were going to happen as rapidly as that of the clash of steel in a sword fight. Worried, out of breath, the spectators remained on the other bank, their bodies leaning forward, their eyes transfixed.

The boat advanced little by little, moving about the turbulence, fast as an arrow, through the rapids between the rock which were pointing like black heads covered with foam-like hair by the waves.

The boat had now reached the middle of the river. It was going to enter the current which was going to push it towards the opposite bank. At that moment, the ferryman stood up suddenly. The Doctor, Na-Indra, and the two Italians let out a worried cry, but their voices strangled in their throat.

Faster than the ferryman, Cicada had extended his arm. The wind brought the travelers the echo of a gunshot. The ferryman, struck by a bullet in the middle of his stomach, remained for a second standing up, moving his hands instinctively over his wound.

Then the young Parisian stepped towards him, lifted him by his legs with one rapid move and threw him into the river.

There was a dull splash, a liquid geyser, then nothing more, but the boat was now turning at the will of the waves, with its two young passengers alone in it. Thanks to his cold-bloodedness, Cicada had avoided the most pressing danger, but it was still necessary to complete the task and cross the river.

He was alone now to direct the boat, alone on the raging waters, alone on a river the challenges of which were unknown to him. But his face didn't express any emotion.

"Don't be afraid, little sister. I have paddled at Bougival. The oars know me."

Then he got seriously to work. His eyes didn't leave the surface of the waters. It seemed he knew the direction to follow. Taking advantage of the currents, he slowly guided the boat towards the right bank where his friends, with beating hearts and fast breathing, encouraged him with gestures.

But a last push of the tumultuous waters carried the boat towards a rock. With a motion of the rudder, Cicada made it turn at the last minute. Instead of breaking apart on the rock, it only brushed it on. However, by avoiding one danger, the young man had thrown them into another. Caught by an impetuous wave, the frail boat now glided on rapidly, getting further away from the right bank.

Cries reached Cicada's ears. He looked behind him. He saw his friends making frantic movements.

"I'm not afraid," he cried out when they could hear him. "This is not as bad as the Bay of Audierne."

And speaking to Anoor, his growling voice softened into infinite tenderness:

"Do you remember, little sister, when I pulled you out of the furious waters? Don't be worried now. Even if we capsize, I'll pull you out."

She shook her pretty head, and replied:

"I am not afraid of anything when I am with you."

"That's the spirit!" he shouted, delighted. "Then it's my turn to play sailor again in order not to avoid these rocks."

His memories of having been a sailor came back to him and he took charge of the maneuver.

"The helm to starboard!... Good! Now to portside! Portside, I said, you damn boat! It's that friggin' whirlpool... Go, girl, go!"

Meanwhile, the Doctor and his companions, seeing the boat carried away by the current, tried to follow it on foot; but the forest blocked their way with its bushes. In a few minutes, the travelers had exhausted their strength against that green, elastic and resistant wall of vegetation.

Out of breath, they threw a last look at the river. The embarkation was but a black dot in the distance and soon disappeared behind a bend. Night was about to fall. From the horizon a shining purple light, the last resistance to the victorious shadows, cast its reflection on the countryside, turning it scarlet like Cesar's robe.

Cicada and Anoor would soon be lost in the shadows in that land peopled with enemies and savage wild beasts. How would the two of them survive?

Na-Indra let herself fall to the ground and hid her face with her hands. Then she murmured desperately:

"Brahma! Brahma! Sublime Force! Why do you attack the weakness of your servant in this way!"

CHAPTER VI
The Balouche Forest

The current was still carrying away the boat. But the same bend of the river that had hidden the boat from Na-Indra's eyes in fact led to the end of its tumultuous journey. The boat was thrown onto a sandy cove on the left bank.

With one leap, the young Parisian was off and then he helped Anoor to solid ground. Left to itself, the boat was seized by another wave and reclaimed by the rfver; it soon continued on its lonely journey.

The two young people were alone. A narrow path, worn without a doubt by the wild animals of the night that had come to drink from the river, led into dark forest.

"We have no choice but to follow it," Cicada decided. "The night is near. We can't think of rejoining our friends for the moment. We must find a place to camp where we can rest, and shelter from animals. I heard it said that night in India is filled with teeth and claws. We don't want to test the truth of that."

Without saying a word, Anoor took Cicada's arm and both of them, young Robinson Crusoes, lost in the virgin forest, began to walk.

The top of the trees kept the last light from the sun from reaching the ground, and shadows were spreading. A frighteningly powerful nature was unfolding under the eyes of the two travelers. Sometimes they walked along walls of vines. Their unexpected spread forced them to stop, their heart jumping, as if they had felt the touch of a snake.

The horizon eventually grew a little wider, the vegetation spacing out into a desolate countryside spread with enormous boulders and strange trees. The plants, the stones, took on horrible forms in the night.

Cicada and Anoor were still walking. She was pressed against him, trembling, not daring to express the huge terror oppressing her. He was concerned for her.

"If this path goes on like this for a long time," he suddenly said, "we will climb into a tree. It will be a bad place to sleep, but we can always sleep again another day. The important thing, at this hour, is to not become a snack for some wandering feline."

The last bright shadows were floating into the summer atmosphere. Cicada and Anoor had the impression that they were moving in the dark. They planned to stop in a clearing ahead. Some distance away, they vaguely made out a structure, which they quickly approached with the hope that someone lived there. But they were deceived in their expectations. It was one of those spacious cabins where peasants deposited rice or cereal after harvest. Erected on solid stakes 4 to 5 meters high, the cabin was covered with a ceiling of dried bamboo. It was perched high with only a door and window accessed via a heavy ladder that they had to raise after themselves.

Inside, there were some dried leaves, a handful of straw heated by the sun, which made for a not particularly comfortable setting. However, the young girl let out a sigh of satisfaction upon getting inside. There, one did not have to fear the tigers that roamed the Hindu countryside. As if to brighten the landscape even more, the moon had risen and inundated the clearing with its bright light.

"Sleep well, little sister," Cicada prayed.

He had shaped the leaves and straw into a bed sufficiently soft for sleeping. She held out her hand to him.

"And you?"

"Me? I'm not sleepy. People from Paris are easily spooked. We don't know how to sleep."

She pressed his fingers more tenderly.

"Parisians may be easily spooked, perhaps," she murmured, "but they're also very brave. They're also more devoted than most men."

He was troubled by the vibrant accent of her voice. She continued:

"You shall never leave me, Cicada."

"But," he stammered, "when you are safe with Mademoiselle Na-Indra..."

"Never," she repeated, with more emphasis.

He tried to laugh.

"I'll be like your butler, then."

"Oh!" she said with shimmering tears in her eyes.

Suddenly the young Parisian mock-slapped himself and said:

"I am an ass! I'm hurting your feelings! Of course, I'll stay with you, right up until your marriage."

He stopped. Anoor was no longer trying to hold back her tears.

"What's wrong?" he asked.

"I am saddened by your words."

"What did I say?"

"You just said that you will leave me when I get married.

"Well, then…" grumbled Cicada, mussing up his hair.

"So what they say is true," she trembled. "Men from Europe do not want to marry young girls from India."

The young Parisian remained silent. A world of thoughts swirled in his head. The brotherly affection that existed between Anoor and himself—had it changed into a more tender sentiment? He did not dare ask himself that question. Then, the light of understanding dawned in him. It seemed that, for the first time, he understood his own heart. Stupefied, he discovered that he too would be torn apart if he were forced to be separated from Anoor.

"The daughters of India," continued Anoor, "have a heart just like the women of Europe. It's the sun's fault that their skins are darker."

"You are mistaken, Anoor!" Cicada replied. "I swear to you that it's false. No European woman would seem to me as worthy of love as you do."

"Then," she said ingenuously, a joyous light in her eyes, "why do you speak to me of my marriage to someone else?"

"Why?"

"Yes, why?"

The girl's pretty voice had inviting inflections and Cicada softly replied:

"You are rich, Anoor... And I am poor..."

"So much the better; so we will both be rich."

"You don't understand," he said.

"On the contrary, I understand very well... Money is very amusing to spend, but it has nothing to do with love."

"Yes, but..." Cicada stammered.

"If you were rich, and I poor, would I please you less?" asked Anoor.

"Certainly not!"

"There! You see? Let's not talk about it anymore... It's understood. You will be my husband and we will live together, one always with the other."

Nature at night now awakened the echoes of the wild. Gloomy calls and plaintive moans resounded in the forest, occasionally dominated by savage cries. Wild beasts, harmless or bloodthirsty, victims or killers, entered the scene during the dark of the night. Fierce shrieks of victory and strident screams of agony mingled under the stars in the voluptuous spilling of blood. The trees and the bushes bent over; the vegetation shook vibrantly, under these storms of shrieks carried by the shadows of the night. Sometimes even stifling the faraway roars of the Indus.

Neither Cicada nor Anoor paid any attention to those things. Only the pounding of their hearts reached their ears, making them conscious only of the harmonies of their first love. But with the delicate intuition of people from Paris, the young man, who had grown up an abandoned child on its streets, where one learned everything, art or subtlety of sentiments, at an early age, guessed, at that time, in that desert, that he should not make his companion aware of his affectionate dreams.

"Anoor," he said gravely, "for the time being, let's forget the sweet words that we just exchanged. We will pronounce them again in the presence of the Doctor and of your sister. And it is they who will decide our future."

She shook her head silently but did not protest. She only said:

"Good night.",

Then she closed her eyes, stretched out gently on her mattress of leaves and straw, tranquil under the protection of her companion.

Cicada stood up softly. He came to sit down by the window through which they had come and, leaning his head on his hands, glanced seriously into the depths of the forest.

The ladder was leaning against the wall. Fifteen feet separated him from the ground. He turned his eyes toward Anoor, whose regular breathing showed her to be sleeping peacefully, and he had a gesture of satisfaction. The young girl was sheltered against the wicked beasts. Another day would come without any unfortunate incident. Reassured by these thoughts, the Parisian boy let himself glide insensibly from drowsiness into sleep, from reality into dream.

Suddenly, the forest seemed to bend over, as if struck by a savage storm. Cicada opened his eyes, ready to defend Anoor. An unforgettable spectacle presented itself in front of him. The bushes which surrounded the clearing, split as if cut by a hatchet; they opened up and vomited a whirlwind of panicked animals. There were galloping antelopes, their necks flung back, their horns stuck into the flanks of elephants, whose trumps were high, letting out piercing cries... In the middle of these herbivores, there were flesh-eaters, panthers, tigers, jumping around as frightened in appearance as their inoffensive companions in flight.

Speeding up like bullets, the animals ran across the clearing and disappeared, back into the forest. Astonished, the Parisian boy wondered if he had not dreamed. The clearing was now deserted again. And if the bushes had not been broken, the ground dug up, the grass pressed down, the faraway noise of the mad race would have been lost in the bushes. In that case, he would have perhaps been tempted to think it all had been a dream indeed.

So, what had happened?

Silence had returned. The young man began to feel reassured, when new noises suddenly made him concerned again. These were discreet sounds. One would have said, that in the hole created by the flight of the wild animals, some beings came forward mysteriously, cautiously, as if they wanted to hide their coming.

From time to time, the barking of a wild dog, the sharp cry from a parakeet, the whistle of an awakened monkey, announced that something that Cicada didn't know, was moving forward.

Intrigued, suspecting some new danger, the young Parisian crawled out of the cabin. He slid down along one of the stakes in the ground and, crawling into the bushes, he moved noiselessly towards the place where the indistinct murmurs had called his attention. Soon, he heard the breaking of dried leaves under many feet. He shivered; his ears could not misunderstand. Those were men walking some yards from him—men walking in the night in this green hell had to belong to some local tribe, not to the peaceful caste of farmers who were asleep now in their cabins after the fatigues of the day, but to some of those fearful cults who hid their bloody customs with a cloak of shadows. That thought, jumping into his head caused him a deep feeling of unease.

Wasn't Anoor and him of the target of the attacks of the Brahmins, now assisted by the Sons of Dheera?

He didn't care about his own safety. Brahmins or Dheerists didn't trouble his confidence; but Anoor, his little sister, who, naively and loyally, had become his little fiancée this very night... Anoor was as threatened as he, more so even...

Cicada stopped for an instant. His teeth were chattering. He felt himself on the point of bursting into tears when measuring the peril in which he found themselves. But he controlled himself. His emotions had to remain under control. There was a war to be fought, and he was about to engage into conflict with the enemy. Nervously, he held back his tears and controlled the trembling of his limbs. On his shoulders, on his knees, he carried on with his slow, forward crawl.

And suddenly, he stopped, astonished by what he saw. The trees, less close together in that spot, raised their trunks like the columns of a temple, and through their branches, the rays of the Moon came down to the ground, creating a milky shadow under their cover. And in that wan light, he could see men moving about.

Alone, heading that troop that he undoubtedly commanded, stood a strange and terrible being, making the wild gestures of a madman. That savage, hideous man looked like one of those stone creatures found in the bas-reliefs of some of the Hindu temples. He had long black hair, falling down in untidy waves onto his bony shoulders. His body was covered with white paint and his frightful, frowning face had his forehead painted with the same coating. His nose, cheeks and chin wore the same pattern in alternating dark and light stripes. He marched upright, alone, followed by a strong pack of men who crawled on the ground, looking like an army of snakes migrating towards the dry plateaus at the season when the torrential rain of winter transformed the lower lands into marshes.

"Who the Devil is this and what are they doing?" murmured Cicada.

Naturally his question remained without an answer, and he had no other resource except to keep looking at the newcomers who had come creeping into the forest.

With sharp pain, he realized that the troop was progressing towards the clearing. There was no longer any doubt; they were following the trail left by the animals whose flight had troubled his rest.

Soon, they reached the clearing. Then, the Chief, who was walking at the head, stopped. He said some words that the Parisian boy did not understand, but his gestures, pointing out the cabin where Anoor was resting, needed no explanation.

At that realization, the heart of the young man stopped beating for an instant. Then it began to beat again madly, hammering his chest with heavy blows. A flow of blood surged to his head, deafening him. The brave boy was about to stand up, to jump on the enemies, prepared to kill in order to defend the woman that had taught love to that disinherited boy. But rapid as a flash of lightening, his best instinct stopped the rapid movement that had begun. The attackers were at least one hundred; the result of a battle could not be doubted. He would be defeated. And with him dead, Anoor would be at the mercy of these men. No, a plan of attack had to be abandoned; a ruse had to be used instead.

But what ruse?

Suddenly, he stifled a cry... A hairy being had slid near him and was licking his hands. After a second, he recognized Ludovic. The little bear, somewhat forgotten during the walk through the jungle, had let his two companions get settled in the cabin in the clearing. As for him, he had found a more convenient refuge in a palm tree, whose fruits he had eaten with delight. As it had done with Cicada, the mad run of the animals had troubled him, and from the height of his observation point, he had witnessed the movements of his young master. He had followed him silently, and finally had come to rejoin him.

In the hours of agony, solitude is the worst of suffering. The coming of Ludovic had brought back all his sprit of resolve to the young Parisian. It seemed to him that he had gained a precious new companion and his thoughts became clearer.

The danger to Anoor is not imminent, he thought. *Those bastards must be on the payroll of the Brahmins. They are preparing some new betrayal against Mademoiselle Na-Indra. Only I can warn my friends. So I must remain free.*

A sad thought made him turn pale.

Anoor will be very afraid, seeing herself-surrounded by those monsters. But he shook his head. *Even if I were at her side, it would change nothing. So, I don't have a choice, I must let things here run their course...*

And crouched behind a bush, he witnessed, impassive, biting his lips in order not to turn red with anger, the execution of the plan of the newcomers. With furtive steps, they silently approached the cabin. They heard no noise. They appeared to look for a ladder in order to reach the platform above. Its disappearance slowed them down somewhat, but they soon regained their composure.

Some of them grabbed the posts supporting the edifice. With monkey-like agility, they lifted themselves off the ground. Cicada saw them reach the opening and disappear inside the cabin. A deadly silence followed, then a terrible stifled cry was heard. It was the voice of Anoor, surprised by her enemies in the middle of a dream.

Cicada's fingers scratched the ground with anxiety. The young man remained frozen with anxiety and did not budge. He saw a movement at the window. A man was positioning the ladder, which one of them had finally discovered, and two of the ravishers came down, carrying a white form which was struggling all the way down. Anoor was their prisoner and she shouted out a desperate emotional appeal:

"Cicada! Cicada! Help me!"

Cicada grabbed some dirt and stuffed his mouth with it in order to suppress his desire to act. Perhaps if that moral torture had been prolonged, the Parisian boy would finally have betrayed himself; human strength, after all, has its limits. But fate had decided that it would be otherwise. A sharp whistling came through the air like a flying arrow. A disturbance was produced among the newcomers and everyone disappeared as if by magic, swallowed up by the darkness of the jungle. They had abandoned the clearing, and were taking their prisoner to an unknown destination, from which Cicada hoped to free her.

With a bound, the brave young man stood up and caressed Ludovic's soft fur:

"Let's go, Ludo," he said. "Now, we're all alone, just like we were when we were traveling across France as street artists. It's a question of not losing trace of those villains."

The bear truly seemed to understand him. He emitted a little low growl and, pressing his nose against the soil, started out on the trail of the enemy.

At first, Cicada followed him cautiously, afraid to run into an ambush. Soon, however, he grew reassured. Probably the Sons of Dheera believed him lost somewhere in the jungle, because they took no precautions. They were walking straight ahead, without care, without even hiding traces of their passage.

"They don't think much of me as an adversary, do they?" grumbled the young man. "Well, let's wait a little and they'll see how a French sailor does when he grew up on the streets of Paris. "

And he picked up his speed.

Ludovic trotted happily alongside him, showing him the way. His carefree attitude indicated that they had nothing to fear. His subtle instinct would have warned him of any ambush.

Soon the jungle began to change. The trees became rarer, replaced by thorny bushes which could not be gone through, but without great care, Ludovic lifted invisible scents, and their fast pace continued, but at the cost of some scratches.

Thus, man and beast arrived at a steep slope filled with stones, which took them to the bottom of a deserted gorge that the locals called the Ravine of Dee-rut-Typhum. They had to climb a sharp escarpment which was but a dried riverbed and ran through some dark bushes. The ascent was rough until they reached a higher plateau.

Cicada, despite his courage, felt himself filled with fear. It wasn't unreasonable fear that he felt, but one inspired by some sublime horrors of nature, that the ancients correctly called "holy terror."

Around him spread out a wasteland, frightening to see under the light of the moon. It was a plain of shadows, a field of death, under the Heavens full of stars. There were hundreds of sculpted rocks standing up, petrified representations of monsters and demons, arranged in a wild and formidable chaos, created to serve as a background for abominable crimes, or blood sacrifices. Surrounded at its base by a circle of shadows, each of those blocks carried at its top a luminous point. One would have said it was cruel eyes of a wild beast of the night.

Stumbling on the stones under his feet, that were hurting him with their sharp angles, Cicada still stepped forward. Ludovic went ahead of him, but the progress of the intelligent animal had become more cautious.

Careful! thought the young man. *The enemy must not be very far away.*

He heard the sounds of water running, still went forward, and suddenly arrived at a large platform. He had reached the edge of the plateau. He looked down into an abyss... A drop of sixty feet towards a torrential current. Cicada recognized the Indus. Following the bandits, he had come back to the banks of the river, likely upstream from the place where they had crossed. The general look of the countryside did not suggest any alternative; besides, the young man knew that the Indus was the only river of that size in their vicinity.

The cornice on which he found himself seemed to be a bridge between two cliffsides: one went up from the river, the other continued upward onto the plateau, and became lost in shadows. Sometimes, that transition path was hardly a yard wide, sometimes, on the contrary, it spread out like a public square.

Cicada was going to enter one of those larger spaces, when he stopped and quickly hid behind a boulder. The opening to the temple of Typhum stood in front of him. It was a large, polygonal excavation, cut out from the wall, opening like a dark and frightening mouth, the muzzle of a monster of granite. A series of bas-relief sculptures decorated it.

Typhum was represented, and near him was Rama portrayed as a child. That second statue, although it had not given its name to Temple, was the object of veneration by the faithful. It was recounted, in fact, that during an Afghan invasion, the King of Punjab, Thaouh,[106] captured by the invaders and was taken

---

[106] I couldn't find any reference to that king.

into that place in order to be tortured, and that he owed his life to the intervention of Rama, whose statue came to life, and the Afghans were so terrified that they freed there captive and returned quickly to their mountains.

Kidnaped by the fanatics, Anoor had been taken to the temple of Typhum. In front of the gate, she had given a last, long look to the surrounding countryside. She thought she was seeing the skies and the green plains for the last time. For an instant, she thought of Cicada, whose disappearance, unexplainable for her, filled her with worry. But tenacious hope whispered in her ear:

Perhaps he is free! Perhaps he is working somewhere to free you!

But she chased away that idea. As courageous as the young man was, what could he do against the band of crazy men who were growling around her, and she answered: *He could only die!*

She was hoping, with the unconscious devotion of loving hearts, that the young man would not find her trace, and in making that wish with fervor, she willfully ignored the fact that, by so doing, she was renouncing her last hope of escaping from torture. Goodbye to the things of the earth. Goodbye to her dear companion... Everything had been said, everything had been done. With the feeling that she had already left life, Anoor entered the temple with her guardians. In the subterranean maze they walked for several minutes, then a massive door opened, groaning on its rolling hinges.

"Enter!" commanded a voice.

The prisoner obeyed. The door closed behind her and darkness surrounded her. Deafened, surprised by the shadows, the captive remained motionless, not daring to step forward, held back by that imprecise fear of invisible obstacles in the dark. Where was she? Was this one of those prisons from which one could never escape?

Perhaps in taking a step forward, she was going to fall into a pit? A cry, a rapid touch against the damp walls, a terrible shock... And then nothing. She would be erased from the living, and her body would be broken down little by little, her grimacing skull lying on top of the skeletons of the previous victims. That made her shiver. She closed her eyes but reopened them quickly. Under her closed pupils, her overexcited imagination had showed her an army of bones, a sinister heap of death. She trembled and started walking, because it became too much for her to stay in one place.

"Brahma, protect the innocent child," she said in a loud voice.

Surprise! Suddenly, she heard her name:

"Anoor, my sister? Is that you?"

"Na-Indra!"

"Yes, over here."

The two sisters searched for each other in the dark, talking constantly in order to guide themselves. They reached each other and hugged.

"My sweet Na-Indra!"

"Anoor, my dear sister!"

And then there were questions:

"Are you a prisoner too?"

Anoor told her of their walk across the jungle, her surprise at being kidnaped, and her pain at being in the hands of the Sons of Dheera.

The story of Na-Indra was somewhat similar. At sunset, Doctor Mystery, Timoteo and Graziella had elected to camp right on the bank of the Indus. The gracious Italian woman had offered to share with her the shelter of her blue tent. Towards the middle of the night, the tent was suddenly taken down, covering the young girls with its heaviness. They could almost hear, in a confused way, the sounds of a fight with much cursing... Then silence fell... They felt themselves being lifted and carried away. The tent was rolled up with them inside it, and their mysterious ravishers had not let them out, except to deposit them in the prison where they currently found themselves.

The Doctor and the two Italians, immobile and silent until then, came forward out of the shadows.

"My dear little one!"

"*Povera Signorina!*"

"*Cara puerita!*"

"My dear father!... Mademoiselle!... Monsieur!"

They shook hands and exchanged kisses in which tears mingled with bitterness. Anoor was almost happy. She had forgotten the danger; she only understood one thing: that she was no longer alone.

Then a light lit the prison. Man carrying torches put down in front of the captives some rose-colored candles, some fruits and vegetables. They also offered them jugs of water. At the Doctor's request, they left the prisoners a torch. At least now they could see. They would be spared the horrors of constant darkness. On the Doctor's advice, they ate, but very little and forcing themselves. Still, the food gave them strength. Their ideas became clearer. Anoor expressed her astonishment that anyone had dared to put their hands on Na-Indra.

"Mindless Ones are worshiped," she said. "Those who dare torment them are cursed by Brahma until the fifth generation. Where did they find the audacity of seizing you?"

"I don't know," replied the Doctor with a thoughtful expression.

"But," interrupted Timoteo, "why is my Graziella put in this harsh prison? I can't figure out why."

"Like you, Timoteo, she is paying for the generous impulse that made her decide to help us.

"Oh! For me, it is not important."

"Nor for me either," interrupted the Italian woman, "I think those men are despicable bandits, and I feel only contempt for them."

She had no idea of the tortures that the terrible Sons of Dheera could inflict on their victims.

Everyone looked at her with sadness, and no one had the courage to paint the situation as it really was.

"If my beautiful lady wasn't there," Timoteo whispered in the Doctor's ear, "I would weep for her because our dreadful enemies will not spare her."

"I fear that is true; they have to avenge their comrades." And with a hint of pride, he added: "Not a surprise; we must have killed a dozen of them."

That was true. The former Italian student had fought bravely at the side of the Doctor, and the victory of the Sons of Dheera had cost them dearly. From that point, there was only one thing left to worry about for the two men. What horrible combination of tortures their jailers had in store for them, when they already used infinite refinements of cruelty on more innocent victims!

The conversation stopped. The day continued slowly, seemingly endless. Twice, the guards brought them food, their visits suggesting to the prisoners how many hours had elapsed, and they were astonished to find it had gone so slowly.

At about 9 o'clock in the evening, the sun descended under the horizon. The rapid twilight gave the stars time to display their light one by one against the indigo curtain of the heavens. It was the time when the tigers and the Sons of Dheera shed blood.

Doctor Mystery knew those things; he understood India as if he had always lived there. He tried to listen to the noises outside. Suddenly a shiver went through his entire being; he had heard footsteps almost soundlessly gliding near the door. It opened with a metallic groan, letting in a flood of light. The captives immediately stood up.

Several cultists entered and formed a circle around the prisoners. Their hands gripped curved bronze daggers. On the threshold stood the Brahmin Arkabad—their nemesis, always following them without rest, having sworn their death. He entered slowly, came to stand near the Doctor, and in a serious voice, said:

"Doctor Mystery, Chosen of Vishnu, I greet you."

His voice sounded ironic. The Doctor remained silent, waiting.

"You are accompanying a young woman whose mind the Father of Beings has taken away," continued the Brahmin. "And using the sacred shield that Divine Law has granted to such Mindless Ones, you have dared oppose the wise ones, the Brahmins, who in solitude ponder the frightful problems of the Infinite."

The Doctor shrugged and said:

"I thought that the priests would respect the law that they say is Divine. I believed that the Mindless Ones were considered sacred, and that whoever brought harm to them should then fear the wrath of Brahma."

"You were right to believe that because that is the truth."

"So you say!"

"Why do you doubt me?"

The Doctor pointed to Na-Indra and replied:

"Because the insanity of that woman did not prevent her from being arrested and thrown in this prison. Let the offenders tremble! Brahma knows how to avenge such offenses."

With those words, he hoped to create division in those present. To his surprise, no one seemed to hear. Like bronze statues, the cultists remained immobile. Their faces expressed no emotion. As for Arkabad, he smiled disdainfully.

"You are attempting fruitlessly to frighten those faithful ones. I, Arkabad, who carries out the will of the Sacred College of Ellora, have taken upon myself alone, before the Creator of the World, the responsibility for arresting she who is called Na-Indra."

"So there are some bargains to be made with Heaven?" asked the Doctor sarcastically.

But Arkabad did not react at the sarcasm and instead continued:

"If I behaved as I did, it is because I love justice."

"Ah! That's something new!"

"...And I couldn't allow some villains to use a disingenuous imposter to challenge the sacred words of the Vedas."

"Some villains?"

"Yes, villains."

The Doctor looked around him with astonishment, and with an incisive tone, replied:

"I look at all those present and I saw but one villain: you. Are you the person that you are talking about?"

A threatening murmur rose from the circle, but Arkabad made a gesture and silence was re-established.

"Useless insults!" the Brahmin proclaimed. "You are calling a quick death, the one that you give to an enemy in anger, thus sparing him a long torture. But we shall not let ourselves be taken in by your ruse."

And when the Doctor made a gesture of protest, he added:

"I have reasons to believe that Na-Indra is faking her insanity."

"Is she really?" said the Doctor.

He turned quickly towards the young girl. He was afraid that she might have made a mistake and exposed herself. But no, she had taken again her air of being detached from everything, and at that critical moment, she was playing with one of her bracelets.

Reassured, the Doctor returned his attention to the Brahmin.

"It is easy to say: 'I have reasons to believe,' but that is not enough to break the Divine Law."

"And I shall not break it."

"Nevertheless, the arrest of that poor child..."

"...Was necessary in order to allay my suspicions or turn them into certainty."

"Then you are claiming..."

"I am only attempting to find incontrovertible proof."

"And if it turns out that you made a mistake?"

"In that case," replied the Brahmin in a loud voice, "she will be as free as all of you who are accompanying her. I will put at your disposition some horses, and I will offer gifts to Dheera and Brahma in order to obtain pardon for my mistake. Is that not, Brothers, what, in my loyalty, I promised before you, before asking for your cooperation?"

"Yes," answered the fanatics.

The Doctor bowed his head.

With devilish cleverness, Arkabad had found a way to thwart the Divine Law, while appearing to respect it. But what terrified the Doctor most of all was the calm with which their enemy had spoken of the experiment that he was proposing to conduct. If it failed, he would free the prisoners. He had promised it to the fanatics whose help he had enlisted; therefore, he would be bound to do it. But that means that his experiment would certainly be rigged in his favor. What Machiavellian schemer had he found in order to make Na-Indra admit that her madness was faked? In vain did the Doctor ask himself that question. The tongue of the Brahmin cut short his train of thoughts:

"The hour has come," said Arkabad. "Take the prisoners to the appointed place. By the end of night, they shall either be freed or convicted of being imposters."

In a minute, the captives were all separated from one another, surrounded by guards, and pushed towards the door. In slow succession, they crossed all the rooms of the temple, walking towards the exit. They finally reached the main entrance on the cliffside. The moon threw a hazy white light on the landscape. The captives all had the same exclamation.

There, between the crowd and the esplanade, stood a metallic armature, like that of a giant portcullis. Outside, barely six inches away, was like a round metal cage, opened to the sky, measuring roughly sixteen feet in diameter.

"Go ahead," ordered Arkabad.

Seized roughly by the Sons of Dheera, the Doctor and Anoor were pushed towards a door which opened in the portcullis and, almost carried by their guards, thrown inside the metallic enclosure.

Anoor, her face glued to the iron bars of this new prison, saw in front of her, behind the portcullis, the entrance of the Temple of Typhum and the masked faces of all the Sons of Dheera.

"What does this mean?" murmured the Doctor. "Nothing would be easier for us than to climb up these bars and escape from this enclosure. Gates like these which enclose the gardens of the wealthy have never stopped thieves before, and would hardly hold prisoners..."

He did not finish his thought. The trembling bellowing of a baby goat was suddenly heard.

"A baby goat!"

Anoor turned towards him. Her face contracted in a wordless terror.

"See! It's a baby goat... Over there, near that pillar... They are pinching it in order to make him bellow..."

The Doctor looked at her, not understanding.

"Is that what is giving you such terror, Anoor?"

"Yes."

"Why?"

"Why? How can you ask? But of course! You don't know... That baby goat, it is..."

The voice of the young girl strangled in her throat.

"What is it?" the Doctor insisted.

"The bait for the tiger!"

The Doctor turned pale in his turn.

One of the ways to kill a tiger in India is what one might call the "killing cage."

A solid enclosure, similar to that which held the Doctor and his young companions, is erected in a clearing in the jungle; a baby goat is placed inside and tied to a stake. A brave attendant, armed with a spear, is placed in with them. Once inside, he pokes the goat and makes him cry out. The sharp cries attract the tiger, always wandering about in search of a prey. The dreaded feline soon appears, walks around the cage, irritated by the obstacle. Then he begins to think. He realizes that, with one jump, he can get inside that inconvenient enclosure, and devour the goat which is now shivering with fear.

Then the tiger rears up and jumps in the air. He comes down right in the middle of the cage. But the attendant has seen all his movements. His spear is ready, and it is with a strong hand that he receives the wild beast, piercing him, and throwing him back outside, mortally wounded.

The Doctor and Anoor were living bait, and they had no spears. The bellowing sound was calling the tiger, who was set to devour little Anoor and the man that she called her father under Na-Indra's very eyes. That was Arkabad's scheme to force the girl to reveal her true state of mind!

The goat was still trembling.

A few seconds passed. The Doctor was debating with himself. Not being near his electric vehicle, all his weapons were not at his disposal. To fight a tiger was nearly impossible. Ah, if only he had kept one of his pistols filled with pyric acid! But he had nothing! He said to Anoor.

"Whatever happens... We must get out of here... To stay here would be tp condemn Na-Indra with us."

But he didn't continue. The arm of the little girl was stretched out. Towards the place where the plateau spread out. He looked at the spot.

"Too late! He's coming!" she stammered.

266

Yes, the tiger was coming. His head was lowered. He walked with sideways steps, hitting his sides with his tail, the sound of which resounded in the silence. He was an enormous cat, one of the old males, in peak condition, one of those terrible adversaries, the encounter of which would have worried even the most skilled of hunters. The animal advanced cautiously. Sheltered behind a rock, he looked at the cage, then at the entry to the temple. Before attacking, he studied the terrain with caution.

He remained there, during a length of time which seemed unending in the eyes of the two unfortunate would-be victims. But, however keen the sight of the predator was, other eyes were following that same scene with even sharper concentration: Na-Indra's.

Sheltered by the portcullis, Na-Indra, like her sister, had guessed Arkabad's diabolical plan as soon as the little goat had bellowed. But, at that important instant, she again found the energy that, during so many long years, had allowed her to hide her sanity. Her heart, although crushed by fright, her face, remained calm, expressionless, impassive. Nothing on the outside showed the agony inside. She remained at the place where she had been put. Ah! The cruel minutes!

The tiger hesitated. Soon reassured, he took a few steps onto the platform. He stretched himself voluptuously, lifting his supple spine. With his muzzle opened, he smelled the scents of his victims. Then he lifted his head, and from his half-opened muzzle, escaped a raucous joy.

Horror! That was a call! Hardly had the sound ceased to resonate that three monstrous beasts came to join the first one. All four now looked in the direction of the cage. Their nostrils sniffed the air in a gourmet fashion, and a strong concert of sounds broke out. The beasts were celebrating their impending feast. And crawling forward rapidly on their stomach, they silently approached the iron enclosure. There, they hit the iron bars. With their powerful paws, the tigers tried to knock them down, but the strength of the metal was superior to their own, a resistance they did not understand. They were astonished! They tried to put their muzzle between the bars. The barrier still did not give way.

Then, there were angry growls. Like spoiled children, the felines were angry for not being able to reach the things they coveted. Terrible blows of their paws made the metal bars vibrate. Finally, the older male realized that, in order to get at his preys, he would have to jump. There was like a growling conversation between him and his companions. Those who were close moved away. He moved back some steps and observed his surroundings. Finally, the distance seemed right to him. He raised himself up, ready to jump across the bars in a gracious arc, at the end of which his claws would dig into the panting flesh of his victims.

It was almost over. The Doctor and Anoor were lost. The Doctor valiantly placed himself in front of the little girl. But what protection was a mere human against the furious attack of a hungry tiger?

Ah! But moral strength had its limits. Na-Indra had used all her strength. In front of that terrible scene, she finally gave in. She forgot that Arkabad, standing behind her, didn't miss even one of her movements. More ferocious than the predators, he had planned the operation which would release the poor child in the monstrous hands of the Brahmins.

Near her, a Son of Dheera was holding a rifle in his hands. Na-Indra grabbed it. She took aim and fired. One bullet flew through the air; one bellow answered it.

The tiger turned around. He now attacked the portcullis from where the bullet which had hit him—but not injured him seriously—had originated. He jumped, growled, howled, bellowed, shaking the grate with his powerful blows. The bars seemed ready to break. Arkabad put his hand on the shoulder of the little girl and shouted triumphantly:

"You gave yourself away, Na-Indra. You are not insane!"

Like the wild beasts of the jungle, this wild beast of the temples worked at the destruction of a defenseless child.

At the sound of the gunshot, the other tigers had fled. Only the older male continued his futile efforts.

Suddenly, a light whistling sound was heard. The beast stopped suddenly. Shaking on his enormous paws, he fell on his side and did not move again.

"What's the matter?" asked Anoor. "Is he dead?"

"Yes," replies the Doctor.

Minutes passed and the tiger had not moved at all. With their suspicious eyes, the Hindus were watching the animal. He wasn't faking; he was no longer breathing.

A cry of joy came out of every mouth. The door of the portcullis opened and the Sons of Dheera rushed outside. They went to touch the wild animal's corpse. It was still warm.

Arkabad, holding Na-Indra's hand by the wrist, came out in his turn. With the help of a few men, he released the Doctor and Anoor from their prison. They had escaped the teeth of the tigers, but only to be freed by the executioner of El-lora.

Na-Indra was sobbing.

"Pardon me, Anoor, pardon me! I couldn't contain myself. To live without you now is impossible. I have condemned myself in order to reach with you the blue heaven of Indra."

She made excuses for herself, the poor and generous child, who had just given away her life. Arkabad was triumphant. He laughed. He joked. He led his prisoners to the temple from which they would never come out again, except to go to their deaths. But suddenly, he stopped, staying still, as if he had looked into the face of Medusa herself. The Sons of Dheera also no longer moved. They fell silent.

All of them looked at the sculpture of Typhum which dominated the entrance. A growl came down from it. As everybody looked at the stone god, it extended his arm in a threating gesture.

"Bring horses for the strangers. Rama wants them to leave and he will take vengeance if they are killed."

Was the miracle of the statue of Rama coming to life happening again? The Sons of Dheera threw themselves on the ground, their face in the dirt. But the white form which, under the light of the moon, had a ghostly appearance, continued:

"Bring the horses; then enter the temple and pray. Vishnu is angry that someone raised his hand against his Chosen One."

Arkabad wanted to resist the orders of the god. He tried some juggling, but the Sons of Dheera did not allow it. They, themselves, with all of their stubborn small-mindedness, believed in fantasies. Despite his recriminations, the Brahmin was forced into the temple. Some of the Sons brought the horses, then dashed away to rejoin their companions, who were already praying.

The Doctor, Anoor, Na-Indra, Graziella and Timoteo watched the situation in amazement. Was it a dream? No. Then, the statue began to speak again.

"In the name of God, don't waste any time! Get on the horses and go as quickly as possible!"

What familiar tone was Rama! Their confusion only increased. The god moved about. He ran along the edge, then jumped to the ground in one leap, followed by some kind of roly-poly black shape.

"On the horses! Na-Indra, Anoor, share the same horse in order not to leave me behind!" cried the strange figure.

The same cry came out of the lips of all those present.

"Cicada! Ludovic!"

The Parisian boy—for it was he—jumped on one of the horses, indicating that the moment wasn't right for long explanations. Everybody followed him. Soon the little troop was underway.

Finding themselves on the crest of the clifftop, in all haste, they took the road towards the West, to the Afghan territory, where they wouldn't have to fear the tyranny of the Brahmins.

The methods employed by Cicada to rescue the travelers was then explained.

After arriving at the temple, the young man, wanting to see without being seen, had observed the giant bas-relief and had used it as his observation point, accompanied by Ludovic, who never left him for a second.

From that elevated post, he had been present at a counsel held by Arkabad and the chief of the Sons of Dheera. He had observed the construction of the metal cage. Some passing conversation he had overheard had informed him of the legend of the statue of Rama coming to life, and, in his wild imagination, he come up with the fantastic idea, which had just saved his friends.

Using the dust accumulated behind and between the sculptures, he had disguised himself as one of the gods. An acid pistol he had kept had caused the death of the tiger.

After putting several kilometers between the fugitives and the temple, and being warmly praised for his efforts, Cicada replied:

"It was a simple joke... Any Parisian could have done it. But since you are so pleased, I'll take advantage of it and admit something..."

"What?" asked the Doctor, whose curiosity was now greatly piqued.

"Here it is. When we left the electric car, you, my dear Doctor, my adoptive father, had ordered me to put the bags which we used in the Zapolaki cave back..."

"Yes, I did."

"Well, I disobeyed you."

"You kept the bag?"

Cicada burst out laughing. He replied:

"No, but I filled it with stones and gave it back to Kéradec, who has religiously kept it."

His hilarity caused everybody to laugh.

"But," the boy concluded, "I did pocket the pyric acid gun, which certainly proved useful!"

"Indeed."

"And furthermore, I possess a little box. I don't know what it does, but I will give it back to you, because I think it might come in a handy sometime."

CHAPTER VII
An Alcohol-Powered Warrior

"Dear me... that gentleman..."

"That's the Director of the Electric Hotel."

"You recognize him, Wilhelmina?"

"Perfectly, Jeroboam."

"That's him! That's him!" shouted a dozen young, but irritated, voices.

Such were the exclamations which greeted Doctor Mystery and his companions when they entered the courtyard of the fort of the Peshawar Cantonment, established on the border of the Kabul River, which empties into the Indus near the border at Attock.

The Sanders-van Stoon family, father, mother and little misses, menacing, squeaking loudly, surrounded the travelers.

How did the Anglo-Dutch tribe had found itself there?

After the events at Amritsar, the young girls had decided unanimously that they could no longer stay in a city where Lord Farren and his son were constantly present and walking about half-naked in the most ungentlemanly fashion.

The English officers, furious at having been deceived by the Doctor and his friends, were eager to take a resounding revenge. They did not insist on holding back the visitors who had arrived at such an inconvenient hour.

So the united family of Sanders-van Stoon had retired in a dignified fashion. Understandably, the twelve attractive girls, who had become chatty because of their dashed matrimonial hopes, were in no hurry to return, fearing to be ridiculed. So, after a family vote, they had decided they would return to Europe by way of Afghanistan and Persia. They had taken the train to Peshawar, the terminus station of the railway line, and for two days since they had arrived there, they had been busy with the many administrative formalities imagined by the British Government.

These two days had been difficult.

Full of anger, forced to stay in this place with only the most rudimentary comfort, the dry Wilhelmina and the opulent Jeroboam had been further torn apart by the continuing Anglo-Boer conflict, sharper than ever. The military occupation of Bloemfontein, of Johannesburg, and of Pretoria by the English had exalted the patriotism of the former Member of the House of Commons. But the Dutch woman had praised the courageous pugnacity of the Boers, of President Paul Kruger and of General Botha, who had abandoned the cities in order to begin a terrible and murderous guerrilla war.

"Ah!" she shouted! "The English haven't won yet! Now, the real war, the war of extermination, begins. Everywhere, in the North, in the South, in the West and the East, Boer Commandos are going to hold the countryside. Patrols and convoys will be attacked. Plus, the Afrikanders at the Cape will rise up. The British army, harassed by an uncatchable foe, overcome by sickness, will melt like a piece of butter on a hot skillet."

Beginning with that tone, it can be judged the height to which that conversation mounted. The dozen attractive girls of those combative spouses lined up in order to stand guard between their respective parents. They could not keep them from insulting each other at a distance, but at least, they made it impossible for them to be in contact with each other. That would have had the most deplorable consequences.

Jeroboam was tearing out his hair because he had tied his life to that of a woman who had no affection except for the military. He called on his dead wife, who was taken too soon from his affection, and what a folly, which surely could not be explained, had pushed him to replace her... sequentially at least, because an angel cannot be replaced.

On her side, Wilhelmina vomited fire and flames against civilians, inferior and ridiculous beings, who didn't understand anything about military genius. Those pusillanimous non-entities, especially English ones, whose courage was limited only to insulting a poor widow incapable of defending herself.

In her turn, she groaned about the late Claudius van Stoon, that magnificent and well-meaning Dutch Warrior, whose presence would have chased away all the uncouth civilians of Great Britain. At that moment, the two who had once been joined together were disjoined by politics, and prevented by their daughters from being rejoined. They would have ended up tearing each other apart if the sight of Doctor Mystery and his friends had not saved them.

A common hatred against the man who had played such a large part in their tribulations silenced their patriotism. Besides, they were tired of their endless discussions. With an exquisite sense of the situation, from Maude to Anneeken, the young ladies let out a sharp and tortured cry of anger, and the Sanders-van Stoons, angry, squeaking, and menacing, surrounded the travelers.

The Doctor and his friends, asked a hundred meters away by a patrol to identify themselves, state their names, business, etcetera, had complied with the order. They thought of turning around and fleeing, but the heavy wooden gates giving access into the fort were closed and its high walls prevented any idea of flight. In vain, the Doctor, Cicada, Anoor, Na-Indra, and the two Italian fiancés tried to make themselves heard, but can logic calm the fighting enthusiasm of a husband and a wife, glad to divert their bad mood onto a third person, or the anger of sweet young girls who had just missed marriage?

The Sanders-van Stoon became increasingly irate. Red fingernails were threatening to tear out the eyes of the troublemakers, when a loud voice stopped the tempest like magic.

"If you aren't going to stay quiet, I'll put everybody under lock and key."

A strong old man, whose beard had been bleached by the sun, came forward. He was Ar Vindu, a descendant of the Begum of Peshawar, Commandant of the garrison.

"Let's see," he said, "what's the trouble?"

Everybody answered at the same time, each one accusing his neighbor.

"Silence!" shouted Ar Vindu, deafened, "or I'll call my soldiers."

Then, speaking to Jeroboam, who, considering his weight, seemed to be the most important person, he said:

"You, sir, speak."

Flattered by that turn of events, one that would have been applauded by his former colleagues in the House of Commons, Sanders told the circumstances that had led to their presence in the electric hotel. He inflated his voice in order to denounce the judicial mistake which had followed, their subsequent arrest, and their interrogation by the magistrates of Churu, concluding with the succession of events explanations which had finally established their innocence. Finally, he proffered the evident guilt of the Doctor and his companions, who were certainly traveling deceitfully, because both the British authorities and the Baramins were upset by their movements across India.

The Commandant listened without interrupting Sanders. He shook his head like a man who was considering the situation seriously. When Sanders stopped, Ar Vindu pronounced this judgement, like that of Solomon:

"I have understood nothing of what you have just said. My duty is, therefore, to hold you all as prisoners and ask for instructions from the Government of Punjab. You will be locked up in a place that I will provide. Guards will watch the exits. Each day, you will be authorized a two-hour walk in the court-yard. That's all. I have spoken."

A concert of recriminations began immediately.

The Sanders-van Stoon family (who at last were right) would not accept being treated as suspects. As for the Doctor and his friends, who shortly before had escaped from the Sons of Dheera, they saw themselves captives again, this time of the Sepoy. This was akin to moving from the frying pan into the fire.

But the Commandant would not allow any criticism.

"Those who prefer jail to the comfortable bedrooms I have planned for you only need to say so," he growled with a thunderous voice. "What I have decided will be done. Consider that, peace or jail."

Calm returned without delay, and everybody, lowering their heads, let themselves be taken to a barrack set up by the soldiers, summoned by Ar Vindu with a whistle. Installing the prisoners was very simple. They were placed in a vast room with white walls, and a series of screens coming up to mid-height which separated it into two equal sections. The Doctor's company was taken to one side; the Sanders-van Stoon to the other.

"The wrath of Brahma pursues us," Na-Indra said sadly after the Sepoy had gone away. "Another hour and we would have crossed the border. Ahead of us would have been freedom and the Treasury of Liberty. Now, we have to escape again."

"Damned bad luck," growled Timoteo, wringing his hands.

"I understand your frustration, my friend," the charming Graziella said tenderly. "These English that our government presents as being our allies are conducting themselves like bandits."

The Doctor did not say anything. A deeply furrowed brow formed across his forehead, and his eyes, where the flame of reflection could be seen, looked from Na-Indra, to Anoor, and on Cicada, with an expression of kindly pity. He too had to admit that the situation seemed desperate. Captives of native soldiers in the service of England, they would almost certainly be brought before the Lieutenant Governor of Punjab, Lord Farren, with whom they had had a difficult relationship. As a result, the Doctor and Cicada would be thrown into a prison while Na-Indra and her sister would be turned over to the cruel Arkabad.

There was no one, even the gentle and kind Italians, who didn't fear the results of this misadventure.

Cicada's voice suddenly reached the Doctor's ears:

"Mademoiselle Na-Indra," the young man was saying, "I will not ask you where the Treasure is. First of all, that doesn't make any difference to me, and also, you would not tell me. But you can give me some information...?"

"What kind of information, Monsieur Cicada?"

"This: after we cross the border, would we have a long distance to go before we reach our destination?"

Before Na-Indra could answer, Anoor threw herself into her arms.

274

"Speak without being afraid, dear sister. If he is asking you that, it's because he has an idea. He is brave and clever. He will save us."

The young girl had unlimited confidence in Cicada, and she said these words with moving ingenuity.

"I think so too, my dear Anoor," Na-Indra replied. "If I appeared to hesitate, it's because I was calculating the distance yet to be covered!" And looking at Cicada, she added: "We must cross mountains, follow the Kabul River as far as the city which has given it its name. After that, we must travel South toward Kandahar, where the Master..." Here, her big eyes became fixed on the Doctor with a kind of fervor. "...Where the Master has commanded his servants to wait for him. After that, the journey will not be over, but the most difficult part will have been accomplished."

The Doctor shook his head.

"Strange," he murmured in a pensive tone! "The search for that treasure, dedicated to India's liberation, will take us across the same routes followed by the armies that invaded this country: Mongols, Tartars, Aryans, all have come to India by the valley where flows the Kabul river. The Russians, who seem to want to be seen as the allies of the future India, will also come in through the same route... How strange!"

"Very interesting," Cicada began again, "but we have to start by saying goodbye to Commandant Ar Vindu."

"Yes."

"And since that trip is going to take a good number of miles, it's not enough for us to get away; we must also reclaim our horses."

Anoor clapped her hands:

"You have an idea?" she said.

"Not yet," replied Cicada, "but I'll soon find one."

"Ah!" she said. "I knew that you wouldn't leave us in this prison."

"My dear little sister!"

"No longer your little sister," she quickly corrected. "Remember what we agreed to before the terrible encounter with the Sons of Dheera."

The young man blushed and closed his eyes.

"Let's not talk about that again. Once we are safe, we will explain things to our friends. They will decide. For the moment, it's a question of getting out of here." And with pretend confidence, he added: "We shall get out of here. Can you imagine those soldiers able to stop a Parisian from getting out into the open air?"

Then, he began to think aloud:

"First of all, let's go over our weapons. My great friend, my father, I have confessed that I emptied the contents of the bag of tricks you gave me before our expedition in the caves of Zapolaki into my pockets. I think I used or lost most of those items during our previous adventures, but there are two left: the pyric acid pistols which seems to me to be a serious weapon..."

"But which I am reluctant to use against those men," the Doctor declared seriously. "Those are soldiers, serving, a powerful master against their will... Although I am merciless against tyrants, I wish to spare their slaves."

Cicada shrugged and said philosophically:

"OK! I'll put away that pistol for the moment, but I will keep it. It still has 38 projectiles. That's enough to turn this fort into Sleeping Beauty's castle. Now, here is a little box which contains a brown powder. I can't imagine what it is..."

While talking, the young man had taken out of his pocket a little box made of nickel that he presented to the Doctor, who smiled disdainfully.

"Bah! We can't use that. It is anti-ethylene powder."

"What? Crinoline powder," Cicada joked, deciding as always to mispronounce scientific words.

"No anti-ethylene," repeated the Doctor. "It's just a remedy, a simple remedy."

"Against what, if you don't mind? If I am asking, it's not out of ordinary curiosity, but I'd love to learn what that little pharmacy in your pocket does."

"You don't have, and hopefully will never have, the terrible sickness that one pinch of that powder could cure."

"A pinch? And that sickness is terrible?"

"You be the judge. It's alcoholism."

Cicada burst out laughing.

"I see! The sickness is drunkenness! Your powder would keep me from drinking?"

"Don't laugh," the Doctor replied seriously. "Alcoholism isn't something to joke about, it's a sickness as terrible as an epidemic like cholera, the plague, or influenza, the murderous sicknesses of which make fewer victims every year than alcoholism."

"What?" Cicada stammered. "Seriously?"

"Yes. Consider this. In countries where the drinking of alcohol is not regulated, the number of insane people and murderers increase in a terrible fashion, because alcohol destroys and breaks down the resistance of individuals. Our body, my child, can be compared to a fortress, protected by helpful microbes in charge of destroying bad microbes, which constantly try to dismantle its defenses. Alcohol is the accomplice of these bad microbes. The brain atrophies when one drinks alcohol; reasoning faculties disappear. One becomes impulsive, that is to say, one obeys nervous impulses which are irrational. Alcohol causes rages for no reason, in the course of which it might prompt someone to kill without reason. All our organs shut down, undergoing a kind of reorganization, and what is most terrible is that its children can be born with alcoholic inclinations: epilepsy, tuberculosis, hydrocephalies, cretinism, blood diseases of all kinds, muscle diseases and nervous diseases of all types."

"Brrr," said the Parisian boy with a shiver. "And I thought alcohol gave you strength!"

"That's a mistake that is unfortunately widespread. The agricultural worker believes that he is gaining extra strength by drinking alcohol, but that is only an illusion. Whether it is morphine or nicotine, all the poisons, which ignorant humanity uses, have the same results. They have the effect on the organism that a whip has on a tired horse. The poor beast straightens up, makes an additional effort, which leaves him even more tired. But no one thinks that giving him another blow of the whip will increase its strength."

"I'm sure it doesn't"

"Alcohol doesn't work any differently, and a Minister of War in your country, child, did a good action, so good in fact that it makes up for a lot of bad actions, when he forbade the sale of alcohol in military canteens".

"Really?"

"I swear it to you, and all the scientists will confirm it."

Cicada's face expressed disbelief.

"All right, I'll believe you. I am not an educated man, but, while living with you, I have learned many new things. It would be a good idea to teach to all the ignorant people that scientists know a great deal more things than they, who don't know anything."

And as the Doctor smiled, the young man continued with vivacity:

"That seems obvious, yet it's astonishing to see how many people are predisposed to resist science. Maybe it's because they learned too little at school? So, a doctor, who has studied medicine a long time, prescribes a remedy, but then, the first jackass who comes along, and doesn't know anything about medicine, feels entitled to criticize his prescription. As a result, the skeptical patient does not use the prescription but instead takes some snake oil remedy. If he is cured, he makes fun of the doctor! But if he dies, they'll accuse the doctor of having done nothing."

But changing tone,

"And you have found the method of vanquishing alcoholism?"

There was admiration in the young man's voice.

"No," answered the Doctor. "I am simply perfecting a method discovered by three French scientists, Drs Sapelier, Thébault, and Broca."[107]

"And that method?"

"The same as the one used at the Pasteur Institute. They give the disease to an animal: dog, rabbit, guinea pig, goat... Then they draw out the serum from the

---

[107] In 1899-1900, Drs Sapelier Thébault and Broca advised the French Academy of Medicine of their discovery of an antialcohol serum. They stated that their experiments proved that a horse fed for a certain time on doses of alcohol and food mixed with alcohol furnished a serum of antiethyline which injected into victims of the alcohol habit gave them an absolute distaste for the liquor.

blood from those animals and inject some of it under the skin of a human. They developed some kind of vaccine which stops the progression of the disease."

Cicada rubbed his hands with satisfaction.

"I must be becoming smarter," he declared. "It's astonishing how I am now able to follow your explanations."

"Then I will continue. Drs Sapelier, Thébault and Broca, improving on the work of Drs Thulouse, Meramaldi and Evelyn, had the idea of making a horse alcoholic by sprinkling brandy in his grain. The operation succeeded marvelously! The animal developed a fondness for wine and spirits. Now the serum drawn from the animal allowed curing alcoholic humans to whom it had been inoculated, and cure them more completely to the extent that, after the treatments, those men felt an insurmountable distaste for alcohol."

"What? They no longer wanted to drink?"

"Strong drinks, no. The number of those cured was sixty persons out of one hundred. As for the forty who were not cured, it was either because of their lack of cooperation in not following the treatment to the end, or from constitutional defects which made them reject the serum. I have simply taken up again the work of the scientists whom I have just named. Thanks to a chemical preparation, I have metamorphized the serum into a powder, and I have increased its potency. It's enough just to put a pinch of that powder into a glass of water and, with the liquid thus obtained, turn an alcoholic back into a normal person."

At that moment Cicada let out a cry of despair:

"That's admirable, but we're wasting time!"

"What do you mean?"

"Minutes are galloping away, and only one thought should occupy our mind."

"Which one?"

"To get out of here."

That was true. For a minute, the scientific digression of the Doctor had made those present forget the dangerous situation in which they found themselves. The reflection of the young Parisian brought them back to reality.

"I think we need to talk," said Graziella.

"To find a way out of this prison," added Timoteo.

"Yes," murmured Na-Indra and Anoor, and with a look full of confidence directed towards the Doctor and Cicada, who by then had become serious again.

The Doctor bowed and said:

"Let's confer and may Brama inspire us."

They all sat on big ladders that were spread though the room, and everyone was going to take part in the deliberation, when a volley of invectives broke out above their heads. They jumped and turned around. Then, they were overcome with laughter, seeing the hilarious spectacle unfolding in front of their eyes.

After the first moment of stupor caused by their incarceration, the Sanders-van Stoon family had not been slow in listening to the conversation which was taking place on the other side of the separation of the two groups of captives. Then, they saw that the so-called barrier was hardly six feet high. All they had to do was climb up the ladders--there were enough of them—to get over the obstacle of the screens. Everybody, father, mother, daughters, prepared themselves. Their heads appeared above the screens and they looked to their neighbors like a family of decapitated heads. But they were talking decapitated heads. The stentorian voice of Jeroboam, the sharp tongue of Wilhelmina, the silver timbers of the girls mingled in a cacophony of insults, reproaches, and threats.

"You, miserable persons!"

"You rascals!"

"You will all be turned over to the hangman, because you had a British citizen jailed!"

"And a citizen of the Netherlands, too."

"And you broke up the marriage of these poor young girls, who did not deserve such barbaric treatment."

All of that was said at the same time as there was shouting, bellowing and whistles.

Despite the gravity of the circumstances, the Doctor and his companions were still laughing. And the more they laughed, the more the Sanders-van-Stoon became irritated. Jeroboam was purple with anger like an iris flower! Wilhelmina had turned a bilious yellow, like a rose. And the girls' faces were the color of peonies. Fortunately, the excess of their rage was quickly stifled, and taking advantage of an instant when the fourteen representatives of the Sanders-van Stoon were catching their breath, Cicada broke in with his Parisian accent which was inimitable:

"Madame, young ladies, and you too, sir, please close your beaks, so that I can open mine."

The audacity of the boy surprised them. He continued:

"It isn't necessary to explain to you that I am not here for my pleasure. Just like you, I would like to go where I please, freely."

"Freely? Him?" growled those listening to him.

The Doctor and his friends were listening, not knowing where Cicada was going.

"Now," continued the young Parisian calmly, "your cries have interrupted a meeting with my companions. The purpose of that meeting was to discover some way of leaving this prison."

"Leave it?" shouted Sanders, finding again his use of speech. "I myself will oppose that by force—tooth and nails."

"What force?" joked the Parisian. "Is this a nice thing to say to the only one capable of preventing the English authorities from putting you to death."

"To death?" stammered all of the Sanders-van Stoon.

"Yes—to death! All of you were our companions in the Electric Hotel. You then found yourselves at the same time as us in Amritsar. Now you are

Again, just like us, in Peshawar. If it pleases me to tell them that you are our accomplices—the circumstances fully demonstrate that—you will share our fate."

Only a terrified murmur answered that bold statement. The complexion of the Sanders-van Stoon changed. From anger, their faces turned to astonishment. Jeroboam became as green as lettuce; Wilhelmina took on the color of an unripe tomato. As for the young girls, their pretty faces turned to lilacs.

"Therefore," concluded Cicada triumphantly, "my friends and I must leave this inhospitable place and work at the same time toward your deliverance."

That time, the family no longer protested. The Sanders-van Stoon had been overcome.

"Perfect!" exclaimed the Parisian. "Now you are starting to be reasonable." And smiling, he added: "Now that you are calm, let me explain to you why we are followed by the English authorities…"

A murmur of curiosity answered those words. Decidedly, Cicada had the art of catching the interest of the crowd. In a colorful style, filled with picturesque slang, he summed up their adventures: the drama at Audierne, the meeting of Anoor and the bear Ludovic, the search for Na-Indra, the battle at Ellora, the flight from Amritsar, etc., etc.

The young ladies heard the story with growing emotion. Those men, who had been described to them as bandits, were simply people with heart, dedicated to the salvation of two orphans. As for Graziella, with her expansive Italian personality, she exclaimed sympathetically:

"*Povero! Santa Madona! Corpo Santo!*"

Timoteo clenched his fists, murmuring some terrible threats against the Brahmins.

When Cicada had finished, Maud exclaimed:

"My sisters, we should vote to determine if we will or not be the allies of these kind gentlemen."

According to the family tradition, the voting was soon begun and Sanders proclaimed the result with astonishment:

"14 votes cast. 14 in favor!"

The vote had been unanimous. For the first time, a question posed to the household had all rallied all the votes. That was so pleasing to Jeroboam's heart that he forgot the many tribulations that had led him to this moment.

At about 3 o'clock, the prisoners were taken out of their jail. Surrounded by the guards, they were taken into a courtyard and ordered to walk there, two by two. Ar Vindu himself appeared for an instant to tell his captives that he had sent a telegram to Amritsar in order for the government to decide their fate. But the Commandant went away suddenly after hearing some far away cries which sounded raucous and desolated.

The Doctor, who was walking beside Cicada, suddenly stopped.

"What's that?" he murmured with a thoughtful look.

"That," replied Cicada, "is the shout of a man with lungs of steel. He bellows like a bull."

A guard shook his head, saying:

"No, that's a man in pain."

"A sick man?"

"No, a possessed man."

The Doctor commanded silence from the young Parisian, who was about to reply with some sarcasm.

"It is Akkar, the dear son of our Commandant," added the guard.

"And he is possessed?" asked the Doctor.

"Yes. The Djinns have gotten into his body and are tormenting him. That's frightening to see. His eyes seem about to jump out of their sockets; his lips are trembling; his arms and legs are moving about randomly."

"Ah!" And after thinking for an instant, the Doctor asked: "Was Akkar in good health before?"

"He had the strength of a bull!"

"Was he eating well?"

"Like a hungry tiger."

"I suppose he was drinking much, as befits a warrior of his stature?"

"Ah! Ten warriors couldn't have put away the same quantity of liquid. Faced with those bottles, he was no longer a man. You can believe it. He had the thirst of a god."

"Thank you."

The Doctor was continuing his walk with Cicada. When they were some steps away, Cicada asked in a low voice:

"So this Akkar is an alcoholic?"

"Yes, it would appear so."

Another even more lamentable complaint was heard.

"Listen, Cicada! That's the sound of *delirium tremens*. His nerves are burning, destroyed by the poison, no longer responding to his will, leading him to have a veritable epileptic crisis. For two, three, four days, the sick man grinds his teeth, shouts, is prey to terrible hallucinations, and can't stop his body from jumping around. He shivers, dances about, his arms twist, his feet trash around. He wants to resist, to stop those random movements, but he can't—until death finally comes to deliver him..."

"So that's the sickness he's suffering from?"

"That unfortunate man? Yes."

Suddenly, Cicada laughed and made an about-face.

"What are you doing?" asked the Doctor, surprised by this sudden gaiety.

"How can you ask me that?"

"I don't understand."

"I have just found the way to get out of here and cross the border."

"You have?"

"Yes! Thanks to alcoholism, which at least this time, will have a good consequence."

And as the Doctor's face continued to express his puzzlement, Cicada continued:

"Tell our companions to get ready to mount the horses."

"But how…?"

"I will explain later. We mustn't waste precious time."

Then, going back to the guard to whom they had spoken an instant before, the Parisian told him:

"Please call Ar Vindu. I need to talk to him."

The soldier shrugged.

"He is at his son's bedside. He won't come."

"He will, if you add that I know how to conquer the Djinns."

That sentence, pronounced in a firm voice, made the guard jump.

"The Djinns," he said with some hesitation, "laugh at the efforts of men."

"I don't have time to argue with you. Do what I told you to. If you don't, you will cause Akkar's death and Ar Vindu will never forgive you."

The threat immediately overcame the soldier's resistance, and he said:

"Follow me. I will take you to him."

"Let's go."

"But before that, let me warn you of the danger you are going to run."

"Go ahead, speak."

"Ar Vindu is a violent man. If you lie to him, he will not hesitate to blow your head off with his pistol."

Cicada smiled calmly, and answered:

"Is that all?"

"It seems to me that it is enough."

"You have misunderstood me. Let's go, big boy. I forgive you for not understanding. But you mustn't believe that a pistol is capable of frightening me."

Although he did not understand the young man's boldness, the guard did not insist.

Following him, Cicada went across the building which had been selected to be their prison, went through a second courtyard, and then into a dark corridor which came out into a carefully tended garden, at the back of which was a grove of parasol pines and a rustic cabin.

The cries came from there.

Now that they were close, they deafened the ears of the young man and made shivers go down his spine. There were horrible shouts, scraping sounds, jumping up and down, the bellows of a wild beast caught in a trap, the screams which the madness of the brain expressed at the same time as sadness and fear. It recalled the lamentations of the dammed in eternal agony which the great poet Dante Alighieri wrote about in his *Divina Commedia*. The guard became very troubled.

"You hear that?" he stammered.

"Of course! I am not deaf."

"And you still want to fight the Djinns who have entered the body of Akkar?"

"Certainly." And in a low voice the young man finished his thought: "There is only one kind of spirits here who matter: distilled ones."

The soldier finally reached a decision.

"Stay here. I'll talk to Ar Vindu."

"By all means."

Saying that, Cicada sat down on a rattan bench. The guard started walking towards the cabin which he entered. Cicada plugged his ears in order not to hear Akkar's wild cries anymore. The guard wasn't absent long; he returned and invited him to approach. Cicada got up and complied. A moment later, as he was stepping onto the wooden deck in front of the cabin. Ar Vindu came to meet him. Meanwhile, the screams of the sick man had grown louder. At that moment, one would have believed that he was protesting with all his strength against the stranger's arrival. That was at least how the Commandant interpreted that rage.

"Do you hear?" he asked Cicada roughly.

The young Parisian did not smile.

"Why are you asking? Are there a lot of deaf people here?"

But the quip did not register on Ar Vindu's grim face, who asked again:

"Do you hear?"

"Of course, I do!" replied Cicada very serious. "Your son is screaming as if he was being tortured."

"And do you know why?"

"The Djinns are in him."

"Yes!"

"But I will chase them away if you trust me."

There was such assurance in him that Ar Vindu was impressed.

"Can you really do that?"

"Yes, but before everything else, you must correct an unjust mistake that you made."

"What mistake?" growled the Commandant, frowning.

"You are holding here some harmless travelers who should be allowed to leave immediately."

"I am waiting for orders from the Governor."

"You don't need orders to do what is just." And with a carefree expression, he added: "As you wish. Wait for orders. But when they arrive, your son will be dead."

The old man began to tremble when he heard those sinister words. Then he asked:

"You are certain that those travelers are harmless?"

The Commandant was vacillating; Cicada knew that he had to deliver a master stroke. He pointed to a magnificent peacock, three steps away, which had unfurled his feathers.

"You will judge for yourself whether they are harmless, Commandant. They want to owe their liberty only to your goodwill. If that was not how they felt, they would have left your fort immediately. No one could stop their departure."

A smile appeared on the lips of Ar Vindu.

"I see that you are doubtful," continued the Parisian, "but you are wrong. They are, like me, powerful magicians. It would be enough for them to hold out a hand toward you, toward any of your soldiers, and your heart would stop beating and you would be swallowed up by death."

"Come now, you must be joking!"

"You want proof... All right! So be it!"

And seeming to look around, Cicada suddenly pointed to the peacock. The proud bird, once dedicated to the goddess Juno, continued to spread out his multi-colored tailfeathers into the sunlight.

"That peacock is marvelous," Cicada said.

"True."

"I'm going to kill him."

"With a single gesture?"

"Yes. Watch!"

So saying, the young man held out his arm toward the bird, which made a raucous cry, his wings desperately beat the air, then his claws clutched. He palpitated for a second, his stomach on the ground, his beak wide open, and, finally, rolled on his side. One might have guessed that the acid pistol, cleverly hidden in the young man's sleeve, had just done its work.

But for the Commandant, whose did not suspect any subterfuge, the incident took on the appearance of a miracle. He went to the poor bird, lifted it, and, after being certain that life was no longer in it, he returned to Cicada, who was secretly enjoying the situation.

Ar Vindu's arrogance had all but disappeared. He was humbled. In a murmur, he said:

"Command. I will obey."

"And your dear son will be saved."

"I have confidence in you."

"Good. Give your prisoners back their horses, their weapons and their luggage."

The Commandant asked:

"To everybody? Even those who swore at you when you arrived?"

"Even to those. Their anger came from a mistake that has now been erased."

The Commandant bowed and called a servant by striking a gong.

"That will be all?"

"Almost. Let them get mounted, have the gates opened so that when I'm ready to rejoin them, nothing will hold back our departure."

A guard came running, responding to the gong. The Commandant transmitted word for word Cicada's instructions. The soldier left again, trotting, to carry out the orders.

Then Cicada gave a friendly slap on the Commandant's shoulder and said:

"You did the right, Ar Vindu. And because of this, Vishnu, father of the just, will allow me to cast out the demons who have taken up residence in your son's body. Take me to him."

In a hurry, the Commandant led the young man into a room which had been darkened by closing the shutters. Cicada saw, with some difficulty, a man lying on crumpled up mat in the middle of the room. Any conversation was impossible. His vociferations resonated too loudly and too sharply. On a bamboo table, the young man saw a glass carafe with water and four goblets. He went to them, filled one of the goblets halfway. Then, taking the box filled with the brown powder out of his pocket, he threw a pinch of it into the water, murmuring:

"The Doctor was wrong when he claimed that its antiethyline drug would be useless. As it turns out, it's going to save us."

The words, which came indistinctly to the ears of the Commandant, seemed to him to be just another incantation. The water simmered on contact with the powder, then became clear again. The dissolution was completed. Then, with the help of a tiny subcutaneous injector attached to the box, Cicada, with the confidence of an old professor, gave Akkar several shots of the serum. Perhaps the shot was a little stronger than it should have been, but its effect was astounding. Probably the Parisian had unknowingly increased the dosage?

The screaming suddenly stopped. Akkar's eyes stopped rolling in their orbits. His arms and legs stretched out; he closed his eyes and went into a calm and deep sleep.

Ar Vindu was observing the scene. He looked stupefied.

"The Djinns have gone away..." he stammered. "This is miraculous... What else do you want from me, stranger?"

"Nothing. I am just going to rejoin my companions and leave."

"What if the Djinns return?"

"Don't be afraid. I give you my word that they will never return." And mingling truth with fiction to persuade the Commandant, he added: "You see, the Djinns were hiding in the strong drinks that your son was consuming."

"What? Those dark spirits have had that duplicity?"

"Yes!"

"But then, they will return, because I know my son. As soon as he can stand up, he will ask for something to drink. I know that all too well."

The Commandant stopped on seeing Cicada shrug. He said:

"You don't believe me?"

"No."

"But I assure you…"

"Commandant, I know that you are telling the truth, but when I chased the demons away, I also gave your son a strong distaste for alcoholic drinks."

"What?"

"In the future, he will reject them with distaste, and will not want to drink anything but water."

"Can that actually be?"

"Why do you doubt me? Have I deceived you so far?"

The Commandant bowed, almost prostrating himself.

"No, no, you are a great magician! I can't doubt your truthfulness. Pardon me for having doubted you… But I do not share your knowledge of the unknown, and my mind is too small to fathom what is truly incomprehensible."

The good man would have continued talking like that for a long time, but Cicada, although amused, was in a hurry to rejoin his friends. He said goodbye and returned to the first courtyard. Facing the open door to the outside, the Doctor and his friends, the Sanders-van Stoons, were all waiting on their horses. Anoor was holding in her hand Cicada's mount on which Ludovic was already seated. With a bound, the young Parisian was already in the saddle, and with a resounding voice, he said:

"Let's go!"

The little troop got ready, crossed the threshold of the fort with a thunderous noise, and dashed towards the west, towards the border, several kilometers away. Everybody felt strong emotions.

Soon, on both sides of the road, they encountered a with British colors in two languages which read *INDIA* on one side and *AFGHANISTAN* on the other side, towards the west. That was the frontier.

A few more steps and the hooves of their horses would strike the soil of Afghanistan. The travelers had finally left India, the lands of the Brahmins.

CHAPTER VIII
The Road of Invasions

The travelers were now traveling along the valley of the Kabul River. It is a great river, more than one hundred and twenty miles-long, which nature appears to have designed expressly for allowing human migration to pass from the high plateaus of Afghanistan into the fertile plains of the Indus and the Ganges.

Sometimes, the valley was divided in immense circles and spread out widely; at other times it narrowed itself into rocky sections, and at certain spots, the mountain looked as if it wanted to close off all passageways entirely and not even leave open a narrow road that was difficult to cross.

The cedars, the conifers, the oaks, raised their giant trunks and buried their roots into the slopes of the mountain. Now that they had finally left the territories under the authority of the Brahmins, the little troop traveled at a restful pace. They knew that the hooves of their horses were striking the soil at the very same places that, for ten thousand years, various armies from the north had taken to travel south towards India because of the wealth of that gigantic peninsula.

The Doctor explained:

"Here, this tumulus marks the burial place of the Sikh chiefs Waver and Rajni, who, according to Vedic legends, three thousand years before our era, invaded the provinces of Punjab, Sindh, and Rajputana."

A little further on, the Doctor pointed out a monolith on a summit:

"That giant stele was erected to commemorate the conquest of Rajputana by an invasion composed of people from Southern Siberia and the current Turkestan."

Everyone tried to imagine, in this fashion, the past in the same décor where these events had taken place, as the Doctor recounted each event with deep emotion.

From time to time, they crossed path with Afghan caravans. They were led by tall men, wearing shirts with long sleeves which fell down large dark cotton trousers. Their heads were covered with black silk caps, on top of which sat gold brocades made of red silk. On their feet were clouted sandals, which fit those wandering men. On their shoulders rested long guns with silver decorations, and on their belt hung curved sabers. They wore richly decorated cartridge belts on their chest. These people looked at the travelers with suspicion. From time to time, a warrior wearing on his cap the amethyst jewel of the *Serdars* or the garnet stones of the *Khans* questioned them.

And they all walked away, saying in a jovial tone:

"Go to Kabul. You foreigners ought to see our city. Those there will tell you of the victory of 1842."

It was in 1842 that a British army had been annihilated, and the inhabitants had kept a proud memory of this event, mingled with an incredible hatred for the English. Probably in their ignorance, they took the travelers to be English, because, for them, there existed only two European nations: the English to the east; and the Russian to the west.

According to whether a traveler enters Afghanistan from the North or from the South, he is catalogued as either Russian, i.e.: friend; or English, i.e.: enemy. Nevertheless, Doctor Mystery, Cicada, Na-Indra and Anoor, the two Italian fiancés, and the Sanders-van-Stoon family progressed without any difficulties.

The fourth day of the march, towards the evening, they reached the fortified city of Jalalabad. The *Serdar* there, following the custom, invited them to stay at his house. In this hospitable country, having strangers as guests was one of the duties of those who held public office.

The horses were led to the stable. Their host offered them a copious meal, complete with both white and red wines, from the grapes that the mountain dwellers grow on the slopes. Towards the end of the dinner, ten young men and women were brought in and danced the *Attam* or the *Gumboot*. They danced together, executing various figures, pantomiming a hunt, fishing, the whole spectacle accompanied by shouts, clapping of the hands, and snapping of the fingers.

Then the *Serdar* sent away the dancers and, with a note of irony, said:

"I have reserved the most interesting part of the entertainment for you."

"What is that?" asked the Doctor.

"It's a production of our national anthem."

"What is it called?"

"*The Great Victory*," pronounced the chief in a loud voice.

The Doctor, Anoor, Na-Indra, who understood the language of the country, and served as interpreters, smiled. They were going to be shown a retelling of the story of the English disaster of 1842.[108] The *Serdar* shook his head and clapped his hands. Immediately the doors opened. The servants placed benches across the room, across from a wooden stage resembling a puppet theater. On the invitation of their host, the travelers took a seat and the servants stood behind them. Then the *Serdar* stood up and gravely announced:

"*The Great Victory*, a dramatic work in five acts. A faithful rendering of the way in which the noble Afghan warriors chastised the insolence of the English Conquerors."

The cloth curtain was lifted on the candle-lit stage decorated to represent the drawing room of a palace. Almost immediately, two wooden marionettes, painted to represent the English uniforms, came on stage and were greeted by boos. The servants showed their hatred of the ancestral enemy.

Leaving aside the interruptions of the spectators, we are going to give below extracts from that fascinating play which will explain better than long explanations the Russian and English rivalry in Afghanistan.

THE GREAT VICTORY
(*A Play in Five Acts*)

ACT ONE

LORD ROBERT SALE, LORD ELPHINSTONE:[109]

SALE:

---

[108] The 1842 retreat from Kabul, also called the Massacre of Elphinstone's army, during the First Anglo-Afghan War, was the retreat of the British and East India Company forces from Kabul. An uprising in Kabul forced the then commander, Major-General William Elphinstone, to fall back to the British garrison at Jalalabad. As the army and its numerous dependents and camp followers began its march, it came under attack from Afghan tribesmen. Many of the column died of exposure, frostbite or starvation, or were killed during the fighting.

[109] Major-General William George Keith Elphinstone (1782-1842); Major-General Sir Robert Henry Sale (1782-1845), British Army officer who commanded the garrison of Jalalabad during the First Afghan War and was later killed in action during the First Anglo-Sikh War.

Major General Elphinstone, what do you think of the situation?

ELPHINSTONE

It is bad, Major General Sale. These Afghans are real bastards!

SALE

Which we must conquer with our weapons. Let's recapitulate. The Afghan leader, Dost Mohammad,[110] has with him a Russian officer, on the advice of whom he wants to give the province of Herat to the Persians, and take away from England the province of Peshawar.

ELPHINSTONE

That is so.

SALE

We must prevent that. Our troops are assembled. Starting tomorrow we will march on Kandahar, by way of the hills of Balochistan.

ELPHINSTONE

Finally! We are going to crush those bastards!

ACT II
A Place in Kandahar

SCENE I

ELPHINSTONE, SALE, ENGLISH OFFICERS

ELPHINSTONE

We have taken Kandahar and the mountain forces have been destroyed?

SALE

Yes. Dost Mohammad has finally fled into the mountains. We have appointed as his successor Shujah, who is completely devoted to us.[111] Right now, we have to strike terror in the hearts of the population in order to avoid their ever again having an uprising.

---

[110] Emir Dost Mohammad Khan Barakzai (1793-1863) was the founder of the Barakzai dynasty and one of the prominent rulers of Afghanistan during the First Anglo-Afghan War.
[111] Shuja Durrani (1785 =1842), ruler of the Durrani Empire from 1803 to 1809. He then ruled Afghanistan from 1839 until his death by assassination in 1842.

ELPHINSTONE

I agree.

SALE

Bring in the prisoners.

SCENE II

THE SAME CHARACTERS, AFGHAN PRISONERS, A WOMAN.

SALE
(*speaking to the prisoners*)
You are bandits. You have dared to fire on English soldiers.

AN AFGHAN

Why have they invaded our country? Why have they destroyed our fields, and burned our houses?

SALE

You are thinking too much! Cut off his head!

(*An executioner enters and cuts off the man's head.*)

THE ENGLISH OFFICERS

Very good. When one doesn't know how to use one's head to be well-behaved, one should no longer have the right to keep it.

SALE

None of the prisoners have been well behaved. Executioner, cut off everyone's head. You will then give the heads to my soldiers to use to play polo.

AFHGAN WOMAN (*falling on her knees*)

Have mercy!

THE AFGHANS (*with anger*)

Get up, woman! You don't kneel in front of an Englishman.

SALE

Executioner, strike!

(*The executioner decapitates all the Afghans.*)

ELPHINSTONE

Now, let's have lunch.

SALE

Gladly. That little ceremony has given me an appetite,
(*to an officer*)
You, go to the house of that woman. Take her children and sell them as slaves.
We mustn't miss out on making a profit, and we must keep our heads for all
those imbeciles who lost theirs! (*he laughs*)

ELPHINSTONE

If they had been brought up in England, they would have been well behaved and
that would never have happened to them!

(In the third act, the conquering English, masters of Kabul are surprised to discover that the Afghans have returned and are surrounding the city.)

ACT IV

A GORGE IN THE MOUNTAINS

SCENE I

DOST MOHAMMAD, AFGHAN KHANS AND SERDARS

DOST MOHAMMAD

What news from the battle?

A KHAN

Powerful king, our forces are victorious everywhere. The English who tried to
break through the passes have been driven back into Kabul.

DOST MOHAMMAD

Victorious at last! The heavenly sprits have finally taken pity on the oppressed.
The land of our fathers will again be free. The heels of the conquerors will no
longer oppress them.

A KHAN

And you, the exiled Prince, will again sit on the throne from which the invaders
had chased you, and you will again be our venerated king!

DOST MOHAMMAD

Yes, I will be happy about that, but less than about our new independence.

THE SAME, PLUS ELPHINSTONE

A KHAN (*entering*)
O King, whose head touches the stars, the Chief of the impure English has come to negotiate.

DOST MOHAMMAD
What does he want?

A KHAN
Probably to talk about surrendering.

DOST MOHAMMAD
Bring him in.

A KHAN (*calling to the outside*)
Bring the English representative before the King; he has agreed to listen to him.

ELPHINSTONE (*entering, escorted by two Afghan warriors*)
I greet you, O King.

DOST MOHAMMAD
I will wait to welcome you until I know what offers you bring.

ELPHINSTONE
Mind your tone!

DOST MOHAMMAD
Why? It depends only on me to launch my forces against Kabul and destroy your army. Come now! Believe me! The time for threats has passed. Beg my forgiveness and I will probably pardon you, because the poor people that you command obey you, lacking the power to do anything else. They are not guilty, and I hesitate to destroy them.

ELPHINSTONE
It seems that you intend to make me responsible for everything.

DOST MOHAMMAD
Aren't you the head, and isn't that correct?

293

ELPHINSTONE (*terrified*)

So you want my life?

DOST MOHAMMAD

You came into my country like a thief. You killed my compatriots, stole their wealth, set their villages on fire... Still, if it was up to me, I would still pardon you... but I don't have the right. The tribunal of the Khans will judge you, and your fate will be as that assembly decides.

ELPHINSTONE

Listen to me, O King. It will do you no good to kill me.

DOST MOHAMMAD

The judges do not punish the criminal in the hopes of making a fortune.

ELPHINSTONE

But I have wealth... I offer it to you in exchange for my life.

DOST MOHAMMAD

Stolen treasures. In my mountains, we do not accept presents like that.

ELPHINSTONE (*begging*)

No, not from here. In India, I possess properties, elephants, rice fields, wheat fields, which feed many herds. All of that is yours if you allow me to leave your country safe and sound.

DOST MOHAMMAD (*turning towards the Khans*)

Vaillant Chiefs, you heard what the Englishman offers. What is your decision?

THE KHANS

He killed our brothers. He must die.

DOST MOHAMMAD

What good is the blood of that man to you?

A KHAN

Nothing. It isn't for his value that we seek it. It is to put to rest the spirit of those whom he killed.

DOST MOHAMMAD (*to Elphinstone*)

They don't want any of your gold. It is the river of blood that flows in your veins that the Afghan warriors want to see spilled out on the ground.

ELPHINSTONE (*with despair*)

So, you are without pity?

DOST MOHAMMAD

If only you had fought like a warrior, we would pardon you. But your government did not order you to massacre the prisoners, to slaughter the women and children.

ELPHINSTONE

I did not do anything like that.

DOST MOHAMMAD

You are trying in vain to deceive me. (*calling*) Bring the sorcerer here!

SCENE III

THE SAME, PLUS THE SORCERER, THE GHOSTS

THE SORCERER

The King of Kings needs me?

DOST MOHAMMAD

Yes, Sorcerer, look at that man... Do you know him?

THE SORCERER

Yes. He is Major General, Elphinstone.

DOST MOHAMMAD

Good. He is asking pardon for his life and those of his soldiers, claiming, according to his word, that he has never murdered any innocent people.

ELPHINSTONE

I swear it!

THE SORCERER
(*Holding out his arms and casting a spell*)

May your eyes see your victims! May the blood shed by your cruelty cry out!

ELPHINSTONE (*shivering*)

What is this that I am experiencing? ...It's as if my spirit was escaping from my body... Ah! (*With horror*) Tombs are everywhere, everywhere, all across the landscape... They are opening... The belly of the world is throwing up the corpses of the dead...

*(Enters a procession of ghostly men, women, and children. All have been decap-
itated and are carrying their heads in their hands.)*

THE MALE GHOSTS

We are the prisoners that Elphinstone slaughtered without a trial. We were only
guilty of having fought for the independence of our country.

THE FEMALE GHOSTS

Our crime was for weeping over our dead husbands, killed in the war. It was for
that thart Elphinstone had us decapitated.

THE CHILDREN GHOSTS

Elphinstone had us put to death! Having made us orphans, he judged us unworthy of life.

ELPHINSTONE *(kneeling)*

Take away those ghosts... Thake them away... Have mercy!

ALL THE GHOSTS

May he be granted the same mercy that he gave to all of us.

(The ghosts disappear.)

DOST MOHAMMAD

Get up, Major General. You came here to negotiate in good faith, so your person
is sacred. Return safely to Kabul; but remember my words: Before the end of the
week, you and your men will be dead.

ACT V

THE BATTLEFIELD. ENGLISH CORPSES ARE STACKED UP EVERY-
WHERE

SCENE I

DOST MOHAMMAD, THE KHANS AND THE SERDARS, AN ENGLISH
SOLDIER

DOST MOHAMMAD
(speaking to the English soldier)

Do you, see?

THE SOLDIER

I do.

DOST MOHAMMAD

Of the insolent English army, there doesn't remain anyone alive, but you.

THE SOLDIER

That's true.

DOST MOHAMMAD

You are free to go. Return to your own people and tell them how the Afghans punish thieves and vagabonds."

(*The curtain falls*)

Shouts, applause and stamping of feet greeted the fall of the curtain.

All the Afghans, standing up, applauded wildly that naïve play, which related the splendor of their glorious campaign of 1842.

The Doctor, Na-Indra and Anoor added their applause to those of the Afghans. Their companions imitated them.

The astonishment of the head of the village was brought to its height by that manifestation, and he couldn't avoid asking the Doctor:

"You must not be English, since you are applauding their defeat?"

"Indeed," replied the Doctor. "We belong to another nation, a friend and ally of the Great White Tsar."

It was under that title that the population of Asia named the Emperor of Russia.

"You are a friend of the White Tsar?" asked the Chief.

"Yes."

"Then, you are a friend of the Afghans?"

"Entirely."

With that affirmation, the *Serdar* stood up, and, in an enthusiastic harangue, announced to all those present that his household was honored to receive the strangers whose hearts beat in unison with those of the Russian and the Afghan people.

There was general joy; dances began again and did not finish until well after the night had ended.

The weary travelers could finally go back to their rooms, accompanied right to its threshold by the *Serdar*.

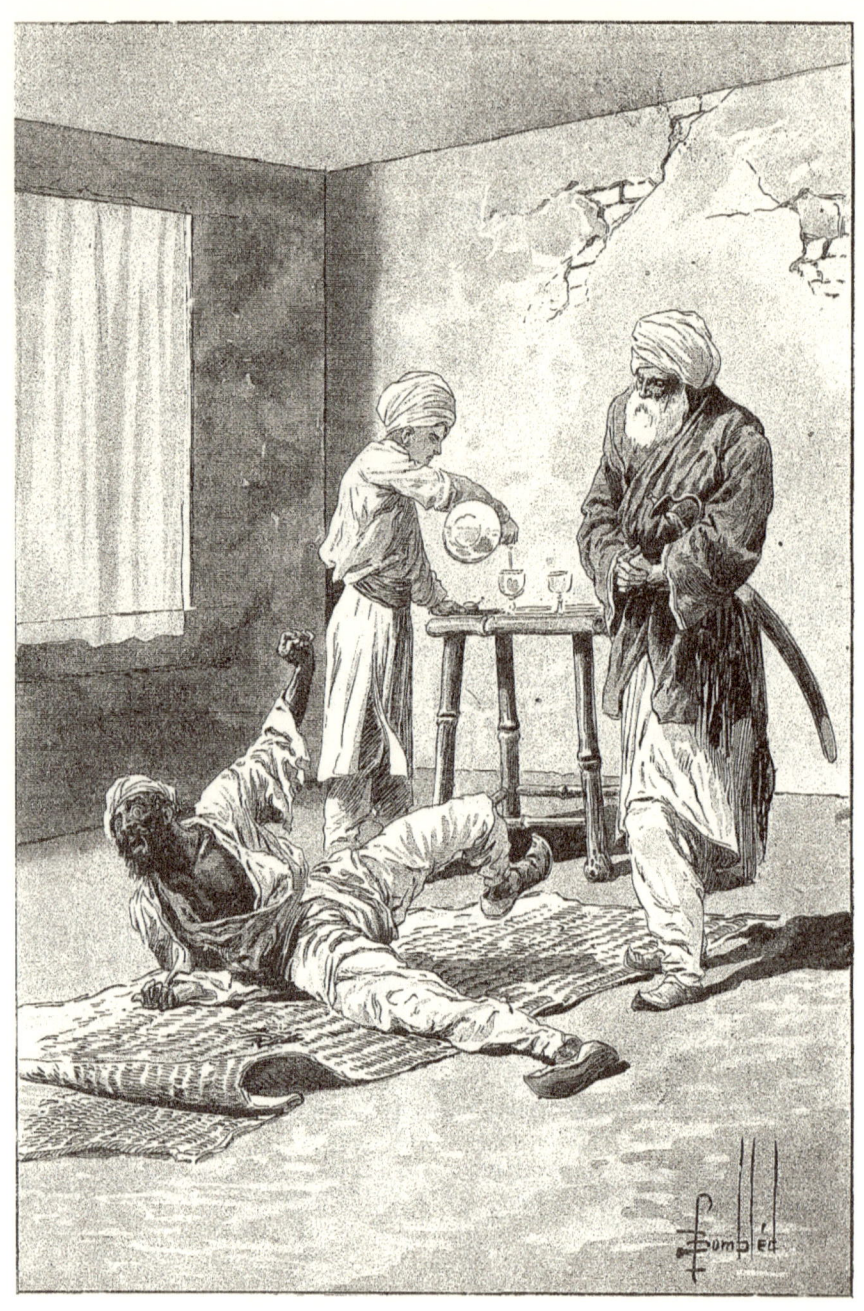

CHAPTER IX
Galloping Hearts and Horses

After that dramatic interlude, the Doctor's companions slept soundly. And the next day, they were escorted for several miles by the *Serdar*, and the warriors even shot off their guns to honor them.

They again started down the road to Kabul. At about 5 o'clock, they stopped on a plateau which was shaded by big trees, located between a plain and a little slope a few hundred yards away.

Led by Wilhelmina, the dozen Sander-van Stoon young ladies went down to the river in order to bathe. Na-Indra and Anoor went with Graziella. Cicada and Timoteo lost themselves in the bushes, chasing Ludvic, who himself was chasing wild bees. The Doctor remained alone, guarding the tied horses. He took advantage of that moment to take out his notebook and complete the notes he had been taking since they had crossed the Afghan frontier. Sketching notations of latitude and longitude, he covered the pages with tight writing. On a blank sheet, he began to sketch a topographical map, on which someone familiar with the terrain would have easily recognized the road taken during the day.

He was absorbed by his work when a voice attracted his attention. He turned around. Holding a superb horse by the bridle, a hunched-over old man, clothed in the Afghan style, came up behind him.

"My Lord," said the newcomer in a shaky voice, "I greet you."

"Greetings, Father," the Doctor answered, using the polite formula employed when one spoke to an old man.

"You have manners, My Son, despite the fact that you're a stranger. I hope you will grant my request."

"Speak, Father."

"I am tired from a long journey, I was once a famous warrior, but age has turned my blood cold, and destroyed my strength. Let me rest in your camp. I will be safe there. If I were alone, taking care of myself, I would be an easy prey for wolves. My weak arms could no longer defend me."

The Doctor smiled kindly.

"Father, tie up your horse near ours and wait for the return of my friends. You will share our meal and we will watch over you."

Thanking him profusely, the old man did as instructed and the Doctor returned to work. Almost immediately Na-Indra reappeared. The young girl had left her companions at the edge of the water in order to return to talk to the Doctor. Absorbed in his work, he did not notice her return. Fearing to disturb him, she stayed at a distance. Her eyes were fixed on him, with an expression both melancholy and tender.

The old man watched her. Suddenly he made a brusque gesture and said very low:

"Young girl," he said, "your friend has permitted me to shelter my weakness in your camp. But he is absorbed in his thoughts. Come and liven up the ears of the old man with the music of your voice."

The pretty girl came to sit near the old man.

"Here I am, Father. Would you like me to tell you the beautiful legend of Rama, conquering the Kingdom of Lotuses, in order that all the flowers would belong to Aiputra, his fiancée?"

"Yes, my daughter, but before that, let me give you a present to thank you for your kindness toward an old traveler. In the pockets of my saddle bag, I have some precious jewels. A pearl, less pure than your smile, will make a delightful addition to the jet-like color of your hair."

Saying that, he stood up with difficulty and walked towards his mount. Na-Indra followed him, murmuring thanks. What young girl would not be grateful when someone offered her a jewel to show off her beauty?

Very happy about the encounter, she did not notice that the old man very cleverly was untying his horse. That was done so rapidly that even a suspicious person would not have noticed it.

"Look, my daughter, does that pearl seem to you worthy to shine on your forehead?"

Na-Indra remained silent with admiration. The pearl that the old man held out to her was the size of a hazelnut, the most marvelous of jewels. As she looked at it, she felt herself suddenly seized by the waist, lifted off the ground, and thrown backward on the horse. Then the "old man" jumped onto the saddle with the agility of a much younger man.

Stupefied, not understanding, Na-Indra lifted her eyes toward her kidnapper and a great despair took over her. The snow-colored beard of the old traveler had gone and she stared at the cruel face of Arkabad the Brahmin. The same Arkabad, whom she thought she had been delivered from forever! He had, in fact, followed the travelers' trail and he put into execution a new, diabolical plan.

Na-Indra let out a terrible cry; a sad whinnying answered her. Arkabad had just pushed long spurs into the flanks of her horse, and the poor beast was now racing away at a wild gallop.

"Doctor! Doctor! My only friend... Save me!"

The young girl was shouting this, while the horse's gallop was pressing her against the hard wood of the saddle. Her young body was bent as if it were about to break.

When he heard her shouts, the Doctor raised his head. At a glance, he understood the situation. He was stunned as if by an electric shock. Without even thinking to alert their companions, he raced to his mount, untied the reins and jumped in the saddle. A second later, he raced to follow the ravisher in the midst of a dust storm.

As a man who knew the region well, Arkabad had gone onto a little path which, in appearance, seemed impracticable. A short, steep slope brought him onto a plateau where his valiant mount, whose speed he was increasing with his spurs, could go full rein. As Na-Indra was still crying out, he interrupted her roughly:

"Be quiet, girl!"

"Doctor! I'm here!" she shouted without paying attention.

"Be quiet!" he ordered again, rudely. "Or I'll stab you to death!"

She looked at him straight in his face.

"What does that matter to me! If you do this, I will carry with me to the grave the secret that you covet so greedily."

She was expecting an explosion of anger, but she was mistaken. The Brahmin smiled ironically and said:

"He matters a great deal to you, doesn't he?"

"No."

"You are mistaken, Na-Indra, or at the very least, you are trying to deceive me."

She murmured without lowering her eyes:

"Na-Indra does not know how to lie."

Arkabad again laughed ironically.

"Is it possible that you have not yet acknowledged what resides within your heart?"

The girl blushed; her eyelashes fluttered, and her shaking voice betrayed her emotion.

"I do not know what you mean," she said softly.

With a motion of his wrist, the Brahmin corrected the course of his horse which had just hit a stone; then, he leaned towards his prisoner, and said:

"Na-Indra is the guardian of the Treasure of Freedom."

"Its faithful guardian, yes. Who would sacrifice her life not to betray the hope of the oppressed in favor of those who would crush them under their yoke."

"Indeed, girl, that's what you believed—in the past."

She coughed loudly.

"I have not changed."

"Ha! Ha!" laughed the Brahmin, picking up the reins.

In front of him there was a rocky bank, which would have seemed unpassable to many sportsmen, but Afghan horses "swallow up obstacles," according to the expression of these marvelous mountain men.

Controlled by a firm hand, the horse, despite its twin burden, passed like an arrow above the barrier of rocks. The path at the top continued in a straight line across a plain.

Arkabad looked behind him. The Doctor remained invisible. He let out an exclamation of triumph. He believed he had finally outdistanced the man pursuing him. He took up again the conversation where he had left off.

"You claim that you have not changed, Na-Indra?"

"Yes. I have remained faithful to my duty, as you yourself remain a villain."

The Brahmin shrugged philosophically:

"I serve Brahma. All means are good when they are used for the glory of the Creator. You're a feeble female; you would not understand those things. And I feel nothing but contempt for your insults."

"Contempt is the refuge of the guilty. Those who have been accused unjustly do not disdain to defend themselves."

"As you please, girl. But it is not about me that I want to talk, but about you."

And spurring his horse, whose brown body began to run with sweat, he shouted:

"One more effort, Tadgiri! We will soon be out of danger."

As if the generous animal had understood, he started again at full gallop.

"You changed without knowing it, Na-Indra," Arkabad continued, with renewed emphasis as if to give his words more weight. "Before, you would have died bravely in order not to divulge your father's secret."

"My father—murdered by your people!"

"Today," continued Arkabad, without paying the least attention to her interruption, "you reject the idea of death."

"I do not."

"Ha! Why try to hide the truth? I am the Executioner of Ellora—I can read the truth that is in your heart! You are now afraid of dying, I tell you, because your beautiful eyes will then close and, in their clear mirror, they will no longer reflect the features of a man who has stolen your soul…"

He took his time and finished without pity:

"…The man whom, only a while ago, you called to your rescue."

All the blood of the young girl flowed back into her heart. A mist obscured her eyes and her lovely face suddenly changed colors. From her lips came out a heavy sigh, and now inert, without a voice, she remained stretched across the saddle, carried exactly like a corpse by the gallop of the horse

What the Brahmin had said was true. Arkabad had seen clearly into her heart. As the flower opens its bud to the rays of the sun, so her love too had grown without her thinking about it, without her being able to defend herself against that mysterious passion. At first, she had wanted to fight it. She had wanted to snatch it away from the person of that Doctor who had protected her from all those villains who had destroyed her childhood, her adolescence, and condemned her to a life of sadness and pretended insanity.

In the past, she had seen herself differently; a defensive virgin, having no other goal but to give her life in martyrdom for her homeland, its freedom. Having to fight constantly to defend herself, she had picked up the habit of thinking like men. Her spirit had never learned the delicate female subtleties. She had never had the vague dreams of young girls, the hope of someday having a smiling fiancé, of marriage among singing stars and flowers of harmony.

Then Doctor Mystery had appeared before her.

And her warrior heart had softened; Na-Indra had become a woman; with agonizing and delightful slowness, love had found its way within her heart. So, like all women who encounter love without having thought of it, to whom its divine law is suddenly revealed, she had surrendered entirely, without restriction, without hesitation, to that new emotion.

That had been an intense and hidden joy. Her passion came up from the depths of her soul as a fresh source comes out of a dead land, causing all of the niceties, graces, and charms unknown until then to flourish. Yes, the cruel Brahmin had accurately seen within her heart. Death now horrified her. It was henceforth the black cloud which blinds the stars, the murderer of hope.

Upside down, her head bouncing with each gallop of the horse, Na-Indra looked at the surface of the plain which seemed to glide below her with rapid dizziness. Suddenly, she received a violent shock, and, almost immediately, she heard a shot.

The horse had made a sudden turn, but, brought back by his rider, it started again towards the horizon. Only the poor beast watered the path they were traveling with blood. It had been wounded!

The girl looked to see who had shot the animal. She finally spied him a hundred yards away, coming like the storm, with the mane of his horse ruffled, its nostrils dilated, letting its breath come out with great snorts.

That was the Doctor.

At first, outdistances by Arkabad, he had finally reached the plateau. He had been aware of the superiority of Arkabad's horse. Continuing the chase in those conditions would have been madness. It was necessary at any price to slow down the faster horse.

The Doctor had then seized his weapon. Twice he had positioned it on his shoulder, but then then lowered it, not daring to fire for fear of hurting Na-Indra. His heart was beating rapidly; his eyes were troubled; yet, it was indispensable for him to be calm in order not to hit the girl he sought to save.

And at the time when the cruel Brahmin had revealed to the hapless Na-Indra, the unacknowledged love she felt for her traveling companion, a similar revelation had taken place in the Doctor's mind. He had discovered very clearly that his anxiety did not come from any fears he might have had about the fate of the Treasure, but from the danger that she was under... He would have gladly given up all the treasures in the world for her to be safe. He became rapidly aware of this newfound emotion, caused by the fact that a young girl with a harmonious voice and a charming look was being carried away by a horse dashing like a bullet on a plain which unfolded before him like an endless ribbon of dust.

Only her beauty and her charm preoccupied him. He thought of nothing else.

"If she dies, I will never know the hiding place of the accumulated gold to free our people," he murmured, out of breath. "If she dies, I will die too, because life without her dear presence would be an unbearable torture."

For these two beings petrified with patriotism, for whom the dream of freedom had been their only aspiration, there had been a similar evolution at the same time. The danger run by Na-Indra had been the determining trigger in an explosion of feelings that had been far too long held inside her

"It's necessary, however, that I slow down that horse," grumbled the Doctor, whose pale face, tight body, dazzling eyes bore a frightening expression of terror and hatred. "I must! I must!"

His will tightened his nerves to the breaking point. He made himself remain calm, commanded his heart to slow down, and, for the third time, took aim at Arkabad's horse. For a second, he remained that way, waiting for a propitious moment; then, his thumb pressed the trigger.

The shot burst out, making the weapon on his arm vibrate; with the hissing of a snake, the bullet went on its trajectory.

The Doctor leaned over the shoulder of his mount. His heels had been laboriously hitting the flanks of his horse.

He saw Arkabad's horse deviate from its path, its gallop broken for an instant. Then, it began racing again, because of the blows from the fist of its rider.

Rage led the Doctor to the spot where the horse had been hit. He saw a large spot of blood on the ground. A red trail started from it, so the wound was serious. Soon, the faster horse, made weak by the loss of blood, would have to stop.

The Doctor let out a savage bellow. Finally, he was going to crush under his heel that miserable priest who had pursued him for weeks, had made his young friends desperate, and, most of all, be reunited with the one that he had kidnapped... Na-Indra... Which means a kiss from heaven."

"A kiss from heaven," he murmured, with fervor. "What name could be more fitting!"

But his thoughts ended with a cry of horror. As he had foreseen, Arkabad's horse was tiring. The Brahmin understood that his foe would soon catch up with him... The outcome of the chase was no longer in doubt... It was simply a question of minutes. Then, he, Arkabad, the Executioner of Ellora, would be vanquished. He would be forced to return to the Brahmins, his brothers, and tell them that Na-Indra, Doctor Mystery, and Anoor had escaped him, that they were free, beyond any attempt to capture the holders of that huge treasury, the clever use of it would upset the established order of India...

No, a thousand times no! If that gold would not belong to the Priests of Brahma, so be it, but at least, no one else should ever profit from it. It would remain buried in its unknown hiding place. Since the fortune would not belong to Ellora, at least it would not be a menace in the hands of their enemies. Those reflections spelled the death of Na-Indra. If the young girl disappeared, the secret of the treasure would disappear with her. Also, wouldn't it be a magnificent vengeance than to create the abyss of a tomb between her and the Doctor, guilty of having challenged the power of the Brahmins? Arkabad turned around in his saddle. The Doctor was but fifty steps away.

"Good!" he said. "I still have enough time."

And with a sudden gesture, he pulled out his dagger...

Na-Indra had seen nothing. Still lying across the saddle, she was looking at the Doctor, who was getting closer at every second. After her initial fright, she again had found her confidence. In a few seconds, the two horses would be side by side. Deliverance, after that horrible ride, would surely follow. The Doctor's face was visible. Suddenly, she read terror on it. She could see his desperate gesture, the meaning of which escaped her, but which seemed to her to be a warning. Her eyes went back to the Priest of Brahma.

Then, she understood: The dagger, the blade, shining in the sun, the satanic twist of his mouth, spelled out his intentions.

At the same moment, his left hand dropped the reins of his horse and tried to prop up his prisoner in order to better stab her.

To die... No, Na-Indra didn't want to die! Now that her heart had opened to love, she no longer felt her haughty resignation in the face of death. She would defend her share of happiness. A new energy came into her and she bit Arkabad's hand cruelly. The Brahmin threw himself backward and cursed loudly. Without caring about the danger, Na-Indra's only idea was to escape from the Priest. With a violent effort, she succeeded in throwing herself off the horse.

Arkabad reigned in the animal, as if he intended to come back for his victim, but the Doctor arrived like a clap of thunder. The kidnapper abandoned his original intention and left as fast as possible. He thought that the Doctor would not follow him., and he was proven right.

Upon seeing Na-Indra rolling in the dust, the Doctor slowed down his horse. Once near the body of the young girl, he stopped so suddenly that the animal almost fell back on his haunches. Then, jumping to the ground, the Doctor kneeled at the side of his traveling companion.

The head of the unfortunate girl had hit a rock. Under her dark hair flowed a trickle of blood. She didn't move anymore, and her dark eyelashes covered her silky eyelids on her discolored cheeks. Was she dead? Had these two beings, lost on the Afghan plateau, guessed their mutual love, only to abe so cruelly separated?

The Doctor did not move; nor did Na-Indra. He remained kneeling near her, his concerned eyes fixed on her pale face. That exceptional man seemed to have lost in one moment all of his will power and courage. The thought that she was dead had destroyed him. How long did that mute scene last? During how much time did dark thoughts of despair raged like a thunderstorm in his brain? What ghosts emerged from the abyss of the past while he floated half-way between now and nothingness? He himself would have been unable to answer these questions? What he remembered later was that, under his hand, which tightly gripped the wrist of the young girl, he felt the weak beating of her pulse. That was because her lips suddenly half-opened to let out a sigh; then it was her eyes' turn, before closing again because of the light.

The Doctor sprang up like a madman, his arms extended towards Heaven, and he let out a strange, superhuman cry, the echoes of which rolled on the desert surface of the prairie.

Then he appeared to collapse again under the weight of the emotions he felt. He found himself near Na-Indra, still lying on the ground. But now, he had recovered his intelligence, which came out victorious. He leaned over the young girl and found that her wound was not serious. Her temporary loss of consciousness would be the only consequence of her fall.

For the first time, he thought about Arkabad. He looked for him but in vain. The Priest had disappeared. So, the miserable had escaped punishment, but he had also failed in what he had attempted.

The Doctor decided to ignore Arkabad for the moment in order to concentrate only of the care that Na-Indra needed. With gentle movements, which a mother would have envied, e picked her up in his arms and carried her right to his horse. The animal's bleeding flanks drenched its robe with sweat and stained the long grass of the plateau. He placed the wounded girl, as well as he could, on the shoulders of the horse; then, taking the bridle in his hands, he started to walk back towards their encampment.

He traveled slowly, carefully following the road, upset that he wasn't able to spare his dear companion more bumps in the road. However, she seemed to be asleep. A rosy tint had returned to her cheeks. Suddenly, her lips moved. She spoke softly. The Doctor stopped, his stomach filled with anguish.

Was her delirium coming back?

He made sure that hers was not the trembling voice of a person suffering from a hallucination. No, Na-Indra spoke like a child dreaming...

"Yes... The lake with the blue and red lotuses is like a mirror where Heaven is reflected. But that is not the azure of the sky, the white of the clouds upon the horizon, nor the green top of the trees, leaning above the clear waters that I am looking at..."

There was a silence; then, she continued:

"That's him, the man whose goodness, whose courage led him towards me from the end of the world, as if Brahma had wanted to say to me: 'Here is the one man that I created so that you could unite your life to his, so that you could be the tender caretaker of his household. He's the one whom I see, and I see only him. My eyes may henceforth be lost, as his image is engraved forever on them, and they can no longer see any other? If that is true, may Brahma be praised. What land, what mountains, what oceans, what stars would be sweeter to behold than the image of my beloved?"

Hearing this, the Doctor's steps became heavier, more stumbling. A terror weighed over him as he heard the melodious song of love flowing from the lips of the dreaming girl. He thought:

Her heart is filled with love; but it belongs to someone else... I learn of this just as my own heart, which I thought was dead, is coming out of its lethargy... Was I born only to suffer?

"Here he is, always here, yet everywhere. Far from me, he is still present. In the solitude of my home, he fills my thoughts with words from the past, which I had forgotten, but live again to delight my ears. He is here, always here..."

The wounded woman suddenly opened her eyes. She looked around her with astonishment. Her eyes then became fixed on those of the Doctor, who was looking at her sadly. And in the unconsciousness of the awakening, still half wrapped in the cloak of dreams, Na-Indra murmured:

"Yes, everywhere... Yet, he is there, near me, and his eyes bathe me with their pure radiance."

The Doctor paled; his legs trembled. That rival whom he had been cursing a moment before, was him! Carried away by an unexplainable joy, overcome by that truth which had come to him on the wings of a dream, he stammered:

"Na-Indra! Na-Indra! Am I in my right mind? Can the unbelievable be true? Is the impossible being realized? Are your eyes, gates of a heaven where shine these twin stars, illuminating for me, a forlorn creature of the night, a new promised land?"

She made a gesture of surprise. Raising herself up on the shoulder of the horse, she said slowly:

"So it is true?"

"Ah! Dear child. Desperate, alone in the world, I tried to reattach myself to life by traveling and helping others achieve the same happiness that I thought had long been denied to me. But now, near you, that happiness has been realized. My heart, once buried in a tomb, is born again, and blossoms at your sight and under the sweet music of you voice."

Na-Indra held out her hand to him. He hesitated to take it:

"Take it," she said simply. "I am giving it to you."

He seized it with passion.

"And now," continued the young girl, "lets continue on our way... Let's not talk. To hear the dear words of the heart requires the silence of lips. Silence, my dear friend. Sadness must be forgotten. We must feel that we have always been close."

They managed to return to their camp without exchanging a word, as agreed, but there was such joy on their faces that their companions noticed it immediately.

"What's happening?" asked Cicada.

"I heard a gunshot," added Anoor.

The Sanders-van Stoon girls all talked at the same time.

"We were all very afraid."

"I, too," Graziella said. "I thought our enemies were about to attack us."

The Doctor and Na-Indra, still under the effect of their newly-released emotions, hesitated to answer. But suddenly, Anoor spotted the blood of her sister's head and let out a little cry of fright.

"Are you wounded, my dear sister?"

"Wounded?" shouted all the others.

"Yes, there, on her head, look... There's some blood..."

Everybody pushed forward, their questions crisscrossing each other. Surrounding the pretty girl, they grew curiouser as they were not getting answers.

"What's wrong? Did you fall? Was that a criminal who shot you?"

The Doctor was about to tell his friends of the terrible danger that had threatened the Guardian of the Treasure of Freedom, but Na-Indra kept him from doing that.

She pulled Anoor close to her heart, embracing her for a long time, and, with an adorable smile, she explained:

"Sadness had become a part of me. Thanks to that wound, I was able to escape it and replace it with happiness."

Everybody looked at her in surprise, not understanding. She took the Doctor's hand and, with her head high and a mysterious respect, she said:

"Legends say that Brahma once created a being so pure that she seemed superior to him, the master of the world, worshipped by all, and he adored his creature. It was she whom we encountered today."

"What's her name?" asked Cicada, unable to remain quiet any longer.

"Her name is the sweetest in the world. No light shines with more brilliance; no perfume has a smell as sweet. Her name, my sweet little sister, my friends, is love."

A silence followed.

Everyone understood, and in the eyes of the Parisian boy, fixed on Anoor, in those of the other girl responding to his mute appeal, in the fluttering eyes of Graziella, and the little Sanders-van Stoons, a humid cloud passed by.

The rosy wings of the Love Fairy had just touched all the young people, their new hearts opening to the notion of true love.

CHAPTER X
The Secret of the Tombs

"How lugubrious this countryside is!"

"It's truly a land of horror!"

These exclamations that came from the travelers were justified by the appearance of the countryside that they beheld.

After a short stop in Kabul, they had resumed their journey South, towards Kandahar, where the Doctor had agreed to meet with his sailors. The looks of the countryside had changed. It was no longer the gloomy valley of the Kabul river, but the semi-desertic plateaus of East Afghanistan. Everywhere, there were shades of red until the end of the horizon. No tree showed its green limbs, bringing the gaiety of its verdant plume. Some bushes, turned red by the sun, stood here and there, bent by the wind, nestled in rocky crevices, where the shadows had retained a semblance of moisture. Not a murmur of flowing water disturbed the deadly silence of that arid country. Sometimes, they came across sharp ravines, the beds of torrents that flowed one month of the year, at the time of the great rains, but which at any other time offered only dry rocks heated by the heat of summer. It was necessary to go long distances before encountering a well, usually located under an enclosure of wooden joists inside which hung a leather bucket, thanks to which one could parsimoniously sip some water.

The inhabitants of this region were nowhere in sight; perhaps the tribes of nomadic shepherds had already left it and gone towards the distant and fertile valleys in the center of Afghanistan. The travelers were disheartened by the general desolation of the country; never had they seen such barrenness before.

At the intersection of two ravines, cut evidently by ephemeral rivers, extended a triangular plain, covered with stones and boulders. At its center stood a low hill on which were lined up a number of *ekbas*, burial mounds indicating that there were tombs in that area. The Afghans, like most people of central Asia, customarily built tombs of this kind. Each passerby piously added a rock on the pile of stones, said a short prayer, and went on his way without worrying about which dead person he had paid homage to.

The Doctor and his companions had stopped on arriving onto that plain because everyone had been affected by the sadness of the landscape; each had expressed his thoughts by exclamations which all could be summed up like this:

"This region is very strange!"

Only the Doctor had not joined his voice to that of his friends. With an emotion that he could not explain to himself, he looked at the Hill of Tombs. Na-Indra, who was riding beside him, said:

"You knew those sleeping here when they were alive?"

The Doctor shook his head.

"No, but I am sorry for those unfortunate people, buried in nameless graves, far from where other men are living. I am truly sorry for them."

He was not looking at her when he said this. You might have thought that he was answering his own thoughts rather than her question.

Suddenly, he frowned, having forgotten the presence of the adorable girl, who heard him sigh with heartbreak.

"Where are sleeping those whom I loved? In what unknown place are they buried, those who are still waiting to be avenged?"

Na-Indra was trembling. The man to whom her heart had been given, was suffering. She heard an almost superhuman sadness in his words and wanted to console him, obeying her sublime instincts. She put her hand on his shoulder and said:

"Brahma has permitted that our paths be joined together when both of us were lonely. He has united us in order for us to walk side by side. Your heart is swollen with tears; let me weep with you."

The Doctor looked at her with unexplainable tenderness. He took her hand, and carried it to his lips, and slowly answered:

"You will know everything one day. You are the ray of light that has revived my dead soul, but now is not the time for you to know the nature of my sorrow." Then, shaking his head as if to chase away an unwelcome thought, he added: "It is getting late; we should camp here."

Ten minutes later, a camp had been hastily set up in the shadow of the hill of the sinister tumuli.

The Sanders-van Stoon young ladies, helped by Graziella, prepared the evening meal while the men took care of the horses.

The Doctor himself was away from his companions. As if pushed by an invisible force, he had walked slowly up the hill. A difficult pathway ran on its edge. Na-Indra was following him a few steps behind. She worried with her big dark eyes full of sadness. She, who had suffered so much, recognized in her friend a limitless grief. How dark his mood was! What had he suffered to drive him to such despair?

She was shivering at the memory of the surprising words he had said just before they went on this walk:

"Where are sleeping those whom I loved? In what unknown place are they buried, those who are still waiting to be avenged?"

Who were those dead? What enemy had struck them down?

While thinking about this, she climbed to the top of the hill, still following the Doctor. He had not turned around once. He thought he was alone; his preoccupation had prevented him from noticing her presence.

They came in this way to the summit. In front of them there was only the rocky plateau. Seven *ekbas* were lined up on the ground in front of them. An eight tomb lay to the side, but the arrangement of its stones, in an elliptical wall, indicated that it was still empty of the body that it was supposed to hold.

The Doctor stopped, very pale. He was counting the *ekbas*.

"Seven," he trembled. "Seven! The number of those who disappeared! And that eighth tomb still empty… Is it was waiting for the one who is still alive? How strange… Why does this image, which revives my regrets, find itself across my path? Did the souls of the dearly departed fear that my will has grown soft?"

He remained silent for a moment, and then began again:

"No, no, you who are sleeping under these stones, whoever you may be, hear this oath: Na-Indra's love will not diminish my memories. She, too, belongs to a race of victims. Her life, united to mine, only creates one more duty for me."

The scene had a troubling grandeur.

Immobile, as if her feet were riveted to the ground, Na-Indra was listening. Her eyes were fixed with suspicious terror on the tombs. With her lively imagination, she was almost expecting for the graves to open, the dead to stand up to receive the terrible and mysterious oath that her friend had just made.

Now the Doctor remained silent; his head was bowed as if he was meditating. What thoughts were stirring inside his head? To what memories had he abandoned himself? Those insoluble questions made Na-Indea tremble. To know that he was unhappy, but not to know the words that might help him, was an insupportable torture.

Suddenly, her whole body shook. Something, or someone, a bizarre figure had just slid by, almost touching her. She did not have the strength to cry out. The apparition seemed to be a mummy escaped from a tomb. It was a little old man with skin like parchment. He was walking bent over, his legs trembling, his naked feet coming out like the legs of a spider from the tunic of white cloth which shrouded his body.

The young girl believed he was the spirit of the tombs.

The strange person approached Doctor Mystery. He stopped near him and, with a broken voice, growled:

"Stranger, add your stone to these *ekbas*, and your action will calm the spirits of the dead."

Troubled, the Doctor addressed the old man.

"Who are you?" he asked.

The old man stayed bent over, his eyes riveted on the ground without looking at the man he was talking to.

"I am the guardian of these tombs. I live over there, in that ravine, from where I can watch over these *ekbas*."

"Forever?"

"Forever."

"Undoubtedly, those were the members of some powerful family?"

"Yes, they were powerful. Now, they are stripped of humanity, and when Shiva will have cut off the end of my days, there will no longer be anyone, or anything, to remember that they ever existed."

There was silence.

"No longer be anyone," repeated the Doctor in a trembling voice. "No longer be anyone…"

Na-Indra, approached cautiously without making any noise.

"There will no longer be anyone," the Doctor said for the third time. Then he asked brusquely: "Are you a Hindu, old man?"

The guardian murmured: "Yes."

"What made you live here, so far from your country?"

"Remorse."

"Remorse, you say. Then you are guilty of something?"

"Yes." Then in an even more broken voice, the old man added: "I knew that those that lie there were about to perish, but out of cowardice, I let the crime happen and did nothing. The devotion that I didn't know how to show to the living, I am now giving to the dead. I have devoted the rest of my life to these *ekbas* of those that I didn't know how to save." And he concluded sadly: "But shall it be expiation enough, and will they ever pardon me?"

In his voice vibrated a desperate anger. The Doctor sought to change the course of the conversation.

"And what about that opened tomb?" he said pointing out the eighth grave. "Is it waiting for someone still alive?"

The old guardian shook his head:

"No. That one, too, is no longer alive. Like the others, he has entered the bosom of Brahma. Only, I have not been able, as I did with the others, to find his body, embalm it, and rub it with spices. His remains lie I don't know where."

And twisting his thin hands, the old man added:

"That is what is tearing me apart. I have begged the Creator of the World to let me know by some sign that he has judged my expiation to be sufficient, to allow me to find the missing body of that man, so that I can give him a proper burial. And the day that he will allow that, then I shall understand that His pity has now reached me. But doubtless, my sin is too great, and Brahma has remained deaf to my prayers. I have searched in vain; I have not been able to find the missing body."

Na-Indra heard the complaint of the servant who made himself keep watch over his dead masters. She had an impression of a dream made of pity and horror. That lonely existence spent in face of the tombs was terrible and desolate! Now the old man no longer frightened her. She was sorry for the misfortune that had condemned him to a life of isolation, horribly face to face with his remorse.

Probably the Doctor was having the same thoughts because he asked:

"Would death seem easier to you if someone else were to watch over these *ekbas*?"

The old man clasped his hands.

"Ah! To not leave them alone, abandoned in this dessert... Yes, I would wish for that... But who will think of those who can no longer pay for the service of anybody?"

"Who else, but me."

"You?"

"Let me know their names and I promise you, old man, that these *ekbas* will not be abandoned."

But the guardian shook his head.

"No, it must remain a secret... Those who killed them are powerful and vengeful. If they knew the truth, they would come and scatter the ashes of the dead to the wind. Their names are already forgotten; may that forgetfulness also protect them against profanation!"

The Doctor smiled and he held out his hand to the old man and showed him the figurine that in the past had commanded the obedience of the fakirs and the Companions of Shiva and Kali.

"By the Golden Tiger, I wish that you would trust me and tell me the truth."

The effect of that gesture was striking. The old man stepped back. His eyes were fixed with surprise on the Doctor and out of his mouth escaped a heavy startled sound. He remained there, like a statue, his weak body shaking. Terror, surprise, joy, appeared on his face in successive expressions.

"Do you trust me?" The Doctor finally asked.

The man bowed and, in his shaky voice, replied:

"The Prince has come out from the Kingdom of the Dead to tell old Ahmad that he has been forgiven at last."

Na-Indra avidly listened. Why did that poor devil, living isolated in this desert, seem to recognize in the Doctor a familiar figure?

She looked at the Doctor. He had turned pale.

"Why are you calling me Prince?" he asked brusquely. "Princes don't exist anymore. Tyranny had turned them into fugitives."

But the old man was not listening. His face in the dust, he said, as if reciting a psalm:

"Rama, Rama Sahib, the last of the Princes of Rundjee, now stand in front of the tombs of his parents. That, O divine Brahma, I never dared to hope."

Rama Sahib! Those words went through Na-Indra like a ray of fire. Rama Sahib, the Princes of Rundjee... These were names venerated throughout India as symbols of liberty, of devotion to the oppressed. And this old, prostrated man had called the man to whom all her love had been instinctively given by that name. Was he then, too, a martyr of the same cause for which she had also suffered? Were they souls who had recognizing the same destiny in each other? Had their affection gloriously risen from the same ruins?

The Princes of Rundjee were famous in Punjab, Sindh, and Rajputana. Their history was that of the India herself. Everywhere where they had fought the English, the Afghans, the Persians, and even the Brahmins, that illustrious progeny had been, spending without counting both its blood and its gold.

Then, a terrible disaster had struck down that heroic lineage.

In a few months, all eight representatives of the Rundjee had been overcome by death. The oldest had fallen first, then the father, a renowned warrior, soon followed by the mother, then their four brave sons—except for the last, Rana Sahib who, before disappearing, had had the horrible sadness of receiving his wife's last breath after only a year of marriage.

Was he the one whom Na-Indra saw in front of her, that silent effigy of desolation?

The Doctor suddenly straightened up.

"Old man," he said slowly, "you have spoken too much now not to tell me everything. If these tombs are those of the Rundjee, why are they here, more than one hundred miles from where these unfortunates passed away?"

The old man slowly stood up.

"Sahib, no need for threats. The old guardian of the tombs is now your slave. I will talk since you desire it; but before that, let me destroy the sepulture that I had prepared to receive your remains. You are alive; there is no need for an eighth tomb..."

While speaking, he went towards the last tumulus whose stones were distributed differently from the others. He knocked them down with a blow from his feet, then returned towards the Doctor.

"Sahib, you are alive. It is therefore the sight of an avenger that rejoices my old eyes. Let me tell you more about my sin and the duty that I have imposed on myself..."

He was expressing himself with real majesty, and an indescribable emotion was expressed in that scene between the two men leaning over a barren hill in the middle of a desert on a high plateau.

Troubled, the young girl had the feeling that she should perhaps not listen to this conversation without the permission of her companion, and, trembling, feeling her heart beating, she approached the Doctor and placed her hand on his arm.

He jumped at that slight contact. His surprised look met the imploring expression of Na-Indra. He understood and said gently:

"Stay, child, stay. Struck by the same enemies, Brama has pushed us towards the other from the extreme opposites of the world in order to encourage us to accomplish the mission which has now fallen on us. I know everything about you. Destiny has now set up this instant where, in your turn, it is necessary that you must know everything about me."

Saying that, he let her sit down on the ground beside him, and, at the end of the day, in the violet light of the twilight created by the purple and gold rays of the sun descending on the horizon mixing with the first blue rays of the moon, Ahmad began telling his story in the third person:

"A dozen years earlier, this poor devil was one of many servants in the Brahmin community of Ellora. He lived in the midst of the temples and the sacred caves, with the mission of gathering the offerings of the faithful and restoring them in one of the vast underground storerooms where the priests kept their treasures.

"He went to sleep one day in one of chapels of the mountain and forgot himself there well after the hour when he and the rest of his caste were supposed to leave the holy place.

"A confused number of voices woke him up. Feeling himself to be in the wrong, fearing one of those punishments that the priest of Brahma inflicted voluntary on their servants, Ahmad did not make any moves that might have betrayed him.

"An enormous column filled the shadows of the corner where he was lying and the speakers found themselves on the other side of that mass of granite.

"Ahmad shivered when he recognized one of the voices. It was the voice of a man, dry, rough, authoritative, that belonged to a feared Brahmin because he was charged with carrying out the arrests and executions in Ellora.

"He was the executioner. That was a terrible and terrifying position. In the obscurity of the caverns, without witnesses, without arguments, the Brahmin tribunal assembled. There, they accused a certain individual, or a certain family, of

317

a crime against the divinity, or against the interests of His servants, and passed a judgment without appeal.

"The Brahmin whose words came to Ahmad's ears spoke like this. By some mysterious ways, he struck the victims designated by that somber tribunal and no one knew what spell had struck them when they died.

"Amongst the highest castes, they knew the hand which committed these deeds, but no one ever dared raise his voice. No one fought against the all-powerful Brahmins., for whom religion was but a pretext, and domination was everything.

"Now the Executioner of Ellora was speaking:

" 'The Rundjees have come to stay in Nizam,' he said, 'and even though they don't pay homage to the Brahmins, and they are affiliated with our rivals, the Companions of Shiva and Kali, we have not bothered them. We were hoping that time would open there eyes and they would be grateful for our leniency.'

" 'They certain are,' murmured the soft voice of a woman.

" 'You believe that, girl, but you are mistaken. The Rundjees claim that we are the accomplices of the British, and that all of our efforts tend to counteract the efforts of those who are dedicated to chase the conquering invaders.'

" 'They cannot be saying that, O wise Brahmin.'

" 'Yet that is exactly what they are saying.'

"The woman questioning the priest moaned.

" 'Why are you confiding these things to me, whose weakness will not allow to remedy?'

" 'Why? Because the priest of Ellora are watching over you.'

" 'They are good and kind to me.'

" 'They don't want to see you enter a doomed family.'

The girl moaned again.

" 'Holy Brahmin don't talk like this. My soul has flown to Rama Sahib; even if I were to call it back, it wouldn't come back to me.'

"'Yet you shall have to do that."

" 'No, please, don't require this. If you knew him, my Rama, you would judge him differently then you do now. He is handsome, his eves shine like black diamonds, and his heart is noble, his thoughts elevated...'

The sarcastic laugh of the executioner interrupted the girl.

" 'You must have drunk a love potion in order to want to resist my orders.'

" 'It was Vishnu himself and not I, a weak creature, who decided what would happen. You want to make me marry a Rajah for whom I have only aversion.'

" 'He is a friend of the Brahmins.'

" 'I know that, and I have done my best to draw my heart close to him, but I have failed.'

" 'Is it so necessary to feel affection towards one's husband?'

" 'Oh!, Brahmin, you are so absorbed by the study of the divine mysteries that you don't know the life of ordinary people. Be good enough to lower your mind for a moment towards things mundane. Let your reason guide you. Can one live under the same roof, be interested in the same things, fight for the same causes, share everything: joy, sadness, duties, without the powerful bond of affection shared?'

"A silence followed; then the Brahmin took up again in a menacing tone:

" 'Then you persist in wanting to be the wife of Prince Rama?'

" 'Yes,' the woman he was talking to answered ,very low.

" 'Go ahead then. But the day when tears flow from your eyes, blame only your stubbornness.' "

At that point, Doctor Mystery interrupted Ahmad to ask:

"Old man, can you put names on the faces of those people who spoke thus in the caves of Ellora?"

"Yes, Sahib."

"Please do so."

"The Brahmin executioner is named Arkabad."

A double exclamation burst out from the lips of Na-Indra and the Doctor.

"Arkabad!"

The same man who had attempted to kill Anoor, who had relentlessly pursued Na-Indra... So it was the same man who had once condemned the Rundjees.

"And the young fiancée?" asked the Doctor in a lowered voice.

"That was an orphaned girl from the noble line of the Feliardit, and her name was Diarmida."

"Diarmida!" repeated the Doctor in a heart-breaking tone.

The old man climbed on one of tombs and said:

"She lies here!"

Na-Indra leaned her head on the Doctors shoulder.

"The spirit of Diarmida is in me, my friend. Don't weep. Don't let yourself go into despair about the past. Brahma in his infinite wisdom has allowed one flower to remain on the dried stem. He has wished that, for you, everything would be replaced by me, and that you be everything for the one who lives only for you."

"Ah!" he murmured. "Diarmida... Na-Indra... Two angels with the same soul."

Then, suddenly shaking his head, he looked at Ahmad and ordered:

"Continue. I want to know everything. I still don't know who struck them down."

And extending his hands above the graves, he said:

"Sleep, you that I loved so much. Sleep... I will stand watch in order to avenge you."

And Ahmad continued speaking in the third person:

"A fortnight later, they celebrated the wedding of Prince Rama Rundjee and Diarmida Feliardit in style. With the happy couple, one noticed the presence of the noble Dekan, the grandfather of the groom. His tall stature, his white-as-snow beard and hair, attracted much attention.

"Diomi Rundjee and Lenoor, his wife, came next. The happiness that lit up their son's face was reflected on their features.

"Finally, Rama's three brothers, robust young men, proud of their ancestors, walked side by side with him—Iglir to the right, Banium on the left, and Dogmar in the middle.

"On the steps of the palace thronged a crowd of guests, servants, and just curious people. Ahmad had managed to slip in among these last. Alone, perhaps, he noticed the veil of melancholy spread over Diarmida's sweet face. Did I say alone? No! Another stared at her with piercing eyes, like those of a vulture seeking to fascinate a dove. This was the Brahmin Arkabad, Executioner of Ellora.

"For a second, his eyes met those of the young woman. She quickly shut her eyes and a deathly pallor spread over her cheeks. But very quickly, she opened them again and looked towards Heaven.

"The poor child had just begged Brahma, Creator of All, who, alas! could not grant her prayer.

"Ahmad had taken a strange interest in those people over whom the wrath of the Brahmins was suspended.

"Certainly, he would done a good deed if he had gone to the palace of the Rundjees and told them about the dark plot that luck had revealed to him. But he was afraid of the vengeance of the Brahmins, and so he had said nothing.

"Besides, circumstances at first seemed to support his belief that he had been correct in his careful reserve. Six months had gone by without anything troubling the peace of the Rundjees.

"A foreigner, little aware the Brahmins' customs, might have believed that they had forgotten the offenses and that their anger had disappeared; that Rama Diamida no longer had anything to fear.

"The young woman had entertained that very illusion. She laughed, she was happy, all worry had vanished from her mind.

"Poor credulous woman! The priests of Brahma do not know forgiveness; they never pardon. Lightning was going to break out in the midst of a pure blue sky.

"Each day, the noble Dekan took a long horseback ride. He mounted a black horse, a faithful companion from his last campaign, and seeing them pass by on the dusty roads, the people in the fields bowed with admiration as if before the incarnation of courage and liberty.

"Now, one morning, when Ahmad was busy on his ordinary job, Arkabad came to him.

" 'You are faithful?' he asked Ahmad.

" 'Yes, my Lord,' Ahmnad answered.

" 'And you know how to be silent?'

" 'Yes, my Lord. I will be whatever pleases you, my Lord.'

" 'Good. You are going to accompany me. Bring a spade and a pickaxe.'

"Ahmad went to the temple's store and brought back the two items and met Arkabad at the edge of the sacred gorge. Two other men were waiting with him. One of them was a servant like Ahmad; the other was unknown, with a cruel face. A belt of red silk was wrapped around his fist; he was a strangler.

"Arkabad ordered in his sharp voice: 'Let's go!'

"Everybody followed him. He was leading the way. They went around the enormous rocks defending the sanctuary of Ellora. They reached the thick forest which extended to the north and soon stopped at a ravine where there was a running stream.

" 'Here,' the Brahmin said.

"The man with the red silk cord nodded, smiling an evil smile, looked at the bushes that surrounded them like a green wall, and disappeared into them.

"The Brahmin Arkabad followed him, after having ordered the two servants: 'You two! Start digging a grave!'

"Ahmad and his companion immediately attacked the ground which was covered with a thick carpet of moss. The earth was dry, crumbly, made of sand, with lumps of rock salt that shone when the tools exposed them.

"Without too much effort, the two improvised gravediggers finished their task, then put down their tools, lay down in the shade, and waited.

"They thought they heard the sounds of a horse galloping at some distance, then it stopped abruptly. A long silence followed, then the gallop started again, at a charging pace. It was no surprise for the two servants, since they knew that the main road was not too far away; so they did not pay it much attention. And yet, the first act of the drama which was to bring the doom of the Rundjee family had just been accomplished.

"Arkabad, knowing that Dekan would travel for his morning promenade in that direction, had arranged his ambush accordingly. Lying on the ground, pretending to be hurt, he had called for help as the horseman was just passing by. Dekan had jumped down from his horse and rushed toward the villain in an effort to help him. The strangler, lurking behind a bush, had then taken advantage of this moment to wrap the fatal cord around the neck of the old warrior and, with the infernal skill that characterized his wretched kind, had killed him without mercy.

"The Brahmin then returned to the two servants.

" 'Come,' he said only.

"Passively they obeyed and arrived at the place where the body of Prince Dekan lay.

" 'Carry it to the prepared grave,' commanded Arkabad.

321

"And the servants carried the warrior and buried him. On the filled grave, they placed patches of grass and moss in such a way as to hide any trace of their work.

" 'Very well,' said the brahmin then. 'Let us return to Ellora.' Then, he said to the servants: 'Let oblivion fill your mind. A memory of this event would lead to your deaths.' "

Ahmad fell silent for a moment. Beads of sweat rolled on his forehead. Finally, he stretched out his hand towards the first tomb, near which he sat facing the Doctor and Na-Indra, and said slowly:

"The noble Dekan lies there... and for years I have ensured that travelers pay honor to his remains."

"Right here?" interrupted the Doctor. "But you just told us that the murder had been committed near the sanctuary of Ellora?"

"Yes, Sahib, it was."

"But then, how...?"

"How is the corpse in this place? I will tell you presently, Lord. Let me continue my painful confession..."

The old man remained for a few seconds with his head bowed, as if trying to recall long-forgotten memories, then he continued:

"After this expedition, I returned to the sanctuary filled with horror. I had become the accomplice, the instrument, of a crime, and I had to keep silent. What could I do? I was too weak to try to thwart the evil plans of the Brahmins. And then, my love of life was more powerful than remorse. I knew that talk would inevitably lead to death. Those who dare strike at the greats of this world are crushed mercilessly, and I, weak worm that I was, kept silent, although I despised me for doing so. I felt my heart writhe in my chest when chance put me in the presence of one of the Rundjees.

"The whole princely house was in mourning. A mountain of rupees had been promised to whomever would find Dekan's body, for there was no doubt about his fate. His horse had been found riderless, ten miles from Ellora, and had been brought back to the palace. People thought the old man had been the victim of an accident.

"They searched the countryside, the forest, the mountain gorges without finding anything. The precautions of the murderers had been well taken.

"Then, little by little, the searches stopped. The people lost interest in the disappearance of old Dekan and moved on to other concerns.

"I saw Arkabad quite often. Now, he showed me some unusual benevolence. I couldn't read my thoughts and saw in me only a devoted and discreet servant. If I had known, I would have let him see my anxieties, so I would have avoided being involved in the atrocious scenes which were about to happen; but as I confessed to you, I felt cowardly in the face of death.

"How silly I was! What is death but the passage from a minute of life to the infinite of the afterlife? Instead, I reaped years of expiation during which I wept over these tombs!

"It had been about two moons since the old prince had been murdered when a dust-covered courier arrived at the temple of Ellora. This man brought grave news.

"A wealthy rajah was near death. Rajah Paohm, sensing his impending end, had asked that a Brahmin call on him in order to sweeten his last moments by entertaining him with the promises of afterlife that Brahma makes to us, poor humans.

"To my great surprise, Arkabad volunteered to go to attend the dying man himself and ordered me to accompany him. My role was to carry the holy book of the Vedas, translated from the Sanskrit manuscript.

"We both left Ellora. On the way, Arkabad gave me his instructions:

" 'When I give you a sign, you will come and take my place at the bedside of the Rajah. You will continue reading from the sacred book. I know you to be discreet, yet I do not recommend that you see anything, or hear anything, of what will happen around you.'

"A shiver ran through me. What was the sinister Brahmin plotting? In what new scheme was he planning to make me his accomplice? Vain questions! Poor wretches like me never learn the secrets of their masters.

"We arrived at the superb palace of Rajah Paohm. Everywhere there was confusion, agitation, as is always the case in houses, when death knocks at the door.

"A young woman with disheveled hair, her clothes torn according to the custom, received us. She was called Sokoum and had been wed the previous year to the Rajah, who had elevated her from the status of slave to wife.

"Doubtless, the hand of the Brahmins had been no stranger to this decision, because the former slave was filling the temple with princely presents. Also, I often saw her in the sanctuary having long conferences with the priests.

"She bowed down before Arkabad with all the signs of the deepest affliction:

" 'Honored representative of Brahma,' she groaned, 'my soul is in mourning.'

" 'I believe so, beloved daughter of Heaven. So I came to bring you the consolations that the Lord of Creation reserves for his chosen ones.'

"That was a banal sentence. Many times, I had heard similar ones without paying any attention to them. Why, on that day, did it make such a painful impression on me? The Brahmin's intonation may have been slightly different... In any event, young Sokoum suddenly seemed appeased. The confusion in her countenance disappeared. Her dark eyes flashed joyfully. Arkabad's words had no doubt a mysterious meaning for her that escaped me. She got up, preceded us through the apartments and ushered us at last into the spacious room where the Rajah was stretched out on his couch.

"Livid, already half paralyzed by death, Paohm had a faint smile when he saw us enter.

"Arkabad advanced gravely, drew on the Rajah's chest the triangular sign, emblem of the Brahmanic trinity, then sitting down, he took the Veda book from me and began to read slowly, in a deep voice, the sacred verses, which tell the progression of the soul through the deserts of infinity.

"In a corner of the room, Sokoum squatted on a pile of cushions, and from time to time, chanted:

" 'Brahma! Vishnu! Shiva!'

"Her monotonous voice thus punctuated the verses.

"Motionless, I watched. The Rajah was breathing heavily; greenish hues marbled his skin; his eyes were losing their glow. Obviously, the awareness of his surroundings was abandoning him.

"Such was probably the opinion of Arkabad, for with an imperious gesture, he called me to his side. He passed me the sacred book, pointing to the verse where I was supposed to take over, and I started reading:

" 'The third heaven whose clouds are made of fragrant rose petals will open before the wandering spirit, and harmonies emanating from invisible orchestras will plunge him into the necessary ecstasy for one who wishes to cross the barrier of stars, luminous abode of the *Talamidas*.'[112]

"Here I paused for a second, waiting for the usual response, 'Brahma! Vishnu! Shiva!' but the beautiful Sokoum remained silent. I threw a glance toward her and saw Arkabad sitting next to her and talking to her animatedly.

"I resumed my reading, but now I couldn't concentrate on the meaning of the words my lips spoke. An ardent curiosity had seized me, and listening intently, I tried to overhear the conversation of the Brahmin and the desolate wife.

"To us, humble creatures to whom the Creator has refused a great intelligence, he gave as compensation, senses more acute than those of the great thinkers. So I soon overheard their conversation. Besides, deceived no doubt by my monotonous delivery, the Brahmin spoke in a low yet understandable voice:

" 'So, beautiful Sokoum, your husband's family, arguing your former status as a slave, intends to quarrel with you about Paohm's legacy?'

" 'Yes, Father of Ellora. In vain have I been the soft light that has embellished his last days; his greedy parents want me driven out of this palace where I have lived as sovereign.'

" 'What do you intend to do?'

"She made a desperate gesture and replied

---

[112] Note from Paul d'Ivoi: *Lower spirits charged with guiding the soul through the maze of infinite space.*

" 'I don't know! You are my only hope. Please remember that I am pious, and that I have never hesitated to bring royal gifts to the temple. Consider that Paohm's fortune in my hands will be your fortune, revered Brahmin, and protect this unfortunate woman from these greedy relatives.'

"I was beginning to understand. Arkabad was not unaware of the embarrassment that the death of the Rajah would bring to his widow. That's why he had wanted to come in person. But to what end? This is what I was dying to learn. So I redoubled my attention, while continuing to read in a monotone high voice. The Rajah no longer moved; his gaze was extinguished, and the sound of his breathing no longer reached me. Maybe his soul had already flown away, but I was still reading and I was listening.

" 'Do not believe, woman, that the priests of Ellora have abandoned you,' continued Arkabad. 'They love you for your kindness and your respect for the gods, and they have already thought of assuring you the wealth of which your piety shall make good use.'

"Ah!' she said reassured. "Will you defend me?'

" 'Yes. Listen. Your husband's relatives would triumph in court if we let them proceed. The laws of Nizam are clear: a slave who becomes heer master's wife cannot inherit, except in one case...'

"Sokoum veiled her face with her hands, and in a trembling voice, stated:

" 'Except in the case where she has a stake erected on which she will be burned alive in honor of the deceased.[113] Then she can bequeath her husband's treasures to her children, if she is a mother, or to her family and friends, if she is not.'

---

[113] *Sati* is a Hindu practice, now mostly historical, in which a widow sacrifices herself by sitting atop her deceased husband's funeral pyre. It probably developed into a real sacrifice in the medieval era within the northwestern Rajput clans to which it initially remained limited, to become more widespread during the late medieval era. During the Mughal period of 1526-1857, it was notably associated with elite Hindu Rajput clans in western India, marking one of the points of divergence between Hindu Rajputs and the Muslim Mughals, who banned the practice. In the early 19th century, the British East India Company initially tolerated the practice; in 1803, William Carey, a British Christian evangelist, noted 438 incidents within a 30-mile radius of Calcutta. Between 1815 and 1818 the number of incidents in Bengal doubled from 378 to 839. Opposition to the practice by evangelists and Hindu reformers, such as Ram Mohan Roy, ultimately led the British Governor-General to enact the Bengal Sati Regulation of 1829, declaring the practice of the burning or burying alive of Hindu widows to be punishable by the criminal courts. Nevertheless, isolated incidents of *sati* were recorded in India in the late-20th century, leading the Indian government to promulgate the Sati (Prevention) Act, 1987, criminalizing the aiding or glorifying of *sati*.

" 'Exactly,' said the Brahmin with irony.

" 'What! You, a priest of Brahma, would order that I be burned at the stake of the widows?'

" 'Yes.'

" '' But I don't want to die like that!' Sokoum cried out.

"Arkabad seized her hands and in an authoritative tone said:

" 'Silence, you madwoman! Listen to the advice of the wise. The law of Nizam says: *The slave, united to his master by the holy ties of marriage, will inherit his property if she steps on the pyre of widows...*'

" 'Yes.'

" 'But the law does not say that the slave must perish on it.'

"And since the beautiful Sokoum did not seem to understand the Brahmin's astute interpretation, the latter explained:

" 'We thought of using this loophole in the law to secure the riches of Paohm for you. You will lament, you will declare that you do not wish to outlive him, and that, according to the custom of inconsolable widows, you desire to be stretched out beside him on the funeral pyre. Thus you will order the preparation of this bonfire...'

" 'Yes, yes,' she stammered, 'but afterward... What happens afterward?'

" 'On the appointed day, you will appear in the costume of the victims. But fear not, we'll be there to prevent the sacrifice, and on the evening of the ceremony, you will thank us for having kept you in good health, while ensuring your fortune.'

"She still hesitated.

" 'His relatives will sue. They will argue that being near the stake is not enough to create rights... That the intended victim must burn...

" 'But the judges will defer to the interpretation of the Brahmins who alone are able to perceive the true meaning of the law better than mere individuals.'

" 'What, revered father, you would consent...?'

" 'To testify in court? Of course. my daughter.'

"Sokoum knelt down in front of Arkabad and said:

" 'How can I reward so much kindness? What devotion will be worthy of such radiant protection?'

" 'Continue to be pious and to open your heart to the voice of Brahma, delivered to you by His representatives on Earth.'

"I admit that this conversation left me perplexed. I didn't see what advantage the priests of Ellora would have in helping Sokoum inherit from the Rajah. The family of the dying man was generous towards the temples too, as generous as the former slave. Was it possible to guess that the intrigue hatched seemingly to favor Paohm's widow was in fact aiming to deal another blow to the Rundjees?"

The Doctor made a gesture of rage at this moment.

"Ahmad, doi you mean to say that Arkabad at that very moment was already planning…?"

"The death of Diomi, your father? Yes, Sahib."

The Doctor shook his head doubtfully.

"Just listen, Lord, and you will believe…"

"We stayed all day in the palace of Rajah Paohm, who had breathed his last while Arkabad and Sokoum were discussing the capture of his heritage.

"The former slave affected an inconsolable pain, and in front of her servants assembled, in front of her friends, she declared that life would be unbearable henceforth. She announced that she would follow her beloved husband to the land of azure birds, whose golden eyes contemplated Brahma, and whose songs, sweeter than the sweetest harmonies, celebrated the power of the Creator of the Universe.

"This comedy of sadness sickened me. But the entourage, not being in the confidence, believed the widow's words. They tried to dissuade her from sacrificing her youth and her beauty, but she was steadfast in her resolve, and for good reason.

"Eventually, Arkabad and I returned to Ellora when Sokoum's prayers had overcome all resistance. Three days later, when the sun would rise, then the pyre would be raised up and consume both the corpse of the Rajah and the body of the former slave.

"On the way back, the Brahmin, not suspecting that I had overheard his conversation, asked me rather abruptly:

" 'Ahmad, are you faithful?'

" 'Yes, Sahib,' I answered without hesitation.

" 'I know it, so I will confide in you.'

"I bowed.

" 'Despite my exhortations, the unfortunate Sokoum wants die in terrible agony…'

"Again I bowed. It would have been impossible for me to utter a word. I knew my interlocutor was lying. I rejoiced to learn towards what sinister goal he was working, but at the same time, I trembled that he might discover that instead of being his blind and deaf instrument, I was a thinking creature.

" 'To let her perish,' continued Arkabad, 'would be unjust. She who honors Brahma, who venerates his priests, should not undergo the torture that only criminals, who have to expiate their crimes, deserve.'

"I nodded confidently.

" 'So,' he continued, 'I have resolved to save her in spite of herself.'

"He was waiting for an answer. I had the strength to stammer:

" 'You are good, like Brahma himself.'

"The traitor smiled. The compliment had flattered him. He continued, even condescending to lean on my arm:

327

" 'And you will help me, Ahmad.'

" 'Yes, Sahib.'

" 'This is what I expect from you...'

"I opened my ears. I was about to find the key to the mystery!

" 'You will go to Aurangabad...'

" 'Tonight?'

" 'Yes. You will go to the residence of the English Governor...'

" 'Yes.'

" 'And you will tell him this: *Arkabad, Executioner of Ellora, informs you that, within three days, Sokoum, the widow of Raja Paohm, will voluntarily burn herself on the pyre of her dead husband. He will be glad if you can prevent that barbaric execution.* My sacerdotal ring here will assure you that the Governor will truszt you—and my message.'

"The English, at that time, were making laudable efforts to reduce the number of such sacrifices, but, in most cases, were powerless when confronted by the fanatism of the crowd. They could only intervene effectively when the Brahmin supported them.

"The purpose of my mission seemed very clear. Certain of the assistance of the College of Ellora, the British would take the necessary measures to prevent the death of Sokoum. But I had some doubts. I felt vaguely that the Brahmin was looking for another result, and nothing in his attitude reassured me. However, I put on an expression of faith.

" 'I thank you, Sahib, for entrusting me with a mission of such importance. I will leave as soon as you order me to.'

" 'Wait still,' he said.

"And we continued to walk in silence. It was only when we reached the entrance to the sacred gorge, that Arkabad pointed tat he road to Aurangabad, and commanded:

" 'You may go now. On your return, report to me about your conversation with the Governor.'

"I don't need to add the Governor received me perfectly. I had brought him the certainly of a moral victory, something of which he was very fond.

"The next evening, I returned to Ellora.

"Arkabad made me report on my trip in great detail. He praised me for my intelligence and the zeal that I had used in the circumstances, and even gave me some rupees as a mark of gratitude. Such generosity was rare; the Brahmins willingly received presents, but were very slow to give them. It must be then, I thought, that he had derived great pleasure from saving the beautiful Sokoum from the flames.

"However, the hours went by. The time for the funeral services of Rajah Paohm came. The Brahmins, clothed in white linen, crowned with blue flowers, carrying the sacred statues, walked in a procession to the palace of the dead ruler.

"In a huge court of honor encircled by the tall trees of the park, a giant funeral pyre, rising to height of the first floor of the palace, had been set up. Already the body of the dead Rajah clothed in his finest attire had been stretched out on a precious rug covering the platform which the fire was going to devour.

"An attentive and troubled crowd was waiting before that sinister altar. On the first row was a delegate of the noble caste, Dioni, your father, Lord, now head of the Rundjees. He stood almost god-like, wearing the warrior armor, an invaluable memento of the past, that only he had the right to wear in ceremonies such as these.

"The Brahmins made a living chain around the funeral pyre. At their appearance, a heavy silence had fallen upon the crowd. The tragedy was about to begin, and everyone felt their hearts tighten at the thought of the flames which were about to consume a living woman at the same time as her dead husband.

"Suddenly, gongs sounded, gloomily, and on the terrace which dominated the courtyard, Sokoum appeared, surrounded by her servants. She was very pale. Despite the promises of the Brahmins, terror showed on her face, making the blood from her heart drain out. Her eyes, wide open, were fixed with a terrified expression. On her white flowing robe that fell right to the ground, her loose hair twisted like black snakes, and the roses peaking out of her dress seemed to be staining it with blood.

"She walked slowly. A murmur of compassion, immediately stifled by respect, had greeted her arrival. With an automatic step, she went towards the funeral pyre. When she reached the steps set up for allowing her to climb onto the platform, her courage failed, and she stepped back.

"But Arkabad was there. He had chosen that spot, foreseeing exactly the last revolt of his accomplice. Smiling, he held out his hand to her, and, as if the presence of the executioner had given back all her energy to the widow, she bravely put her foot on the first step.

"Lightly, as if she was going to a party, the young woman climbed the funeral pyre. In an instant, she stood at the top, saying a last goodbye to the crowd, then she lay down on the cloth of the funeral pyre which had been thrown over the wood to receiver her, wrapping herself modestly in the folds of her tunic.

" 'May Brahma look kindly upon this scene,' sung the priests. "One of his children is going to enter into his bosom before the hour fixed by nature. May he receive her among his Chosen Ones.'

"The gong sounded again, like far away thunder. Four men came forward. Each one brandished a torch whose red resinous fumes rose in the air before floating away. They placed themselves on the four corners of the pyre. There was to be a signal and then, they would set fire to the dry wood of which the funeral pyre was made.

"But the signal was not given. Instead, a sonorous voice shouted with a strong British accent:

" 'Sacrifices such as these are forbidden by English authorities!'

"Soldiers jumped out of the bushes, ran towards the funeral pyre, seized Sokoum, dragged her away, while others lit the wood as quickly as possible. Soon crackling noises were heard. The Rajah would be burned, but his soul would not complete his journey through the twelve heavens in the company of the beautiful Sokoum.

"In the crowd, there was at first amazement. To prevent a voluntary death is a sacrilege, an act of profanation. All were frozen with horror, then cries of rage break out. They rushed on the English soldiers. A furious melee ensued.

"But after a few minutes of struggle, the Brahmins intervened. They spoke to soothe the crowd's anger. Brahma, no doubt, wanted, this they said; he wanted the good and charitable Sokoum to go on living in order to do more good, to practice virtue, to serve as an example to all women; she deserved to die only on the day fixed by destiny, and then sit at the right of the Creator of the World.

"Everyone calmed down. Friends, curious, servants, allowed the English soldiers to occupy the palace. The Brahmins presented them as the instruments of the will of Brahma, so they no longer were profaners, but obedient slaves of the god. As the incineration of the Rajah ended, the assistance dispersed.

"Only, during the fight, assassins in the pay of Ellora had killed the leader of the Rundjees and taken away his body!

"Nobody had noticed that. As his family, his wife, and his sons were worried about not seeing him return to them, I was digging in the valley of the forest, near Dekan's tomb, a new grave, where the hatred of the Brahmins had condemned Diomi to sleep, without his descendants being able to lavish pious care upon his final resting place."

And pointing to the second mound, Ahmad concluded sadly:

"Here lies the valiant Diomi."

CHAPTER XI
The Blood Trail

"Arkabad! Always Arkabad!" growled the Doctor, gritting his teeth. "To think that I held him within reach of my arm and did not crush this wretch!"

Tenderly, Na-Indra leaned towards him and said:

"My friend, I thought I had suffered more than any other creature on Earth, yet, I see now that you are to be pitied more than me. The abyss into which I whimpered was nothing compared to that into which you were thrown. I will no longer speak to you of my sufferings, but only of my pity."

"Poor child, the same demon is bent on destroying both of us."

But she shook her head, and with a sudden exclamation proclaimed:

"We were saved by each other! Brahma wanted us to hear his will. He gave both of us a single heart, a single love, but also a single hatred."

Ahmad watched them with inexpressible anxiety.

"I hear what that girl is saying," he finally whispered. "She is as beautiful as the spirits of light, and she forgives the weak, who obeyed the orders of the mighty. She understood that this fragile earthen vase could not clash with a steel jug. But you, Lord, you, Master, to whom my thoughts flew during all these

331

years of solitude, will you not speak to your servant the comforting words that will soothe his remorse?"

Calm again by a terrible effort of will, the Doctor held out his hand to the old man and said:

"I have no anger towards you, who were only the passive instrument of the Brahmins. In my name, in the name of all those who are no longer and whose spirits undoubtedly wander around us, here is my hand as a pledge of forgiveness."

Ahmad seized it and raised it devoutly to his lips.

"Go on with your story, Ahmad. I am certain that my mother Lenoor, my brothers Iglir, Banium, Dogmar, and my wife Diarmida, were struck by the same enemies, but I want to hear from your mouth the bloody tale of a dreadful past."

"Diomi," Ahmad continued, "was nowhere to be found. Like the brave Dekan, he seemed to have left the Earth like a cloud crosses the sky, without a trace. Diarmida was soon to be a mother. We took pity on her. They hid that new misfortune from her.

"The days flowed by, and your wife, Lord, gave birth to a son, who according to our custom received as a name derived from yours. You were Rama; he was Ramani.

"At the sight of the baby, your mother appeared to forget her sadness. The child brought with him all those little ones spread around them. The fragile creature replaced the spaces left empty in her heart by Dekan and Diomi.

"It was only then that your mother was told of the disappearance of her husband. The blow was hard. The young woman had the intuition of the calamities which were going to fall upon her new family. In a secret conversation, she recounted to Lenoor what had happened in the temple of Ellora before her marriage.

"At that revelation, your mother was awestruck. So the hatred of the Brahmins was bent against the Rundjees. They were impossible to fight; defeat was certain; annihilation assured. For a long time, the two unhappy women talked.

"They didn't dare warn, you, Lord Rama, or warn your brothers. They knew you were valiant men, fearless. In all likelihood, you would have attacked openly the College of Ellora..."

"That would have been better," interjected the Doctor.

Ahmad shook his head sadly and replied:

"Perhaps, Lord; but your mother judged differently. The Brahmins planned—that was obvious—to add to their treasures the riches of the Rundjee and Feliardit families. The only mean of disarming them was to take away those who would inherit them..."

Here, the Doctor let out a heart wrenching cry.

"So that's why my mother encouraged my brothers to take a trip to Europe. 'You are not still bound by marriage,' she said to them, 'so it is good that you learn about those things which assure the power of the Westerners. Perhaps one day, you will have to fight for the independence of our country. To win, you must become the equal of our oppressors.'"

"Yes, Lord, I know," said Ahmad.

"And Diarmida supported her view."

"Yes, Lord."

With horror in his trembling voice, the old man continued:

"There were Brahmin spies in your house. Your servants betrayed you, reporting all your words, your gestures your very thoughts. You did not suspect their betrayal. However, on the evening of the day when your brothers were supposed to go to the Feola Railway Station to travel to Mumbai with the intention of taking passage on a steamer to Europe, one of your *mahouts* [114] came to the temple.

"I recognized him right away and my whole body was suddenly bathed into a cold sweat. I asked myself: *Am I again going to fill the function of a gravedigger?*

"That man had a long conversation with Arkabad, then he went away. Some minutes later, the Executioner of Ellora had me summoned.

" 'Ahmad,' he said, 'dress like a farmer. The service of Brahma calls me far from here and I am taking you with me.'

"My foreboding had not deceived me. Oh! I had an instant of revolt. In my sleepless nights, Dekan and Dioni appeared to me, reproaching me for having buried their remains in a desolate place. Would others soon join these reproachful ghosts? But like always, I hid my true feelings; courage was lacking in me.

"Therefore, the Brahmin Arkabad and I departed. We did not go to Feola, but to Adigar, a monastery located twenty miles to the west, close to the railway line. It was a Brahmin property, surrounded with thick woods and fruit trees which bordered the road and provided the monastery with much of its food.

"They received us with the honors to which the high rank of Executioner entitled Arkabad. However, he cut short the ceremony and summoned Aïtar, the head of the monastery, and shut himself in a meeting with him for more than an hour. I waited for the results of their conference all day.

"That night, a message arrived from Feola addressed to Arkabad. It was a copy of a cable sent by a spy of the Brahmins. He read its content to me: *Arrived at Feola with luggage. Taking first train at 4:30 a.m.*

"Various tools had been laid out on the table there... A wrench, a pick and so forth.

---

[114] Elephant rider, trainer, or keeper.

" 'Take those tools and follow me,' ordered Arkabad.

"I obeyed. We left the monastery and went into the thick woods which surrounded us.

"A quarter of an hour later, we arrived at the train tracks. At that point, the line was built on an embankment, and, by the light of the moon, I could see the rails extending as far as the eye could see like a silver ribbon.

"The Brahmin pointed out to me the bolts which tied the rails together and ordered:

" 'Unscrew them!'

"I shivered down to my very bones. The Executioner of Ellora was commanding me to cause a catastrophe. With the rails unbolted, the train would derail. I foresaw a heap of broken cars, decapitated bodies, and blood flowing everywhere in crimson streams.

" 'I'm waiting,' continued Arkabad.

"Ah! One would never guess how much suffering even the most cowardly of persons may endure! We were alone. If I had possessed any courage, I could have given a blow with my pick to that monster right in front of me. The idea of that act of justice certainly went across my mind, but it was only a fugitive thought, and instead I bent towards the rails.

"The terrible priest made me remove the ballast, lay bare the wooden sleepers on which the rails are fixed, and separate from the wood the iron legs affixed there like iron claws. Then, I put the ballast back. The most experienced eye could not have suspected the dreadful work which I had just executed. However, according to the engineers' expression, one of the rails was now 'crazy,' or loose, and it would surely give way under the sudden thrust of the train.

"Arkabad tapped me on the shoulder with a satisfied expression.

" 'I am pleased with you ,Ahmad,' he said. 'The time is not far off where from simple servant that you are now, I will promote you to the rank of novice. You will have your part of the power that your devotion assures in the College of Ellora. Go back to sleep now; I will call you when the time comes.'

"And bending under the weight of my tools which were killing my shoulders, I returned to the monastery. I ran to shut myself up in my bedroom and wept like a child. Oh! Coward, coward that I was! In that terrible night, my cowardice had made me part of a crime, the horror of which tormented me endlessly.

"Then I fell into a heavy sleep without any dreams. In the monastery, no one had to right to shut their doors, and at any hour of day and night, the members of the congregation could enter freely into any room. I was awakened by the noise of several persons entering my bedroom. While shaking me awake, they said:

" 'It four o'clock in the morning.'

"Four o'clock! In half-an-hour at most, the train would reach the section of the line where I had prepared the catastrophe! I got up quickly, shivering.

" 'Why are you trembling?' one of the monks asked med.

" 'Because I am cold,' I replied.

"Following those who had awakened me, I went into the woods until we reached the railway. Arkabad was waiting there. Leaning against a tree which was strangely lit by the approaching dawn, he appeared to me like the genie of destruction.

" 'Take the torches,' he ordered.

"My companions searched the bushes. There, on the ground, were torches made of resin. Everybody picked up one. There was one left on the ground.

" 'That one is yours,' said one of the men. 'Pick it up.'

"I obeyed mechanically, then found myself back along the railroad with the others. No one was talking. One would have said that nature itself joined the solum silence which preceded the desired cataclysm. There was no wind and the leaves looked heavy, leaning towards the ground, perfectly still.

"We were waiting for those who were about to die in total silence. Suddenly, my heart stopped. Far away I heard a groaning rumbling sound in the distance. Arkabad stood up again. A cruel smile contracted his face.

" 'The train,' he said.

"The men bowed their heads.

" 'Do you remember my instructions?' he asked.

" 'Yes, Sahib.'

" 'Then, pay attention and make sure that everything is carried out properly. '

"A soft whistle came from the bushes, echoed by another from the brushes in front of us. That signal—because that's what it was, I was certain of it— seemed to have awakened the forest. Then there was silence again.

"Now the roar was louder. The train was approaching. Every puff that it let out led the travelers closer to death. I didn't move. My hair stood on end, running with sweat. I looked with terror toward the spot where the train was going to appear.

"There it was. The lanterns in front of the locomotive shone like the eyes of an enormous monster.

"A few more instants and it would be right in front of us. And suffering from a vertigo-like effect, it seemed to me that it came even faster and with more rage towards the fatal spot where the iron supports were secretly missing from the rails. In my head, there was the confusion of madness; my thoughts swirled in the grasp of fear and the dull striking of the pistons.

"Then I saw a vision from hell. There were screams, the screeching sounds of metal and wood being broken, the sudden release of vapor in the air. And above all, the whistle which continued blowing in a manner that was both horrible and irritating.

"The train had derailed. The cars were piled one on top of each other . There was no order left, just a pile of debris from which came heart-breaking cries.

"Then Arkabad stepped forward. The torches held by my companions lit the sinister shadows. The servants jumped onto the railway. What were they doing? I didn't know. A dark veil floated in front of my eyes. My legs were stiff. My feet, suddenly turned heavy, could not get off the ground. I had the impression that they were held back as if by deep roots.

"I saw human forms run by me, carrying the wounded, whose blood flowed like crimson fountains.

"Suddenly, tongues of flame dazzled me. Fire had broken out in the wreckage. And everything became clear to me... My companions had torches. Thery had started the fires! I fell to the ground, unconscious.

"When I came to, daylight lit up a scene of utter desolation. The locomotive on the embankment was surrounded by broken cars pointing toward the heavens and clouds of thick black smoke. With a cry of horror, I stood up, shaking, and ran back towards the monastery.

"Three days later, the Governor of the province sent a note olf thanks to the Brahmins of Adigar for having shown "a devotion beyond all praise" by bringing help to wounded caused by the tragic derailment which had happened near their monastery.

"Arkabad and I returned Ellora. This time, we traveled by way of cart and oxen. The floor of the vehicle was covered by straw, and four bodies were stretched out. Those of Lenoor, your mother, and of your brothers, Iglir, Banium, and Dogmar.

"It turned out that Lenoor, with motherly solicitude, had wanted to accompany her sons right to Bombay. Everyone believed that their bodies had been consumed in the fire which had destroyed the train. It was a mistake. In reality, they had been stolen by the Brahmin, and at present, I was going to go back to the ravine in the forest of Ellora to bury them next to those of Decan and Dioni."

On the plateau of the tombs, no one spoke. His head bent, his face hidden in his hands, Doctor Mystery, whose real name was Prince Rama Rundjee, last surviving member of his line, appeared devastated.

Na-Indra, too, was weeping.

As for old Ahmad, his hand pointed automatically towards the remaining four tombs. His gesture was explicit. It said, here lie the four victims of the derailment which I caused.

And that gesture, which had punctuated each chapter of his story, took an even more tragic turn. But suddenly, the Doctor raised his head. His pale face was calm and only the bluish circles around his eyes betrayed his superhuman suffering.

"Ahmad," he said slowly, "answer my questions."

"I am yours, O Lord," replied the old man. "Tell me what you wish to know."

"One last thing." And after a pause: "Arkabad was everywhere, and he was always the creator of these misfortunes?"

"That is correct, Lord."

"Was he also the one who caused Diarmida's death?"

The old man shrugged sadly.

"I do not know, Lord."

"What? Weren't you a part of that too?"

"As for that, no. Diarmida was found dead at the Temple of Ellora, strangled by the red cord of a killer. I buried her body in the same fatal ravine, but I don't know how or why she had come to be in that sanctuary."

"So you wouldn't be able to confirm that she was brought there by the miserable Arkabad?"

"I can only guess."

"Guess what?"

"Arkabad's function at Ellora makes him the prime suspect."

"His function?"

"Yes, to be the executioner and to carry out the sentences of the College of Ellora."

After these words, the Doctor remained thoughtful. Then, he murmured:

"That's how it must have been. It must have been him who, hidden under a mask, took part in the horrible scene which I beheld."

He then took Na-Indra's hands into his own.

"Na-Indra, who is to me like a kiss from heaven, the star of my life, you must learn how they had killed my first love. You who have tended my wounds, who have given me back the ability to love and to hope in the future, Na-Indra, you must hear the death song of the Rundjees…"

She didn't say a word, but leaned her head on his shoulder, and her big black eyes fixed themselves on his, as if to give him with her pure grace the courage to tell everything, and the will to begin his life again.

"My despair," began the Doctor, "at the news of the horrible catastrophe, which had taken at the same time my mother and my brothers, was immense. But as horrible as it was, it did not equal that of Diarmida.

"I was even surprised by it, but could have I ever suspected then the true criminal nature of what had been for me a horrible accident?

"She changed and became grim. Her baby in her arms, she wandered about the palace, aware of the slightest noise, defiantly looking at everyone and everything. She sent away the servants who were supposed to guard our son. Henceforth, she alone took care of him.

"Also, she did not allow me to leave her anymore. If I had to go out, she accompanied me, our child held against her breast. And when I tried to lessen her terror, alas! I could not do so. She answered me, the poor gentle martyr:

" 'Let me alone, Rama. I am obeying an inspiration from above. As long as we are united, we have nothing to bad fear. Our separation would be fatal.'

"*Madness*, I thought. However, she was right. Down in the countryside, a rumor was growing. People were accusing the Brahmins of the calamities that had struck the Rundjees. But the cleverness of the wicked priests could not be so easily thwarted. And Diarmida's precautions only inflicted me the most grievous pain that a man could suffer.

"One evening, when we were dining out on chaises lounges, we remained there, without talking, overtaken by the calm of the night. Diarmida kept her eyes on our child, asleep in the next room. A delightful feeling took hold of me; it seemed to me as if my blood was being refreshed in my veins. I experienced a delicious fatigue, a physical wellbeing, a peace if the mind which I hadn't felt in many weeks. And this moment of rest delighted me, like a traveler-tired takes joy in a halt in an oasis in the desert.

"Suddenly, a shadow stood before us. I felt myself trembling. It was a Brahmin whose face was hidden behind a ritual mask with three holes for the eyes and the mouth. Diarmida had seen him also and cried out:

"'Rama! Rama!'

"And she threw herself between the stranger and our child.

"I wanted to do the same, but then and there I was the victim of a strange and terrible phenomenon: my arms and legs were suddenly stiff, petrified. The least gesture was impossible for me. One would have believed that an iron armor was imprisoning my body. I made a superhuman effort to overcome my paralysis, but remained unable to move. I tried to talk, to shout, but my tongue remained silent and no sounds came out of my mouth.

"Diarmida, who was stupefied to see me thus, repeated in an agonized voice:

" 'Rama', get up!

"The Brahmin, whose eyes were shining behind his mask, began to laugh.

" 'Don't tire yourself out calling your husband,' he chuckled. 'He can't answer.'

She made a dull cry and leaned towards me.

" 'Rama, I ask you, speak! Danger is hanging above our very heads.'

"But I remained silent. It was awful; I could see, I could hear, my head was free, but my nerves, my muscles, refused to obey my will.

" 'Brahma! Brahma!' shouted my poor wife. 'Are you inflicting your wrath on the last of the Rundjees?'

"The masked Brahmin laughed and said:

" 'Not yet.'

"She turned towards him and asked:

338

" 'What do you mean?'

" 'That Rama can still be saved.'

" 'Oh!' she begged, 'let him live, and my fortune shall belong to you. I know that is what the College of Ellora wishes. I will let you take all these riches which have brought me only unhappiness. Let me live out my days poor and destitute near my Rama.'

"The masked man shook his head, and in a harsh voice, said:

" 'He will live, but you will be separated from him.'

" 'Separated?'

" 'Remember: you married him despite having been forbidden to do so by the Brahmins. You have disobeyed your orders. You must bend before the law.'

"Diarmida trembled and replied:

" 'But I wouldn't know how to live without him. To see him, to hear him, is as necessary for me as the sun is for the flowers.'

" 'The suffering of a human,' the mysterious Brahmin said, 'is sweet to the gods. Their cries of agony are more like perfume than the smell of incense from the sacred candles. Your obedience will perhaps lead you to pardon. You sinned against Brahma; you must pay the price.'

"And as she remained paralyzed by terror, the Brahmin approached me and raised a dagger with a shining blade over my chest. Then, with a gesture, he stopped Diarmida who was ready to jump to my aid.

" 'You are three steps away from him; me, I have only to lower my arm to cut the string of his days. So be quiet and listen...'

"My unfortunate wife bowed her head, vanquished by the cold logic of my assailant. To tell of the rage which was boiling within me would be impossible.

"As I said, I saw that man defy my wife. I heard his cruel words, and yet an invisible force paralyzed my body. But my mind was not calm; ideas turned and twisted in my head like a pack of wild goats in a clearing. I was suffering the torture of the damned, but the gesture of malediction, the shout is of anger, of pain, were all but denied to me."

For an instant, the Doctor remained silent. He mechanically wiped the sweat from his forehead, and then continued in a lower voice:

"The Brahmin was enjoying his triumph. The three of us were as still and silent as statues. Finally, the masked man said:

" 'Diarmida, listen to me attentively...'

"The poor soul made a sign that she was listening.

" 'The knowledge of the Brahmins,' he declared with pride, "their science, has no limits. It allows us to do the impossible, to understand the infinite. The life of the planet, of the animals, the lighting itself, are our servants. We wanted Rama to become as weak as a child, for his body to be paralyzed. Some drops of a vegetable extract mixed with his food were enough. That brave man, that accomplished warrior, was rendered powerless; he lies under my blade not knowing how to avoid it.'

"Diarmida covered her face with her hands. She was crying; she felt as if everything was lost; that she was alone and defenseless in the hands of her butchers. And that knowledge tore through my spirit like a hot flame. Ah! To regain my freedom of movement, just enough to crush that miserable Brahmin and die afterwards, but die avenged. I called on all my nerves, my bones cracked, my muscles extended, but alas, the force which condemned me to inertia could not be overcome. From that terrible inner resolve, nothing appeared on the outside.

"That last attempt crushed my spirit. Was I therefore to remain impassive before the torture of my beloved spouse and the destruction of my happiness? No doubt that our tormentor was reading my mind, because he continued:

" 'Rama has realized that human energy is nothing compared to our power.'

"A shiver was Diarmida's only answer.

"At that very moment, in unison, as if he had wanted to share our despair, our child started to cry. At the sound of his sweet voice, my wife forgot everything. The woman became a mother, and with a sudden gesture, she seized the baby and began rocking him slowly. Ah! The adorable scene. Most ordinary criminals would have been softened by the view of a young mother comforting her child. But the Brahmins are merciless. Their hearts are made of steel. They have only one emotion: Domination. They do not think like other men do, of affection, goodness and devotion... These, they call weaknesses. They work only to enslave others, and renounce their own families... By placing themselves outside society, they claim to be above it.

"The masked killer continued with a nuance of impatience:

" 'Here are our conditions for your husband to go on living...'

"Suddenly brought back to reality, Diarmida looked at him, aghast.

" 'Do you understand me, woman?'

" 'I do.'

" 'You will leave this house with your child...'

" 'Yes, but what about him?'

"She pointed at me with a fierce gesture.

" 'He will live. I have promised you that. I am strong enough not to have need of lying.' Then, the Brahmin added casualty: 'If you hesitate, I will revert to my previous plan.'

"And he made the motion of stabbing me in my stomach. Diarmida let out a heart-rendering cry.

" 'I will leave! I will!'

"The masked man shook his head with satisfaction.

" 'Right away. Tonight?' he insisted.

" 'Right away,' promised my wife in a broken voice.

" 'Then sit down at that table.'

"Again, she obeyed.

" 'Here is a piece of paper and a pen. I am going to dictate… Write.'

"The pale victim, like a living cadaver, threw me a long sad look. Then her trembling fingers picked up the pen and she waited. The Brahmin spoke thus:

" 'I, Diarmida Rundjee, have left the palace in mourning, never to come back. All those whom I loved have been struck by the wrath of Brahma. A curse extends to all those who carry my name, so I must flee. Perhaps my submission will appease the wrath of the Creator of the World.'

"The forlorn woman wrote. The Brahmin was watching over her shoulder, to be sure she did not leave anything out. When she had finished, he said"

" 'Good. Now, sign it.'

"Diarmida signed.

" 'You are free to go.'

" 'Where shall I go?'

" 'Wherever you please. The Brahmins, whom you blame, despite the fact that they are only carrying out the will of the gods, will be merciful. They don't want to see you impoverished. Take this bag; it contains some diamonds, the purest ever extracted form our soil. Their value exceeds twelve million rupees. So you can see that wealth is not what motivates the actions of the College of Ellora.'

"Mechanically, my beloved spouse took the little bag.

" 'Now, go,' ordered the priest. The hours are flowing by, and if you are too slow, I will not be able to save the life of Rama Rundjee…'

"As I said, the Brahmins are known to be so unforgiving that even the bravest of the braves do not dare to disobey them. Diarmida gave in under the will of the masked man. She came to me and embraced me for a long time, drenching my face with her tears.

" 'Goodbye, Rama, my beloved. It is in order that you live that the guardian of your household is condemning herself to solitude. Your son will grow up praising your memory, I swear that to you."

"Suddenly, she interrupted herself and looked at the Brahmin straight in the eyes.

" 'Rama will know that it is out of kindness for him that I am depriving myself of his dear presence?"

" 'What for?' mocked the priest.

" 'In order for him not to suffer additional useless pain. If he were to believe himself to be abandoned by me, it would be better for him to die, and for myself and my child to follow him into the shadowland where there is no more suffering.'

"The Brahmin felt that nothing would change the resolution of the dear creature, so he gave in.

" 'So be it. He will know.'

" 'So he will live, yes, saddened by my absence, but certain that in some unknown retreat, my thought will be with him and that our son will grow up to give back to the name of Rundjee its former glory.'

" 'He will live knowing this.'

" 'Then I will sacrifice myself.'

"After a halting last kiss, as if she feared lacking courage, and with her child in her arms, Diarmida went away.

"Ah! How horribly I felt! It was as if my heart was going to break, but that was an error of my senses. My heart, like the rest of my body had been muted by the poison of the Brahmins and beat slowly but steadily. The emotions that moved my thoughts did not have the power to move my body.

"Leaning forward, the Brahmin listened her go. Finally, he stood up. He looked at me through his mask and said:

" 'Prince Rama, the hour has come for you to repent for having dared challenge the power of the Brahmins, and for having devoted your loyalty, and given your offerings to the Companions of Shiva and Kali.'

"My eyes, the only active part of myself, expressed all my contempt.

" 'Yes," laughed that miserable man, "you are prideful; your family bows to no one. But now, you are in my power, even if you will not beg. That is of little importance for a man who can tear apart your brain and torture your soul...'

"And with cruel slowness, drawing out the horror of each of his pronouncements, he said:

" 'I promised to that fool Diarmida that you would live, but that is the only thing I promised. You, last son of the Rundjees, shall live prisoner in an underground cell where you will never see the light of the day and never receive a visitor until you die. You will live knowing that the foolish creature who left here only added to your suffering because her useless devotion will have served only as a substitute for a quicker and more merciful death.'

"He remained silent for an instant. He probably wanted for each of his words to bury into my mind like a poisonous dart.

" 'For months, years perhaps, you will live begging for death.' He then leaned over to my ear and whispered: 'And then, like all the other fools who walk around on the surface of the Earth believing in affection, believing in love, you think you might find a consolation from your insanity in thinking: "I suffer, my heart beats, I have been erased from the ranks of men, but Diarmida still lives; and our son will believe in strength and wisdom. The future of the Rundjees comes forward when the child becomes a man." Yet, that false joy, you will never have...'

"My eyes closed; a dark cloud spread over my thoughts. I felt a sadness deeper and more terrifying than everything I had felt during the last hour. Nearer still, the Brahmin murmured in his strident voice, like a human tiger:

" 'Tomorrow, the farmers going to work their fields will find on the road near the Fountain of Allimilad the lifeless body of Diarmida, your wife, killed on the order of the College of Ellora.' And after a pause: '"Tomorrow, your son shall be brought up by faithful servants in the temple. He will grow up to take his place among the Brahmins, and, like us, he will become the fierce enemy of that ridiculous liberty upon which your family concentrated all their efforts. Here is what you will think of in your underground prison. I have prepared the most horrible cell for you, without light, without joy, and most especially, without hope!'

"The pain which had invaded my thoughts as the accursed Brahmin had talked, suddenly tore something in my very soul and the stars dimmed in front of my eyes. Was I dead? Was I still alive?

"The sharpness of my pain, combined with the drug that the Brahmins had given to me, produced the most unexpected phenomenon. I was in a catalepsy, a strange state where my heart hardly beat, where blood circulation was almost nil, that same state that fakirs reach through hypnotic means. I no longer thought; I no longer suffered.

"I was a dead man living in a vegetive state."

Na-Indra let out a deep sigh and said:

"My friend, my friend, can my love ever make you forget that past so full of horror?"

The Doctor looked at her with affection.

"In the darkest sky, a star may appear and the shadows will be vanquished. You are that star, Na-Indra, and from the depth of the shadows, those who are no more will bless you for having brought some light to the one who is to fight against the dark."

Then, changing tomes, as if courage had been reconfirmed with those few words, he said:

"Let me finish my tragic tale, so that nothing in my life is hidden from you."

"I remained in a catalepsy for a long time.

"One day, however, I emerged from that state. My eyelashes could move; my eyes had regained their sight.

"My first clear impression was that of cold. I was inside a kind of box made of stone, through the walls of which a draft of cold air passed through. Above me, through a see-through lid, I could see a golden ceiling decorated with lively images.

"My thoughts, which were confused at first, became clearer little by little. I recognized the paintings on the ceiling, the columns carved with petrified flowers with long stems. I was in the holy of holies of the Temple of Ellora. But why was I in this stone coffin? Why was I dressed in sumptuous clothes?

"I was pondering these questions when I heard footsteps.

"A sense of caution prevented me from calling out. My memories had returned, but still felt like a far away dream, and inspired in me a feeling of melancholy. But there was something else that was strange. It seemed as if my whole being had been renewed. My father, my brothers, my mother, Diarmida, my son, all passed through my mind without awakening the horrible sadness that I had felt before. Perhaps my heart itself was still asleep?

"Still, I had the clear feeling that every man in this temple was an enemy and I remained stiff, motionless, my eyes slightly open, allowing me to slip a look across the veil of my eyelids.

"And above me, looking at me across the glass lid, I saw two men. However, they were humble servants, not Brahmins.

" 'Pardon me,' murmured one of them. "Pardon me, O last victim, for not having yet buried you alongside the others. But the work is heavy and it is more difficult to expiate one's crime than to commit it.'"

Here, a dull cry from Ahmad, interrupted the Doctor. The old guardian of the tombs had stood up as if prodded by a stick, and his hands were trembling convulsively.

"Ah, Lord! Lord!" he stammered. "So you heard these things!"

"Yes, but why are you so troubled?"

"Because the person who spoke thus…"

"Yes?"

"That was me!"

"You?"

"Yes, Lord. For two years, you remained plunged into a sleep that we mistook for that of death."

"Two years, you say?"

"Yes… And during the long months that passed…" Ahmad stopped. "No not like this," he said as if he were talking to himself. "Nothing must remain hidden from the Lord who has returned." And turning back towards the Doctor, he asked: "Do you know, Lord, what happened during your sleep, when you were not able to hear or see?"

"No."

"Well, Old Ahmad will tell you."

The old man leaned back and spoke:

"After you lost consciousness in the palace where your ancestors had lived, Arkabad—who was the masked Brahmin, I am sure of that—clapped with his hands. Some servants of the Temple who had been posted in the neighborhood came running.

"They wrapped you with blankets and carried you to a waiting chariot stationed outside. Hidden between bales of freshly cut maze, you were taken to the

Temple of Ellora and thrown into a dungeon, a place where other people before you had suffered atrocious agonies just for having attracted the wrath of the Brahmins.

"None of your servant appeared. They had been gathered in the kitchens by the Brahmins, and when the British authorities investigated your disappearance, these unfortunate men could swear on the sacred books that they had seen nothing, and that they had heard nothing.

"All of that, I learned later, from the mouth of those who had been employed on this expedition, because at the time, I had been occupied in the ravine of the forest of Ellora digging a new grave.

"That grave was soon filled with its own body: that of Diarmida, caught in the countryside, strangled by the same assassin who had killed your grandfather..."

The Doctor was listening without moving. It seemed that he no longer had the strength to mourn. He had drunk the cup of despair right up to the top.

Meanwhile, Ahmad continued:

"The bag of diamonds, the wailing child, those two treasures that the woman had been carrying in her flight were brought back to the Temple.

"The Brahmins reclaimed the precious stones. As for the poor little boy, he was taken to a slave nurse and, soon, in his growing hair a scared barber was called to cut a tonsure in the form of a star, the emblem of the Brahmanic trinity.

"From that moment, he was consecrated to Brahma. But Death took pity on that poor boy doomed to betray everything his ancestors had fought for. He passed away a few weeks later and his little body was buried by me in the same tomb where his mother had been laid to rest..."

And with strange authority, Ahmad pronounced:

"The gods have willed me to oversee that new, horrible work. They have wished that I fulfill the duties which were given to me; to assure those noble dead graves before which passersby bow and pay a respectful tribute.

"Digging through the soil, I reached the body of Diarmida that I had previously buried. What horror did I feel in seeing again her dead body under the pale light of the moon in the great silence of the nigh. I wanted to place the remains of her son in her dead arms. It seemed to me that, in this way, I was doing a pious duty, one which would bring a smile to the spirit of the poor martyr from the heights of Heaven.

"In the end, that sight was even more terrible than I had thought. She was beautiful, just as I had buried her. You would have said that she was sleeping. Trembling, I placed the child near her, and then I filled the hole.

"Only one thing puzzled me, and I never stopped thinking about it. How had her body remained intact? A careful examination of the soil explained the phenomenon. The ground was mingled with rock salt in strong proportions. Thus, the bodies were preserved.

"And I thought I saw in there an opportunity to better fulfill my duty. We, servants of the Brahmins, traveled a great deal. Constantly, we were going down many paths and roads in order to carry out the orders of our masters.

"Every time that I could, with the help of the companions of Shiva and Kali, I took one of the Rundjees' bodies out of his or her forgotten tomb and carried it here. After I had them all reburied here, I told myself that I would come to this forgotten corner of the Earth, and would consecrate the rest of my days to honor those that I had not been able to save.

"Laod, a poor devil like me, who had also been mixed up in that sinister business, decided to come with me. Seven tombs had been dug and an eighth one had been prepared. Yours, because we intended, Laod and I, to reunite you with your parents. But the job was difficult...

"The Brahmins, accused silently of having destroyed the line of the Rundjees in order to steal their wealth, had schemed to stop that unpleasant rumor. They took your body out of the hidden cell where they had let it, and pretended to find it on some lonely road. They had placed the bag of diamonds which had formerly been given to Diarmida on your belt. As you can see, it still had its uses. The Brahmins declared that you were not dead, but taken with lethargy. They asked for, and obtained the guardianship of your body, and placed it in the Temple. At the time, I believed that they engineered your death-like sleep with methods known only to them.

"They proclaimed very loudly: 'Those impious people who attribute the deaths of the valiant Rundjees to us... Well, if Rama awakens, he will speak, and the wicked who accuse us will be confounded. Why would we kill the Rundjees in order to steal their fortune? Rama carried it with him in a sackful of gems and we didn't steal it. The faithful can see for themselves that it is still attached to his belt.'

"Spreading their lies to disculpate themselves, they nevertheless claimed the fortune of the Rundjees easily, since the Temple of Ellora inherited it, following the death of your son, whose life had been dedicated to Brahma.

"Mind you, they only took control if it as its 'guardians,' claiming that they would give it back to you when you have awakened...

"So you had become some sort of a precious hostage., one that Laod and I had sworn to free and bury here in the eighth grave, in a land over which the power of the Brahims does not extend.

"That is why, leaning over the glass lid which closed the stone coffin where you lay, unconscious of your existence, dead to all, we were asking pardon for our past cowardice.

"An opportunity to execute our plan finally presented itself. The procession of the Jagannath was supposed to take place in the sacred city of Delhi that year. The Brahmin of Ellora went there *en masse*, leaving the guardianship of their temple to their servants. We had several days in front of us. We resolved to act. And while looking at your face, we loosened the glass, making sure that no one could detect our work…"

"Except," the Doctor said, "that I heard each of your words. You said that horses were waiting outside the sacred gorge. You were planning to return at midnight. The sacred tiger would be locked up in its golden cage for the night, and you would have nothing to fear from it. With a slight effort, you could slide back the glass and take away the body of the last of the Rundjees."

"Yes, Lord, this is exactly what we said that day," murmured the old man joining his hands. "But, when Laod and I returned, the glass had already been lifted and your body had vanished."

A sad smile passed over the Doctor's lips.

"Because I had escaped. Standing next to the doors of the temple, I waited for you to return and open the great bronze doors so I could slip out, I ran across to the sacred gorge. There, I saw three saddled horses, I chose the best one and I left at a gallop.

"At dawn, I had succeeded in reaching one of the lairs of the Companions of Shiva and Kali. They received the fugitive, furnished me with some clothing less striking than what I was wearing, and even gave me some money, because I didn't dare try to sell even one of the diamonds from the little bag that I had taken with me. Then I went for the border.

"Since then, there hasn't been a day when I haven't dreamed of freeing the Indian nation. Vengeance did not enter my calculations; it was a nobler sentiment, a more elevated thought which motivated me. I traveled the world without rest, learning much knowledge from the Westerners. I became one of the most learned. Then the time came when I thought I was prepared to take up the battle again."

And turning Na-Indra, he said:

"It was at this moment that I met Anoor, who later took me to you, dear one."

"As for us," finished Ahmad, "we were surprised to find the stone coffin empty. We assumed the Brahmins would learn of our plan, so we prepared to flee. Laod died along the way, and I arrived alone here, and have stayed since on this plateau, living here in repentance."

Then everyone fell silent, reflecting on all the strange threads that had been woven by fate. Long minutes went by in this way, silent and pensive, when suddenly the ironic voice of Cicada was heard from the plain below:

"Hello! The table is set! Who wants dinner?"

The Doctor and Na-Indra, startled by the young man's voice, were pulled back into reality with a jolt. The Doctor replied in an indistinct tone:

"Let's go back and rejoin our friends."

"Yes."

347

"They still do not know what you have learned, my dear fiancée. Everything is all right this way, and the truth is known only to you, who are the only one who should know it."

"I will not say anything."

Then pointing out the tombs with a gracious gesture, she added:

"This is the twilight of days long gone. Night is coming, and with it, its unavoidable gloom." Then, she put her hand on his arm and concluded: "Still, the dawn will appear in the middle of even the darkest shadows. Having the same duties, Brahma has reunited us in order that we share the same fate."

The Doctor leaned forward and softly kissed her on the forehead, saying: "Come..."

But he stopped suddenly in front of Ahmad, who was still bowing and immobile.

"Let that humble man who felt pity in his heart partake in our meal. May he become our friend and feel himself forgiven."

"You are right," she said. And with her soft voice she called out: "Ahmad!"

The old man did not answer.

"Ahmad! Ahmad!" she repeated, louder, but with no results.

The Doctor put his hand on the shoulder of the old man. But as soft as was his gesture, it disturbed the balance and the poor old man fell to the ground. Surprised, the Doctor leaned over him.

Ahmad did not move. He was dead. He had devoted his life to guarding the tombs of the Rundjees: He had just helped the last survivor of their line. His task completed, he had gone into the unknown which grants lasting peace to all those who have suffered. The two fiancés exchanged a long gaze.

"My love," said Na-Indra.

"My kiss from heaven," replied the Doctor.

"With his hands, this poor man gave a decent burial place your loved. ones"

"Yes... You mean to say that it is right that I dig his tomb?"

"Yes. And it is right that I should help you."

He opened his arms to him:

"Tonight, Na-Indra, we will bury him in the tomb he had dug for me, as a dear member of our family."

Again, Cicada's shout resounded in the dark:

"Hello! Hello!"

The Doctor, wiping a tear, answered:

"Hello!" Then he said to his companion: "Come. They too love us."

CHAPTER XII
In Herat

"They must be massacred, my brothers!"

"It will be done."

"These enemies of the Great White Tsar and of the Russians are unworthy to live."

"Don't worry, you who have come from the far away country of India to warn us, you will see how Afghanis punish traitors."

And the one who had just spoken extended his hand solemnly, as he pronounced, very low, the words of an oath. He was a handsome young man, with regular features, and a fine black mustache—the very type of an accomplished Afghan Warrior.

Near him one of his fellow officers, somewhat older, approved with a gesture. Both of them looked at a third person who began to speak:

"Now that you have been warned, O Supreme chiefs of the noble city of Herat, I do not regret any more the troubles I suffered in order to join you. All of us Indians are the bitter foes of the English, who are oppressing us mercilessly. When I learned that they were sending across your country an assassin whose task it is to murder the general of the Russian armies camping in the north of your city in order to allow the British troops to come and occupy Afghanistan, from Kabul to Kandahar and Herat, I did not hesitate. There were more than six hundred miles to travel, endless dangers to face, but nothing stopped me. Now, my mission is complete."

The chiefs held out a friendly hand to him.

"We thank you."

"Your confidence has repaid me for my trouble."

"However," continued the youngest of the warriors, smiling, "I would like to honor you even more. In our country, when a man has rendered an unusual service to his country, it is the custom that every night, the watchers who go through the city, repeat the worthy name of that individual. To their normal cry: 'Ten o'clock, eleven o'clock, midnight, all is calm,' they add 'You who are not asleep, think of one who has merited the praise of the Afghan people...' I would like for your name to be proclaimed in this fashion. What is it?"

Without hesitation, the man answered:

"Arkabad. I am a Brahmin from Ellora, who vowed that Afghanistan united with Russia shall triumph over the rapacious English."

"Excellent! Then the name of Arkabad shall be proclaimed by all our people." Then, he asked: "When do you think that that traitor who calls himself 'Doctor Mystery' will arrive in Herat?"

"Perhaps this very evening, surely by tomorrow. I left Kandahar only a few hours before him."

"Then, rest your tired body, Arkabad. I am going to gather my warriors and it is here, near the venerated ruins of the temple of Kelatni (here, he gestured towards a little mosque with dilapidated stones in the shadows of which they stood) that he will end his miserable journey. Rest yourself, friend. My servant will bring you cool drinks, food, whatever you need in order to replenish your strength. We ourselves will rejoin you soon, with the brave men which we have assembled."

With this, the young chief saluted Arkabad with a noble gesture and, followed by his silent companion, walked towards the village whose crenelated walls, flanked by high square towers, stood about fifty yards away.

The Gate of Kandahar opened his ogival arch in the brick wall and, though that opening, one could see a narrow street, dirty, paved with irregular stones, where moved a colorful population. That was one of four entrances of Herat, a major city in Western Afghanistan, a few miles away from the Russian railways station of Kushka,[115] the terminus of a line which connects to the Trans-Caspian Railway at Mary.

---

[115] Today, Serhetabat (formerly *Gushgy* for the Turkmen, and *Kushka* for the Russians; a city and administrative center of Serhetabat District, Mary Province, Turkmenistan, in the valley of the Kushka River.

The Chiefs walked under the gate and disappeared from sight. Arkabad sat on the crumbling steps of the mosque and said:

"This time, they won't escape me. At Kandahar, they used their damned rolling house. Now, they're here... But why? To join forces with the Russians, I'd bet. Those barbarians only dream of invading India and destroy the influence of the Brahmins. This Doctor Mystery is a dangerous enemy. What weapons is he bringing to the warriors of the White Tsar? I don't know, but I am guessing that if I get rid of him, I shall be destroying a powerful enemy."

And shaking his head, he continued:

"As for those two girls who have deceived me, perhaps they will carry with his destruction the secret of the Treasure of Freedom..."

He made a violent gesture; his closed fists threw out an empty threat into the air.

" But why should it matter! Our temples are already filled with treasures. Let that wealth be lost forever rather than used against us."

Lazily, Arkabad stretched out on the ground. His head resting on his hands, he closed his eyes. But the expressions which flowed over his face indicated that his cunning mind was not at rest.

Suddenly, he stood up. He had heard the sounds of trumpets coming from the center of the city. He listened for a moment, then an ironic smile came to his lips.

"Good! Good! The chiefs are gathering their warriors. They are working for me, those idiots. Ah! Doctor Mystery, are you ready to face fifty thousand fanatics?"

The evil Brahmin was not wrong. An hour later, two or three thousand Afghans, rifles swung across their shoulders, bandoliers around their chests, came out of the city and took up a position on the plains to the right and left of the mosque. Tents were set up, and a few fires were lit. An army had miraculously surged out of the ground at the call of the Brahmin.

Arkabad observed all this with a mocking eye. What results had come of his duplicity! He felt an immense pride swell in him. He had finally created the obstacle which could not be overcome; he was at last about to destroy his heretofore uncatchable adversary.

And his eyes themselves full of eager hate turned towards the south, to the white ribbon of the road to Kandahar, with an ardent desire to see the appearance of the vaunted aluminum house.

But night came on without any trace of the vehicle.

In the plains, the fires danced in the same way as the winds. The clanking of steel resounded through the air from time to time as the Afghan soldiers patrolled from one spot to another.

Then from the terraces on top of the walls of the city came dull metallic rumbling sounds. They were putting the artillery in place.

Arkabad rubbed his hands. The entire city had become his ally in his scheme to stop the Doctor! In the midst of shadows cast over the earth, he dreamed of finally conquering his foe.

Midnight!

Far away on the horizon, the light of a lantern had just appeared. One might have mistaken it for a capricious star descending from the heavens in order to bathe the land with its light.

Arkabad stood up, looked, and listened. The same star went across the horizon in an inexplicable zigzag. Inexplicable? Not so! All day long, the Brahmin had studied the countryside. He knew all the twists and turns in road to Kandahar. These were the same pattern followed by the star. So it wasn't a star at all, but a lantern with a powerful reflector. And given its intensity, Arkabad no longer doubted it was the lantern in the front of the aluminum house!

A thrilling feeling made his nerves vibrate. He was finally going to triumph! Standing up on his tiptoes, filled with hate, he shouted into the night:

"Alert! The traitors are coming!"

It was true: the Doctor's rolling house was indeed approaching Herat. They had finally reached Kandahar, and there had been joyfully reunited with the rolling house, its equipment, and the worthy Captain Kéradec and his crew, always faithful to their leader.

It was a great pleasure to board again the fantastic vehicle which, during the first leg of their journey, had helped them so much.

Cicada found all of his gaiety again, and while the aluminum house rolled rapidly down the highway towards Herat, he leaned over the platform on the front as he had in the past on the prow of the *Saint-Kaourentin*, and chanted at the top of his lungs the refrains of a sailor.

Anoor, who never left him, mingled her sweet voice to that of the young Parisian. Na-Indra, her big sister, sat next to the Doctor, looking at him tenderly.

The Sanders-van Stoon family had, without resentment, occupied again their former bedrooms, and the nice couple Timoteo and Graziella had joined them, admiring the technical wonders of the vehicle.

Their plan was to return to Europe by way of the Trans-Caspian Railway.[116] Their marriage would be the last most amusing chapter of their trip.

Now, everybody had been told by the Doctor that they were expecting to arrive in Herat shortly, so they had taken the precaution to take a long nap in the

---

[116] The Trans-Caspian Railway (also called the Central Asian Railway) is a railway that follows the path of the Silk Road through much of western Central Asia. It was built by the Russian Empire during its expansion into Central Asia in the 19th century. It was started in 1879, following the Russian victory over Khokand. Originally, it served the purpose of facilitating the Imperial Russian Army in actions against the local resistance.

afternoon so that the night would find them gathered on the platform in order to observe their approach to the city. The lanterns lit the road a certain distance and the eyes of the passengers were trying to see further to make out the walls of the city. Suddenly Cicada let out a cry:

"There! Just in front of us!"

Nothing showed yet, but they all scrutinized the blue depths of the shadows. The young man was right. About half a mile away, a black mass showed up on the horizon. Soon, they could see the crenelated walls of the towers.

The Doctor stood up; he was going to talk. But Na-Indra was faster than him.

"Herat!" she said with deep emotion. "We have arrived."

And leaning towards him, she finished her sentence so low that only he could hear it:

"Tomorrow, the Treasure of Freedom will be in our power, and henceforth, there will be two of us to guard it."

She had hardly finished when a red light lit up the sky.

"What's that?" shouted Cicada. "Are they lighting up in our honor?"

A rumble passed in the air above the heads of the travelers. A mass struck the ground and there was a deafening explosion, while a geyser of fire rose from the ground as if a volcanic crater had suddenly opened.

Everyone cried out in fright. Timoteo, into the arms of whom Graziella had ran, murmured:

"But that was a shell!"

"A shell!" repeated Cicada. "Are we going to be bombarded?"

A second shot came from the ramparts and a shell landed not too far in front of the aluminum house, covering its passengers with stones. The cries of the Sanders-van Stoon redoubled but were soon cowed by the Doctor's voice who ordered:

"Shut off the lantern!"

That order made sense. The electric lantern offered the enemy an easy target. The darkness became suddenly total. But almost at the same time, they heard a new noise, even deadlier. It was like the crackle of hail falling down. Some of them easily recognized the whistling sounds that accompanied it.

Guns were now employed by their unknown enemy from Herat who was firing a hail of bullets at them, which could prove very dangerous. There was no hesitation, no possible explanation; it was necessary to fight.

In the sharp, masterful tone of his greatest days, Doctor Mystery shouted:

"To the mirrors!"

Cicada, Anoor, and Na-Indra shivered. This man of genius, who had found a way to trap and control the power of lightning, was now going to use it.

Meanwhile, the rolling house was backing up, leaving the immediate danger zone that exposed it to the enemy's fire. After it was out of range, the Doctor asked:

"Kéradec, are you ready?"

"Yes, Master!"

"Have one of the mirrors target the top of the wall, and let the other one go around the plain, near the city gate."

"Understood!"

A minute later, one that seemed like a century, there was a sharp explosion, and, in the distance, a red light broke through the shadows.

Then, the countryside lit up. One might have believed that the Spirits of Fire had set fire to the Earth after escaping from their prisons as is recounted in Indian mythology. Blue, red, and green lights crossed each other with sinister, short explosions.

It was like an unparalleled firework display, but one of death and destruction, generating not applause but the horrifying sounds of agony. The destructive rays of the Doctor's parabolic mirrors went across the land covered with shadows and the black lines of the ramparts, everywhere spreading death in its wake. No heavenly storm could equal that artificial lightning that destroyed everything in its path.

The guns, the cannons had all stopped firing had stopped. A deadly silence followed the clammers of the crowd.

"Stop!" commanded the Doctor.

The fiery mirrors no longer spat death. The nightmarish battle was over. The deep silence of the night, an instant troubled by the anger of men, fell again on the countryside.

Everyone was quiet, horrified, but also awe-struck before the awesome power of Doctor Mystery. Only Cicada had the strength to talk, to throw out an ironic comment worthy of that Parisian gadfly:

"Now that the enemy has been obliterated, what will you have, ladies and gentlemen? Absinthe, sherry or whiskey?"

But nobody laughed. Laughter died on their lips when they saw the Doctor, calm, cold, as if nothing unusual had happened, seemingly oblivious to the fact that he had just ordered the creation of a firestorm, one more terrible then those which nature for so many centuries had monopolized.

No one slept a wink that night onboard the rolling house. Everyone was eagerly waiting for dawn. There was haste and fear to find the effects of the electric fire which had reduced to silence an enemy of which they ignored the number and the purpose.

Finally, dawn broke. Slowly, the pale light of the new day lit the summit of the hills and slid towards the valleys. At last, the battlefield was revealed.

Hundreds of dead bodies were stretched out on the ground. The walls of Herat were empty of their defenders. It was the gloomy and sad solitude of desolation after a prodigious battle.

"Forward!" ordered Doctor Mystery.

And the aluminum house went forward. They went through the zone that the shells had ravaged. Large craters opened to the left and the right of road. If one of the deadly projectiles had reached their vehicle, it would have reduced it and its passengers to atoms.

That thought filled the passengers with anger. Still, pity for the vanquished also filled their hearts. They had been forced to defend themselves; after all, wasn't that the right of every creature?

Now they saw lines of riflemen sheltered behind rocks. Many were still kneeling, their rifles on their shoulders, ready to fire; but their hands could no longer press the triggers. The light of the mirrors had passed by there, and everyone was dead. They were locked in battle for eternity.

Everywhere, they saw melted weapons, twisted steel, destroyed by the artificial lightning.

The Sanders-van Stoon family, the two Italians, even Na-Indra and Anoor, would prefer to flee from that spectacle of carnage. But they could not leave the platform. It was if an inner voice was shouting at them: "Look! Look!"

A will stronger than theirs forced them to go across that sinister landscape were death reaped until even He was exhausted.

"What's that little temple?" asked the Doctor

"Kelatni!" murmured Na-Indra who had become pale, and whose hands trembled.

"Yes, you're right… But what's wrong with you, my sweet fiancée?"

"There! It's there!" she stammered.

"What is there?"

"The Treasure of Freedom!" And suddenly, she spoke hastily with a nervous volubility. "It is there, in its crypt, that the chariots transported it in the past, all the gold that the patriots of Punjab gave... It's from there that caravans left to go and took the bags of coins to the great merchants of Asia and exchanged them for precious stones, diamonds, pearls, sapphires, which are all less cumbersome and easier to carry on the day when such wealth will be needed! It's there! There!"

On an order from the Doctor, the rolling house started towards the temple. As they were approaching, they saw a body stretched out across the doorway. They stopped. Everybody jumped down to the ground, and a cry of stupor came from their lips when they saw who the dead man was who seemed to guard the entrance to temple.

It was Arkabad!

He was there, rigid, his face was convulsed by the hateful passions which still agitated him at the instant where life left him. On his temple, they saw a small black spot surrounded by a white circle. That's where the lightning bolt struck him, destroying his evil, scheming brain forever.

Now, the travelers understood the reason for the attack of which they had been victims.

For the last time, the Executioner of Ellora had been thwarted in his attempts at destroying them.

An hour later, a rather heavy coffin was removed from the crypt of the temple of Kelatni and taken inside the rolling house. They opened it and saw a wealth of precious stone of an inestimable value. There was enough there to pay the ransom of an empire. Everybody marveled at those riches amassed by the patriotism of the inhabitants of Punjab!

At that moment, military music came to their ears. Pipes mingling with drums. It didn't sound like Afghan music, but more like Western tunes.

Everyone rushed outside, and they stopped on the road, astounded. A Russian regiment, music at the head of them, was advancing in good order towards the Gate of Herat.

The soldiers had also spotted the aluminum house, because a murmur rose from their ranks. Almost at the same time, a horseman rushed at full gallop toward the travelers. Two steps away, he stopped suddenly and the horse kneeled down.

"General, I salute you," the Doctor shouted joyously.

"You?" replied the General, holding out his hands. "I had an inkling of it yesterday, when at Kushka, someone came to tell me that the people of Herat were trying to block the passage of strangers. As fast as I could, I brought together a regiment to help you. But obviously, my help was not needed," he added with a smile, "because you treated them in a very harsh way."

The Doctor had a melancholy smile:

"They forced me into it, General... But let's not talk about that. A year ago, I told you that two roads led to India, that of Kabul, and that of Kandahar."

The eyes of the Russian soldier were shining:

"Yes, you did tell me that."

"Well, these two roads have now been mapped, and if you to do me the honor of accepting the hospitality of my electric house, I will show you the topographic photographs that one of my inventions automatically took when moving through Kandahar. I myself mapped the road to Kabul."

Sanders was listening. He exclaimed:

"Ah, so I traveled with people who were busy preparing a Russian invasion?"

"That's alright by me," interrupted Cicada that Anoor thanked with a sweet look.

But the Doctor commanded silence from his young companions and, with a friendly gesture, turned towards Sanders, once a member of the British House of Commons, and said:

"Who knows what tomorrow will bring?"

And walking ahead of the Russian general, he went back inside the Aluminum House.

Afterword
Cicada's Destiny
by Marie Palewska

The street urchin Cigale, whose name means "Cicada," and who is said to speak with a Parisian accent, is first introduced in *Doctor Mystery* as "a kid, almost a child," a mere cabin boy aboard the ship *Saint-Kaourentin*. The character had everything necessary to seduce Paul d'Ivoi's youngest readers: he was their own age, cheerful, resourceful, and funny in his use of street slang and his spontaneity. He also aroused admiration by heroically coming to the aid of innocent people in danger. His youth, his orphaned status, and his generous nature thus gave him the required characteristics to reappear in "*The Eccentric Voyages*" as a new recurring character after the Lavarèdes.

Cicada plays a major role in the next volume in the series, *Cicada in China*. The story takes place during the famous Boxer Rebellion, which had just occurred, and which d'Ivoi chronicled as seriously as he could despite a few changes made for the purposes of dramatic development, and unsurprisingly, an overall political outlook that is clearly pro-western and anti-Chinese.

The story begins in Beijing in May 1900. We find a still cheeky but more mature Cicada who is now "sixteen or seventeen years-old," who has just arrived from Moscow. He is working as the Tsar's courier having brought to the Russian ambassador an ultimatum from Nicolas II to the Emperor of China demanding that he puts down the Boxers who have shed the blood of European missionaries and are inciting the Chinese to kill foreigners.

We learn that it was Cicada's mentor, Prince Rundjee, a.k.a. Doctor Mystery, who found him this job in order to distract the young man from mourning the beautiful Anoor, who died while attending a boarding school in Saint Petersburg, one year after moving to Russia following their trip to India and Afghanistan.

This loss adds a certain depth to the character and helps to make him even more endearing. It also underlines his natural generosity, when he fosters the budding love between his two new companions in adventure: René Loret, a French attaché, and Princess Flower Reed [*Roseau-Fleuri* in French], the favorite of Chinese Empress Cixi. Imprisoned in the Forbidden City, Cicada and René meet Emperor Guangxu, his mother Empress Cixi, Prince Tuan and other nobles of the Imperial Court. During a banquet, they are unable to prevent the torture of western missionaries. They eventually escape thanks to Cicada's skills; then, working for the French Legation, they travel to Tien Tsin, then to Takou, where they bravely succeed and assist in the taking of the forts blocking the access to the Pei Ho river.

Cicada has his baptism of fire and is among the first in the attack on the enemy forts. He again distinguishes himself by his bravery at Tien Tsin. But René is taken prisoner by Tuan, who seeks revenge and condemns both him and Flower Reed to death. As the two young people are about to be fed to panthers and snakes in the arena of the Forbidden City, Cicada manages to save them by impersonating the Living Buddha. They then return to the French legation on the symbolic date of July 14. After a month of siege, during which Cicada again displays his courage, the Allied armies arrive on August 14, 1900 to free to besieged.

While the victorious troops march through the Forbidden City, Cicada suddenly discovers with amazement Prince Rundjee, accompanied by Na-Indra and Anoor, who is alive and well! His mentor reveals to him that he was put to a test for his own good: "The world would have been hard on a lost child from Paris marrying the heiress of one of India's noblest families."

While Doctor Mystery's methods may seem harsh, the reader is now satisfied to learn that, since Cicada has now demonstrated his heroism, nothing stands in the way of his marriage to Anoor.

Yet, Cicada is still single in the next volume, *Massiliague of Marseille*, published a year later. This time, D'Ivoi's spotlight is on a colorful Frenchman from the eponymous southern port, obviously influenced by Alphonse Daudet's classic novel *Tartarin de Tarascon* (1872). The Provençal town of Tarascon is so enthusiastic about hunting that no game lives anywhere near it, and its inhabitants resort to telling hunting stories and throwing their own caps in the air to shoot at them. Tartarin, a plump middle-aged man, is the chief "cap-hunter," but following his enthusiastic reaction to seeing an Atlas lion in a traveling menagerie, the over-imaginative town understands him to be planning a hunting expedition to Algeria. So as not to lose face, Tartarin is forced to go. His gullibility causes him to have a number of misadventures until he returns home penniless, but covered in glory after shooting a blind lion!

Here, our native southerner, Massiliague, is bombastic but not ridiculous, and shows courage and ingenuity. In Mexico, he offers to assist a young Peruvian patriot, Dolores Pacheco, in her search for a sacred necklace, the possession of which shall seal an alliance amongst all the native peoples, uniting them to rebel against the domination of the United States. Cicada, who had left Asia to return to France to perform his military service, joins the expedition.

It turns out that the young man decided to cross the Pacific in order to finish the world tour he had started when he left for India. On his way from San Francisco to New Orleans, he stopped at the hacienda of the planter Fabian Rosales. There he met Massiliague and his companions and decided to help them in their quest, which the American Joe Sullivan seeks to hinder.

If Cicada rarely plays a leading role in the many adventures that the heroes encounter while traveling through Texas and Mexico, he nevertheless makes a fateful discovery: his real identity! While injured after a final confrontation with

Sullivan's men, Fabian Rosales discovers the letters F and R tattooed under Cicada's arm, proving that the young man is his son! Rosales' real name is Roseraie; he emigrated twenty years earlier from France, with the aim of starting a new life in America after his jealous brother had taken his son away from him and destroyed his life.

In this book, his third appearance, Cicada is reunited with his long-lost father in Mexico and acquires three half-sisters, Inès, Vera and Annina, from the second marriage of Fabian Rosales to a Mexican woman. Vera has taken part in the search for the sacred necklace, disguised as a *peon*, out of love for Massiliague, who plans to ask Fabian for her hand at the end of the novel after her subterfuge has been revealed.

As for Dolores Pacheco, she succeeds in her quest, but faces a different fate. As a descendant of the Incas, brought up in a Peruvian temple according to their sacred rites, instead of being the symbol of their emancipation, she is fated to be sacrificed on the altar of her ancestors!

However, the so-called "Mexican Virgin" is rescued in the next volume, *The Sowers of Ice*. Her sister, Stella, arrives to rescue her from her dreadful fate. She is accompanied by Massiliague, a Canadian, Francis Gairon, and a young French engineer nicknamed Jean *Ça-Va-Bien* [Jean All'swell], who had previously saved Stella from the eruption of the volcanic Mount Pelée in Martinique on May 8, 1902. Jean forces his authority upon the Inca priests by performing the seeming miracle of petrifying the temple's hot spring by using vials of liquid air.

This novel makes good use of the news headlines of the day, cleverly exploits the picturesque secrets of the Inca civilization, while featuring the return of the clever and jocular Massiliague. However, Cicada is nowhere to be seen—except for a brief passage at the end, which reads:

In fact, two months later, not three but four marriages were celebrated in Sao Domenco. [Stella and Jean, Dolores and Francis, Vera and Massiliague.] *Cicada, released from military service, married Anoor.*

This is accompanied by a brief footnote referring the readers to *Doctor Mystery, Cicada in China, Massiliague of Marseille*, and previous episodes of the series. This is quite the rushed ending for our hero, but at least it is a happy one in the "they lived happily ever after" tradition that was always the case in Paul d'Ivoi's books.

www.ingramcontent.com/pod-product-compliance
Lightning Source LLC
Chambersburg PA
CBHW060414030726
47495CB00003B/570